REMNANTS

Ready for New Life

Kiki Swanson

Happy reading!
Kiki Swanson

Remnants: Ready for New Life

For information about this title or to order other books and/or electronic media, contact the author or the publisher:

www.kikiswansonbooks.com and email kikiswan@cox.net

Brooks Goldmann Publishing Company, LLC
www.brooksgoldmannpublishing.com
7970 E. Camelback Rd., 710
Scottsdale, AZ 85251

Library of Congress Control Number: 9009933302
ISBN: 978-0-9817881-4-2
Printed in the United States of America

Book and Cover design by: 1106 Design

Ten percent of sales
pledged to
the after-school program at
The Boys and Girls Clubs of Greater Scottsdale

Dedicated
to
all those
who
face the decision
of
where to live
in
their senior years.

May
they find
joy
in new life
together!

Acknowledgments

I APPRECIATE ALL THE STORIES I've heard from residents of retirement communities. My favorite characters on these pages are telling real stories, filled with genuine anxiety, concern, love and joy. Their memories reflect the lives of my dearest friends, along with a few of my relatives and neighbors. Some are parents who thought those demanding years were behind them. Others are lonely and wish their offspring were closer. A few are alone in the world. In my ministry to senior adults, I've been privileged to share in family grief and happiness, in problems with destructive habits and in celebrations of newfound relationships.

I hope you'll find yourself and your friends among these remnants who are ready for new life. A creative friend like Daisy can see the possibilities in people just as she has shaped pieces of fabric into sources of happiness for children.

I've studied people as they age. Some have practiced an old attitude for years and enjoy complaining. Others have scarcely noticed time passing and marvel at their blessings of long life. Fear has overtaken a few. What makes the difference? I believe the magic word is *together:* together in faith, together today and together in all the surprises ahead.

— Kiki Swanson, 2009

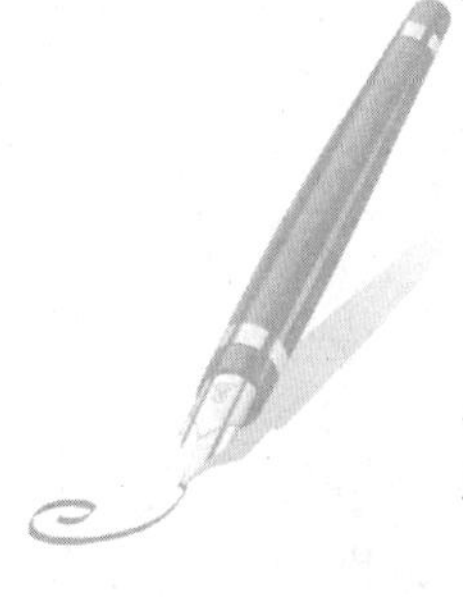

Can a Christmas letter change the lives of friends?

December 5, 2002

Dear Friends, near and far,

Once again, Christmas awakens my warm memories of all of you. I hope this year has been a gift to you. I don't need to tell you what the past two years have been like for me. I've finally admitted I'm lonely in the evenings, most of all at meal time. I sew in the daytime, but after dark, my eyes are better at reading than embroidery.

So, I'm sending out my greetings early this year to tell you my news. I've decided to move to a new retirement village called La Ventura right here in Scottsdale. I never thought I'd leave the dream home Scott and I built ten years ago, but I think he'd approve of my choice. It's a beautiful place, with red geraniums at each doorway and rose gardens along the walks. The managers are a young and energetic couple.

Why don't you consider joining me here? Wouldn't it be fun to be neighbors again, going to the same meetings and drinking coffee together at ten? Remember those years? I'm really serious about this. A sign at the main door says "Welcome to Your New Life." Just think, no more pool to clean, no more leaves to rake, no snow to shovel, and someone to cook dinner every night. Sounds awfully good to me.

I miss you, and I hope you agree with me that we could have years of fun together, even if we're "single." I'm moving on January 10, so note the new address.

With love and hugs for a Happy New Year,

Daisy

*Daisy MacDuff**7375 N. Via de la Romeria*
Scottsdale, AZ 85250

Daisy sealed the ninth envelope, stamped it and said to Curly, "There! That's the best thirty-seven cents I've ever spent on my old friends. Think they'll come and join us, Curly?" Her Golden Retriever crooned a low tone as he always did when she asked his opinion. While she fixed Curly's dinner, she remembered how this idea started, back in October during the sale at the Fabric Farm.

CHAPTER 1

The Idea Blossoms

BIG SALE ! End of Season
REMNANTS
Great Variety Available!

FOR YEARS, DAISY HAD haunted the sale tables at the Fabric Farm for materials to make children's toys and quilts for the church bazaar. That day, she wanted something for herself, a new dress to wear to church or for a luncheon. The fall colors seemed drab, so she browsed through the clear tones of summer cottons. In the full length mirror at the back of the store, she held up to her face a remnant of aqua linen. She looked around and realized she herself was a remnant of her generation's sewing homemakers. Only one mother and daughter were poring over pattern books, and a young woman was choosing nursery curtain cloth. She recalled the excitement of meeting friends at the store for these clearance sales, but where were her friends today? Were they feeling like remnants too, vestiges of a thrifty generation? A few had moved away, one had died, but had the others given away their sewing machines? Did they just order from one of those glossy catalogs? "It's strange how silently things change," she thought.

She moved closer to the glass and saw that sixty-eight years of smiles and frowns had left permanent records on her face. "Permanent?" she asked that face. "Nothing's permanent; there's always a chance to change." She sucked in her tummy and carried the yardage to the cutting counter.

The young clerk measured it and said, "Three yards in this piece."

"I'll take it," Daisy replied. She thanked the girl, took the fabric and the bill to the front counter and paid for her purchase. Then she saw the sign again. *Great Variety Available!* She thought, "Variety is what's missing in my life. I need to think about that."

Back home, she put her new fabric on the washer for the next load and hurried to the kitchen to fix a sandwich. She needed to be at the church by two. The Seasoned Seniors program committee was planning the next meeting at a new retirement center as a preview to its grand opening. "Can't be late for this meeting," she said aloud as she locked the back door and raised the garage door.

It was half past four when she let herself into the back hall and heard the telephone ringing. "Hello," she said breathlessly. "No, I'm fine, but I just came in from the car. How was your day at the hospital?" She listened to her daughter. "This was a busy day for me too. Thanks for the call, Julie. See you soon." Daisy hung her keys on a hook by the door and took her mail to her desk. This was her least favorite time of day, when there wasn't much to look forward to, except the evening news at five and fixing some food. Then she always had a good book and a comfortable bed. She knew she was lucky in many respects, but her grief was never far from the surface of her life.

Scott had been a pillar of the church, the head of the men's club and an elder. When Julie and her younger brother Pete were in elementary school, Scott was superintendent of the church school. He coached Little League, and he took Julie on the father-daughter camp-out. More than all those things, he'd been Daisy's one and only love, from college until his death a year ago March. "My whole life revolved around that wonderful man!" She sighed, as she often did, and moved ahead to her TV chair with parts of the morning paper she hadn't read.

On October 18th, the Seasoned Seniors toured La Ventura. Each walkway was manicured, the gardens ablaze with new red geraniums. The trees were still staked, and the newly sodded lawns showed their seams. Most of the couples strolled over toward the free-standing units, or casitas, as they were called.

Daisy watched as Sara and Ted Harvey walked slowly, hand in hand. She sighed. "They're such a nice young couple. I wonder why they're interested in this place."

"C'mon, Daisy. Let's take a look at the pool." Jane pointed to an area where tables with umbrellas and lounge chairs were being set up. "I don't think it's finished yet, but I want to see how deep it is."

"It's big enough for me." Swimming was not Daisy's favorite sport.

"Not deep enough for diving. Oh, well, we'd never move here anyway."

"You never know when it might seem like a good idea."

"Nah, we're not ready for this. Maybe someday, if I break a leg or something bad. I couldn't even get Joe to come along today. In fact, he didn't even want me to come on the tour."

The others had moved on to see the apartments in the first two buildings. "Now that's what I want to see." Daisy turned and followed the group. "Nice little private patios. That's good. Oh, and I like these doorknobs."

"C'mon, Daisy. They're getting ahead of us again. Don't dawdle."

"Slow down, Jane. We're here to see the place; let's see it."

As they came around the end of the building, their guide was holding open the door to the main hallway. "The common rooms are open twenty-four hours a day, just like your living areas at home. Someone's always on call at the front desk. These smaller rooms are for meetings or social events, whatever you might need."

The Harveys came in from their tour of the casitas. "Daisy MacDuff, how are you? Are you going to move here?"

"I don't know. I always attend these senior meetings. It's good to know what's going on around town."

"We've never come before, but this sounded so inviting." Sara went on, "I'm sick of cleaning the pool. The dust storms hit our patio and pool full blast last summer when we were on vacation. We had to have some serious cleaning done."

"I've lived here a long time, and you're right. It's a big job to keep things clean. I love seeing my pool company's truck pull into the drive."

"But that's expensive," Sara added.

"I know, but after I lost my husband, it seemed like a worthy expense." Daisy pointed to the casitas. "Were they nice?"

Ted nodded. "They're beautiful. I didn't think I'd like the granite counters, but they're light tan."

"I liked the bathrooms. And the new carpet. Gee, I didn't realize ours looks so beaten down."

Coffee and apple cider were offered in the main dining room, and everyone was ready to sit and talk. A young man joined Daisy and the Harveys. "Welcome. I'm Malcolm, and my wife Bonnie and I are the directors here. Do you have any questions I could answer?" Ted made some comments, and Sara admired the light fixtures.

Daisy turned toward her church friends. "Did you see the movie theater? And the library?"

Sam agreed. "Wouldn't that be nice to have all those books and DVDs in the next room?"

"I'm impressed with the craft room. I know it won't always look that neat, but it sure looks spacious." Everyone knew about Daisy and her sewing.

Malcolm moved along the table. "It's great to have a post office station right here beside a bank, and then the barber shop and beauty salon. The soda fountain keeps late hours too."

It was an amazing place. No one spoke about buying into the village, but everyone took home a brochure along with a clear impression of polished new floors, plush carpets, shiny counters and sparkling light fixtures. The gentleman who had guided the tour invited them to come again and bring their friends. "Remember, we have lots of variety in the rooms and casitas, as well as in the residents coming here." He chuckled and beamed beneficently over the group.

On the way back to the church, Jane asked, "What's our next meeting about?"

Sam answered, "The hospital chaplain's speaking; he told me to call it *Look Ahead and Take a Chance.* He's a great guy; it'll be good. November 22nd."

At home, Daisy noted the next meeting on her calendar and then surveyed the month. Every Tuesday, the craft group. Every other Thursday, P.E.O. The last Friday, the bugman. Every Saturday, check the choir robes. "Add laundry and pressing every Monday, and it's De-pressing! When did we get in such a rut, Curly?" His tail fluttered once in response; he was content with the rut.

"A month until Thanksgiving." Daisy's words hung in the air as she poured herself a glass of tea. "And then what? Another month until Christmas." She knew she shouldn't indulge herself with thoughts that all led to one conclusion: "I'm all alone!" She shook her head, breathed deeply and had a new thought: read the brochure from La Ventura.

The next half hour flew by as she studied each picture carefully. She figured in the margin of the newspaper what her fixed monthly expenses were. As the brochure reminded her, *Living in your present home is not free.* She added insurance, the year-round weekly lawn care, the monthly bugman, the new security system, the window washers, and the trash pick-up. Could she afford living somewhere like La Ventura? Maybe.

By Thanksgiving, she decided to tell Pete and Julie and their spouses about the center, but only the fact that she'd seen it and liked it. They might jump to conclusions. They'd probably picture their modest inheritance flying out the window. They might think she was ill. They might offer to take her in. She dreaded the scene, and yet she felt excited about making a change in her life. She didn't want to go on like this much longer. She also didn't want to live with either of her children.

Instead of all the questions she had anticipated, they simply wanted to see La Ventura, soon. Daisy felt exhilarated by the possibilities. Only Pete's wife Susie frowned and seemed negative about Daisy's decision.

"Why would you want to leave your nice home? Where will we have Christmas dinner? This feels like home."

Pete quickly said, "Sue, Mom's given this some thought. Let's go see the place."

Susie persisted. "I just don't think she should move so soon. You're her advisor, Pete. You know how your dad loved this place."

"Sue, please. Dad would have trusted Mom to make up her own mind."

"But she's still all sad and weepy. That's not when you make good decisions."

Pete put his hand on her arm, drew her closer and said firmly, "Sue, that's enough. Mom, we'll see it tomorrow. It must be beautiful or you wouldn't be willing to move."

Daisy smiled and said, "It's not an easy choice to make, but sooner or later I'll have to give this up, and I'd rather do it while I'm well."

During the following week, she chose a model she could afford, one with a partial view of the McDowell Mountains beyond a small garden patio. Julie offered to help her pack boxes, and Pete agreed to help her move when the unit was ready. She was walking on air, almost breathless. "Curly, you're no help at all." He rose from his usual evening spot, stretched and came over to sit close to her knees. His chin rested heavily on her lap, and she could not resist his beautiful brown eyes pleading for a little love. "Curly, I'd never move if you couldn't come with me." At night, Daisy prayed that Scott was watching over her decision.

The next morning she had spent at her computer, composing her annual Christmas letter. Last year's had been short and sad. Nine months a widow, she wasn't able to say much else. But this year's would wake up her friends in nine cities in eight states. "Tomorrow I'll check on the temperatures in those places. Hope it's chilly and wet." She stacked the envelopes by the back door.

CHAPTER 2

The Response Begins

DAISY KNEW FROM THE weather report that it was snowing in the East, so she smiled at the Boston postmark of the first envelope.

Dear Daisy,

What a wild idea! You know I would never leave Boston. My two boys live so near. They would think I'm crazy. I'm glad you look forward to moving, but all my extra money goes to the Jewish Relief Fund in Jerusalem. I think these retirement homes are for selfish people who have no relatives. What's the matter with Julie? Won't she take you in? Well, dear, happy holidays and don't wreck your back lifting boxes.

Shalom, your old friend, Sue

Daisy laughed when she read Sue Senderman's reply. "Good old Sue; she always said what she thought. Her boys would manage just fine without her, Curly. They must be forty by now! Well, you and I are moving anyway."

Daisy's days had a new sense of excitement as she began to think of things she'd give away and items to be packed with care. Memories came to life as she opened drawers and cabinets that hadn't been disturbed for at least two years.

She decided all the photographs would go with her. Big and little, they all went into two boxes marked FAMILY PIX — SAVE. Then she had to face boxes of legal papers and tax records. She dragged them one by one to the family room where she could sift through them while she watched TV.

Among the memories were a few mysteries. The copy of Scott's speeding ticket in Tempe amused her, since he always reminded her to slow down. She was more puzzled by a photo copy of a check for $2,000 to an attorney at King Legal Services. That office was well-known for handling D.U.I. cases. It was dated 1999. She wondered if their son Pete had been in trouble, but why hadn't Scott told Daisy about it? Had Scott needed a lawyer?

On Saturday afternoon, the telephone interrupted her task. "Hello? Yes, this is Daisy." She listened and began to smile. "My son said a realtor would call soon. Why don't you come and see the house this week so we can decide what to do next? Yes, Tuesday will be fine."

She felt a little shaky as she put down the phone. "Oh, Curly, this'll be the hard part. If I let go of the house, will I let go of my best memories?" Curly groaned, shifted position, and then came close to her. "You know what I mean, don't you, Old Boy? Dear Scott is everywhere in these walls."

Christmas mail brought more news from her special friends. Eagerly, Daisy opened the card from Madison, Wisconsin. She knew Martha hated winter weather, so she mentally crossed her fingers as she read.

> *You surely knew the right person to invite to Arizona! Your P.S. was right on target, because I haven't written anyone except Mary Ann for years. After Frank left us in 1994, I went to work at the Med. Center. I was drinking a lot and was really lost. The people at work got me the help I needed. Now I do addiction counseling at Aldersgate, and I love it! In fact, I'm afraid to leave it. It's kept me sober to help others battle their demons. I wouldn't expect you to understand. What an awful confession to make to a dear friend like you. Please let me know if you still want me. I love you, Martha*

Tears clouded Daisy's eyes as she finished reading Martha's note. "Curly, you and I have been so lucky. I love my tea, morning, noon and night, and you're addicted to those chew bones, but we've never had to admit our weaknesses to anyone else. I hope she'll join us," she said with passion. "I'll write her again tomorrow."

A business envelope from Oklahoma City contained a typed letter from Donna Krueger.

> *Dear Daisy, hello to you too! Our lives have certainly taken different turns, haven't they? Until last July, I was still on duty at St. Ambrose. But a case of shingles really knocked me flat. I've tried to get my strength back, but I'll never do floor duty again. I'm thinking about going into real estate where I could set my own hours.*
>
> *I always wonder if these retirement places are worth the money. What about Terri, my beautiful Angora? She's my family since Rudy left ten years ago. I still wonder why I stayed with him so long. Well, that's not your headache. Terri's so old, I doubt if we could move. But who knows? Hope your holidays are warm. Write more about your new place. Send a brochure, O.K.?*

"Well, Curly, we're up to one NO and two MAYBEs. We're moving anyway, Old Boy." Daisy sank into her easy chair and prepared to spend an hour with TV.

The telephone jangled into life around seven. "Hello?" Daisy strained to listen while muting the TV. "Oh, Beth, how in the world are you?" She listened for quite a while. "That's a big change for you; I always admired your career. And how's your brother, the handsome devil?" Beth's stories continued. "And your hip surgery was a success?" She nodded. "Lots of my friends here walk with canes, Beth. That's not a problem. Why don't you think about it? I'll send a brochure that tells the costs and all."

When she came away from that call, she patted Curly and said, "Finally, Curly, we have a taker! Beth O'Donnell wants to come and live with us. Hooray, hooray!" Daisy waved her arms over her head, and Curly rose to the occasion with a swishing tail.

Daisy was thrilled with Ellen's note from Atlanta.

Dearest Daisy, You are still rescuing me! Right after Christmas, I'll call you for more info. I'm definitely looking for someplace where my knees won't ache so much. It might just be a trial run for a year or so. I'm sort of a leftover around the church now. The new pastors are doing very well. They don't need me any more. I'll call. Happy New Year, dear friend.

"Curly, we have a new tally: one NO, two MAYBE and two YES! Dear Boy, we'll have such fun. I wonder if any of them has a dog." His tail thumped on the floor in response to the lilt in Daisy's voice.

The next note came from Evelyn in Bettendorf, Iowa. Daisy expected it to be a sad one, because Evelyn and Joe had been caring for a disabled daughter as well as her mother for more than ten years. After reading it, Daisy shook her head. "Curly, her mother must be ninety-eight by now and Charlotte must be almost fifty. Maybe I shouldn't have sent them an invitation, but I never wanted to leave them out of any plans, even back in Davenport. How sad."

Just before Christmas, Daisy's mail included a letter from an attorney in Poulsbo, Washington, Richard McKinnon.

Dear Mrs. MacDuff,

I am writing for my aunt Clarissa Benton, because I take care of her business matters. She was pleased to be invited to join you in Scottsdale. My wife and I want her to relocate to a warmer, drier place, but it is difficult to persuade her. We hope she could spend the winter months there, returning to us for the summers. Would this be possible?

Her hands are quite crippled from arthritis, so she needs help in housekeeping and cooking. She plays bridge every day and enjoys friends. Please send me more details. We would appreciate your encouragement.

"Well, Curly, Clarissa may be another YES to add to the count." She set aside the address to mail a brochure. "Imagine the piano teacher with crippled hands. Life is not always kind, Curly."

CHAPTER 3

The Big Move Is a Challenge

UNDERLYING THE EXCITEMENT of moving and hearing from old friends was the fear that Daisy couldn't sell her home. She scrubbed it up to the best condition possible, and her realtor assured her it was priced just right. Maybe Christmas wasn't the best time to be selling. "I've signed the listing agreement, but what if it doesn't go soon? Oh, Scott, why did you leave me with this mess?" She looked around at all the furniture she wouldn't need. "Pete thinks he can sell this after I make a list of what I want to take with me. I wonder."

This major sorting of things was far more difficult than she had imagined. There was no holiday spirit in the cardboard cartons stacked in the hall. It was the second year she hadn't trimmed a tree. The fireplace looked lonely without the usual red candles in brass holders on the mantel. No evergreens were draped over the picture windows. "Oh, Curly, here come those tears again."

Two days before Christmas, the realtor called to say he was bringing a client to see the house in an hour. On an impulse, Daisy pulled a box of red velvet bows out of the garage. She stuck one on every carton, on the lampshades and on the white cabinet doorknobs in the kitchen. She found one of the big red candles and popped it on the mantel beside a green plant. The last red bow was for the front door knocker, and she opened the door just as the people arrived. The realtor told her later that the red bows sold the house. The buyers said the house looked "inviting."

Negotiations were slow during the holidays, but at least one worry was off her mind. Daisy told Curly, "Choosing our unit at La Ventura was one step of about a hundred toward moving. No wonder we haven't heard from some of the others. They know how much work is involved."

In early January, Betty wrote from Santa Fe, New Mexico. Her message was scrawled across the printed greetings in a large card with brilliant abstract designs on the cover.

> *Daisy, my Big Sister in high school would be the only person alive to know I'm old enough to live in a senior place. Good Heavens, NO THANKS! Why would I want a new life when I like my life here? Santa Fe is the place where people come to be vibrant and active after their career days. Of course I've always had a studio here. If I need exercise, I do my ballet routine right here. If I need a church, the Episcopalians are just around the corner, and the Rector is so charming. I wish you well in rounding up some old friends for this new place. A retirement center sounds so middle class to me. What will you do with that dog you always write about? Happy New Year, Daisy.*

"Middle class? I certainly hope so!" Daisy studied the picture again and noticed the initials E.P. in the corner. "Elizabeth Parsons. I should have known it was one of her own paintings. What will I do with that dog, indeed!" Curly seemed to know his welfare was being considered, so he tilted his head slightly and looked expectantly at Daisy. "Well, of course, that dog will retire with me. Right, Curly?" Then she remarked, "Three NO votes, two MAYBE and three YES. And no word from one. Not bad."

Daisy's friends in her church circle registered a whole gamut of comments when she announced her upcoming change of address at the January eighth meeting. Many of them had no idea she was considering a move. "I suppose that house of yours is too big to take care of?" Another comment was, "I always thought you'd move in with Julie's family, since they both work and you could take care of their boy." Someone else asked, "Did you talk it over with the pastor?"

Finally, she spoke up. "You know, until I went through these last two years, alone, I didn't know how important it is to be able to make decisions. I'd forgotten how to weigh the pros and cons of a situation." She looked around the quiet room; everyone was listening intently. "When I saw that new place, I could picture people reading in the library or eating a cone with a friend in the ice cream parlor. I realized how solitary my life has become."

"But Daisy, you have all of us and the church. Seems to me you're there every other day."

"True, but that's not the same. I needed something new that represents my present life. I was falling into the habit of relating the present to the past without much thought of the future. I think my grandson would say I was just hanging on. One day he asked me if I was going to date again. I about choked at the thought, but it gave me his view of my being alone. 'Available' as he put it." Almost everyone chuckled. "So, I feel very good about making this decision all by myself. My two kids approve of the place, and they're helping me with the process. Only Pete's wife has some reservations, but that's normal for her." She took a big breath and thought to herself, "That's the longest speech I've ever made."

"Well, if you're sure about it, we just wish you well. Right, Ladies?" They all nodded, and Daisy sat down.

Another voice asked her, "What would Scott have said?"

Daisy paused and then said, "I don't know. The couples moving out there are lucky; they can talk it over. I bet they don't all agree, and yet they may agree to give it a try. It's a harder decision when you're alone."

Then she stood up again. "Are you all going to quiz the other people from the church who are planning to live out there?"

"Who are they?"

"I don't know yet, but I saw others out there when we toured the place, and there's a brochure in the church office. You know, that nice couple, Ted and Sara Harvey?"

"Oh, they're too young to move there, aren't they?"

Daisy looked a little indignant and said, "How come I'm old enough?"

"Because you're alone now. It's safer for you to be there."

"Sara Harvey told me she's tired of keeping up the yard and patio. That's a good enough reason, isn't it?" Several murmured in agreement, and Daisy sat down.

Jane piped up, "Shirley Lott and her cousin are moving out there, next week I think."

"But they look old," someone said. Daisy smiled to herself. It was definitely a hot topic, and she felt very good about her decision.

Friday, January tenth, was the big moving day, and Daisy felt more energetic than she had in years. She drove a load of small things over to La Ventura, unlocked her Unit 7 and realized it would be home from then on. Her son-in-law Matt brought her furniture in a rented truck, with his son Mark to help. By noon, everything was in its place, except for a mountain of thirty-three cartons. Pete and Julie left the unpacking for Daisy, and that was good. She could take her time and sort things as she went along. Julie had organized a yard sale for Saturday, and Daisy had hired a cleaning service to make the house ready for the buyers.

At the end of the day, Pete put his arm around her shoulder and said, "This chapter of your life is closed, but you can always re-read the story in your memories and all those photo albums and Dad's videos. It's time to move on, Mom."

Daisy remembered how she had lectured her kids about adjusting to college life. She even recalled her definition of being homesick. "It's a yearning to return to your old comfort zone, and it sneaks up on you at the most embarrassing moments." Yes, she found herself longing for *home*. "I need space to wander around and think. We need a kitchen big enough for both Curly and me. Everything feels close." Then a nudge from Curly cured the blues. Mailbox time also broke the spell and brought her into the present. "Things are looking better," she told herself.

Unit 7 was not far from the dining hall, and Daisy had a clear view of people wending their way toward the good aromas of dinner. One pleasant surprise was seeing two women from the church walking along the path one evening. "Shirley, is that you?" she called out.

"Of course, Daisy. We heard you were moving here, but never knew when. You know my cousin Jenny, don't you?"

"We've never met officially, but I knew you were related. So, does it take everyone as long to unpack as it does for me?"

They laughed and agreed. "Makes you wonder if you should have bothered to move, but once you're settled, you'll be glad you're here."

"That's good to hear. I was a bit blue this afternoon, already missing my family room."

March brought back the sad days of March 2001 when Scott died. With Julie and Pete's help, the weeks passed. Daisy had never been a weepy person, but Scott's life had been so intertwined with hers that her life still seemed out of balance. She often found herself gazing intently at her wedding ring. The facets of that diamond led her into a comfortable land of memories where nothing ever changed. She wondered how widows could give up wearing that sign of identity.

April warmed up to ninety degrees early, and Daisy hated to see her geraniums wilting already. She had brought them from the old house, little plants she had started herself. But her patio offered no shade, and the walls held the heat inside.

CHAPTER 4

New Friends and Old Friends Meet

BETH'S ARRIVAL IN MAY was a blessing. Daisy marveled at how healthy Beth looked. She'd put on an inch or two in the waistline, but her beautiful white hair was still thick and well-cut. Her dark eyes and high cheek bones had always reminded Daisy of the blessings of her Irish heritage. Beth was eager to learn all about life in the hot desert. Daisy couldn't afford to be glum about the heat, since she was the resident cheerleader for the place.

Ellen flew in from Atlanta on her son's pass to look the place over, and she loved it. Ellen was as cheerful as Daisy remembered her and still had a gentle confidence about life. This decision to move west fell into place with all her previous moves. "I'll be back right after Labor Day," she promised Daisy.

In June, Mary Ann Martinez drove from Roswell, New Mexico to see La Ventura. That was a real surprise, since Daisy had never heard from her. She kept Daisy moving to show her every amenity and every inch of the town. She liked the casitas so much that she coaxed her sister Martha into building one with her. Those units wouldn't be ready until October, which gave the sisters time to sell their homes and make the moves.

By September, Daisy and Beth adjusted themselves to the new life, like the rules and regulations of college life. Meals were at definite times; they shared laundry rooms; they had to learn a hundred new names all at once. People with pets were all on the first floor, and Daisy and Curly had settled into a new routine for their walks. "That's part of the variety we needed, Old Boy."

Beth observed, "The toughest part of this summer was having people tell me when to do things. I didn't realize how long I'd been on my own schedule or none."

Daisy nodded. "I can see that's harder for you than me. I've only been alone for twenty-nine months."

Beth picked up on the reference to Scott's death. "Daisy, for Heaven's sake, stop counting months." Then she looked at Daisy's injured expression and said, "I'm sorry I hurt you, but it's time to move ahead. We were both blessed with good husbands when we needed them most, to be good fathers and good partners. Now we have good friends, like each other."

"I know you're right." She sighed. "I'll be glad when it gets busier around here. Too much time to think now."

Once Ellen arrived, the three of them were inseparable for a week. "I think the fun started with that card you got, Beth, you know the one about congratulations on moving, as if we were newlyweds buying our first place."

"Well, in a way, we are. We're just castaways together on a new island."

"That's good, Beth. Just think, I'd have never known you if it weren't for Daisy. Say, I need to find a new church."

"You know, the van goes down to that big Catholic church. It's much closer than Daisy's Presbyterian, and we'd be glad to have you."

"No, you can't have her. My Ford out there is a Presbyterian car, for little old ladies going to church. Of course, when Clarissa gets here in December, we'll have to drop her off at the Episcopal church. No telling what Mary Ann and Martha will do."

As the casitas were finished, new faces came into the dining room, some for lunch or dinner and some for both meals. Daisy met the Chisholms at the door one evening. Paul was gracious as he introduced his wife Anna. "We've moved a whole mile today, but you know we're as tired as if we'd come from New York."

Daisy nodded knowingly. "I moved from Hayden Road over here, and I agree. It's still moving day, and it's no fun."

"Do you have family here?"

"A son and a daughter, both married."

"Nice to have your kids nearby. Ours are scattered around."

"Most of the time, it's wonderful. Once in a while, I feel as if my nest isn't as empty as it should be." They smiled, and Daisy led the way to a table. "Would you like to sit here? These are two of my friends. Beth O'Donnell and Ellen Crane, meet the Chisholms, Anna and Paul." They exchanged greetings and sat down. Bonnie came around to meet everyone and said she was sending over another newcomer.

"Hi, I'm Sandra Menkoff, and I'm alone, just me. Bonnie sent me over to sit here." Daisy took care of all the introductions again, and soon the conversations began.

"We've all been waiting for October when the casitas would be ready. I have two friends coming to live in Casita 33."

"Are they retired?"

"Oh, yes, one from Madison, Wisconsin, and one from Roswell, New Mexico."

Paul laughed. "Boy, that's a long distance marriage!"

"No, no. These are sisters who haven't lived together for forty or fifty years. I can't wait to see them."

Daisy asked, "Sandra, tell us where you're from."

"Oh, lots of places. Most recently, from Las Vegas."

Anna asked, "Why would you leave such a fun place?"

Sandra's face started to blush. "It's a great place when you're real young, but it gets kind of tiresome later on. I had to buy a house somewhere, so I chose to come to Scottsdale and retire. It always sounded friendly."

Daisy assured her she was right. "We came to Scottsdale about thirteen years ago, and I've never regretted it."

When Martha's sister, Mary Ann, moved from Roswell, she was the first resident to speak Spanish fluently. She reminded the dinner crowd one night that *ventura* is a word for happiness and good fortune, but also can mean a chance or a risk, maybe even a danger. That provided a lot of good conversation for everyone. To her table she added, "When my sister Martha gets here, we must make sure it isn't a danger for her. She's fought so hard for sobriety."

Ellen assured her, "I'll be right there to help her. My husband was a pastor, and we both did addiction counseling."

"She's really steady now, to a point of attending parties where the refreshments include beer and wine. Don't worry. I just mentioned it after I explained about *ventura.* She took a long time to decide to come here. For her, any move is a risk."

Mary Ann met her sister at the airport, since they had agreed Martha would sell all her things, including her car. She wanted to make a completely new start, and Mary Ann's furnishings would be enough to start their joint household.

On the following Tuesday at the usual Happy Hour at five, Martha was introduced as the newest member of the Ventura Managers' Team. Every resident had a vote in major decisions, so they were known as managers, all of them. She told where she was from and about her past employment, the usual information about children, marital status, and so on. Then she asked if there were any friends of Bill W. in the group. A hush came over the room as people looked puzzled and exchanged glances. She smiled and said, "That's all right. I always ask."

From the far side of the combined library and computer room came a soft voice. All eyes turned to see Tom Gable rise, lift his glass of cola and say, "My toast is to my new friends who don't seem to care what I'm drinking as long as I'm good company. I'm an old friend of Bill W."

Martha returned the toast with an uplifted glass of ginger ale. She turned to Daisy and said through her tears, "Thank you for inviting me here. This is going to be a wonderful place for me." People returned to their little groups of conversation or to the snack table for food. Martha asked Mary Ann if she knew who that man was, and only Ellen knew him as Tom Gable.

"I talked with Tom one day at the mail boxes. He's from California, somewhere north. He owned a restaurant, I believe, and came here to join his brother running a place called 'Mom's Office & Grill' on 68th Street. Last fall when his brother died and the place was sold, he was interested in getting into a comfortable place to retire."

"Well, he may be my partner in a new twelve-step group."

When Daisy returned home that evening, she found Curly anxiously waiting at the door. She snapped on his leash and tried to let him out. Instead, he romped back into the living room and stood at attention near the telephone. Sure enough, the light was flashing on the answering machine. She chuckled as she pushed the button to play. Pete's voice, so like his father Scott's, started his message with "Hi, Curly, how's the Old Boy?" Curly's tail swept back and forth. They listened to the whole message, and then she coaxed Curly out the front door. She tried to tell Curly what a nice social hour she'd had before dinner, but his entertainment had been in hearing from Pete.

They returned from their walk, and Daisy confided in Curly, "I have a feeling something new and exciting will keep us busy this week."

CHAPTER 5

The Strength of Friends Surfaces

BETH CAME TO DAISY'S DOOR one cool morning, and Daisy saw she looked troubled. "Come in. Is something wrong?"

"Very wrong. You can't imagine how wrong."

"Here, sit and tell me." She stayed close to Beth.

"I need to find a surgeon. My doctor called and gave me one hour to find a surgeon in Scottsdale or he wants me back in St. Charles Hospital by tomorrow afternoon."

"Whoa. Why?"

"My mammogram came back with significant changes. That's what he called it. Likely a malignancy."

"You had it done before you left Geneva in May? And it took him six months to tell you?" Daisy's voice was rising as her anxiety grew.

"I just now notified everyone of my change of address. I know I should have done it earlier, but I never thought of the mammo." She moaned and bowed her head. "Oh, Daisy, why this? Why now? I'm over the hip surgery and the big move out here." By now she was crying, and Daisy had her braced with an arm across her shoulders.

"Maybe that's why you're here, Beth, where you're with an old friend to get you through it. We'll find a surgeon. Let me call my daughter; she knows all the medical people here." Quickly she went to the kitchen where she could talk softly to Julie. When she returned, Beth was gazing out the window in a trance. "Julie recommends Dr. Vithon. He's supposed to be everyone's favorite for smooth recoveries, and that's what you want."

"I don't know, Daisy. Do people recover from losing these?" Involuntarily, her hands were holding her breasts, as if to protect them from removal.

"Yes, I'm sure they do. Who needs breasts any more?"

That brought a smile to Beth's face, in spite of her tears. "I always kind of liked my figure. Maybe I was vain."

"No, you're not. You were the prettiest girl in Geneva, and once your hair turned white, you were the prettiest lady. And you don't even wear glasses yet. Now, let's concentrate on finding Dr. Vithon."

"I don't think I can make that call, Daisy."

"I'll do it. I'm going to pretend to be desperate, so brace yourself." In a matter of five minutes, they had an appointment for the next morning. "Amazing how many names I dropped in those few minutes," Daisy said with a chuckle.

"Can you tell Ellen and the sisters? I'll listen, but I don't think I can say that awful C word about myself."

"Let's both talk to Ellen. C'mon, let's go over to her place right now."

"This minute?"

"Yes, Beth, now." She opened the door and urged Beth to follow her. As they walked, she said, "Then we'll go to your place, and I'll hold your hand while you call your doctor back home. If you want, I'll write down what you need to tell him."

Four days later, four of the five friends were clustered in the surgery waiting room. The 7:00 a.m. surgery was in progress, as they huddled there waiting for news. Each one reacted according to her own experience of bad news or a medical crisis. Daisy had taken Beth to the doctor and to check in at the hospital at 5:00. Mary Ann and Martha had both suffered tough decisions in hospitals with their parents. They were prepared for the worst and were praying. Ellen was calm, watching for any movement around the nursing station.

Daisy's chair faced the hallway to the operating room. She kept her eyes on that double door. After an hour and a half of this tension, a doctor in scrubs came out and walked toward them, meeting up with Julie outside the door. They came in, smiling. The doctor announced she had come through it very well, and she would be in the recovery room for several hours. He said Julie would explain the follow-up treatment.

Julie hugged them all and then sat down to explain. "The double mastectomy or bi-lateral removal of all breast tissue was needed. Three lymph glands on one side were involved and two on the other, so chemo is recommended. Anything beyond that will be up to the oncologist. She'll be able to go home with all of you tomorrow."

Ellen choked over that. "Tomorrow?"

"Yes, she'll be fine. The nurse will show her exactly how to empty the drains, and she can have pain meds as she needs them. Many of our patients find Tylenol is enough. She can eat anything. Probably none of your wild cocktail parties for a few days, Mom."

They all laughed at that. "Should one of us stay at night?"

"I don't think so, but if she'd feel better, you might take turns. We have to remember, it's a terrible shock that she's been through so fast. Be compassionate and help her, but don't do everything for her. Part of her recovery in strength will come from doing the usual stuff she does every day. The best part of recovery comes from your friendship. Patients with loved ones do the best. Some laughter every day will lighten her fear of being scarred or handicapped. She needs to watch her posture. It's easy to hunch over and favor those incisions.

"When will she need to see the doctor?"

"I'm guessing in a week, to Dr. Vithon. Then she'll want to see the oncologist, who won't want to start treatment until she's well healed, maybe after the holidays. One of you should go with her to hear about the treatments. There's a lot of information about side effects, so it's wise for someone else to hear that. Mom, why don't you wait for her in her room, since you're her closest buddy? Just one visitor today." She excused herself, and the others moved toward the parking lot and Mary Ann's car.

Three weeks later, the five friends met at the Tuesday evening social hour to celebrate Beth's recovery. The drains and bandages were gone, and the doctor had dismissed her for another month. She was radiant in a pink shirt with a red and pink silk scarf under her collar. "This is one scar I'll never show anyone," she said emphatically. "It has to be the most crooked incision ever made."

"Julie says it will all disappear when you have the reconstruction."

"Me? I don't know. It sounds ridiculous at my age."

"She told me you should not decide anything for three months. Julie's always right." They all nodded, knowing Julie's positive approach. They sipped their drinks in a toast.

Beth smiled at her new friends. "You gals have pulled me through this, you know. I never knew the meaning of a support group until this hit me. What if you hadn't written your Christmas letter, Daisy?"

Daisy shrugged and replied, "What if you hadn't accepted my invitation?"

Mary Ann chimed in and said, "Why did you write us?"

"Remember I told you I knew something had to change in my life? That day I went to the remnant sale did it. I love making something new out of remnants."

"So? Go on."

"Well, we're all remnants, survivors of divorce or spinsterhood or widowhood, but we're not ready to give up living."

Ellen spoke up. "It's Biblical! The answer is in Romans 11:5. We're remnants, chosen by grace, by God's grace. We still have things to do in this world."

Martha frowned and said, "Yes, but some of us thought we'd found something good to do. I didn't know we might need new friends to help us."

Ellen went on, "Isn't it amazing God chose a mixture of people like us for Daisy to write to?"

Daisy replied, "I wrote nine letters, but you were the only ones with enough courage and vision to say yes."

Beth added, "Here's to Daisy still putting remnants together to make something new."

Daisy was delighted with the way her friends had met and melded together into a group. The variety in their ages hadn't been noticeable. They combined blonde and grey hair with salt and pepper black, and Daisy wondered if Clarissa's red hair had turned yet. They agreed they must get to know other residents too; but they decided to have a Thursdays at Three meeting, just the five of them, to talk about issues or politics or a new book, just good conversation. Before long, other small groups formed around special interests too.

CHAPTER 6

Another Remnant Arrives

THE DAY AFTER THANKSGIVING, Daisy and Curly were returning from their walk when a shiny black limousine drew up to the main entrance of La Ventura. The driver moved to help his passenger out, and Daisy watched as a fashionably dressed, beautifully coifed white-haired lady stepped out. She looked up and called out, "Daisy MacDuff, I'd know you anywhere! How in the world are you?"

Curly's tail went into action, but Daisy frowned slightly as she focused on the lady's face and her bent shoulders. "Clarissa? Clarissa, is that you?" They came together in a big hug. Curly tried to join them.

"This must be your famous dog who gets to retire with you." She bent to give Curly a pat. Then she gestured toward the driver who was watching with amusement. "And this young man, Tommy, is doing just what my nephew ordered. Isn't he a darling boy? Now where should he leave my things?"

Daisy directed him to the lobby where one of the assistants would put them on a cart. She was laughing at the memory of years of easy friendship with her flame-haired friend. Clarissa dismissed the driver with a twenty-dollar bill and blew him a kiss with a flourish. Daisy caught a glimpse of Clarissa the Performer.

"All right, dear, show me where to register and let's get this new life of mine started."

Curly and Daisy led the way, with the luggage cart following. On their way to Unit 17, Daisy tapped on Ellen's door. She called out, "Be there in a minute."

Daisy watched as the bags were piled in the living room. "Fourteen bags, Clarissa?"

Ellen came in and they exchanged names and laughed as Clarissa explained, "Dick said I should pack everything at once so I wouldn't have dribs and drabs of possessions getting into holiday mail. He even loaned me the suitcases. That's why he got the limo!" She looked around at her rooms and was all smiles.

"We got excited last week when all this nice furniture arrived," Ellen commented. "How did you get it down here?"

"Oh, I didn't. Dick just asked me what kind of things I'd like and said it would be waiting for me. I like what he chose, don't you?" She looked into the bedroom and nodded appreciatively. "He has good taste. And this is a pretty place. Daisy, you knew I'd have to have greenery around me, didn't you?"

Soon they heard the chatter of the dinner procession and they took turns washing up. As they walked, Clarissa said, "Now you understand, Daisy, I'm only here on a trial, just until the hot weather starts. You know I can't stand to perspire."

Daisy chuckled and said, "I do remember that. You were always afraid your hands would slip and you'd miss a note."

Clarissa's face clouded over and she nodded. "How I wish that were the reason now. But I guess it wouldn't be ladylike to get the cards sticky either. You know, that's my life now."

"I've already warned the bridge group that you'd be here by Christmas. They reminded me they play for fun, and I told them you'd try not to convert them into duplicate fiends."

"No promises." Clarissa looked out over the crowd as Ellen moved ahead of them. "Daisy, did all these friends of yours know Scott as well as I did? I mean, I was worried about your note when you said I might find some surprises in packing, like you did. Was it something about Scott?"

Daisy sighed. "Clarissa, you were always so perceptive. Yes, I found some things among his papers that shocked me. Secrets. Some things that dated way back to when we were first in town here. I guess he drank more than I knew. I was always busy with my sewing and church stuff. Maybe I should have helped him adjust to retirement, but he seemed so confident and ready for anything new. First I was hurt; then I was mad. Then my regrets made me sad. Finally, I just threw all those records away. What good would it do to keep that bitterness? It was hard enough to lose him. I couldn't go through that grieving again."

"I think you made the right decision. He was such a handsome man. He was bound to have some flaws; no one is perfect! My dad's old records were dismal. I wonder that the I.R.S. didn't come after him for years. He just kept terrible records."

"And you were always so precise, Clarissa."

"Right, and I could have helped him, but he'd never tell me anything about his investments. That's not how I want to remember him, either, so I put all those papers through the shredder and kissed the past good-bye."

"Clarissa, it's good to have someone here who knew me 'way back when." Daisy dabbed at a tear and smiled.

Over the weekend, the halls and common areas were transformed into a holiday setting. "I can't believe the variety of wreaths," said Beth. "And all the twinkling white lights. No way anyone could feel glum around here."

Ellen agreed. "I thought I'd miss the festivity around Atlanta, but it's going to be Christmas here too. The sunshine helps, doesn't it?"

Beth put her arm through Ellen's and whispered, "I thought life looked pretty grey for a while, but you know, Daisy was right. There is life without breasts." She laughed out loud and Ellen squeezed her hand and nodded.

"You're making a wonderful recovery. We're so proud of you. By the way, are you writing a Christmas letter this year?"

"No, but I always put little personal notes inside the cards I send. I have to admit, I send fewer cards each year. I've lost touch with a lot of old pals. That's why Daisy's letters were so welcome."

Ellen thought about that. "Maybe I should write more notes. I wonder what Daisy's writing this year." They walked on toward the dining room.

Christmas and Hanukkah decorations soon became a topic of conversation. Daisy brought this up at one of their Thursday meetings. "This season may be a test of how we're growing together. So far, people seem a little tentative in talking about their holiday traditions. Accepting each other is what I hoped would add variety to my life."

Ellen spoke up first, as she often did. "The church helps me the most in December. But, I do miss sweet Emily and her parents. This new church isn't quite the same."

"Boy, is that the truth!" Beth shook her head and continued, "I don't even recognize the music anymore. The words are sure simple; every verse gets sung three times it seems. It's just not my old St. Timothy's, but it meets the requirements."

When they met the next Thursday, Mary Ann proposed the day's topic. "Doesn't it seem as if we ought to be involved in making the holiday for someone else?" The room was quiet, so she went on. "I know we agreed not to exchange gifts this year, and we've already mailed presents to our families. But there must be hungry kids around here, maybe some without parents."

"My priest begged us to remember the street people in Phoenix."

"Yes, but Beth, Scottsdale has them too. Right downtown in the after-school programs, there are kids who need warm clothes and food or toys." Daisy shook her head sadly. "We could drive over to Walmart or someplace big like that and buy some gifts. We could do that today, and then take them to the Boys and Girls Club or Vista del Camino. Kids play there during their vacation."

"You don't think it's too late?"

"No, around here the stores are open even on Christmas Eve. Would food be better?"

"One of us should call and ask what they need the most. Daisy, you call. You know which clubhouse is nearest us."

Daisy called several numbers and learned that games and four new basketballs would help the kids at the Boys and Girls Club, and hams, beans and cookies were needed at Vista. "The directors said the cold weather has hurt a lot of families, and the food supplies are short for the migrant workers out in the orange groves."

Mary Ann spoke up and offered to drive, because she could also speak Spanish if there were people waiting for help at Vista. "I spent years talking with those workers around Roswell. We should have been doing this weeks ago. I don't know why I forgot all my previous mission work."

"It's easy when we live in such a comfortable place," Ellen consoled them. "This past year has been such a change for all of us. The move made us focus on ourselves, and that's not bad. But now that we're settled, it's time to reach out."

"All right, I'll drive too, since we have such small cars. Let's meet at the front door at 4:00 so we'll be back in time for dinner." They hurried off to get their purses, and Daisy thought, "The holiday spirit momentarily overcomes arthritis, loneliness and the prospect of chemotherapy. Thank Goodness!"

CHAPTER 7

Happy New Year, 2004

THE NOTICES WERE POSTED at every corner:

> **2004 IS THE YEAR TO LEARN!**
> **NEW CLASSES START THIS WEEK!**
> **Knitting & Crochet**
> **Computer**
> **Wood Carving**
> **Pottery**
> **Writing Your Life Story**
>
> **Tuesdays at Two**
> **Locations to Be Announced**
> **Sign up in the office, NOW!**

Martha was the first to see the notice and tell the others the news. "I want to write my life story. Do you think I can?"

"Of course." Daisy was always the one cheering them along. "It would probably be good for all of us to do that one.

But I'd like to do some knitting again. Heavens, I haven't made anything for a baby for years."

"I wish I could use my hands like that," Clarissa said wistfully. She sighed. "I guess I could talk about my life, maybe use one of those dictation things Dick uses."

"Why don't you offer to teach bridge, Rissa? Or any card games. You seem to know them all."

"Hm. I could. Would they mind if I volunteered?"

Daisy said emphatically, "Of course not. Go to the office and talk with Bonnie or Malcolm. They just don't know they have a pro of a teacher right here."

Beth's doctors recommended chemotherapy as a preventive measure as well as a way to seek out and destroy stray cancer cells. "I like that idea," she explained to the friends. "I want to fight whatever invaded my body, just when I thought I had a happy new life starting."

They all agreed and offered to be her drivers. "I'll draw up a schedule, so we can sign up. We'll need other new friends since we only have two cars among us. When do you begin?" Martha sounded eager to organize the group.

"I'll find out exact dates and times tomorrow. I think the Ventura van will drive me."

"Well, I'll check on that too. Let me know tomorrow."

The Tuesday classes began, and conversations about the classes kept the residents mixing in new ways. "Isn't it interesting to find out that some of our residents are retired from fascinating work? Gustav, the wood carver, used to sell his carvings in an elegant shop in Door County, and his father did it before him. And our writing teacher used to be the Food Editor of the newspaper."

As spring came to the Valley of the Sun, the heat became the main topic at dinner. Some of the residents were returning to northern homes, especially in Michigan and Minnesota. Two Canadian couples divided their year half and half for tax and insurance benefits. Many of the singles were planning to stay in Scottsdale, except for short visits to relatives or tours to Europe or Asia. The Bunch of Daisy's, as they had sometimes been called, decided to share their writing projects on alternate weeks during the hot months after the class schedule closed on May first. After that, they would pick a current event to discuss.

At one of their meetings, Ellen asked Martha how the twelve-step group was progressing. She was quick to explain she couldn't really say much about it, but she went on, "The fact that the same people continue to come, never miss a meeting, tells me I'm doing the right thing. You know Tom's my strong helper, so at least you know two of us."

"I just learned that he worked in his brother's bar, so he must really be committed to the program."

"I know. I think he was the one who added the word 'grill' to the bar. He told us at dinner one night about developing a signature sandwich down there and some special coffee blends."

"How long has he been in town?" Daisy inquired.

"Ten or twelve years, I think he said. He used to go to an AA group over at your church, Daisy, and sometimes to one at the Temple on McDonald."

Mary Ann joined the conversation. "Martha, I think Tom's kind of sweet on you."

Quickly Martha blushed and protested. "Heavens no. He's just a kindred spirit. We understand each other."

"Sure, sure." Mary Ann laughed and said, "That's why his face lights up when you and I come into the dining room."

"Maybe he's interested in you. After all, you've been alone a long time and look so slim and young."

"I'll bet you girls have been teasing each other over dates since high school days." Everyone enjoyed their banter.

Sales of the casitas and apartments had been brisk in the spring, although many of the new owners planned to move in after the August heat. The directors had a reception for all the owners who were still in town on May first. The decorations included a May basket on each of the main doors and flowers in baskets on every table. The place had never looked better, and Daisy was especially glad she was considered one of the "original" members of the Managers' Team. The director Malcolm introduced her as a volunteer in public relations, and her friends clapped and cheered.

One of the new owners, Dave Olson, used a white cane and told several others he lost the sight in one eye in an accident in 1999. "But I could have drowned, so I'm lucky to get around this way."

Mary Ann asked more about the accident and learned it was where 68th Street crosses a canal. Daisy watched as Tom moved over to talk with them, and she drifted toward a group wearing the lavender name tags indicating the most recent owners.

A gentleman from Tucson introduced himself, saying, "I'm Alexander MacPherson, and it sounds as if I ought to speak to a MacDuff."

Daisy noted his strong handshake and handsome smile. "Welcome to our home, Mr. MacPherson. We need more Scots around here."

"Always, but are you that formal all the time?"

She smiled and agreed that first names are the norm. "Have you lived in Scottsdale before?"

"No, but I like the looks of the place. My son and daughter-in-law live up in Carefree, so this is nearer them than Tucson. My wife died a few years back, and the kids have been urging me to move up here when I retired. We lost our retirement place to the fire on Mt. Lemmon last summer."

"And you retired from what?"

"Law practice, mostly taxes and family law."

"You'll be very popular around here if you tell the others your experience."

"Right now, I'm retired, really retired. I'm mostly just tired. And I still have to clean out the Tucson house by June fifteenth."

"I don't envy you. That was the hardest part of the whole move. I thought the decision was tough until I started to thin out everything. I hadn't thrown anything away since my husband died two years earlier." She shook her head sympathetically.

Another new owner came toward them. He announced he too had to empty a house this week. "Andrew Mason here. My wife didn't come with me. She's in Eloy, taking her time to pack some of the delicate stuff. She, uh, she doesn't really want to move yet."

Daisy sensed the situation, as did Alex MacPherson. He shook hands and introduced himself to Mr. Mason. "But she signed the papers and all?"

"Oh, yes. She didn't think we'd have to move right away. When our house sold fast, and the people wanted it right away, it set her back a bit."

"I hope she adjusts to the idea soon."

"Sure, she will. I brought the dog and as much stuff as I could in my truck. I'll go back tomorrow and see what's holding her up."

Daisy asked gently, "Please tell her that we're anxious to meet our new neighbors. Lots of us had some days when we weren't sure we'd made the right move. Now it seems just fine. How long have you lived in Eloy?"

"Ever since we got married. Let's see, 1952. I was the town vet."

Daisy gasped quietly. "This may be a difficult move."

Alex asked, "Did you sell your practice?"

"Yup. Nice young guy bought me out and bought the house too. The new doc and his family have their stuff coming on Monday."

With that, he turned away and headed for the food table, leaving Alex and Daisy to share a smile. They moved on and met some other new people.

As the number of residents grew, so did the number of pets. Cats outnumbered dogs so far, but Daisy and Curly walked morning and evening with quite a group. All the ground floor units were sold, not just to pet owners, but to people who knew their neighbors might be four-footed.

Malcolm asked Daisy if she and Curly would like to be a visiting team once the dementia wing was completed in the care center. "We're told that canine visitors are very soothing to many patients. Both you and Curly seem to be the right disposition for that mission. You know, there's a training program over at the college."

"Let us know when it's time to train for it. We'd be glad to take a stroll over there. Curly's never been in an elevator, but we can take the stairs if he balks."

"Curly would balk at the elevator? Not this gentle giant."

Back in Unit 7, Daisy rewarded Curly with a chew bone. "We're needed in a new way. Isn't that amazing? We may have to go to school together!"

CHAPTER 8

Introducing Clarissa Benton

On May thirteenth, the Thursday at Three friends met for the first reading of a life story. They had agreed at the last writing class to go in alphabetical order, by last names. As usual, Daisy acted as the moderator of the group. Clarissa asked if she could sit down to read, since her back was her weakest part. Daisy did a drum roll on the table, "He-e-e-r-e's Miss Benton," and sat down.

"Alphabetically speaking, I'm often first, so today, I'll start by introducing you to Clarissa Benton, born in Cleveland, the youngest of five girls. Father was a science teacher, and Mother was a church volunteer in the Altar Guild. We were all red heads; my elder sister Elizabeth was a strawberry blonde; then Margaret had curly dark red hair, just lovely. Next was Louise, and her hair was almost orange, terrible! Then Florence was a light red head. I hated being called 'carrot top' and 'Orphan Annie,' but my hair was flaming red and curly.

"In 1929 when I was six, Father moved the family to St. Louis. He explained it was to find students more interested in science, but I think he was a restless man. We stayed there eight years, during Depression days. Finally in 1937, he decided to teach high school in Seattle, the cleanest city in America, according to him. He was worried about pollution and war; he was an anxious personality, always talking about protecting his girls.

"In 1942, we moved again, away from the big city that could become a target for enemy bombing. We moved out to the Olympic Peninsula where he taught in Silverdale, a new and growing community. He wouldn't let my sisters go to college in Seattle until he was sure the ferries were safe.

"Finally, Elizabeth and Margaret lived together at the university until Liz got married. Then Louise was allowed to move in with Margie. All this time, Florence and I stayed home, went to school and made music. She played the violin and I, the piano. As a senior, I was asked to take over my teacher's students when she had surgery. She never really recovered, so I had twenty-two children coming to our home for lessons after school. It was wonderful to be earning money doing what I loved.

"Once the war threat was past, two of my best students took over for me, and I got to go to Seattle with Flo. We each helped a professor and earned some of our expenses that way. Flo was engaged but waited a long time to get married. I entered graduate school and taught undergrad students on the side. Mother grew more and more sickly. When I was twenty-seven, I came home to take care of Mother and the house. She died before Christmas, 1950. Father retired and stayed upstairs. He became a recluse, a sad and lonely old man.

"I advertised for students and before long had a thriving group of talented young ones. Father claimed he loved listening to my music lessons. So, I bought a second piano and converted the downstairs into my studio. When he died, of a broken heart I think, in 1952, I took up bridge in the evenings. Several neighbors and I played a couple of times a week.

"Life went on smoothly, for eight or ten years. I attended symphony at St. John's and had lots of friends. I accompanied the Kitsap Glee Club and kept it going and growing for over twenty years. People used to ask me when I was going to get married, but in my forties, I wasn't interested in giving up my way of life. I had all day to myself, except for my own practice routine. About 2:30, my students started to come; by 6:30 or 7:00, I was finished. Time for a sandwich and some cards. Two of my sisters had died; I had bought the other sisters out so I owned the house. My bills were small, and my freedom was huge! I could decorate and dress however I wanted.

"The arthritis started when I was sixty-five, as if I'd hit a wrong note in a concert, bang! Within two years, I had to send my students to one of my best former kids. She was delighted, and it pleased me to start someone's business the same way mine had begun. I kept a couple of beginners and coached two of my most advanced ones. But I could never again play second piano at the recitals. I was famous for my June recitals. I'd rent the Baptist church with its broad stage, have my two grand pianos moved there and tuned. Each year, I bought a new formal dress. Monday, Tuesday, and Thursday nights we started with the littlest ones and finished with the most accomplished. It gave me such satisfaction to see those children blossom with poise and skill. It was hard to let go of recital time.

"Then another door of opportunity opened. The new YMCA director asked me to come and teach beginning bridge in the senior program. It was great fun and kept me on a teaching schedule. It didn't matter my back is bent and my fingers gnarled.

"Liz's son Dick is my attorney and takes care of my business matters. I remember when he was a youngster and wanted to be a doctor. He promised he'd take care of me, do all my operations. He became a lawyer instead, and thank Goodness, I've never needed an operation. Between us, we've arranged all the family funerals; I've survived my parents and all four sisters. I am the last of the redheads!

"Our writing teacher suggested we close with a recent experience of great joy. Mine came just a few days ago, as I was counting the months I've been here: almost six. I was all alone in the game room and felt drawn to that lovely little piano. I sat down, rubbed and flexed my fingers and struck a chord. No pain, just stiffness. I couldn't believe it. I trilled a few runs and remembered some favorite passages. I made it all the way through the second movement of the 'Pathetique' and felt tears pouring down my cheeks. It was a moment of such joy that I wanted to share it with you.

"These months with Daisy's other friends have been so happy, but I never thought a climate could be such a blessing. Believe me, I'll visit Dick's family from July to September, but when the clouds move in, I'll be back."

Clarissa set aside her papers, about twenty pages written in a large sprawling hand. The others stood and huddled around her, thanking her for her whole story. Daisy led off with, "Clarissa, as long as I've known you, I never knew the rest of your life. Thank you for being our number one writer! We'll meet our next writer in two weeks; now don't forget!"

CHAPTER 9

Hi, I'm Martha, and. . .

"THE REST OF THAT LINE will come later. In 1933, I was christened Martha Joan, after my aunt and Saint Joan of Arc, born into our typical Italian family, the Morellis, in Chicago. My older sister is Mary Ann, and we had an older brother Paul who was killed in Korea and another one, Guido, we've lost touch with. I grew up in St. Teresa's church and school. Public high school was pretty intimidating to me. I was an average student, sheltered at home and aware of what I would probably grow up to be. I learned to cook, clean, baby-sit the neighbors and cousins in that expectation.

"Frankie Costello was the same age and the same background. He assured me he was God's answer to my prayers for the future. We graduated from North City High on Wednesday, the twentieth of June in 1951 and were married on Saturday, June twenty-third. Frankie prided himself in making me pregnant by Sunday the twenty-fourth.

"His first job with a trucking company required a week of training and a transfer to Madison, Wisconsin in six months. Paul was born in March 1952, and young Frank in 1954. We built a house in a new subdivision, and I thought we were doing everything right. Then we had Louis in '56 and Mary in '58. Our home was pretty happy, busy and always full of kids and their activities. When I wasn't carrying a baby, Frankie apologized for me to our friends and neighbors. 'Soon, she'll look productive, if you know what I mean,' he'd say and laugh. Having a pregnant wife was all that mattered. I had made up my mind that I was through having children. That enraged him, and we had lots of arguments about who could decide that.

"When the kids were all in school and they were able to be alone for an hour or two after school, I said I'd like a job, something where I'd learn some new skills. 'Over my dead body' was his usual veto. In front of the whole family one Thanksgiving he proclaimed that no wife of his would ever work. I remembered that a few years later when he walked out on us, moved to the Milwaukee district and moved in with a woman working in that office of the company. It was O.K. for a mistress to hold a job.

"After he left, Mary and Frank stayed with me while Paul and Lou sided with Frankie and moved to Milwaukee. He vowed he'd never divorce me. Well, he didn't have to; I divorced him. I got a job at the big Medical Center, transcribing records. The people there were wonderful and helped me sober up. Then I went to Methodist Hospital to make a new start. Our parents had died, and I became a Methodist, and I've never regretted my choice. I eventually found a whole new career in counseling.

"Young Frank was married in 1976 and still teaches school in Neenah, Wisconsin. His daughter Jennifer is twenty-four. My Mary was married in 1984, and they've opted not to have children. She's a nurse, and her husband is a pharmacist. They have a very stable life.

"Paul, who went with Frankie, has never really been happy, according to his brother. He's a policeman in Milwaukee, married with no kids. I've lost touch with Lou, except through the others. He married in 1978, and they had two little boys, little Lou in 1979 and Mario in '81. As far as I know, he's still a bartender in Milwaukee.

"Moving here is the bravest move I've ever made. With Mary Ann's guidance, I sold everything from my old life, except personal treasures. I look back on my early life and wonder why I was so dependent on my family and then on Frankie. He hurt my feelings all the time, and I had never been treated that way at home. Why did I settle for cooking and cleaning for him? I loved being a mother, and yet he almost ruined that for me too. He'd ridicule me in front of everyone. I remember one evening when he pulled me up out of my chair at dinner and shouted, 'Kids, take a good look at this woman. Does she look dumb enough to forget to buy my beer?'

"And yet I felt so guilty about failing as a wife that after he left, I began to cry and drown my sorrows every night until I fell asleep. Now I can see what was wrong, and I've helped lots of young women to see themselves as worthy people again. I don't know what was wrong with me. I could have had several careers, each one rewarding and teaching me about life. I could have made some money to save for the future.

"My most recent joy? The Christmas letter from Daisy. I had let all my old friends slide into the past. I wonder if some of you have done the same thing. I was ashamed of my old life, but Daisy seemed to remember me as a person she'd like to see again, maybe even as a neighbor again. That lifeline to bridge the bad years was just what I needed. I called Mary Ann, and she was still thinking about the letter. She drove out here, and began to put the pressure on me. She knew I couldn't afford it all at once, so she offered to lend me half of the down payment. It's awful to be so dependent! Secretly, I decided to try it for three years.

"Living with all of you and starting a new recovery group are my joys. Oh, yes, now I'll finish that sentence. My name is Martha, and I'm an alcoholic. And you're all supposed to say 'Hi Martha.'"

The friends clapped and laughed as they chimed in "Hi, Martha." There were hugs and tears, and Martha was the most radiant of the six. Daisy closed the meeting, saying, "See you on June tenth right here, to meet Ellen. I'll see you all at dinner tonight too, and next Thursday for other talk."

CHAPTER 10

Meet Ellen Ferguson Crane

THE GROUP MET PROMPTLY AT three in the coolest room at La Ventura. By now the afternoons were so warm that Daisy had requested a tray of iced tea and extra ice for their meetings. Martha was the first to speak up. "I can hardly wait to hear Ellen's life story. I'm so relaxed today."

Ellen smiled and began. "I grew up in Louisville, Kentucky, in a happy family where I was expected to be a good student like my parents before me. My father worked for the *Courier-Journal* as an editor, so I often heard wild stories around home and was sworn to secrecy. I started young to dream about finding a lost child's mama or curing a dreadful disease, doing something heroic.

"It was assumed I would follow tradition and graduate from Indiana University up in Bloomington. World War II was winding down as I started classes, but of course it took a long time for the world to settle back into a relaxed routine. The sororities rushed us, and my girlfriend and I pledged Theta. Dates were pretty sparse since we girls outnumbered the boys about eight to one. I did like one boy whose asthma had kept him out of service, so I felt lucky to have Joshua Crane squiring me around campus. When we graduated in 1948, we got married right away. It must have been a surprise for my folks, and his up in Indianapolis, but we thought it was thrilling. I moved with him to an apartment near the Louisville Seminary.

As a student's wife, I could take classes in religious studies and Christian Ed.

"In 1951, after his graduation, he got a call to Red Hill, Kentucky. We were so excited! We stayed there until 1958. Seth was born there, and the people cried when Josh accepted a call to Scottsburg, Indiana. I still hear from one man who was on the session that first called him. Then Peter was born in 1960, and we just loved being a cozy little family. I helped out around the church whenever a volunteer was needed, and the boys did too. Trouble was, I was having such a good time being the preacher's wife, I forgot to keep the boys in order. By the time we left there and went on to Oak Park, Illinois, those boys were terrible pranksters, galloping through the sanctuary, playing hide and seek in the parking lot, hiding the key to the organ and tying up the telephone lines with the hold buttons. Josh's dad said Josh was just as wild.

"In 1974, Josh was called to Minneapolis to the largest church we ever served. Our long-haired boys were sixteen and fourteen, Seth driving too fast and Peter chasing every girl he could see. When the MacDuffs moved in, it was like having some angels dropped into the neighborhood. Scott took the boys fishing and taught some good lessons out in the boat. Seth tried dating Julie and being 'the boy next door,' rather than trying to be the coolest kid in Central High. Daisy dragged me into her kitchen for tea whenever she saw me fraying at the edges. Josh could relax in their home with Scott, without feeling he had to be the perfect pastor. We stayed there at Knox Presbyterian for ten years. The boys did college there, and those were years of many blessings.

"I taught adult classes as well as the four-year-olds, and I learned how to encourage other women into leadership. I always led a group to the national meetings of women at Purdue. We all found we could make things happen with our minds and hearts, as well as our money. They were stimulating years for those of us in our forties and fifties.

"Then right at the peak of my feverish activities, Josh was called to Atlanta. Along with his call came an invitation to serve on the Board of Trustees at the seminary in Decatur. He couldn't resist such an exciting opportunity. While we were there, his first book was published. His uncle was a poet and Grandpa was a minister. Josh was a good writer! When he went on sabbatical in 1995, he wrote another book aimed at helping parents of teenagers. I was still typing that manuscript when he died in 1997.

"I think his work in family counseling and listening to young people's needs made our churches grow. He always seemed to have time for everyone. I never knew how he did it. Fortunately, I too believed he was meant to give one hundred percent of himself to being a pastor. I read books by the bushel and was always willing to do anything helpful around the church.

"God blessed our sons with loving wives. Seth married Marie in 1983 at age twenty-five, and they had handsome Nick in 1986 and dear little Emily in 1990. At thirty, Peter married Jane in 1990, and they adopted a Korean girl named Kim who is now ten, a terrific student and a musician. Funny thing is, I've looked like everyone's grandma since I was about fifty; you know, white hair and overweight. I've worn glasses since college. When someone asks if anybody remembers some event in history, I always remember!

"Once again, I'm willing to do anything to make our latest adventure as friends a success. My most recent joy is being able to walk without pain. I'm in a dry climate, and some medical wizard created a new anti-inflammatory pill I can take. That's about all it takes to keep a smile on my face. Thanks be to God!"

The others were nodding in agreement. "Ellen, you described yourself perfectly! We love you, Grandma!" Questions kept them talking for another half hour. Finally, Ellen said loudly, "Let's see; we'll hear from Daisy on June twenty-fifth, practically the longest day of the year."

Daisy added, "Very possibly the hottest day of the year too."

CHAPTER 11

We All Know Daisy Jones MacDuff

"OUR WRITING TEACHER ASKED us to do the hardest thing in the world for me. I could draw it or sew a quilt telling my life story more easily than writing it. But just like school days, I'll try.

"I was born June fifteenth in 1934, into the First Presbyterian Church of Franklin Falls, Iowa, along the Mississippi River. The manse was a bleak sort of a house with no frills. Mother worked hard to keep it perfect, because as she said, it wasn't ours. Everything belonged to the people of the church we served. Believe me, it kept us humble.

"I had to amuse myself a lot of the time, since church activities kept my parents busy and involved with helping others. I had an imaginary friend, Ona, and a baby doll, Rosie. My cat was good company, as long as she wanted to be. I had colds all the time, probably not helped by the drafty, chilly house. In spite of wearing glasses from age four, I read voraciously. I learned to play the piano early, and that helped me all through life.

"Dad moved us to the church in Davenport, and that manse was lovely. I graduated from Davenport High School and went on to the University at Ames to major in home economics with a minor in food chemistry. When I learned to sew, that became my creative outlet. I wanted to teach everyone to sew, to make clothes and stuffed toys and household things. That goal kept me studying! The fabric stores were my favorites, and I soon had a room filled with bundles of matching materials and shoe boxes of half-completed future projects.

"I kept running into this handsome, older student when I went to the chemistry building. We began to meet for coffee before class, and gradually I realized I dearly loved that sturdy, blond senior named Scott MacDuff. He was president of his fraternity and active in Young Republicans. From a Scottish family in Bettendorf, he was filled with energy and ambition. His love of life was catching, and I was caught! We had lots in common. He was in civil engineering with a chemistry minor. He'd already been in the army after high school R.O.T.C., so when I graduated in 1956, and he got his degree, we were married. He already had a job, so we couldn't wait. Dad married us. Everyone in the church was there, and it was a traditional June wedding. In a shower of rice, we set forth for Poulsbo, Washington, where he had been hired in a government project. A fellow worker had found us an apartment over in Silverdale, and I began to practice my new skills on my husband.

"I joined the Women's Chorale in town and met Clarissa who accompanied and directed the volunteer group. After I had Julie in 1958, Clarissa urged me to return to sing. She wanted me to bring my baby to practice. She'd play, keep Julie beside her on the bench, and direct, all at the same time.

"Then Scott got a new contract back in Davenport. Our families were thrilled we'd be there for four years. We had Peter in 1960. I had lots of friends once again, plus afternoons free enough to sew and help Mother around the church. Even then, I knew I had already made some of my most long-lasting friends. There's something powerful about the bonds you forge in sharing marriage adjustments, small children, ailing parents and sibling relationships. I looked ahead at the itinerant life we were slated to have, and I knew all four of us had to be adaptable. That had been one of Mother's pet theories: learn to adapt without losing your own character. I was starting to expand on her wonderful gifts of maternal wisdom.

"After the four years in Iowa, we were off to Oklahoma City. Life there was oriented toward the oil business, and Scott's assignment was providing roads and bridges for new traffic needs. He even consulted on pipelines and such. During our four years there, I grew close to a neighbor, Donna Krueger, whose son Franz was in Julie's grade. She was a nurse at a big hospital and worked different shifts. I was often Franz's cookie mom after school. They were Lutherans, and we had tied in with the Presbyterians again. Her boy was just a genius, and eventually went into international relations. Anyway, those were good years too, awfully busy with our two in school, and I was a Brownie mother. After we moved, I lost track of Donna. I invited her to join us here in Scottsdale, but she didn't seem interested. Maybe tempted is the right word. She asked if her cat 'Terrific' could come too. I wrote her again and invited the cat too, but haven't heard a thing.

"Scott's next contract was with the University of Massachusetts as a teacher. He found he loved that job. I fell in love with all the quaint towns and loads of antique shops. People were a bit cautious about receiving new neighbors from Oklahoma; it was almost laughable to have them ask exactly where is Oklahoma, 'on the west coast?' I met another new resident named Sue Senderman, and she hated living in a small town. All she could talk about was Boston, as if she owned it. Her husband taught Hebrew, and their two sons had always been in boarding school. They never seemed terribly orthodox, but she said her greatest fear was that her sons would marry outside the faith. I just hoped and prayed mine wouldn't marry too young. She was my first 'no' about moving here.

"I keep getting off the track, but all these moves tie in with how I met each of you, so bear with me. When Julie was fifteen and Pete was thirteen, Scott was restless and ready to get back in the field. Minneapolis hired him as a consultant on its transit system and traffic problems in general. It was a very progressive city, and we loved its vitality. We joined the Presbyterian Church, and I suppose you can guess that the pastor was Joshua Crane. Ellen was trying to raise these two boys who were wild and woolly p.k.'s. I knew what that meant, so I tried to befriend her and defend her against all the free advice she got from the congregation. With long hair and loud music and fast cars, they were pretty scary kids, weren't they, Ellen?"

Ellen nodded and then patted her forehead, reliving that painful age.

"Those boys had the same threat over them that I'd had: be good or else! Well, we were neighbors and good ones. Their Seth dated our Julie for a time. We pretended not to notice, hoping they'd stay together, but they went their separate ways. Both of us had a son Peter, the same age. Ellen had always read the latest books on psychology or mysteries or Bible studies. I missed her when we moved on, missed her intellect and gentle wisdom.

"After those six years, we were sent to Madison, Wisconsin, not too far away. We moved into a brand new house with new people everywhere. The Italian family next door, with four kids younger than ours, happened to be Frank and Martha Costello. Students kept coming and going, with huge baskets of laundry to be done, always eating something and mostly trying to make it through the University. Her Mary and our Julie got along beautifully and still exchange Christmas cards. Often we were included in a summer picnic when her sister Mary Ann came for a visit. She was a social worker, and knew all the problems of growing kids. I was so shocked when Frank moved out, and two boys sided with him and left home for good. But Mary Ann seemed to understand and be a comfort to Martha. We were only there four and a half years, and we didn't put down roots as we did when the children were younger, but we kept in touch with the neighbors. Before we moved, Julie was married at the University Chapel, and Pete was engaged to a girl from Los Angeles.

"I wasn't too disturbed when Scott wanted us to go to Aurora, Illinois. It's a small city, very busy with manufacturing and transportation. The house we chose was in Geneva, and that town became my all-time favorite place. When we asked our new pastor for a reference to an accountant, he chuckled and said he used one who was not in the congregation. We agreed that was O.K. The name we got was Beth O'Donnell, whose husband was ill, so she had moved her CPA office to her home, not far from us. It was love at first sight, and we became close friends. I envied her skills and how she could work at home. She was confident and looked so professional, always wearing a beautiful suit. We had four of the happiest years there along the Fox River. Once again, I found antique stores and clever, crafty artisans with new ideas. That town spurred my creative juices into action, and I loved it.

"But before long, Scott decided to retire. I thought Geneva would be perfect for that mode of life, but he had started to suffer from sinus headaches. Everything he read promoted a dry climate for chronic sinus problems. Our parents were gone, and Pete urged us to try Scottsdale. We gave it a month in the winter of '91. Scott wanted us to build a home to settle in permanently, and he began to sketch ideas. We returned to Geneva and said farewell to Beth and other friends. It was a sad farewell for me.

"After seven houses around the country, we were finally home in 1992. Julie and her husband Matt had a chance to move here when he decided to go out on his own in law practice. I felt so blessed to find property we loved and a design we agreed on, plus having the children nearby. Then we found a wonderful church. That made it even better, and for nine years we reveled in contentment. He had his golfing friends and a retired engineers' club; I had my circle of friends and sewing buddies, plus a couple of neighbors from Iowa.

"Disaster hit in March of 2001. Scott was tired all the time and seemed disinterested in keeping the pool immaculate. He had always been so proud of the yard. We went to a dinner at the church, and he suddenly slumped in his chair. He was taken to the hospital where it was diagnosed as a mild heart attack. During that night, he suffered another attack, much worse, and by the next afternoon, he was gone. I was numb with the shock, and I suppose some of you have experienced sudden loss too. The grief comes and goes for a long time. Pete and Julie were all that kept me going, for days and days. Incidentally, Curly became pretty darned important to me too!

"That summer I learned all the lessons I should have known for years, how to do everything around the house, the car, the checkbook, etc. Other single women helped me. It wasn't a good year for a Christmas letter, but I had to tell people what had happened. Everyone said to be patient and keep busy; time heals all wounds, and so on. But other coincidental things help too. I have wondered if God is another definition for coincidence, because so often some marvelous insight pops up when I'm sitting quietly, open for ideas. The church seniors' tour of La Ventura was certainly providential for me. Even the next program fit into the grand design. It was called 'Look Ahead and Take a Chance.' And the rest, as they say, is history that you all share. Thank God for friends!"

The friends clapped and began to chatter at once. "You were like gypsies moving around the country! I thought ministers moved a lot, but you sure beat us," Ellen exclaimed.

"You know, as I wrote this story, I saw it was a travelogue rather than an autobiography. I never told you what any of my family was really like, or what food we liked or what kind of house we had. Oh, well. The facts stand." Daisy smiled and added, "It was a nostalgic tour."

Beth said softly, "Your whole life was governed by your husband's choices."

Defensively, Daisy agreed. "Of course, and I wanted it that way." A tear glistened on her cheek. "Now, let's see, we're ready for Mary Ann's 'true confessions' on July eighth."

Clarissa reminded them, "I'm staying to hear that one, but the very next day, I'm off to the cool coastline. Hurrah!"

"We'll miss you, Rissa, and don't get any funny ideas about sending for your stuff and staying there. We haven't forgotten those fourteen suitcases!" The group disbanded in laughter.

CHAPTER 12

Who Is Senora Mary Ann Martinez?

MARY ANN GREETED THE FRIENDS in the Hedgehog Room and was pouring iced tea for everyone. "Se habla Espanol?" she asked the group. No one replied, so she answered her own question. "Si, but not today."

"I was christened Mary Angelina Morelli, by an Italian priest in an Italian neighborhood with Italian parents. I was born in Chicago on May thirtieth in 1930, conveniently on a Saturday for my father, an electrician. He was the driver in the family.

"I've forgotten a lot about home life, but I know Mom was a super cook. There were lots of us crowded around the dinner table, so she pulled a kitchen stool up to the corner of the table after she had served everyone else. She always ate in her apron, and she patrolled our eating habits. Clean plates were the norm, and it's a wonder we weren't all fat as pigs. Paul and Guido always had seconds, which pleased her.

"I was lucky in school; things came easily for me. I had lots of energy and loved the little children from next door and across the street who came to play with my sister Martha. She was such a cute little girl, with dark curly hair and a dimple in her cheek. She'd wait for me on the front stoop or in the front window every day until she was old enough to go to school. The boys were gone a lot; in fact, we'd lost track of them until Paul died. They went off to war and never settled back in the city.

"I graduated from high school in '48 and got a scholarship to the University of Chicago. That was a turning point in my life. I worked after school and took every extra class I could. I helped in the after school program at the YWCA and in the University's laboratory school. In the back of my mind was the nursery poem Mom loved to quote.

Monday's child is fair of face,
Tuesday's child is full of grace,
Wednesday's child is full of woe,
Thursday's child has far to go,
Friday's child is loving and giving,
Saturday's child works hard for its living,
And a child that's born on the Sabbath day
Is fair and wise and good and gay.

"She was quick to remind me I was born on a Saturday and was so short, I might never find a husband. Men liked a woman who was strong, could work hard and have lots of children. I understood I was to make my own way.

"The School of Social Work had a placement agency and found me a job in Albuquerque, New Mexico. I'd never been beyond the city limits, so you can imagine how thrilled I was! I can remember writing letters home, and Martha was the only one who wrote back. How I loved seeing her perfect, round handwriting on an envelope!

"The agency there was all directed toward the Hispanic people, many of whom had migrated north from Mexico. It was easy to pick up the language after hearing Italian all my life. In 1960, I met and married a kind, loving older man who was a career military man out at Kirkland Air Base. He was from Mexico and volunteered with us to teach the boys baseball. He was a dear, but when he retired, he wanted to return to Mexico. He had never really loved working in the States. We had no children, so Jaime said I should keep my good work and maybe he'd come back north in a while. He wrote regularly and always asked if I needed money. I was so busy that I wrote short notes to him about our program, but we gradually lost touch.

"My next job opportunity came from Roswell, New Mexico, in the Casa de la Familia office. It was primarily to start a day-care center for working mothers. I called it the Round Up, and we were trying to teach English to both generations. It was a great success. We found so many kids who needed a safe place to play and have lunch too. We began keeping records of birth dates and siblings' names, which the local schools were grateful to have. I knew two generations of these families.

"Every summer I'd go to visit Martha, because she had kids who were growing up too fast and a husband who would never let her come to see me. There were neighborhood cookouts, and one friend of hers I remembered most was Daisy MacDuff! She had been such a special help to Martha that we started sending Christmas cards each year. After hearing her life's story, I realize why I had so many changes of address in my book.

"In 1996, Jaime died, and his insurance money came to me. It was like a windfall, and I could have comfortably retired. But the school was doing well, with government support and a food bank and a clothing closet for kids. Over the years, I had taken in and raised seven little boys until they finished school and got full time jobs. So, I decided to remodel the house from dormitory style to a single lady's retreat. I bought a new car and retired gradually to a consultant's role.

"When Martha asked what I thought of Daisy's Christmas letter, a light went on in my brain. I told her I'd think about it if she would. I'm not sure when it all began to gel, but those news-letters with the activities and menus were tempting. I offered to drive over here and see La Ventura. I loved it and loved seeing Daisy again. Martha and I had houses to sell, like most of you, I guess. It was much harder than I expected to clean out the clutter. The actual real estate part was easier than I had thought. I still can't believe it took nine or ten months to get here.

"Through it all, we both knew it felt right. At seventy-four and seventy-one, I think we were both feeling lonely. I had no family, and Martha's kids are all self-sufficient. Isn't it amazing how much we need companionship when we're little kids and again when we're old kids? Martha agreed to try this for three years. Sister, I hope three years is a charm. I'd like to stay here much longer!"

Mary Ann sat down and leaned back in her chair, looking relieved. The group clapped, and Martha reached over and squeezed her hand. Daisy spoke up, "I think the amazing part of you, Mary Ann, is that you made the transition from living with seven-year-olds to seventy-year-olds!"

Martha piped up, "But Mary Ann, you didn't mention our recent adoptions."

"Right. I've gone from little boys to little cats. You've all heard about Hansel and Gretel, and you'll hear much more since they're getting cuter and cuter. We're revising our wills, so we have to decide which one of you will inherit them. Any volunteers?"

"No," said Ellen, "but that should remind us all to review our legal stuff."

"Gosh, life keeps getting more complicated, doesn't it?"

"You all need a nephew like mine," Clarissa said smugly. "He does it all, and I'm on my way to see him."

They crowded around Clarissa. "You'll be back as soon as your bones start to rebel against the rain, won't you?" They stood close until she promised, and then they offered to help her pack and get ready for her shuttle at six the next morning.

Daisy wrapped up the meeting, reminding Beth to have her story ready for July twenty-second. She overheard Martha tell Mary Ann how she'd always hated that nursery rhyme, because she was born on a Wednesday.

CHAPTER 13

Meet B.O.O.

BETH CAME EARLY AND SAT at the end of the table. Her white hair sparkled in the fluorescent lighting, set off by a vivid Hawaiian print shirt in the colors of pink, red, rose, and a dash of burgundy. Daisy poured the tea, and Ellen arrived with a plate of cookies. "Special, today, since it's our last program about our life stories. Heavens, what'll we do next?"

"After Beth finishes, we'll talk about a new idea; all right?" Daisy settled down in her chair, and nodded to Beth.

"My monogram is BOO. Can you imagine an O'Brien marrying an O'Donnell? Well, I did, and then I realized I had moved from B.O. and the Lifebuoy soap ads to a Halloween scare. I was born in Chicago on Friday, November second, in 1928. Good Irish Catholic parents had two more girls after me, Mary and Colleen, and finally the son they had wanted all along, Sean Francis. I was named for my mother's dear Aunt Beth, who was a spinster aunt who doted on her nieces.

Father encouraged me to study accounting since I was good with numbers. He claimed he had a terrible time finding honest bookkeepers in his insurance office. So, I went to work for him when I was twenty-one, fresh out of Elmhurst College near our home. Right there in a couple of years, I met a dashing attorney named Bruce O'Donnell. There was no mistaking his

Irish background, with a twist in his accent and a charming smile. He knew how to court a young lady!

"After the wedding, we stayed near Chicago only a few months until he broke away from the firm and opened a practice out in Geneva, Illinois. As Daisy told you, it's a delightful town, and the county seat, so Bruce developed a whopping practice in the first year. We still had no children, so I studied hard and became a C.P.A. Sometimes, we even worked together with clients. Things went beautifully for years, with country club dances and Kiwanis Club for Bruce. I kept close to some college friends, since we were less than thirty miles from the campus. I've always loved clothes, so I was in a perfect small town for boutique shops, and Chicago's Michigan Avenue was just an hour and a half away.

"We had some difficult years with our aging parents, maybe more demanding than if we'd had children. We added a small apartment over the garage, but when they couldn't manage the stairs, Bruce and I often ended up spending a week or two in the apartment while they used our quarters. A new retirement center opened in Aurora, and we finally had everyone located there, safe and near us. By 1980, we had lost all four. We had four blissful years, traveled to Europe and South America and Canada. Then Bruce was hit with Parkinson's, and it progressed rapidly. He had to give up his practice in 1985, and that's when I moved my office home into the apartment.

"One day I had a call from new residents, Daisy and Scott MacDuff. He was working as an independent contractor and as a consultant to two companies, so he needed tax advice. We met at our home, and the four of us hit it off so well. When Bruce had a bad day, we'd have to cancel a dinner date or playing cards. But there were lots of times when we'd sit on our screened porch and talk and sip Tom Collins drinks late into the evening. We didn't have children, and theirs were far away, so we seemed well-matched. I remember a lovely Sunday afternoon drive along the river one October, must have been 1988, with the Macs. I think it was the last time Bruce went anywhere. Soon after, just before the holidays, he had to be hospitalized and finally cared for in a rest home in Batavia. In 1990, in the winter he couldn't shake a chest cold and died of complications. He was just short of turning sixty-five. He was the nurses' favorite patient, charming to the end.

"So, there I was, completely alone, my sisters in Florida and Detroit, and handsome brother Sean cutting a wide swath in London. My business always picked up toward income tax deadline, so that helped me to keep going in the usual routine. St. Timothy's became another involvement as they needed volunteers to count the Sunday plate and then do the Monday morning banking. I made some new friends I wouldn't have known as long as I was married. The years passed pretty well. Then I noticed I couldn't climb up to the apartment as easily. Finally not at all. I was terrified of the icy sidewalk in the winter for fear I'd fall.

"My doctor retired and the new, young woman doctor suggested I have a hip replacement. I'd never thought of it, so I investigated the procedure and decided it was worth a try. She sent me to an orthopedic clinic in Aurora, and I started 2002 with a new hip. To me, it was a slow recovery, but the doctor thought I did fine. I had my usual tax clients and a friend who drove me to therapy and helped me shop until I could drive again. By summer, I felt confident and flew to Detroit for a visit with Colleen. Amazing what the airlines can do to help you. But I hated to give up my cane, so I bought some fancy ones to blend with my jewelry and prepared to live that way forever.

"Then Daisy's letter came. I'd been so absorbed with my own life, I had let a lot of contacts slip. But bless her heart, she didn't give up on me. She even told me there were lots of canes and walkers around here. Of course, she's right. Then I found I hardly needed it when I got busy sorting my junk and packing boxes. I hired a student from the church to help me, and we made good time of it. The house sold in a couple of weeks, and I found I was free to do what I wanted. What a discovery! Father James said over and over to me, 'If you don't like it, come back.' I stayed until Easter and then flew here. My car could have been brought too, but I decided to sell it there and buy here if I needed one. I still may buy one. I saw a beauty the other day in the church parking lot.

"Well, of course I had to be the one to test the system by getting sick right away. I still can't believe how that happened so fast, but I'm grateful to all of you, and to Julie, for such kind and loving care. What more can I say, except it's never too late to learn a new lifestyle. If you keep banking on the past for your strength, you may go bankrupt in the future. Any time you need help with your checkbooks, come and see me!"

The four listeners made enough applause to attract the attention of Malcolm as he passed the room. He stuck his head in the doorway and asked what the cheer was about. At their invitation, he came in and had a glass of tea. "You know, you gals are my pride and joy around here. You're all so different and yet you've become quite a team. Do you miss some of your old buddies back home?"

Martha spoke first. "I've made such good new friends, and it was time for my old friends to make new ones too. They're all welcome to come and join me here."

Beth chimed in, "I agree, and it's valuable to offer these classes. I just told my whole life story, and if we hadn't had that class to get us started, we'd never have shared so much."

"I'm glad to hear it. The Book Group is doing well too. The Wood Carvers are meeting three times a week. By the way, what do you hear from your card shark?"

They all laughed, and Ellen answered, "Not much except she's raving about the cool air. We just hope she misses us enough to come back before the holidays."

"I bet she'll be here in October. That's when the showers start up there, with those grey skies she doesn't like. We'll see. I was just talking with a potential resident, and she mentioned her fears about moving into this village. Were any of you worried like that?"

Martha glanced around and said, "I told them I was afraid of losing my support group, but you see I've found a new one. My sister was pretty sure that would happen."

Daisy added, "I knew I was right in my hometown, but I think Beth was the bravest. She came out in May, in time for the summer heat."

Beth smiled and said, "That wasn't my fear. I thought I'd be older and more infirm than the rest of you. I only knew Daisy. You know, you can be real lonely in the midst of a crowd."

Malcolm was intent on Beth's words. "What could we do better to help the new ones blend in sooner?"

Mary Ann took a turn. "Could you have a present resident become a sort of guide, or an instant buddy? Those aren't the right words, but you know, assign a host right away? Then if it doesn't seem like a good match, maybe appoint another one?"

"That could work. I'll talk it over with Bonnie. It wouldn't have to be someone the same age, would it?"

"No, just someone able-bodied to walk easily with the new person."

"Thanks for the tea and the advice, girls. Keep writing! Maybe you could give me something for the newsletter?"

Daisy surveyed the others and summed up, "Not yet, Malcolm." He left with a wave. She went on, "What shall we do next?" She paused. No one spoke up. "I think we've become so much closer telling each other our stories, but maybe we need to mix in with everyone else and find new friends."

Martha groaned and said, "Daisy, we came here to join you and your friends, remember? We have other new friends too, but we have to stick close together on Thursdays at Three. It's special." She looked around, and everyone agreed.

Ellen calmly said, "This bunch of your friends intends to stay close, so you can't get away from us. Don't even try."

Daisy laughed. "I'm not looking for different friends. I just don't want us to get the reputation of being a clique. I know the bridge players keep to themselves, and so do lots of the couples. Now that there are so many of us living here, it's easier to make lots of little groups. If we want to add more women to our group that's fine. It might be fun to add some men."

Mary Ann jumped on that remark. "Heavens, what would Clarissa say if she were here? Aside from her, I've probably been alone the longest, always doing things with the girls."

Beth smiled and offered her opinion. "Let's just be open to everyone and always announce what our little group is doing, in case someone else would like to join us." On that note they disbanded and agreed to think about the next subject for the Thursdays at Three meetings.

CHAPTER 14

The Doldrums Move In

FOR THE SECOND SUMMER HERE, Daisy realized that it was easy for many of the residents to turn the key in the lock and vanish for the hottest months. The office knew where they were, but the rest of the neighbors just noticed how few people were at dinner and at the Tuesday Night Social Hour. Robert Newburn, the retired sailor, called the month of August the doldrums, like his remembrance of a calm sea in a sailboat when there was nothing to do but wait it out. He was philosophic about these quiet times. "This is when you writers have the best of all worlds. You can sit undisturbed and let the inspiration flow. By the way, Daisy, what's the group working on now that the life stories are finished?" He sensed there was no quick answer coming, and continued, "Maybe now you're ready to write what we should all be composing, our obituaries. Who else can write what we want printed?"

Daisy was listening. "Maybe you have a good idea for our next project to share. We did enjoy sharing our life stories. We're searching for a new common topic. Would you like to join us, Captain?"

"I might. It depends. Are you going to advertise what your next 'sharing' will be about?"

"We haven't decided, but maybe one of these longish, detailed obituaries would tie in well with what we've just written.

None of us wants to live with or be completely dependent upon our kids to review our lives." Others nearby nodded in agreement. People enjoyed their coffee, and a low hum of conversation filled the dining room.

As she was leaving the dining room, Daisy was held back by a woman who appeared desperate to talk to her. "I'm Phyllis Fenton, a neighbor of Jane, you know, Jane at your church."

"Yes, I know Jane Simpson. I'm happy to know you too."

"But you don't understand. I'm so lonely here. I don't know any of these people."

"I see. You know, I don't either, Phyllis. But we all share the same address. It's easy to introduce yourself, just like you did to me a minute ago."

"But maybe they already have enough friends, and they won't like me." She grasped Daisy's arm tightly. "I'm afraid to be alone."

"Then you're in exactly the right place. You'll soon have lots of friends, I'm sure. You might invite Jane over for lunch some day soon. I think she worries that we don't eat very well." They had reached Daisy's place. "This is where I turn in. I'm expecting a long distance call so I must say good night, Phyllis. See you tomorrow. Don't forget to call Jane."

"Oh, I hope I get home all right." And she set forth cautiously toward Unit 21.

The happiest event of early September was the grand opening of El Nido, the care center that had been such an inviting part of the package of buying into La Ventura. Assisted Living was the level of care that everyone expected to slip into when absolutely necessary. Then, if health deteriorated further, the concept of "a nest" of skilled nursing was most reassuring. The promise was that someone kind would help a patient evaluate what items could move with her or him into the nest. The rest of the decisions would be made by family or the administrative staff, according to "last wishes." Daisy's bunch of friends read the pamphlets with interest, but at the moment, each one was perfectly content in her chosen housing. However, the words "last wishes" remained in their thoughts.

CHAPTER 15

Fall News Is Good

DAISY INVENTORIED HER SUMMER sewing to see what she had ready for the big mission sale at the church. Seven rag dolls, seven doll quilts, two stuffed and fancy-dressed teddy bears, four chef-style aprons and one single bed quilt. She always tried to make enough things to earn three hundred dollars for the mission fund. It seemed about right for this year. But she was more critical of her hand work than ever before. I wonder if I'm losing some of my sight," she mused to herself. "That would be an awful loss." She promised herself to arrange a checkup with her eye doctor.

The very next *Scottsdale Tribune* advertised the remnant sale at the Fabric Farm. This was an annual "must go" in Daisy's mind. As she studied the ad, she thought again of all her old friends who used to go with her. "I wonder who might be interested in driving over there with me?" She tried to think of other creative women who rose to the challenge of what they could make out of a thirty-five cent remnant that would sell and earn five dollars for mission projects. "I hope there are some young, crafty ones coming along in the church," she said to herself.

"Talking to yourself again, Ms. MacDuff?"

Daisy laughed as Ellen stopped in front of her. "I'm off to the remnant sale. Want to come along?"

"Sure. Nothing else pressing today. Let me get my purse."

Daisy picked up her mail while she waited. "Wow, a letter from Donna. Could she have changed her mind?" Daisy tucked the envelope in her purse; the sale was more urgent at the moment. Ellen returned and they headed out the door.

As they browsed up and down the aisles of bolts, Daisy said, "At the back is the real treasure. C'mon."

"I can't believe the mountain of bundles. Daisy, how do you choose?" She laughed and went on, "You saw each of us as one of these? Let's see, I bet this made you think of me." She picked up a piece of yellow and white gingham marked three yards. "Yup, it's round and looks old-fashioned."

"No," protested Daisy, "but I might have thought of Clarissa in this gorgeous lavender linen. Mary Ann wears so much denim, but of course I didn't know that until she got here."

"See? We are remnants. Now here's Beth, in this Hawaiian print in rose and red and white. Too bad there's not enough in this one to take back to her. Martha wears these bright plaids well, doesn't she?"

"When I come in for dress material, I always look for the easy-care ones. I'm sick of ironing."

"I was about to comment that not one of us human remnants is wrinkle-free!" They continued to poke through the piles until Daisy had eight small packets. They drove back in good spirits.

At four o'clock, Daisy let Curly out, snapped his leash on his collar and tossed her purse and a large shopping bag into the living room. In her hand, she had Donna's letter. As they walked, she read to Curly:

> *"Dear Daisy,*
>
> *I haven't forgotten your invitation to join you, but I thought I could manage my life without moving so far away. However, when I lost my only son to a road accident in France, I discovered I needed friends, serious friends. I thought back to the times when we talked about the really vital things in life, and since then I've never had such a good friend as you. I called La Ventura one day, only to learn that they have a waiting list. I hung*

up; then I called back after I thought about it, and I put my name and application in for their next building. They said it would be completed in 2005, maybe as early as February. Could you accept a Valentine friend with cat at that time? I really need you as a friend. Please write.

Curly, we'll have another friend. She needs us; can you believe that?"

At dinner that night, Daisy shared Donna's interest in coming to Scottsdale. Martha and Mary Ann were sure another cat person would be welcome, and Ellen responded to Donna's grief over her son's death. "Maybe a small group could be offered here to deal with grief. Our churches all offer those groups, but not everyone attends a church. What do you think?"

"Ellen, you've probably had the most experience with ministries like that. Why don't you work out a proposal and talk to Malcolm about it?"

"I think I will. We've had two deaths of residents just since the first of the year. You know, that suggestion about writing our own obituaries isn't a bad idea. At least we should write our last wishes down."

Martha spoke up. "At first I thought it sounded as if we were getting morose, always so aware of death. But when we talk about it, I feel more matter-of-fact about it, not so emotional." After that comment, the ones around the table agreed it was wise to think ahead.

Clarissa's grand entrance, just before dessert was served, energized the whole dining room. "Am I the first snowbird to return?" She went around hugging almost everyone she knew, trailing an enormous shoulder bag and the scent of White Diamonds.

Daisy was laughing along with all the rest of them, enjoying Clarissa's stage presence. She turned to Beth and said, "She's like a gust of wind blowing into the room, isn't she?"

"And yet at the same time, she can be so practical and down-to-earth. You know, she supported herself all her life and never had an easy home life. But she rises above the past."

"I think that's her recipe for success."

"Now Daisy, what are you whispering about me?"

"We're thrilled to have you back! We've needed a spark to get us going again, after a hot summer. Sit down and tell us what you've been up to."

Clarissa plunked her bag on the floor, unbuttoned her suit jacket and took a deep breath. "I learned a lot this summer. Number one, I missed all of you. Number two, it's no fun living in someone else's home, even when it's your own nephew. Number three, my old bridge club has become very stodgy, so conservative and kind of trembling about the future. Honestly, I couldn't believe what they're talking about. No more gossip or jokes or fun stuff. All these politically correct opinions about same-sex marriages, the priest who's been divorced, kids wearing droopy clothes. They wondered how I could get through security at the airport. Did I have to take off my shoes? Of course I did. Everyone had to do it." She paused long enough to ask for a glass of water.

"Didn't they think you looked healthy when you got back there?"

"Oh, and how. They couldn't believe I can play the piano again. Not like I used to, but I had to show them."

"What did Dick have to say?"

"Well, he thinks we have magic in the air here in Arizona. He's coming down here for Christmas this year. How about that!" She sipped. "Now, tell me all the hot news here."

There was a short silence with some exchanged glances. Mary Ann started with the fact that Clarissa had missed Beth's life story. "But you're in time for our next assignment. Same teacher's coming again, next week, and by May, we'll have something new to share."

"Good. Beth, you must have a copy of what you said, don't you?"

"Yes, I do, and I'll be sure to get it, as soon as you're settled in, and before I leave."

"Oh, dear. I walked away from all my luggage as soon as I saw you in the dining room." She started to take a drink and stopped midair. "Wait a minute, Beth. Where are you going?" Everyone else stopped and looked at Beth, standing behind her chair.

"I have to be up real early tomorrow for the van; gotta get my beauty sleep soon."

"But it's only seven-thirty."

"I've made up my mind, so don't try to change it. I'm having plastic surgery tomorrow."

"Tomorrow? What for? Where? Who's the doctor?" Each fired questions at her.

"It's a follow-up on my cancer surgery almost a year ago. It's time to get my figure back." Beth was so positive that no one dared to comment. Only Daisy smiled and was glad she'd suggested it last spring. She hoped Julie had recommended the surgeon. Beth was already halfway across the room.

By November first, the days were crisp with an occasional cloudy day. Daisy was getting ready for the church mission fair and recruited help from Ellen. Martha and Mary Ann took a trip to see the trees turning color in Flagstaff. Within a week, Clarissa had the bridge players organized. Building Four, as it was temporarily called, was rising daily. The place was crawling with workmen and tools. A main floor unit was reserved in Donna's name, although her latest letter sounded as if the cat, Terri, might not live until February. Daisy suspected there would be a replacement, Terrific Two, if anything happened to Terrific One.

The Winter Writers' Class was challenged to write something serious about a philosophy of life. It was Beth who recalled Daisy's words about Clarissa and her "recipe for success." She planned to suggest it to the instructor before the organization meeting in December. She told Daisy, "I've missed getting together, just the six of us. We need to get that started again."

Daisy was pleased. "Let's pick a starting date, and I'll ask the office for one of the common rooms. Do you think anyone else would want to join us?"

"Secretly, I hope not. But I guess we could try to be open to someone new."

When the Bunch of Daisy's talked together about a good week to start meeting, Martha asked, "What would you think if I invited Tom to come sometimes?" Clearly the group was startled at the suggestion.

Mary Ann said, "Would he want to come?"

"I don't know, but he might. We've been sharing a lot of philosophical talk of late. It's just an idea."

Daisy spoke up and told of her conversation with Captain Newburn. I'll see if he'd be interested."

"How about that nice man who's so quiet, the Scotsman you talked with, Daisy."

"Oh, MacPherson. Is he back from the mountains yet?"

"Check up on him. I have a feeling he needs to get acquainted."

Beth changed the subject. "Won't it be wonderful to have the election over and no more ads on TV? I am *so sick* of hearing the same pitch over and over. Even when I mute the TV, I know what they're saying." Everyone chimed in with nods and agreement.

Lunch on Tuesday, November second, was served with tension, since the residents had never known each others' political affiliations. Scottsdale appeared to be largely Republican-minded, but Daisy observed a few bumper stickers supporting the Kerry-Edwards ticket. She recalled her father's Democrat party talk. He never dared speak of his personal feelings from the pulpit, but he grumbled at home about the pep talks he received from conservative church members. "Here I am, being just as secretive about my voting record as Daddy was about his. He must be laughing at me, somewhere up there."

Ellen sidled up to Daisy after lunch and said, "I'll bet you and I are in a minor minority around here."

"Why, Ellen, you must have heard all the same talk I did. Manses are interesting places for political talk, aren't they?"

By evening, the count was becoming decisive, and the President was re-elected and applauded around La Ventura. "To tell you my opinion," said Alex, "I think the people surrounding the President are more important than who's in the oval office. So, I didn't much care who won. I care a lot about the Senate and the House and that Cabinet. We'll see how the second term goes. I have a hunch there'll be some resignations."

Beth returned to her favorite complaint. "At least we won't have to hear those horrid ads any more. Those people who want us to think they're so intelligent stoop to saying the dumbest things!"

During the next week, the churches hosted mission fairs and bazaars; school boards had new leaders, and a cold snap in the weather caught everyone's attention.

Daisy was still recovering from the Mission Fair when her ophthalmologist's office called to schedule another appointment. "Time to remove that cataract" was the diagnosis. Her impending surgery cast a gloom over her "bunch." She kept assuring them that it would be quite routine. "I'm just trying to keep up with all the other residents who've had the same thing done. They all rave about seeing colors better and reading street signs."

Beth chimed in, "That's right. If you're going to continue as our designated driver, we want you to see clearly."

"Speaking of driving, Beth, weren't you going to buy a new car?"

"I keep thinking about it, and they get more and more expensive."

"We could all help you shop for it."

"I've already done my shopping, on the Internet."

"What? You'd shop for a new car that way?"

"Absolutely. Why should I wear myself out wandering around these huge car lots? I'm on a first name basis with a dealer out in Sun City. He has all kinds of low-mileage used cars. When I told him I just needed it to drive to church, he asked whether I wanted a Lutheran or a Methodist car. He said he has all kinds." Everyone laughed at her story. "I told him I'd like a small Catholic Cadillac, and he promised to find me one in a week or so."

Daisy updated the group. "I postponed my surgery until January fifth, a Wednesday. He promised I'd be back at circle on the twelfth. So, I'll need Mary Ann to drive me or maybe Beth?"

"That's what I need: a deadline, a reason to buy. Also a ride to Sun City."

Christmas plans immediately followed the Thanksgiving weekend. For Clarissa, her nephew's arrival was the target. They remembered last year's plan to make a holiday for others. This year's most urgent mission needs were warm clothes and blankets.

"Fortunately, I can really help them out this year," Martha declared. "I haven't worn half of the sweaters and jackets I brought. Remember, I was keeping ready for the possibility of going north in three years? Anyone can add to my stuff." She announced at lunch one day that she would like to deliver the warm clothes to the agency by the end of the week. The pile of garments grew so high that Malcolm had to find cartons for the collection. Finally on Friday, he offered to drive one of the vans down to Vista del Camino. Martha agreed to go along and represent all of them. Mary Ann was already there, for her volunteer afternoon at the desk.

Daisy's friends collected money for hams. Ellen suggested that approach, since she remembered all the canned goods that come in from churches and clubs aren't the main part of a dinner. "The leftovers from hams are so good. If there are Jewish families in need of food during their holidays, I hope turkeys will help them. All these kids will be hungry when they don't get their school meals."

They had trouble choosing a place for their Christmas luncheon, but Clarissa had the biggest influence when she pointed out that La Ventura's excellent diet rarely included seafood of the kind she was used to in Poulsbo. So, Steamers was selected and they reserved their table for Tuesday, the twenty-first of December. Beth very quietly offered to drive, if they would show her the way on a city map.

"Beth, when were you going to tell us about your car?"

"Soon," she said with a little smile, "It's just gorgeous, and I still can't believe it's mine. Do you want to see it now?"

Of course, they all scrambled toward the desk and the main door. In the first visitors' parking spot stood a shiny white Cadillac with a soft blue leather interior. No one commented on the coincidental soft blue sweater Beth was wearing with her white slacks. The car did indeed look as if it belonged to Beth.

"See? I had to have some better news for my Christmas cards than last year's surgery. And I want to help drive our bunch around town too. The dealer even delivered it!"

As Daisy walked home, she realized that she was still driving the car Scott had bought for her in 1991. "I've always wished it had cruise control and air bags, so why don't I buy a new car?" She remembered asking her mother why she never wanted anything new. "The old is good enough for me," was her reply. "That attitude goes beyond humility; it's demeaning," thought Daisy. "I wish I had the courage to go out and do something wild."

CHAPTER 16

The Thirteenth Step Is Love

On Christmas Eve, Clarissa played a selection of carols in the Great Room. People drifted into the area from dinner or as they returned from other gatherings. The old melodies revived memories from Europe and Mexico as well as childhood movies. Her nephew Dick and his wife Jan sat nearby, smiling at their family recollections. Over the low tone of conservations and humming, a squeal and a peal of laughter broke out. Martha and Tom were standing between the Christmas tree and the French doors, facing each other at first and then in an embrace. Then they laughed and hugged again.

"We're engaged," Martha shouted out, and Tom waved one arm in the air in a cheer. The crowd broke into clapping, and Clarissa struck the opening chords of the wedding march. It was the first truly joyous event the whole community had shared. Mary Ann rushed forward to hug her sister and then Tom.

Members of the twelve-step group crowded around the couple, offering to give the bride away or cook the food or provide the flowers. A new resident came to Mary Ann and presented his card to her. "If I can be of any help to your sister, please let me know." Then he vanished behind a row of chairs. When Mary Ann had time to study the card, she saw that he was a retired minister from Montana. Wouldn't it be exciting to have the wedding right there in the chapel. Usually the ceremonies on campus were of a more somber nature, celebrating the dearly departed. "Yes, it's time for some fun around this place," Mary Ann exclaimed to herself.

Only thirty-six hours later, the joy of Christmas was challenged by news of the 9.0 earthquake on the floor of the Indian Ocean and the catastrophe that followed. At dinner, the Captain asked to make an announcement. He described in scientific detail the effects of the tsunami that had devastated the people of the South Pacific countries, those on the Malaysian Peninsula, Sumatra, Sri Lanka, India, Bangladesh and the many islands involved. His grief was so evident that people began to ask what they could do to relieve the suffering of millions of people. The mood became solemn and stricken.

"We're witnessing a piece of history of Biblical proportions when over a hundred thousand people are wiped off the earth. The power of nature in the oceans is beyond compare; it's so fast and so unseen. The devastation will be apparent for years." When he sat down, he was in tears.

Ellen observed softly, "Our lives will go on, but these events show us how we have to reach out to those who need us. The message of our interdependence is clear, here in this room and way over there."

Daisy agreed and added, "We must never let this lovely place isolate us from the world and its reality."

CHAPTER 17

2005 Starts with Success

As Daisy prepared for her surgery, she had time for some serious thinking. She put all her papers in order on her little desk, in case Pete or Julie needed to find something concerning her care. She cried out to Scott when she thought of being alone and unable to help herself. "This is the first scary thing I've had to face," she thought sadly. The quiet time let her review the past two years.

In the fall of 2002, she was focused on herself and her dilemma of a big empty house and no view of the future. Then she was so sure she had solved her own problem that she wanted to help everyone else with their retirement plans. She wrote the famous Christmas letter they talked about. She looked back on it and was amazed that anyone was willing to give it a try. When they arrived, each one had been centered on her own adjustment. The first turning point had been Beth's illness. That jolted them out of their individual concerns, and they had pulled together to support her, even though they didn't know each other very well. Everyone seemed to find new friends in a crisis.

Daisy found tears on her cheeks, as she realized how they had trusted her to draw them together in an emotional but expensive investment. She thought about their arrivals. She had hardly recognized Clarissa when she came, but her energy still propelled her through life. Beth had changed the least, since she had been white-haired so young. Martha's eyes showed the years of her unhappiness and insecurities. Mary Ann had always been energetic, and she'd never concentrated on herself until she retired. She'd been happy in her work and probably still found satisfaction in all the good relationships she had built. Ellen, dear Ellen, was so thrilled with the Arizona climate; she was an inspiration to everyone. Her faith was deep, and she knew how to express it to help others. Then Daisy sat very still and wondered who she herself was. A still, small voice reminded her, "A remnant, saved for a reason."

She went into the bathroom and splashed cold water on her face. In the mirror was the same old face, creased from years of happiness and slightly tanned from the winter sun. She smiled at her hair which was thin, somewhere between gold and silver. She squinted at her bright eyes that certainly needed help. "Thank you, God, for getting me over that spell of fear. I know better. But why did you have to take Scott away? Do you have work for me? For me, *alone*?" She recalled praying for an assignment many years ago, when they were in the East. Her answer then was to be a "catalyst" among church women. She smiled remembering the "Catalyst Corps" traveling around the churches, recruiting leaders and mission workers. Aloud, she said, "Here I am, thirty years later, still trying to change lives, just a catalyst in a new place. Thank you, God."

When Mary Ann took Daisy back to the doctor for her checkup, he announced, "Another success! I'll see you in two weeks. In the meantime, you may have to watch some fuzzy TV and talk with friends. Reading won't be comfortable for a while." Daisy was relieved to be able to tell people that she was recovering and managing the eye-drop regimen well.

The next day, Phyllis sidled up to her on the path and said, "I'm so glad you won't be blind. I was really worried for you."

Daisy explained her doctor's words. "So, see, we need to hope for the best, Phyllis."

She replied, "Yes, but I've heard of so many medical mistakes. It's enough to keep me from going to the doctor."

"I suppose I can't change your mind, but around here we need all the optimism we can get. I'm glad I'm healing, and soon I can drive again. Bye for now, Phyllis."

By the first of February, the Bunch of Daisy's was deep into the next writing class, about a philosophy of life that sustains a person from youth to old age, a recipe for success. Tom, Robert Newburn and Alexander MacPherson were among the writers who offered to read aloud their winter writing in a small group, after the class ended on April twenty-sixth. So, the Bunch of Daisy's was faced with a decision about their future summer Thursday meetings. After some discussion, the three men who sat near Daisy in class were invited into the summer Thursdays at Three in the Hedgehog Room.

The Bunch was anxious to meet Donna Krueger. "When did you say she'd get here, Daisy?"

"Supposedly, on Friday, February 4th. She's driving, and I assume that Terrific is riding with her." Malcolm and Bonnie were ready to welcome her, and her unit was ready. Friday turned into Saturday, and still no signs of a car from Oklahoma. On Saturday evening, when there was often a large group assembled in the card and game room, Daisy found herself wandering through each room, stopping to chat here and there and looking expectantly toward the driveway. Around 9:30, a disheveled woman rushed into the lobby in pursuit of a large white cat. Encountering a group of people in the next room, the cat stopped cold and sat on the cool tile floor, nonchalantly licking one paw. All eyes turned to the woman who was apologizing to everyone for disrupting their party.

Daisy came forward and tentatively asked, "Donna?"

The woman looked at her and said, "Daisy? Daisy MacDuff?"

Daisy laughed and said, "I thought you were having trouble walking, and yet you're running!"

"Oh, thank God, I'm in the right place. That cat'll be the death of me yet. I'm going to write a book about driving with a grumpy old cat for a thousand miles. Daisy, where can I go to wash up and get organized?"

"Follow me." She turned to the others near her and said, "We'll be right back. Watch that cat."

When they returned, the cat hadn't moved, but Bonnie had brought out a small bowl of water and was trying to talk to Terrific. "Ms. Krueger, we have a man who will show you where to park and will help with your luggage. If you'll come over here, you can sign in, and I'll get your keys. Have you had anything to eat this evening? There're a few snacks in the game room."

"Thanks, but I just want to find my rooms and a bed."

"Daisy took care to have your bed made up, and a few supplies in your refrigerator. We'll talk more in the morning. You do have a container for the cat?"

"Oh yes, but she's been in it for three days. I may have to corral her in my bathroom tonight. She might refuse to move if she sees that crate."

By the next noon, Daisy took Donna around to meet her other friends and picked a big table for brunch. "You know, I wrote you and said I'd give this place a try for about a year, but I wasn't making any promises? Well, I'm here to stay as long as Terri lives. I'll *never, ever* drive cross country with her again. I had no idea what it would be like. The rain was awful; snow too!"

Martha was quick to respond. "I only agreed to give it a try too, but I've never been happier."

"Well, I'm glad to hear that. Daisy said someone is a cat lover too."

Again Martha spoke up. "Oh, we are. Many Ann's my sister, and we adopted two kittens that were left under a bush by the pool. They're adorable."

"Once Terri calms down a bit, you'll have to meet her. She's hiding now, but once she gets acquainted and finds her nest, she'll be friendly again."

"Have you met Curly?"

"Daisy's dog? No, haven't seen him yet, but I've heard about him."

"This is one of the few places in town that allow pets. Good thing Daisy found it for us."

"Well, it's too soon to tell. I feel hemmed in with all these walls and roofs. I suppose it's for the shade, but I'm used to the wide open spaces." Donna looked pensive. "I guess I've become a loner, since I was sick and quit work. I don't know if I can learn to share my space this way."

Softly, Ellen said, "It takes time to adjust, time for things to look right to your eyes." They all nodded and knew something of what Donna was experiencing.

CHAPTER 18

Feelings Are Tender

TOM AND MARTHA WERE INSEPARABLE, and Mary Ann came to Daisy with a new idea. "Do you suppose we could arrange a legal transfer of my share in our casita to Tom and then I'd take over his smaller unit? I don't want to mention it to Martha unless it's possible to do this. You know, there's a waiting list for the small units too."

"Gosh, what a noble idea, Mary Ann. I thought Martha would move in with Tom."

"I did too, but these small units are really confining for two adults. I want this marriage to have the best possible circumstances as my blessing. I haven't forgotten Sis' life story and how helpful I could have been if I'd had any idea of what was going on in her young life."

"I don't quite agree there, but we can't rewrite history. It's a super idea, and there must be a lawyer who could arrange it. If it's O.K. with Malcolm and Bonnie. And if it appeals to Tom and Martha."

"Hm. Hadn't thought of that. Maybe they want to be crowded into Unit 19."

"Probably not, but you know, you wouldn't want it to sound like pity or a charitable gift."

"Right. And I keep listening for any doubts on her part. But so far, everything sounds smooth. It would be a mess if they changed their minds."

Daisy smiled. "He seems to be a nice guy. For a while, I felt as if he shied away from me, but I guess it's just because we're both from Scottsdale so we don't have the usual questions to start conversations."

"I'm surprised to hear that, because Martha said something about his having known your husband. You'd think he'd have a lot of conversation starters."

Daisy's eyebrows shot up. "My Scott?"

"Well, I'm sure that's what she said. He could have met him at the golf course or in a store, couldn't be?"

"I suppose. I just wonder why he never mentioned it to me. It would be so logical, since we have nothing else to talk about."

"I may be completely wrong. Listen, it's almost lunch time, and I need to buzz over to our place before the dining room. See you in a minute, O.K.?"

Daisy went in to wash up and touch up her face. Now that she could see clearly, she had decided some blush gave her face a little more life. Mirrors aren't always kind. Right now she was frowning at herself, or maybe at Mary Ann. "Maybe it's Tom I should be frowning at," she thought.

Donna sat down next to Daisy at lunch and had lots of questions. Finally, Daisy said, "Why don't you come along this afternoon to our writers' class. It's a nice way to ease into knowing a few people at a time."

"No, I can't write worth a darn. Don't even want to."

"Well, you commented on not getting acquainted, so I just thought. . ."

Donna cut her off with, "I'll find my own way around."

Fortunately, Ellen joined them right then and chatted on about how good the salad looked. "I've actually managed to lose seven pounds this spring. My doctor back home would be so pleased."

Daisy picked up on the new conversation. "Do you like your new doctor?"

"I do. He's so young, I had my doubts. But then, every doctor our age has retired. I need my glasses checked too, so I'll get the name of your man."

Donna perked up and said, "Don't you people talk about anything besides doctors and aches and pains? I guess I'm just in a grouchy mood today. Think I'll go to a movie this afternoon. Anyone want to come along?"

A new resident named Alice Turner across the table spoke up and said she'd love to see a movie. "Any movie's fine with me. Would I make you grouchier if I take my cane?"

Donna couldn't let that go by. "I promise I won't be sad or mad. Let's drive up to Shea to that big place they advertise on TV. We're bound to find one we like, or we can go to two different shows."

Daisy left lunch with Ellen, grateful to have a steady, cheerful friend like her.

The spring writing class about life philosophies gave deeper insights into members of the community. With new people joining the original group, the teacher could explore a variety of styles as well as topics. The students wrote a lot but rarely read aloud. One newcomer was a published poet, and that intimidated the novice poets. Another man had a tendency to be critical of everyone's efforts, but quick to defend his own words. Finally, the teacher suggested that they review their initial agreement about critiquing and encouraging each other. Guidelines were printed and became a benchmark for future comments.

The retired attorney, Alex MacPherson, wrote about his philosophy during the years he had been a judge in a small county in Texas. It was several weeks before he said, "I might be prepared to read my so-called recipe for success aloud at the next class, the Tuesday after Easter." Daisy in particular was curious about his ideas, because she noticed he rarely mentioned anything personal. He often made good observations about other members of the group, and he always was friendly and open to conversation. But no one really knew anything about him.

Easter Sunday was the wedding date for Tom and Martha, the first ceremony on the premises. Captain Newburn consulted with the County Clerk's office to learn if he could marry the couple on dry land. When the answer was negative, he told everyone of his disappointment. Quietly, one of the new couples came around to his table at dinner and introduced themselves. The Reverend and Mrs. Wilson had spent a lifetime performing marriages in churches in Idaho, Montana and Wyoming. "We'd be happy to be a part of this celebration, even if we don't know the couple. Martha's sister has my card."

Captain Newburn was delighted and jokingly offered to do the premarital counseling, since he had watched the whole romance develop. "I'm really tough on these flirtations." He winked and continued, "In this case, I think the couple has some values in common that may guarantee smooth sailing."

George Wilson smiled and nodded. "So I've heard. When I asked if there was need for a leader of a recovery group, I learned of Martha's good work. Later I talked with Tom and he told me his story. So, I could easily bless their union, if we could put together a nice little chapel ceremony. Marge here is good with the details." He patted her shoulder affectionately.

"Never had an assistant myself. On the cruise ships, the crew did all the detail stuff, and I just had to wear whites and sound official. Always had good food and drink later. Not a bad duty."

"No, I guess not. You never had to counsel them later. Those were the tough cases."

The Captain thought a second or two and nodded. "I often wondered if the shipboard romances lasted. Hated to be a part of the heartbreak, if that's how it ended."

This marrying team of three met with Tom and Martha and made the perfect plan for a two o'clock wedding with a two-thirty reception. Everyone was invited. Ellen remarked that maybe this would start a trend, but no one else seemed to agree. Donna watched all the preparations from a distance, still not feeling quite a part of the community. Bonnie approached her with, "Donna, I have something to ask you. When you're near the office, stop in, could you?"

"Sure. Tomorrow morning O.K.?"

"Fine. Thanks."

Monday, at lunch, Donna sought out Daisy and seemed excited about something. "Daisy, I've been offered a job I can do, a part-time, sit down job."

"Wonderful, and how did you find it?"

"Bonnie asked me to open the first aid station three or four mornings a week. If no one comes in, it doesn't matter. She just thinks it's a nice service to offer the community. You know, people burn themselves or scrape a shin over at the pool. She said some of the folks are on diets, and I could be useful in nutrition."

"That's perfect, Donna. I also heard the lady leading the water aerobics won't be back this year. You probably know about exercise too."

"Well, I do, but see, after the shingles, I lost a lot of strength. I don't know if I could keep up much of a pace."

"But you're younger than some of those who need the exercise. I'll bet you could do enough to keep them going."

"Think so? Well, I'll see what Bonnie thinks about it."

That evening, Daisy felt that at last Donna had joined the group. Maybe after a while, she'd be willing to introduce herself to the writing group or let herself be interviewed, rather than writing her life story.

The wedding changed a few things around La Ventura. The couple and Mary Ann exchanged housing, but Hansel and Gretel were completely disoriented. Both their homes were on the ground floor, fortunately, but neither of the sisters ever knew if both cats were in for the night. Tom had not bought into the lunch meal program, so Martha dropped out of it too. The group adjusted to seeing less of Martha and more of Mary Ann. One of the bonuses was an increase in the twelve-step program. Three couples began to attend, and Martha reported to Mary Ann that she was sure her marriage to Tom had made the difference. The group was bigger, less personal and probably seemed more open to everyone.

Clarissa was thrilled with her bridge group, because she was getting to know some of the couples better. Ted and Sara had become regulars, and they seemed close with another couple from the casitas, Paul and Anne Chisholm. She was still trying to even the number of players and work Sandra into the mix. Martha teased her for being a matchmaker, but bridge remained Clarissa's focus. "Bridge keeps the brain working, and that's my chief goal," she announced loudly.

CHAPTER 19

Summer Heats Up

PEOPLE BEGAN TO TALK ABOUT summer plans to escape the heat. Beth wanted to make her first trip back to Illinois, although everyone reminded her that one can never return and find things the same. "I don't expect to find my old friends waiting with open arms, but my eyes will appreciate the scenery. I'll always miss the river."

Ellen's granddaughter Emily planned to visit Grandma, to stop the letters pleading with Ellen to "come home." "She's going to be so grown up, I'll never know her. I told her to bring her best swimsuit to show off her strokes, but I know what she's going to show off!" They laughed, knowing that her waistline would be about twenty inches.

Mary Ann invited any one to ride with her to Tucson or Alamogordo or all the way to Roswell. There were no volunteers, but Martha offered to keep the cats at their place for the two or three weeks she'd be gone.

No one even asked Clarissa, because she had announced first that she'd be gone from July fourth until October first. "That's like last year, because I miss you all so much. I'll be ready for a few laughs when I get back."

"So, who's going to keep the Thursday at Three program alive?" asked Daisy.

"We'll all be in and out of town, except Rissa. We won't really be gone all the time. Whoever's around this summer can share their recipes for success."

"Next winter we'll work on our last wishes and then follow up with our obituaries. Ms. Leslie is willing to keep teaching the writers, and she likes the subjects Ellen and I proposed."

Martha spoke up and told them again how she first recoiled from the idea of last wishes and obituaries, but then saw it was just a practical matter. "Tom and I will both do it."

Daisy said, "I'm not going anywhere this year, unless over to San Diego with the kids for a long weekend. I have enough sewing projects lined up to keep me cool and busy."

"Your eyes are really good, aren't they?" asked Beth.

"Just amazing. I didn't realize how I was squinting and avoiding hand work."

"Computer's better too?"

"Oh, Heavens, yes. I'm back into writing letters again."

"I suppose you've already written your recipe for success," Mary Ann ventured.

"You know, I thought and thought about it, and finally it came down to four words."

"Such as?"

"Keep praying; keep busy."

"Now, Daisy, you do a lot more than that. What about trying to help all of us?"

"No, I discovered that your coming here did more for me than for you. I wasn't recovered at all when I wrote you. I just thought I was. I was still mad at Scott for departing without warning, and I was still so lonely. Then I thought I had the answer: make a change!"

Martha said gently, "Scott must have been a good husband and father."

"He was wonderful!" Clarissa's words came to mind, and she added, "But he wasn't perfect."

"Did you know that Tom knew him at the grill?"

"The men's grill at the club?"

"No, his brother's place on 68th Street."

"Tom's never mentioned it to me."

Tom arrived in time to say, "Someday Daisy and I will talk about old times. You know we're all going to be late for dinner if we don't get over there right now?"

Dinner was a quiet one for Daisy as she reviewed the conversation with Martha and then Tom's interruption to gather them for dinner. After the meal, they all went their own ways, Ellen falling into step with Daisy. "Something bothering you, Daisy?"

"Not really, just a funny little feeling that someone knows something about me, and I may never know it. But I guess that's all right. I probably need to spend some time with Pete or Julie. It's been ages since we had any family talk."

"You're so lucky to have them here in town. I know they try not to smother you, since you have lots of friends here. But every so often, family is still closer and feels good."

"I'll call them tonight. Thanks for that word, Ellen. Good night." Daisy dropped off the walk at Unit 7, while Ellen continued on her way.

Daisy settled into her favorite chair and dialed Julie. "Hi, dear. I'm fine; how are you?" She listened to the recital of Julie's busy day. "Do you have time for lunch tomorrow? Let's meet at Rob's Place around noon, O.K.?" And so the date was set.

Now Daisy thought about her agenda for tomorrow. "What exactly is bothering me? It's a combination of Clarissa's comment, Martha's remark and then Tom's reference to old times." She still didn't know what old times they shared. "Well, Curly, you're determined to get me up and out the door, aren't you? Let's go for a quick walk before we turn in."

On Tuesday, Daisy signed out for lunch, went to the church for the sewing group, and then drove out to Rob's. Julie was her usual prompt self, and they settled into a booth. "So, Mom, what got you on the phone to make a lunch date?"

"I don't know, but Ellen said she thought I sounded as if I needed a dose of family."

"The blues?"

"Not really, just some strange little feelings." She proceeded to relate the coincidences to Julie, who listened attentively.

"What do you suspect Tom knows that we don't know? Want me to ask Pete if he knows anything about Tom? Or about that place where he worked?"

"Well, maybe. But don't make it sound too serious. It may just be some old office party story or gossip. Your dad really wasn't a great party guy, even back in college at the fraternity. He had to go to all the events, but he was never the life of the party, if you know what I mean."

"I know, Mom. Don't worry. You know, some people enjoy sounding secretive or 'in the know.' He may just be teasing you. But I'll talk to Pete."

They enjoyed their sandwiches and then Daisy told Julie about finding the speeding ticket among Scott's old papers. "I laughed, because he always warned me about driving too fast."

Julie agreed. "We've all had tickets we hid from each other, I suppose."

"But there was also a receipt from a legal firm, that one that's always advertising about getting people out of a D.U.I."

Julie looked surprised about that news. "I don't remember either Pete's or my getting into that trouble. Maybe Dad himself got a ticket or at least a warning."

"For two thousand dollars?"

"Oooh. That's a lot. Was it dated?"

"Yes, some time in 1999, I think. I've forgotten the month, but I think it was in the winter. Do you think that sounds important?"

"Well, I don't know, but it sounds as if you want to know. These days with computers, there are no secrets, Mom. On the other hand, what if you find out something you'd rather not know?"

Daisy pondered that for a few minutes. "I can't buy into that idea. If we want to know something, let's explore. We may find absolutely nothing. Dad could have been fixing a ticket for some buddy of his."

"That's really true, Mom. He'd have done that in a heartbeat. Well, I'll see what Pete thinks." Julie reached for her purse, but Daisy had already snatched the ticket. "This has been a nice visit, Mom. Let's do it again, soon, and I'll pick it up."

"Maybe. We'll see. Thanks for listening." They hugged and went toward their cars.

Donna had shied away from the Bunch of Daisy's and their Thursday at Three meetings, although before each meeting, they all made a point of inviting her. One day, as she was counting her supplies in the first aid station, Beth came in and asked to talk. They sat opposite each other, with Donna being the professional. She could tell Beth had something serious on her mind.

"I wonder why I feel so tired and listless. Do other older people ever complain to you of that feeling?"

"Oh, Beth, I know a dozen reasons why you might feel that way. I think the most frequent cause is boredom or depression. Do you have anything on your mind that you dread or wish you didn't have to do? Are you lonely?" She let those questions hang in the silence.

Beth took a deep breath and said, "I think I'm afraid of more cancer, especially since my nearest sister has it now." She glanced around the little room. "For a long time I couldn't even say the word, but now I know that cancer is more than an illness. It's a shadow that comes over your life and lurks in the closet. Then someday when other things look gloomy, out it pops."

"That's a very real fear to have, Beth, but there are all kinds of tests to rule out your fears. Why don't you call your surgeon's office and ask for a referral to one of these clinics where they perform the tests?"

"Because I don't quite have the courage to make the call. I don't want to admit I'm afraid."

"Would you like me to find out something for you? You had breast cancer, right?"

Softly, Beth said. "Yes. I had a bilateral mastectomy, and I had chemotherapy after it for eight months."

"Did you have radiation too?"

"No, because the doctor said everything looked good."

"That's wonderful, Beth. Do you have any symptoms that worry you?"

"No. I had reconstruction and implants. I suppose it's all in my head."

"That doesn't make it any less real."

"Well, thanks for being so kind and sympathetic. I just needed someone to talk to. I'll think about what you suggested."

Beth stood up to leave, and Donna asked, "Do you like ice cream cones?"

Beth laughed and said, "Sure I do. Do you have time to go and get one?"

"I do. All I have to do is close the door and hang up this little sign."

Ellen stopped to pick up Daisy before dinner that Friday evening. "Boy, it was a hot one this afternoon. The room where we met for the grief support was stifling."

"Try the Hedgehog Room where we meet on Thursdays. I swear it gets more air conditioning. Did you have a good group today?"

"Well, a couple of the men have already gone back east, and that leaves all women. Must have been seven there. I was really pleased that Donna came by after she closed up her office. Alice was there and maybe that's why she came. They've done a couple of movies lately."

"Wonderful. I think she's trying hard to find her place here. Maybe she was right when she said she'd become a recluse."

"Beth went to talk to her about something last week, and she was impressed with how professional Donna was on medical subjects. And she used the word 'compassionate.'"

"I can believe that. She loved nursing and the hospital life. I wonder if she had more than just shingles a couple of years ago. Her legs seem to be her big weakness, and she's so thin." They walked along to the dining room, joining more on the path.

One remarked on all the parking spaces available now. "How many left for the whole summer last year, Daisy?"

"Gosh, I don't know, but I remember the dining room got pretty sparse, maybe only twenty or thirty tables."

Beth joined them and said, "It reminds me of church. Last week, Father Benjamin asked us to move forward and close the ranks so we'd feel more like a church family. But you know, I'd rather be here and all air-cooled than sweltering along the river back home. When my husband was ill, we put in an air conditioner, but none of my friends had it."

"So you're flying back there to visit them and coax them all into buying coolers, huh?" The group enjoyed a few laughs.

CHAPTER 20

Summer Flies By

JULY FOURTH PROVED TO be a beautiful day, surprisingly breezy with fluffy white clouds against the usual dazzling blue Arizona sky. Malcolm and Bonnie had announced a picnic supper with an evening band concert. Malcolm donned a chef's hat and fired up a long grill to cook hamburgers and bratwurst from Wisconsin. The kitchen crew dressed in red T-shirts and white shorts, and flags were fluttering on each building. The music started at 7:30, and the nurses in El Nido wheeled patients out onto their patios or balconies to listen. The little band from the Community College was made up of local students, and their patriotic tunes brought back a lot of memories for the residents.

Daisy had invited Julie and Matt, plus Mark and Pete and Susie, plus Suzette, to come after dinner. They brought lawn chairs and joined some of the other guests around the picnic tables. Some of the residents went inside to watch the televised shows from Boston or Washington, D.C. The rest of the crowd was happy to turn south for a half hour display over Town Lake in Tempe. There were some sporadic flashes of color around the horizon, but early wildfires caused most private clubs to cancel their displays.

La Ventura's third summer sailed along without the sense of doldrums like 2004. Most of the people were content to swim or exercise in the early morning and then play cards and read during the heat of the day. Malcolm rented a lot of good movies for the small theater, sometimes showing a film twice in an evening if a crowd filled the room. The popcorn machine was extremely popular, as well as pitchers of lemonade. As residents returned from a trip, tales were shared and pictures passed around.

One resident had notified the office she was moving. Bonnie came into lunch and explained, "Anne hasn't been completely content here since she arrived in 2002. She was one of our first 'managers,' and she never liked that concept of management. We thought we had such a good idea in giving every person a vote. But she wanted more service and no decisions to make. That's probably why her daughter brought her here to begin with, thinking her mother might be ill or would move on into El Nido. As it happens, Anne is perfectly healthy and just wants a different sort of care."

A voice in the crowd asked, "Where will she find it?" A light chuckle went around the room.

"Well, I don't know. Short of a hospital or a rest home, we think we provide most of the amenities you all request or require. Please let us know if you think of some better way to make La Ventura fit your needs. We're always open to considering a new feature."

Martha commented, "It's sad to lose someone from the community. What could we have done to make her happier?"

Ellen answered, "Probably nothing. Don't you remember neighbors back home who moved out and found some other place they'd rather live? This is just a microcosm of the towns we came from."

Martha pursued the topic. "I still think we need to watch out for people who don't look happy."

At this point, Tom observed, "There will always be people who are restless. Maybe her kids promoted this place, and it wasn't her choice. She never spoke to me, so I suppose she didn't like men."

Donna summed up, "She deserves to make a new choice."

A man in the front table asked, "Are all the units sold?"

"Yes, right now. Anne's will be available to the next person on the waiting list, and then on down the list until someone wants it."

Mary Ann asked a key question. "Anne has such an ideal location. Can one of us trade it for ours?"

Bonnie frowned a bit. "Well, that would require an outright purchase of her unit and then the sale of yours. You know how we arranged your move into Tom Gable's unit. The only difference then was that the next few people on the waiting list were couples, and you wanted a small unit. That's how we moved you into that next place on the list."

"I remember that well. I just thought maybe some others would want to know what they could or couldn't do."

"Right. Enjoy lunch, and I'll see you later."

Daisy said to Alex as they walked along, "Isn't it incredible how fast these weeks go, even when today's the thirty-fifth day over a hundred degrees?"

"I guess the older you get, the faster the time flies. Doesn't seem fair, does it?"

She laughed. "How's your writing schedule? We really appreciated your piece last spring about being a judge. That seems like such an awesome responsibility."

"It is, but you know, after one's practiced law for a few years, it falls into place. It was a small county where my cousins lived. I took some great classes before I went on the bench. I was always open with the press, although those TV cameras and mikes in your face were the worst part of the job."

"What about the election?"

"Hey, if you keep your feet out of the mud, you've got nothing to hide. You have to quit reading the newspaper; it's bad for your blood pressure. But it's much easier to do taxes."

"Well, here's my place. See you later in the writers' group. Hi, Curly. Oh, you look so hot and breathless. You don't want to go out? How about if I put your fan out there for a few minutes?" He watched her dutifully as she unplugged his fan and took it out to the shady part of the patio. Once it was whirring away, he ventured outside, stretching and shaking out his fur. She ran some fresh water in his outdoor bowl and turned to go inside.

"Hm. Message for us." She punched the button and sat down to listen.

"Hi, Mom. Just talked to Julie about your concern over Dad's papers. I'll sure look into it, but I doubt I'll find any problems. I understand you just want some reassurance. Wouldn't want to be sued down the road, would we? Sleep well, and let me do the searching. Love ya. Hi, Curly."

Everyone enjoyed young Emily's visit to Ellen. She was the most popular person in the water aerobics class, or at lunch, or in the ice cream parlor or at the movies. At fourteen, she had the family features of Ellen, a wonderful smile and twinkling blue eyes that wrinkled at the corners when she laughed. Her voice even suggested Ellen's, and during her visit, Ellen became more grandmotherly than usual. The girls in the beauty salon trimmed Emily's long blond hair and gave her a marvelous bouffant twist that lasted just through the dinner hour. At the end of ten days, Emily announced at dinner that in forty-one years, she'd be very happy to move into La Ventura.

Donna turned to Daisy at the table and said, "Wouldn't it be lovely if she could remain so innocent and charming? Next thing you know, she'll be into drugs and booze and smart talk." She looked down and shook her head sadly. "Wait'll she wants to go to London or Paris, get a tattoo or a nose ring or join the Aryan Nation. She won't come to visit Ellen then."

Daisy was shaken by Donna's outburst. She saw tears running down Donna's cheeks and in spite of earlier rebuffs, she put her arm around Donna's shoulders. "We'll hope for Ellen's sake that Emily will stay close."

Donna nodded through her tears. "I'm sorry all that bitterness came out, but maybe you needed to know what I've been through. You remember Franz when he was always the smartest kid in the class, so at ease with adults and so charming. Then in college, he teamed up with a couple of rich kids who knew how to get to Europe and live the high life. Away they went, and from then on, I never really knew my son. His job sounded elegant, and the stories of his social life were reported in *People Magazine*. I'd study those pictures, trying to remember the sweet young kid from high school days. Oh, I know, your kids were model, and your husband was Mr. Perfect. That's why I never wrote you."

"I'm so sorry to hear all this. We can only go so far with raising these kids. From college on, they're on their own really, even when they live at home. Some of the secrets that come out later hurt, but we each get to choose our own mistakes to make."

"I never thought of it quite that way, Daisy. But you're a tough friend to have."

"I am? Why?"

"Because you grew up just right and look good and do everything right. You never seem to have problems. Do you ever get mad? Do you ever cry?"

Daisy thought a minute about how to answer that question. "Not too often, but it's not because I don't have feelings. It's just that crying doesn't help me much. It leaves me feeling horrible. My brain moves ahead to solving a problem. I'm not a fighter, so I have to look for a way out of the pinch."

Donna smiled at the picture Daisy had painted. "I'll bet that's why you were never out on the street scolding the kids."

"Probably. I wasn't a very brave mother."

"My, oh, my, you never told me that before."

"Well, see? I have secrets too."

Donna took a big breath and blew her nose. "Sorry for that scene, but sometimes it's good to clear the air."

"It's always good to clear the air. Let's keep it that way. I do *not* like to have people mad at me. That's one thing I don't know how to deal with."

"I'm always mad at someone. Isn't that funny? Surprising we made it as good neighbors for four years."

The dining room had emptied, so they walked out together, arm in arm.

When Daisy came in from dinner, the telephone was ringing. "Hello? Beth, how great to hear from you." She listened for a long time. "You're coming back to God's country on Wednesday? Wonderful. Wait, let me get a pen. O.K. American? 2:05, O.K. I'll call first and then give you half an hour to get to the curb.

South Side, T 3. You'll get help with the bags, won't you? Right, I'll be there. Can't wait to hear all about it."

She sat down and rubbed Curly's ears. "Beth's coming back; all's right with the world, isn't it, Old Boy? Curly, aren't we lucky to be here?"

Beth was settled in from her trip by Thursday noon, so Daisy called Martha and Ellen to see if they could meet at three. Ellen was delighted to get together, because she had been lonely after Emily left for Atlanta. Donna had to be in the First Aid Station until three-thirty, but she promised to join them then. The four enjoyed their tea and listened to Beth's tales of security problems due to her hip and fighting to keep her cane with her. "But Geneva was still the same quiet little town in the summer, the trees heavy over the streets, white picket fences being painted, and cicadas singing like crazy. It was their seventeen-year peak."

"Makes me a little homesick," mused Daisy.

"Maybe you can come with me when I go again. You'd be amazed at the growth to the west."

"You're going back soon?"

"No, but I'm not ready to say a permanent goodbye to that pretty place. Ellen, tell me about Emily. Is she almost twenty?"

"Well, not quite, but I know it'll happen soon. She's still timid about some of the dangers in the world, like drugs and car accidents. She knows an older girl on her street who was attacked and raped last year. She had a lot to say about that."

Just then, Donna came in and apologized for being late. "I actually had four patients today. It was exciting to be in demand." They laughed and asked what accidents she'd treated.

Martha engaged Donna by asking her advice on losing some weight. "I can't believe how much fun I've had cooking for someone, even if it's just breakfast and lunch. But both of us have gained eight or ten pounds."

Donna was quick to answer, "Nothing like contentment for putting on some pounds. You wouldn't want me to prescribe against that, would you?"

Martha laughed and said, "Oh, no, but I could use a hint or two about lo-cal breakfasts."

"That I can do. Stop over at the office in the morning."

"Thanks."

Daisy assumed an organizer's role for a minute. "Since there are five of us here, let's decide what to do in two weeks. We need to get back on our schedule."

All agreed, and Martha offered, "Do you think Donna could tell us about herself? Maybe we could each give a short synopsis of what we said last summer."

"Wow, I didn't know you talked about yourselves."

"We had each written a short 'life story' of just the facts of our lives in class. So, it was fun to read them and get to know each other better."

"I don't think I can write like that." She paused and seemed to be weighing the possibilities. "Then again, I'd like to know where all of you knew Daisy, and I suppose you'd like to know where Terri and I blew in from." They chuckled, remembering her entry one night in February.

"Try it, Donna. We found it was hard to get started, but then it rolled along. Write it out and read it."

"Did you just go from when you were born up to now?"

Ellen spoke first. "That's right, and I had the longest story since I've been around so long."

Finally, Donna agreed that in two weeks, she'd "tell all," as she put it.

Martha announced she'd heard from Mary Ann. "She'll be with us at the next Thursday meeting. She's had a wonderful time, visiting all the kids and the staff people at the Roundup. I asked her if she missed them a lot. She said the visit was nice, but she was ready to get back here. Isn't that great? Tom suspected she might stay in Roswell."

"Really? I thought she was happy here."

"She is. I guess he was thinking how things had changed since we first got here, but she's coming back to us."

Daisy grinned and said, "Those words are music to my ears. You can't imagine all my doubts about how this idea would work out."

"Really?"

"Gosh, yes. I figured we'd all try it for a year or so, but maybe some of you wouldn't want to stay. I wasn't worried for myself, because I'm in my hometown. I knew I'd like it."

Donna reported, "When I asked where most of the residents came from, Malcolm told me seventy percent were from right around here, you know, the Phoenix area. But he was sweet; he said it was important for people to come from far away to spice things up. That was when I called 'way back in late September, almost a year ago. Heavens, where does the time go?"

CHAPTER 21

Donna Tells All

On Thursday, Daisy directed Donna to the head of the table. Clouds had moved in from the southeast, and everyone was hoping for rain. Monsoons were coming into the area, a pattern the old timers kept reviewing. Daisy flipped on the lights while Ellen poured the tea. They settled in to listen to Donna's life story.

"I was born Donna Franzel on April twentieth. Do I have to say what year?"

"Yes," they chorused.

"O.K. It was 1936 in Oklahoma City. My father was an oil driller, wildcatters they called them. Mother worked around at whatever job she could get. He left her when I was still small and went to Texas. Never heard another word from him. Mother divorced him and then married a man who said he was an important tractor dealer.

"Life was pretty rocky at home. He had a terrible temper, and they both drank a lot. I often stayed at a girlfriend's house to avoid the late-night scenes. But he paid for my schooling, so I try to forgive him and forget the rest.

"I did pretty well in school, and I loved nursing. I could hardly wait to get into a hospital and live on my own. Then I met Rudy Krueger at the Lutheran church. He was a distributor for Wheat Gem Bakeries statewide. He absolutely swept me off my feet. He loved to fish and had a small trailer parked on a lot out at the lake. By Christmas '56 we got married. I got a job right away at University Hospital and loved it. Things looked so good, and I was so trusting it would last forever. Franz was born in 1958, and I stayed home for about six months. Then I found a nice neighbor lady who kept him so I could work three days a week.

"We bought a cute little ranch in a new subdivision. We were faithful at St. Paul Lutheran Church close by, and Franz started school. Everything still looked marvelous.

"That fall, 1963, our new neighbors were Daisy and Scott MacDuff. They were such nice people, and their little girl Julie was about the same age as Franz. He went there to play after school on days when I had the late afternoon shift. Rudy sang in the choir, and I was camp nurse during the Sunday School summer camp. I was a room mother and then a den mother. Franz was the best student in the class, so I felt as if we were doing everything right. Sad thing was that the MacDuffs were only there three and a half years. I was never a letter writer, but Daisy inspired me to at least answer her letters, sometimes with a postcard. I could never tell her everything.

"I'll never forget the eighth grade graduation when the church organist came to sit with us. She gave Franz a nice card with a big check in it. I thought that was strange since he'd never been musical at all. He was just brainy in numbers and history. That was in 1971. The next day, Rudy told me he was in love with Joy, the organist. He said he'd be moving out in a month. Well, I was never much of a diplomat, so I told him in a big, loud voice he'd better be gone before the sun set. And he was. Franz was furious with me and didn't speak for days. It was just a horrible time.

"Rudy divorced me and married Joy. There they were in the same church. Well, I left that church in a hurry. In the settlement, I must admit he was generous. He gave me the house and the place at the lake, promising to pay for Franz' schooling, including college. He and his new wife moved to Tulsa.

"I went out to the lake the next summer just to see what I owned. I found two years' worth of love letters from Joy and some pictures of them in a hotel in Tulsa. I burned all of that, then wished I'd kept the stuff to convince Franz that I was the one who was hurt. He always felt sorry for his father that I yelled at him that day. I sold the lake place as soon as I could and bought a new car with the money. I'm sure Rudy had a more elegant place to go fishing.

"Anyway, I was promoted and had a wonderful job. Franz graduated with distinction and went on to the university. He made some bad choices of friends, and after he graduated in three years, the buddies went off to live in Paris. I hardly ever heard from him. Once in a while, he'd send me a newspaper picture of him at some fancy party, usually with a terse note saying he was fine and it was too bad I was stuck in Oklahoma; I should see the world.

"We had lived together for his seven years of school, just the two of us, and that was about all I could take. I've often wondered why such a brilliant person could be so hard to like, let alone love. He could hurt people's feelings and put you down in the blink of an eye. He thought sarcasm was so smart and witty.

"I sold the house and found an apartment close to the hospital. I took some night classes toward a B.A., in literature and history, things I'd missed in nursing. I became a member of the art museum and went to a few plays on campus. I joined a fitness club and watched my weight. The years were pleasant; I was proud of myself for managing life alone.

"Then I got the shingles in late 2001. I had no idea how people suffered from that virus. I was miserable for months. The pain was so intense, I had to take a leave of absence from my job. Later, I decided I could never do floor duty again, even for some of my private patients. Depression was the second worst condition I ever had. That's about when Daisy caught up with me and invited me to join all of you. I told her I couldn't then. She sent more information, and I kept it.

"Last summer Franz was killed in an automobile accident outside of London, forty-six years old. He had been in the social swing for several years; I'd read about him in *People Magazine.* It hit me hard, and yet it seemed kind of logical after what I knew of his lifestyle. I wasn't surprised, just terribly sad. What a waste of genius mental ability, which the world needs desperately.

"I guess you know the rest. I called and then made a reservation for the new building, and here I am. Imagine my leaving Oklahoma after sixty-nine years! Thank you, Daisy."

The others clapped and praised Donna for telling such a painful story. Ellen, always the most expressive one, said, "Donna, that was a beautiful story of your life. You have reason to be proud, but you left out the good part about maintaining your fitness and about driving a thousand miles to get here. You didn't even tell us where you got Terri."

"Oh, that's true. I'd been thinking of getting a dog, a companion but also a watch dog. Then I was in an apartment and figured a cat would be easier to care for. A patient of mine was so worried about her cat at home that I offered to care for the cat at my place until she was well. As Fate would have it, the patient died. She told me the cat was terrific but never used a name. So, I named her Terrific."

"And the cat is eleven years old?"

"The vet thought she was about a year old when I got her in 1994."

"Amazing how she's adapted to life here." Martha and Mary Ann were the cat experts in this group.

"Who has your kittens now?" Donna asked.

Mary Ann shrugged and said, "It's the price I paid to go on a long vacation. They're permanent residents with Tom and Martha now."

Daisy got the conversation back on track. "What shall we discuss next time?"

"How about sharing our recipes for success, since they're already written? When everyone's back, we can start something new."

"Anyone else want to promote an idea?"

Donna surprised everyone by saying, "I think the obituaries would be a fascinating topic. How did you think of that? The obits in the Phoenix paper are pieces of history. I love them."

Daisy added, "It was a suggestion from the Captain, but we too had thought of something along those lines. So start saving some of those long, newsy obits as samples, and let's do that after the winter class on last wishes."

Martha spoke up, "I think Tom would like to be a part of that project, and he also wrote his recipe for success."

"So did the Captain, and Alexander too. Let's include them."

Ellen offered to read Clarissa's recipe as the first one. "I think she wanted someone else to read it aloud."

CHAPTER 22

Recipes Are a Success

CAPTAIN NEWBURN WAS THE first in the room on Thursday. When Daisy arrived, he said, "It's sure nice to be included with you girls. Everyone's envious of me."

"Now, Captain, you know this isn't a closed meeting. Who else wants to join us? We've tried hard not to be a clique."

"I don't think anyone wants to write or think very hard in the summer. I strained my brain to write this when it was cooler."

The others drifted in and stopped for a glass of tea before settling around the table. By the time Alex arrived, the only empty chair was at the head of the table. "So, I'm the Officer of the Court, am I?" He laughed and pounded his fist on the table, calling the group to order. "Who's going to volunteer to read first?"

Ellen spoke up, "Clarissa is, since she's not here. She gave me this recipe in longhand, so I typed it up for her."

"Great! Read on, Ellen."

"This is what she wrote: 'I've never had children to inspire with my philosophy, but if I had, these are the things I'd want them to know. First of all, trust your parents, because no one knows you better. Second, you must rise above the past, however difficult it may have been. Third, learn to adjust to change. And finally, life is more enjoyable set to music. As long as one has life, there is always a way to move ahead, even when everything is against you. Listen for the music!' Isn't that one hundred percent Clarissa?"

Mary Ann said, "I'm sure she had days when responsibilities were heavy for her, but she always seems to be radiant when she appears."

"She has marvelous stage presence," was Beth's remark.

Alex cleared his throat officially and asked, "Are we supposed to discuss each one, or shall we just read on?"

Daisy looked around and said, "It may vary with the recipe, but since Rissa isn't here, we can't ask her to expand on anything. We'll tell her we loved her and missed her."

"O.K. Who wants to pontificate next?"

Ellen waved a piece of paper and said, "This is mine. While I'm in voice, why don't I read it?" Heads nodded and she continued. "My husband was so able to state his beliefs and opinions, but I've never had to think about my personal recipe for success. This isn't for my success, because it's too soon to know if I've been successful. But this is what everyone ought to know. As part of God's world, we're responsible for ourselves and as many others as we can help. We've been given a gift of faith, a capacity to trust in a powerful God who listens to our prayers. We're never left alone to face our fears. Faith keeps our feet on a steady path. Be careful what you pray for, because prayers are answered, not always as or when we imagine they will be." Ellen smiled around the table and said, "That's it."

Alex assumed the leader's role and thanked her. He looked around as if waiting for comments. He called on Beth who said, "Ellen, you don't realize how articulate you are. That was beautiful and so reassuring."

She smiled and said, "Maybe all those years side by side with the pastor rubbed off on me."

"Now who's going to keep us going?"

Martha said, "I'd like to continue in the same vein. Be grateful for every day of life. You will have choices to make, and your choices will move you closer to your goals or in the wrong direction. It's all up to you. Blessedly, current choices can reverse the bad choices you might have made in the past. God always seems to provide a place in life to stop, evaluate and turn around. Accept that opportunity when it comes to you; repent, and then move ahead. This recipe may be doubled or tripled, and it keeps well." She smiled over at Tom, and he gave her the thumbs up sign.

Alex nodded and said, "Martha, you speak with the voice of experience and success. Our choices make us who we are. I often regret some of my early choices, but I still approve my later ones, as I know you do." He searched the room for the next volunteer. "Tom, how about your words next?"

"O.K. Here's my concept of what someone needs to do to achieve success. Trust in a higher power, and that works its way all through life. Trust in God; trust your superiors in business; trust your parents' advice; trust your older brother. I resisted that attitude all my life until I found I needed help. I thought I had all the answers. But I couldn't stand alone because I had no self-esteem. Now I know the meaning of loving your neighbors as yourself. I didn't like myself, so I had no confidence that anyone else would like me. When you trust others, they trust you, and then you think better of yourself as a result. Then you can be generous to your neighbor. If your trust is misplaced, don't be bitter; just evaluate your needs and find another mentor or mate. It's all a matter of trust."

Martha reached over and squeezed his arm. "Tom's so right. A lot of my choices were bad because I hadn't found someone I could trust. I just let others talk me into anything. I had no self-respect."

Donna had come in late and sat by the door. Now she asked, "Could I comment on what Martha said?" Daisy motioned for her to continue. "Trust is between equals, I've learned. What I thought was trust turned out to be just leaning on someone, becoming dependent on him. So, he always had the upper hand. My self-worth just dribbled away."

Alex said, "Donna, come up here to the table. I didn't hear you come in."

"I didn't mean to come in, but I was curious what you had written. I figured I might learn something about success."

Alex said, "Well, remember, we're just giving free advice. We're not saying we have been a success because of a certain idea."

"I know, but your ideas come from experience."

"True. Just didn't want anyone to think we feel like a big successful bunch of retirees. That sounds so arrogant. So, who's next? Robert, how about you?"

"I don't know, Alex. I may have written this in a different way. When I was growing up, every teacher was talking about the importance of making decisions. I had a logical mind and wasn't afraid to size up a situation and then announce what I had decided. So, my statement reads this way: Learn to make sound decisions based on fact, tempered with experience. Set your sights high, study hard and lead the way. Always be a part of the solution, not the problem." He looked at Alex and added, "Do you think that's enough?"

"Sure I do. It sounds like the captain of a ship. You were probably a good one."

"The best."

Alex chuckled and said, "You know, we each have individual ideas, don't we? This is good."

Daisy interrupted to say, "We're running out of time. Can we continue this in two weeks?"

"Couldn't we meet next week?"

"I'm sure we can. I'll reserve the room. All right with all of you?" She turned to Donna. "Did you enjoy listening?"

"Yeah, it was great. I might have to put some words in writing myself. I hated writing assignments in school, but I do have some ideas."

"Good. Writing is hard for me too, but these short statements aren't too bad."

"I think they're the hardest. It's much easier to wander on and on, trying to explain or justify your idea."

A week later, the Thursdays at Three group met again, this time without the Captain who was on vacation and knowing that Martha would be a little late. They looked to Alex, since he'd been the moderator of the last meeting. "All right, I'll be the judge, but remember, no verdicts or opinions. Just listen!"

Mary Ann offered to be first. "My statement is pretty boring, so let's hear it before anyone else has a fancy one." Several voices objected, but she began. "My best approach to being successful in life is to be responsible. I know that sounds heavy, but it's so satisfying to identify a thing that needs doing and to do it. I love to organize people or plans or food. That's always been my best way to help people, to show them how to get where they need to be going. That may not be advice for someone else, but it's my recipe to keep me happy." She folded up her paper and sat back.

"Thanks, Mary Ann, and I couldn't agree more with the business of being organized. I've seen more people lose their way, because they couldn't set priorities and focus." He shook his head and frowned. "Wasted time and talents."

Daisy spoke up, "Mary Ann, it's wonderful you found how to help people and enjoy what you did as a career. I always admire that."

"Daisy, you're good at keeping people in order. How about going next?"

"Well, I guess I could. I agree with Alex about the need to know your priorities and to set goals. I'm not sure where it fits into a recipe, but being realistic is part of good goal-setting. The other advice I gave my kids was to be good students and share whatever they learned with their own kids or with others. I hoped they might become teachers or preachers, but I guess a lawyer and a hospital administrator use similar skills. What my mother really harped on was being resourceful, since they were busy, often absent parents. One-and-only children have no one to entertain them, so I had to learn young how to amuse myself. That's where I learned how to make things, how to recycle materials and try new crafts. Busy hands and a busy mind focused me on growing up to be productive. That's how it adds up to me."

"That's why some of you are here, isn't it? Daisy knew how to recycle her friends and make something new of them."

"Right," exclaimed Beth. "And aren't we glad your mother taught you how to save remnants and be resourceful?"

Martha and Tom both chimed in a loud "Yes!"

Daisy laughed and agreed. "It's kept me happy all these years. I think another valuable idea is to keep in touch with old friends; never let them get away."

"Even when they try to resist your greetings?"

"Yes, Donna, even if you call at a bad time. Risk it!"

Alex took charge again. "Well, Donna, did you write something to share?"

"I did, much to my own surprise. All the reversals I've suffered made me look back to my nurse's training to keep myself healing. One of the most important people in my first year said a patient must, *must,* get rid of all resentment and anxiety in order to heal. That's a big order when you're down and out, but it's so true. I've always been angry about someone or something, kind of mad at the world when I lost my way. But I set aside all those thoughts when I decided to drive out here." She seemed to be finished speaking.

"Tell me, Donna, are you glad you joined us at La Ventura?"

"I think I am, Alex. I've been feeling more optimistic and hopeful, so I know that's a good sign. I still can't get used to a few of the people here. They mope and wander around looking lost. So many complainers at the meals. Sometimes I'd rather eat alone at home."

"That's hard to get used to, I agree. I always try to change the subject." Ellen was the most tactful member of the group, they all knew.

"O.K., troops, let's finish this up. Martha, glad you got here. Beth, we haven't heard a word from you. Surely that white hair of yours indicates wisdom we need to know." Alex's words brought smiles all around.

"Alex, you're a charmer or I'd never let you get by with that. I earned that white hair, one at a time, over tax deadlines, slippery clients, ailing parents, a sick husband and cancer. But maybe some wisdom came too. My precious little brother accused me of always looking for the sunshine in life, and back in the Midwest, believe me, that's a favorite indoor sport. Maybe that's why I love this climate. But if I had to name one quality I think is vital to successful living, I'd say it's resilience. The ability to bounce back from grief, pain, loss or sudden change is the key to moving ahead. If one can't get over a problem and close that chapter of the book, he's apt to repeat the whole experience."

"Amen to that, Beth. Resilience is a word we don't use every day, but it's a good one. My mother loved stick-to-it-iveness. Do you remember that expression?"

"I do. That's perseverance which may encompass resilience. But let's not forget your recipe, Alex. You can't get by without writing one."

"I wrote and then read mine in class, remember? Then this summer I rewrote. Finally I came up with three qualities required for success. One is respect for others; a second is respect for the law; and the third is honesty. The first respect keeps you related to humanity, your own family included. The second respect protects your freedom. Honesty is simply the basis for all relationships. Life is complicated enough without trying to maintain a false image of yourself or anyone else."

"Those are lofty goals, Alex. They fit with your career," said Daisy.

"Well, I'd like to have added a spiritual purpose which I believe is terribly important. But I couldn't get it worded quite right. I wanted to mention vision too, you know having a vision of what needs to happen in this world."

"We were just asked to state a simple pattern that someone else might like and decide to copy. There isn't time to cover all the bases. People write heavy books to do that."

"I'd like to write a book, but my wife used to say it would be too pretentious."

Ellen started to object and correct him, but Daisy cut her off. "Alex, thanks again for moderating the group. It's been fun to hear everyone's thoughts on a serious subject. With this storm coming in, we should probably get home as quickly as possible." Her words were drowned out by a rush of wind blowing leaves and pebbles against the sliding glass doors. "Monsoon's back," she declared.

"You're sure it's not that newest hurricane?" The light changed into a yellowish cast as more dust was picked up.

"Let's hope this one brings us a shower." The lights blinked off and on.

No one was quick to leave the room and go out into the wind. Ellen said, "Is this a good time to think about our next project in writing? Wasn't it the last wishes topic we postponed?"

"That's what I thought we were doing this summer," said Tom. "I felt more urgency in thinking about that than this philosophical bit."

"I enjoyed this talk about values. I'm amazed at how similar our thinking was. We could probably have put all our paragraphs into one long page of wisdom." Alex hated to let go of this meaty subject.

Martha brought up the last wishes again. "Based on our life stories and now the statement of what we think is most important to success, don't you think it'll be easier to evaluate what we leave to relatives or how we want our days to end? I feel strongly about the medical care part. I want to be sure that's kept someplace near where everybody can find it if I get sick."

Tom agreed, "We're going to start with that, honey. I feel the same way."

Ellen recalled, "I suggested the topic to our teacher, and she liked it. Trouble is, those classes don't start until after the holidays."

"Maybe we could do the medical directives during October and early November, just here in our little group."

"Good idea, Daisy." The wind subsided so several of them collected their papers and hurried out. Others drifted toward the office and mail boxes.

In four days, news about the recent Arizona dust storm and monsoon was lost in the awesome reports of Hurricane Katrina, beating its way toward the city of New Orleans and the surrounding Gulf Coast. Pictures of devastation, lost lives, evacuation routes and violence obliterated local news stories. The La Ventura family drew together in amazement, sympathy and support. As September dawned in Louisiana, the effect of the disaster spread across the country. "I know we can't do much physically," commented Alex, "but let's find out how to direct funds and prayers to those who can. Daisy, find out over at your church what the channels are."

"I will, Alex. Right away."

CHAPTER 23

Pete Uncovers the Secret

DAISY WAS DELIGHTED WITH Julie's invitation to dinner on Sunday, the fourth, after the second church service. Labor Day was a strange holiday now that school opened in mid-August. It used to be such fun to close up the vacation place and anticipate the school routine for Tuesday. Now it was an interruption in family plans, an extended weekend in the hottest, most humid part of the year for the valley. Daisy tried to dress in something bright and cool.

"Not many in church today," she said. "I s'pose the winter residents are still up north. What was the early service like?" Daisy's grandchildren preferred the chapel service.

"Maybe fifty were there, but that's not many. I saw two of those gals who live with you, Mom. Isn't one of them Shirley?"

"Oh, you mean Shirley Lott and her cousin Jenny. They've stayed real active at church, but I only see them at one of the classes at La Ventura, the Bible Study."

Julie called out, "Matt, I'm ready for you to put the meat on. I just heard Pete's car in the drive."

"Will do. Send him out to help me, with a couple of cold ones."

Mark came down the stairs as Susie and Suzette came in, followed by Pete. Hugs and kisses went around the room, and Julie sent Pete out with the beers. Daisy loved being in the midst of them. "Well, how does it feel to be seniors this year?"

Suzette beamed and said it was wonderful. Mark shrugged and said, "Hey, it's a heavy responsibility. Coach is already scouting my replacement, and Mr. Hanson made an appointment to see me next week."

"He's your counselor?"

"Yeah. Said it's time to talk college again."

"I thought you'd made up your mind on ASU."

"I have. He's still promoting U of A."

The youngest ones were gone after lunch, leaving Daisy with her four favorite young adults. Peter started the conversation with, "Mom, I got hold of the police report on that ticket of Dad's. It was in February, 1999, the eighteenth, at 7:15 p.m. Seems kind of a strange hour for Dad to be out driving around, but that's what it said. He was stopped just north of Chaparral on suspicion of driving under the influence, weaving on 68th Street south of Camelback."

"Really? Weaving? How odd." Daisy stared at Pete. She looked around at the others and could tell they too were surprised at what Pete had learned.

"Then it said that the car behind him stopped too, and the passenger, a young man with a valid driver's license, offered to drive Dad home in his own car; he said he knew him and lived near him. The patrol car followed them until they were safely home."

"Did the ticket say who he was?"

"Yeah, name was Tomás Gomez. The car he'd been riding in evidently drove on."

"Do you recognize the name?"

"No, but I can pursue it if you want me to. Lots of Gomez listings in the phone book, but a few calls might find him. The court appearance was set for Thursday, April twenty-second, but there's a note that a lawyer requested an earlier hearing, and it was granted for April first."

"Can we find out how the hearing turned out?"

"I went over to the city offices, and the records show he was represented by Earl Baker, attorney-at-law, and paid a fine of $650. License was not forfeited, and there was no jail time. The charges were expunged from the record. Nice for Dad, huh?" Julie nodded in agreement.

Slowly, Daisy replied, "Sure, but how did all that happen without my knowing it?"

"Beats me. You were probably at some meeting, and he didn't want to worry you. Don't worry about it now, Mom. It's ancient history."

"Hmmm. Why didn't I see that check in the checkbook?"

"The one for $650.00?"

"That one and the one for $2,000.00."

"Whoa, I don't know anything about that one. You have a receipt for that amount?"

"I do, or rather I did. I got rid of a lot of stuff that I wanted to forget or ignore. Now I see I should have kept it."

"Do you remember the date on it?"

"It was clipped to the copy of the ticket; I just remember 1999 and maybe winter."

Julie was quietly following the conversation until she asked, "Mom, are you O.K. with this? Pete's right that it's long gone."

"I know. But if you think of it someday, see if you can find that Gomez person."

"Not to worry. I'll keep it in mind."

As Daisy drove home, she kept thinking, "So how does Tom Gable figure in all of this?"

Mid-afternoon on Tuesday, Pete called, and she put the call on speaker phone to amuse Curly. "Hey, Mom, I found Gomez. Tomás was a busboy at that bar and grill down on 68th Street, north of Thomas. He remembered Dad; he called him Duffy. He said he was getting a lift home from one of the managers, Tom Gable. They were driving north about a block behind Dad and saw the whole thing."

"You mean they saw the police lights and all?"

"Yeah, but I could tell he never knew how it ended, so if Dad wanted it kept secret, I guess we don't need to make an issue out of it, do we?"

"O.K. Pete, but Tom Gable is the man who lives near me, and he said we would talk over old times one of these days. It may not be over yet."

"Well, at least you know the facts, Mom. No more surprises."

"I hope not. Thanks, dear."

"Talk to you soon. Bye."

Daisy sat back and sighed. Curly ambled over to her knee and rested his chin there. "Why wouldn't Scott have told me about this? We never had secrets. Oh, Curly, if only I could ask him now." She sniffled into a tissue and mopped a tear in the corner of one eye. "C'mon, Boy, let's go for a walk. That'll get us both perked up."

CHAPTER 24

There's More to the Story

LIFE WAS QUIET AROUND La Ventura. These days, more time was spent comparing notes on temperature readings and post cards from friends in Canada. Lots of discussions were held in the shaded end of the main swimming pool. People always marveled that September is a summer month in Phoenix.

The dining room seemed noisy one evening near the end of the month. Ellen commented, "All of a sudden we seem to have a crowd here for dinner. I'd forgotten how big a family we are now."

"I heard Bonnie say that we're sold out, so I guess we'll have more tables filled."

"Kind of exciting, isn't it?" When Daisy didn't reply, Ellen continued. "You're off in another world tonight, friend."

"You're right. My mind is all mixed up with a pattern I'm working on for a pillow and with news from the kids. You know, just the usual mishmash of stuff."

"O.K. if that's all it is. Look, there's a limo outside the door. I bet it's Clarissa. Isn't she a kick?"

"Her nephew knows just what pleases her. If she has all that luggage again, she'll miss dinner."

"Nope. She's coming right this way, and the driver is stuck with the boxes and bags. Bonnie just caught up with her and slowed her down. I always forget how bent her back is, but she hustles around anyway."

"Girls, I'm back," shot through the noisy room, and all eyes were upon her. She had a long lavender scarf floating around her neck and back over one shoulder of her pearl grey suit. Her shoes were purple suede, and she was the picture of elegance. "Oh, I'm just exhausted, but I'm so hungry I couldn't go right to my place." Hugs were exchanged and everyone was talking at the same time. Tom pulled an extra chair over to Daisy's table and urged her into it. Bonnie herself brought a table setting and glass of water for her.

After the dessert, the Bunch of Daisy's gathered around one table and listened to Clarissa's travel tales. The summer had been cool, but the garden was beautiful. Jan and Dick were the perfect hosts, but she missed La Ventura. Her bridge cronies were glad to see her, but they had become even more narrow-minded and fearful. All in all, a story similar to last year's.

Later, Ellen and Daisy were walking along when Donna and Alice passed them and said they were going to catch a film over at the senior center on Via Linda. "They've hit it off so well," Ellen observed. "I think Donna's moving around much better since she got into the water aerobics class."

"I can't believe how popular that class is. I still remember a friend of mine from the church said she could never live here, because the pool isn't deep enough for diving. But it's just right for the exercises."

"You have so many projects going, Daisy. Aren't you about out of remnants?"

"Just about. It's time for the annual sale. Want to go with me?"

"I might, to remember what inspired you three years ago."

On Sunday, October 2, Martha invited friends over to celebrate Tom's seventy-fifth birthday. By the time she gathered the Bunch of Daisy's and the minister and his wife, plus Alex and Robert, she had a dozen. A neighbor loaned some folding chairs, and Daisy brought a card table. It was a beautiful day, so people spilled out onto the patio. Mary Ann took the cats to her place for safekeeping. Tom was actually jovial as the gracious host, a role no one had seen before. "Just like Mom's Office and Grill," he said. "We used to ask if guests wanted smoking or non-smoking. Here, there's no choice. So, what would you like to drink? Red or white wine, sodas, coffee or tea?"

Tom served easily, and Martha filled plates with canapés and chips and dips. "Don't eat too much, because when the pizza gets here, you'll need to be hungry."

Pizza was an old favorite, but never served as a meal in the dining room. Tom promised it would be the best pizza, because his old buddy at the grill was fixing it. He turned to Daisy and asked, "Were you ever inside that place?"

"No, I don't think so, but I know my husband loved it. Said it was the 'Cheers' of Scottsdale. That was a great compliment in his mind."

"Yup, 'Where everyone always knew your name, and everyone was always glad you came.' I'll tell you some stories about the place, one of these days."

"Fine, I'd like that."

"Pizza's here, folks." Martha's shout cut off their conversation, and that was all right with her.

True to his word, Tom caught up with her after dinner the next day. "I thought maybe I'd stop over tomorrow afternoon. Good time?"

Daisy thought about her Tuesday schedule and nodded. "That's a good time. Bring Martha too."

"I will if that's O.K. with you."

"Of course."

Around three-thirty, they knocked at Daisy's door. After they were seated, Daisy started out by saying, "Tom, you must know something about my husband Scott that I don't know. It's painful to admit that, but I've been thinking about it, and I want to know what it is."

"Well, Daisy, you've become such a leader around here and such a dear friend to bring the two of us together, that it's hard for me to tell you this. But I'm sure you should know this story. One evening, I finished my shift about seven and offered Tomás, our busboy, a ride home. Pulling out of the parking lot ahead of us was a nice little car with the license plate 4DAISY. Young Tomás commented that it was Duffy's car, and I remarked, 'Probably his wife's.'

"We both drove on north, hitting a green light at Osborn. At Indian School, Duffy got through on the yellow, but I caught the red. I stopped, and we were both looking straight ahead. Tomás said, 'Watch it, Duffy. Slow down.' The light changed and as we moved ahead, Duffy crossed the center line in the block ahead of us. A southbound car had to swerve abruptly to avoid him. Camelback was green, so Duffy got way ahead of us. By the time we got up to Scottsdale House, I had to pull over for a cop behind me with his lights and siren on. He pulled Duffy over, right at Chaparral. After the stop sign, we crossed the road, and Tomás said we should stop. 'You know, they won't let Duffy drive himself home. I'll get out here and drive him home. I live just around the corner from them.'

"I told him that was a nice idea, and I waited for a while to make sure it worked out. It did, and I went on home. Next day, I checked with Tomás, and he said there was no big problem. Duffy was way over the thirty-five limit and the cop smelled booze, so he gave him a ticket. Tomás had a license and Duffy knew him, so the cop let Tomás drive and followed them home, to your place."

"That's pretty much what our son found out about that ticket. Scott hired a lawyer and chose not to worry me, I suppose. By the time I got home, he had probably made popcorn and was reading the paper, doing the usual things."

"Yes, Daisy, but what none of us knew at the time, was that the southbound car swerved in and out of the Lafayette intersection, then spun around and ended up teetering over the edge of the canal bank. That one-car accident was in the next night's Scottsdale paper. The driver was in the hospital for a week, and he lost the sight in one eye. I know it was the same car, a sporty convertible with top down, bright blue."

Daisy was gripping the arms of her chair as the story unfolded. "You're telling me that Scott *caused* an accident?"

"I don't know, Daisy. He was never charged with it; in fact he told us at the grill that his record was clean, thanks to a good lawyer. I doubt he ever knew another car was involved."

Daisy groaned. "Weren't there any witnesses to report him?"

"Evidently not. We were close, but we never saw anything. We were just watching Duffy. Never heard another word about it, until I got here."

"Here? Where?"

"Here at La Ventura. Have you met Dave Olson?"

"Maybe, sounds a bit familiar. Oh, I know. He's the one with the cane and. . ." Her voice trailed away into a groan. "Oh, no, no, no. It can't be true." She buried her face in her hands.

Martha moved right over to Daisy's side, crowding out Curly. With her arm around Daisy, she said softly, "It's all part of the past, but we didn't want you to hear Dave telling his story. He often tells it, because it's when he quit drinking. He's proud of that, and he's just fine with his disability; he never complains. He has no idea of how the accident happened. He was cited for 'speeding and losing control.'"

"Yes, but now that I know I can't just ignore the truth."

"Yes, you can, Daisy, because we don't know positively the cause, and it serves no purpose to bring it up. I didn't want you piecing it together some late night all by yourself. Believe me, it's ancient history."

Daisy shook her head. "How did you connect it to me?"

"When you moved in, I saw the license plate." He leaned back and added, "Dave was cited for driving too fast and being too impaired to control his car."

"Yes, but he could have, if Scott hadn't crowded him."

"We don't know that, Daisy. He'd been drinking a lot."

"But all those hospital bills and the pain." She sobbed convulsively.

"Insurance covered everything. He's made a super recovery. He thinks he's lucky he didn't land in the water. He always says he can't swim so it would have been the end of him."

Daisy tried to deep breathe and sit up straighter. "It's going to take some time to get my head around this. I guess I thank both of you for explaining it to me. Scott was an angel in my mind, for many years. But as we both aged, we knew each other's weak spots. I knew he sometimes drank an extra one, but I always thought that was at home."

"As a matter of fact, his D.U.I. charge made my brother and me change one of our old, bad habits. We cut out our roadies completely."

"Roadies? Meaning what?"

"If a customer had to leave and hadn't finished a drink, he could pour it into a plastic cup for the road. Or if he wanted another drink to sip on the way home, we made it in a plastic cup. No extra charge for the service."

"So you don't allow that any more?"

"Nope. And the bartenders are told not to serve anyone who appears unsteady. We've taken keys from a couple of guys and called them a cab. But remember, I've left all that behind."

Martha said gently, "We've given Daisy a lot to think about, and we need to go home ourselves. Daisy, if you want to talk some more, call me. I'll come right over."

"Thanks. I'm not sure what I'll do about this."

Tom said, "Nothing, Daisy. Not one thing. This is just back-up information."

Daisy turned from the door and sank into the nearest chair. Curly snuggled in against her knees. Absently she rubbed his ears and neck, frowning in disbelief at Tom's story. "Curly, what do I do now? Call Pete or Julie? Shake their memories of a great dad? Can I put it aside as Martha and Tom said?"

CHAPTER 25

Last Wishes, Anyone?

THE SCHEDULED CLASSES for Tuesdays at Two in the fall were short series focused on computer topics, e-mail and Internet research. A resident artist promised to teach watercolor technique, and another artisan offered Christmas Gifts You Can Make. The Thursdays at Three group finished the summer with Donna's life story and the two meetings about their recipes for success. Being writing students, they wanted to talk about last wishes, written legally or as family documents. Adding Tom, Captain Newburn and Alex MacPherson gave the group new dimensions.

Daisy said, "It looks as if we'll be a writing and reading aloud group. Any ideas on where to start?"

Robert, the retired captain of a cruise ship, had a suggestion. "Today's September eighth, and already the papers are full of reminders about 9/11 in 2001. I wonder what ever happened to their last wishes or their obituaries?"

Alex looked solemn as he said, "We never know what's next, do we? It's a good reminder to put things in writing."

Daisy spoke up next. "Captain, you suggested obituaries, and I think Ellen mentioned the last wishes idea. But it is an interesting subject. The new pamphlets about El Nido emphasize the need of stating one's last wishes. Anybody else have an opinion?"

Tom said, "I used to think about this a lot. I left my home state to come over here with Al, and when he died, he had no plans made, not even a will. I had no idea about the rules in Arizona. So I learned the hard way, and I think this is a great idea. For us, it comes at a good time, because Martha and I have nothing formal set down in words."

"Alex, can you describe what might be a good form for writing these ideas? I know you were in taxes, but you must be aware of Arizona's laws." Alex nodded and smiled.

So, Alex used the first meeting in October to explain Arizona's laws as a community property state. Such a crowd came to the session, they had to move to the Great Room. Later, when the subject changed to personal last wishes and completing forms for advance directives and Power of Attorney, the group dropped back to the original ten. Around the dinner tables, people occasionally murmured about having wills but nothing else. Even when the La Ventura newsletter encouraged residents to file those directives with Malcolm and Bonnie, the response was minimal.

Alex started another meeting by saying, "Sometimes, the personal letter means more to the heirs than the legal document. You've gotta have a will, but this group should have fun writing the informal stuff. The rest of the crowd will wish they'd stayed with us."

"I like that idea. I'm going to start by going to the bank and looking in the safe deposit box. My old list of what's in there is outdated." Daisy looked satisfied by her decision.

Ellen gasped, "I forgot about that box. It's in Atlanta. Will a bank mail the contents to me?"

"We'll look into it, Ellen. Don't lie awake tonight."

Ellen continued, "I've made an inventory of a few things I brought here that might not look special to my kids, but Emily knows they're for her. I'd feel better having it written in a letter."

"Me too," agreed Martha. "Especially now that I'm married again, and I don't see the boys at all. I want to be sure Mary gets a couple of treasures from Mom."

Mary Ann was nodding. "I want to add to that list. I have things to pass along to Mary. Aunts are important people too!"

Beth, ever the detail person, asked, "Where are we going to file these papers? I suppose I could mail them back to my lawyer in Illinois." She looked thoughtful. "Then again, maybe I need a lawyer here."

Tom spoke up. "Where are you all going to be buried, or where will your wills be read? Have you already decided that? I haven't. I guess that's why I asked."

"We didn't talk about those things before the wedding, did we, Tom?" Martha smiled at the thought of it.

Daisy finally said, "I'm the lucky one with my attorney right here in town, and with two in the family. But I just shudder when I think of something happening suddenly, and the children having to sort through all my stuff."

"You're right. It's the stuff that bothers me. I can write down what kind of care I want or don't want really fast. But it's all the odds and ends. What becomes of the personal things, like clothes and cosmetics?"

Alex cleared his throat and started. "Not to sound like a judge, but you need to know that some kid of yours is going to have to fill boxes with whatever's in your desks and dressers. Then he'll haul the stuff off to the dump, or a rummage sale. It's not a pretty scene. I've written a letter telling my son to call the Salvation Army and clear out my place."

"That sounds kind of unfeeling, Alex, but I know you're right."

"Well, I told him he has the right of first choice, he or his wife or the grandkids. I can picture it happening on a Saturday when they're all going to a ball game and there's no time for cleaning out my place. I'm not a good housekeeper since Doris died. I want the quickest way to get rid of everything."

Mary Ann had been quiet, and then she spoke up. "Most of all, I hope that my things might help someone else who has nothing, maybe a person who has been displaced or burned out. The only way to plan that is to write it down and file it with Malcolm and send a copy to the Boys Club Thrift Shop or Vista del Camino. None of us wants to clean out stuff for another one of us, do we?"

"I'm lucky. My two church friends who live here can take all my craft supplies and fabrics, the things Julie and Pete don't know about, to the church workshops. I've already told them to come and get the stuff right away and get it to the girls who make things for the bazaar."

Captain Newburn finally said, "Who's going to know where to send what's left of me? My kids move around so much, I hardly know where they live. One month they're at the cabin, and the next thing I know they're in Florida, and then back to Maine." He shrugged. "I guess Malcolm will find them."

Martha said with a laugh, "That's the beauty of all their cell phones. They can't get away from family news!"

Beth smiled and said, "I know how you feel. My relations are so scattered. Not likely Sean will ever come back from London." She went over to the buffet. "Anyone want more iced tea?" That was a welcome break in the solemn conversation.

Donna came in and asked why it was so quiet. Daisy responded, "Were trying to be serious for once, thinking ahead."

Skeptically, Donna asked, "About what?"

"Oh, how we leave our affairs in order and such things."

"Ooo, what a dreadful thought. Someone else can do that for me. I won't know the difference."

"What about any relatives? Isn't there anyone who should know if you get sick?"

Donna shrugged and said, "Nope, not a soul." Then she looked thoughtfully at Daisy and asked, "What would become of Curly if you had to go to the hospital?"

Beth jumped at that. "I'll take him. He's the best dog I've ever known."

Ellen agreed and offered to help. Finally the meeting time had run out, and they began to stand and straighten chairs. "Maybe we'd do better with this subject in writing. I can't think of anything else now." Others nodded, and they drifted apart.

CHAPTER 26

A Time to Visit the Hospital

BACK IN HER APARTMENT, Daisy sat down to cuddle Curly under his chin. "You're the only thing I own that people might fight over, Old Boy." She laid her head back against the chair and fatigue took over. Shadows were long when she awoke to the telephone ringing. "Hello? Yes, I'm here, dear. What's the problem?" She yawned and tried to straighten her shoulders. "What? Pete's in the hospital?"

The door knocker clattered loudly, and Daisy walked with the phone to find Suzette at the door. "Gram. It's Dad. He's sick." Tears streamed down her cheeks.

Daisy hushed her long enough to say, "Suzette's here now. I'll get my things and be right there." She turned to her granddaughter and hugged her. "Let's get going, dear. Your mom needs us." They headed out to Scottsdale Healthcare Osborn.

In the E.R. waiting room, Susie clung to Daisy and Suzette. "I should have known something was wrong last night. Pete was so serious, kind of gloomy. He asked if we'd ever written down what we owned and what we owed."

Daisy explained what their summer writing group had been discussing only hours earlier. "People waver between wanting to avoid the subject and knowing they should state their wishes somewhere."

"I know, but Pete deals with that every day. I thought he must have filled out a form some place with all that information. Wasn't his dad careful about that?"

"Well, yes and no. Scott had every blessed detail recorded about the house and the furniture and bills from every can of paint. But I had an awful time finding the insurance policies and stray bank accounts."

Suzette blurted out, "Daddy hasn't died. I wish you'd stop talking that way."

Consoling her, Susie drew her close and said, "Sometimes, we all need a reminder to be more orderly, that's all, dear. Gram and I were just saying how much we rely on Dad to keep track of everything. He's overworked. You and I will have to learn how to help him, won't we?"

A nurse arrived and called them into another waiting area. "In a minute you and your daughter can talk to him, but keep it short and relaxed. He's had quite a shock. He needs to rest a while. In a few days he can go home."

Julie came in and heard the good news that brought smiles to their faces. Then she said, "I'll walk you out, Mom. Did you know the van from La Ventura is in the driveway?"

"Oh? I wonder who needed it?"

"Let me ask at the desk." She was gone only a minute. "A man named Olson, David I believe she said. Do you know him?"

Daisy was overcome with a flashback to Tom's story and all the questions she had put on hold in her mind. "Yes, I know who he is."

"He fell getting out of the pool."

"Oh." Daisy couldn't bring herself to pour out the story to her daughter right there in the lobby of the hospital. "I'll tell you about him some time. Sometime soon."

"O.K., Mom. Didn't Suzette drive you here?"

"Yes, she did. I don't have my car."

"I'll flag down your van. Otherwise, I'll take a break and drive you home." She hurried through the doors and waved at the driver. Then she motioned to Daisy. "C'mon, Mom."

Daisy climbed in and the driver explained, "Gotta finish this entry in my log, Mrs. Mac." Then he closed the doors and turned to her. "You want to go right back? If you've got any errands, we can do them."

"No, I want to go home, thanks. This helps since my granddaughter drove me here."

"Yeah, poor old Dave Olson took a spill at the pool. Skinned up one knee real bad. He's walking fine, so he probably didn't break anything. Maybe needs stitches. Your son O.K.?"

"They're doing some tests. He might have had a stroke or a seizure."

"Well, here we are. Good to be so close, isn't it?"

"Right, and thanks."

Daisy and Curly were several hours late for their dinners, and he crowded close to her knees in the kitchen. "I know you're more than ready, Boy. See if this will make up for the late time." She added a wedge of cheddar to his dry kibble. "Now, Mrs. Mac," she said to herself, "how about some scrambled eggs?" She quickly fixed herself a plate of toast and eggs. "A glass of wine too, lady? Why, thank you, I'd like that." She poured herself a glass, added a couple of ice cubes and adjourned to the table.

As she ate, she reviewed the conversation about Scott's bookkeeping. It had slipped through the years. Looking back on the last couple of years, she couldn't ignore the story Tom had told her. Had Scott had any last wishes? His death came so quickly, who would know? Pete had taken care of all the bills and helped her make decisions for the first month or more. Maybe he'd meant to tell her about pending matters, debts, fines, whatever was left over. "There are surprises every day, aren't there, Sir Curly? And speaking of surprises, David Olson in the same hospital. Now that's a coincidence."

Daisy and Curly's morning walking companions already knew the reason for Daisy's missing dinner. The questions came before Daisy had any report from Susie, so she tried to keep the news tentative. As she let herself in the front door, she asked Curly, "Why is it everyone turns into a doctor with a diagnosis when I said I didn't know what was wrong with Pete?" She plunked down into the easy chair with Curly close beside her knee. "Curly, let's hope he rested well and can come home today."

She dialed the phone and smiled as Suzette answered. "What have you heard from the hospital, Sweetie?" She listened and stroked Curly's head. "Good. That's something he can take in a pill." She frowned. "Well, how about some therapy or a cane?" In a minute she signed off and decided to wait for a call from Susie at the hospital. She knew Julie would call too, if there was any news.

She closed her eyes. "Scott, are you there? What if something happens to Pete? He's been so strong since you left me. I need him. Scott. . ." The telephone cut short her reveries. "Hello, Susie. No news yet? But I can see him tomorrow?" She listened. "All right, dear. Call when you know. I'm here." She patted Curly. "Oh, yes, Curly, I'm always here."

The day dragged by with nothing conclusive. Pete still couldn't stand up straight without help. One foot seemed numb, while the other was weak. He had refused crutches or a walker. The tests continued. Daisy felt helpless and bewildered. The doctors had asked her questions about other members of the family. Whenever there was a reference to Scott, another fear surfaced. She could not delay thinking about Tom's story forever. Pete and Julie deserved to know. Now another piece of that same story was in the same hospital.

She parked at the hospital and walked to Pete's room in a fearful mood. At the door, he greeted her. "Hi, Mom." His strong voice brought her hope, although he reported the doctor's words. "Potassium deficiency, dehydration, overwork, over stressed, high blood pressure. A time bomb waiting to go off. He told me to rest now!"

Later, Daisy left Pete's room somewhat comforted. She was tempted to ask for Mr. Olson's room number. She couldn't understand her hesitant feelings; she'd been a hospital visitor on the board of deacons for three years in Illinois. Why couldn't she just stop by his room as a neighbor from La Ventura? She straightened her spine and took a deep breath. She marched to the main desk and asked the volunteer about Mr. Olson. "He's on the third floor, ma'am, room 3122, and he may have visitors."

"Thank you." The new elevators were across the lobby, and in a minute Daisy was on the third floor. No turning back now. "3122, there it is." She tapped at the half-open door.

"Come on in," was the booming response. It made her smile.

"Hi, Mr. Olson. I'm Daisy MacDuff from. . ."

"Of course, I know. You and your Bunch of Daisy's. Everyone knows you. Sit down." Daisy did as he indicated. He was propped up and watching TV. He clicked it off and said, "How good of you to come and see me."

"My son is down on two, and I heard you were here. Yesterday, I rode home in the van that brought you."

"I was so clumsy, but once again very lucky. I get nervous around water; can't swim worth a damn. That cute thing, Donna, convinced me to come for the exercises, and I was getting a kick out of it. It really felt good, getting out and doing something. Then I missed the top step. That deck is rough."

"But you didn't break a bone?"

"Nah, just took all the skin off one knee and kind of sprained the toes on my other foot. I get to go home this afternoon. Have to stay out of the water for ten days. Watch out for infection. So what's wrong with your son?"

"He may have had a slight stroke; he's lost the feeling in one foot and he speaks slowly, as if his brain is affected. They gave him every test you can think of, but the only thing they know is he needs potassium and needs to bring down his blood pressure."

"He can do that. My wife took potassium all the time."

"Did you live near here, Mr. Olson?"

"Please, Daisy, it's Dave, and yes, we lived down in the Arcadia area for twenty years. When Shirley died, I tried to keep up appearances, but it didn't work. I retired about then, and I played golf three times a week. The other days I was lost. I called my kids all the time, and they finally told me to sell the house and find a friendly place to live. I sure didn't want to move in with them, so they found me this place."

"Do you like it?"

"Yeah, and the food's good. Gosh, I was a lousy cook. Lived on Lean Cuisine that my daughter bought by the carload. She said I'd keep healthy that way. Do you like it? Ventura I mean."

"Yes, I do. We, I lived over on Hayden Road, and the place was too much for me. I was lonely and hated to admit it."

"Isn't that dog yours, that Golden?"

"Thank Goodness for Curly. He's my best friend! I guess that sounds funny, but you know what I mean."

"Sure. I kept Shirley's cat for four years; then finally he got sick and died. It felt good to have something of hers. I drove her blue sports car until I wrecked it. That's when I quit the booze; next big decision was to make this move." Just as he finished talking, a doctor came in and announced it was time to check him out.

Daisy rose and said she'd be going along. "See you at dinner one of these nights?"

"Yeah, I can borrow a wheelchair from Malcolm. Hey, thanks for coming in."

"Bye." She walked briskly toward the elevators, then stopped. "What am I doing? How's he getting home?" She turned back to room 3122. She paused at the door and then knocked.

The doctor opened the door. She blurted out, "Do you need a ride back to Ventura?"

Dave smiled and nodded. A nurse came with a wheelchair. The doctor shook Dave's hand and wished him well. "Be careful, young man." He stepped around Daisy and into the hall.

The nurse spoke to Daisy. "Bring the car to the main entrance. His release will have cleared by then."

"Dave, will you be comfortable in my little car?"

"Oh, sure. It's easier to get in than the van."

"All right. I'll see you downstairs."

Daisy hurried across the parking lot to her car. Inside, she scooped all her papers and receipts off the passenger seat and dumped everything in the back seat. At the entrance, the nurse helped Dave into the car. He was cramped in the seat but in good spirits.

At Ventura, she hailed one of the young staff people who brought a wheelchair and offered to take Dave to his unit. "Bye, Daisy," he called to her. "Thanks a million. See you later."

Daisy drove around to her parking space and sat there, reviewing what had just happened. "Surprising how fast we became friends." She smiled, locked up the car and went to find Curly. "It's a good day, Old Boy. How are you?"

CHAPTER 27

More Problems

THE NEXT DAY, Pete went home, and Susie took time off from her volunteer duties. The Halloween decorations at La Ventura seemed ridiculous, but Daisy knew her view was skewed by Pete's sudden illness. She confided in Beth, "He's been looking tired. He stumbled over Curly when I was there on Labor Day. He's walked around that dog for years, at least eight."

"Has he been told to do anything special, you know, food, pills, more water or anything? Is he dizzy?"

"Not that I know of. You know, I kept wishing I could be in that hospital room when the neurologist was there. But he was very plain about it; only Pete's wife could be there."

By afternoon, Julie came by with an update about her brother. "The conclusion is that he had a light stroke, with mild paralysis that will probably clear up. He might have had others. His blood pressure was awfully high. Didn't he ever know that?"

"I don't know. I haven't been with him at a doctor's for twenty-some years. Your dad took a pill for high blood pressure when he was younger, but after he lost weight, he seemed healthier. That is, until his heart attack."

"Mom, I didn't mean to upset you, but Susie is so concerned. And Suzette is a basket case. I don't know how to help them. They're dependent on Pete more than normal."

"He thinks it's normal to be in charge, dear. Dad did everything too. Susie knows she has to take over some of the paperwork and keep him from worrying right now."

"Well, she's worried they can't pay their bills. Surely he has money in more than one account?"

"Don't know. They spend a lot, and they're so generous to all her charities."

"Let's hope he gets stronger this week. Take care, Mom. Bye, Curly. We'll talk soon."

Daisy was relieved the crisis was past. Friday is always Seasoned Seniors meeting, and she tried not to miss these dates. "Let's see, the topic is 'Don't Let the Turkeys Get You Down.' Might be humorous or else tragic. Behave, Curly. See you later." She drove to the church in good spirits.

The speaker was from Fry's Food Stores, with all kinds of shortcuts on Thanksgiving preparations. "Not my problem," she confided to Jane. "Julie always does the dinner. But I loved what he suggested about make-believe leftovers. I've never tried those packaged gravy mixes, but I'll bet it makes a great hot sandwich with the deli turkey slices."

"We go out. The cheapest big meal is out at the casino, you know." Daisy admitted she'd never been there. Jane couldn't believe it and continued, "What do you folks out there at that ritzy place do for fun?"

"You know, Jane, you didn't like La Ventura from the moment you saw it, exactly three years ago. It's not ritzy, as you put it. Expensive, maybe, but not showy. We have lots of classes and discussion groups. Games and exercises are good too. I read and sew just as I used to do. I miss Scott a lot, but it's so nice to have friends on all sides."

"I s'pose. You have TV? We couldn't live without cable."

"Sure, we have cable and a theater with movies. Lots of things for everybody. The Tuesday Happy Hour is one place we see everybody, even the teetotalers. The appetizers are great."

"Hmph. Well, I heard your old friends were flocking here from all over the country."

Daisy smiled. "Yes, I've pulled together a bunch of the dearest women I'd met through the years."

"Good thing you really like it, Daisy. By the way, how much did you get for your house?"

Daisy's eyes opened wide in disbelief, but she heard herself saying, "You know, Pete took care of that whole deal. Wasn't I lucky?" That ended their chat, and Daisy turned to talk with one of her sewing partners from the bazaar.

Later, she checked on Pete's progress and found he was feeling much more optimistic. His energy was coming back, and he told her, "You know, Mom, I've decided I better take care of myself. Poor Suzette was so scared I'd die. Gotta get into an exercise program, lose the flab and watch what I eat. Cut down on the martini lunches. Maybe it was a good warning. Another stroke could leave me disabled for life! That's grim."

Daisy felt a twinge of maternal concern at the mention of drinks at noon. The word *disabled* stuck with her. "Pete's only forty-five," she whispered to herself.

Daisy awoke one morning with a feeling that today she should pursue her conversation with Dave Olson. Before she could follow through, however, Clarissa called and said she'd be right over. "Daisy, I need help."

"Heavens, Rissa, come in. What's the matter?"

"It's my bridge group. Two people walked out and told me to call them when there's a different group playing."

"Without any explanation?"

"Not a word. Well, I should explain that one of them whispered to me last week that she was sick of playing with Pauline. Sooner or later, everyone has to play with all the others."

"So, what's the problem with Pauline?"

"She's so critical and negative. Last season she told one woman to go and take lessons before she came again. She just can't keep her mouth shut; just has to replay every hand and point out who's wrong. What can I do?"

Daisy took a deep breath and tried to think of an answer. "Maybe you'll have to speak to Pauline."

"Oh, I couldn't do that, but you could."

Daisy chuckled. "Why me? You're the pro. I don't even play bridge."

"But you got me into this. I've never had a problem."

"You know, Rissa, part of the problem is the people who walked out. They should have complained right to her face."

"They're too nice to do that."

"What about me? I'm nice too."

Rissa whined a bit, "But you always know the right things to say to people to keep peace. Everyone likes you."

"You're afraid she'll fight back. I remember that you hate arguments. There must be some way around this. Bring me a list of the players."

Clarissa already had it in her hand. Daisy saw the Wilsons on the list. "Let me talk to the Wilsons about the situation. In his ministry he must have had people like Pauline to counsel. He's a true peacemaker. Marge is too."

"Thanks. I knew you could solve my problem. 'Bye."

"Now, why did she bring me that headache? I'm tired of being everybody's coach or mother confessor. Can't anyone see that I have enough of my own problems to solve?" Curly was listening closely to see if any word applied to him, but, hearing none, he retreated to his corner. "Now I'm not in the mood to talk to Dave Olson. I wish I knew how to handle this, Curly. Scott would know." She paused. "No, it's up to me."

CHAPTER 28

There's a Time to Talk

DAISY WAS READY FOR the big church bazaar this year with a new doll and four tree skirts, plus her usual assortment of doll quilts and quilted place mats. In the tiny kitchen, she stirred up three batches of fudge sauce, filling twelve small jars. Ellen helped her load the car on Wednesday afternoon, so they could deliver the things to the church before five.

"The decorations are awesome," Ellen said.

"The number of tickets sold this year is better than last."

"Why is that?"

"Oh, new pastor, new members, not an election year, maybe the fourth of the month is a charm."

"Pretty scientific reasoning, I can tell," Ellen said with a laugh. "I'll be here, with Beth, nearer lunch time. We already signed out from the village, and she bought the tickets."

"Dave Olson told me he'd bought two tickets for the luncheon. I think I was supposed to ask whom he was taking, but I just couldn't. It seemed too snoopy."

"Oh, Daisy, you nut. He took Donna to a movie last week; well, actually, he went with Donna and Alice. I heard that he asked Donna and explained he couldn't drive. She agreed, but Alice asked if she could go too. Isn't that funny? He seems to be a good sport, probably laughed about it too."

Daisy turned away, wondering if this would be a good time to tell Ellen the complicated story that had been heavy on her mind since early summer. Even Julie and Pete didn't know the story about Dave Olson's accident. She didn't know why it was so hard to talk about an incident that happened six years ago. She summoned her courage, "Ellen, thanks a million for helping. How about stopping at my place for a glass of wine? I've heard a story you need to know, something that's bothering me."

"Sure, Daisy. I'm always ready to listen." They drove home in silence, parked and heard Curly's 'welcome home' bark.

Wine in hand, Daisy started her story with finding the traffic ticket, then the court order and attorney's receipt, Pete's research and finding Tomás, Martha's comment and finally Tom's tale. When she came to Dave Olson's name, Ellen gasped. "No, how could that be the same person?"

"Well, it is. I visited him in the hospital, and he told about wrecking his late wife's sporty little blue car. As a result, he quit drinking and evidently doesn't drive any more."

"Does he know about your Scott's ticket that day?"

"No, no. We got interrupted and just parted as friends. I don't know how I'll ever get back to that subject."

"Maybe you shouldn't. What would it achieve? He's a happy person, and you and Scott were happy until he died. What did Tom want you to do about it?"

"Nothing. It's my conscience that jabs at me. I've prayed about it."

"Dave sees the accident as a turning point in his life. If you take that away from him, he might start to blame Scott. Then it wouldn't be a providential accident. You'd be playing God."

"Thanks, Ellen. That does put it in a different light. Maybe I just have to suffer in place of Scott."

"Yes, but you said Scott never knew about the accident."

"That's what Tom said. Isn't it a strange story?"

"Yes it is. Maybe the best thing you can do is to be friendly to Dave, help him find new interests, things to enjoy."

"He said he'd like to come to the writing group, because he hasn't written any directives."

"Let's encourage that and see where it leads. As for me, my lips are sealed, like a good pastor's wife."

Later, Daisy thought once again how blessed she was to have these friends around her.

After the bazaar, Daisy began to think about the holidays ahead. She was alone but not lonely, and she hoped the others felt that way too. During their Thanksgiving feast, Daisy's family enjoyed an expanded number of Mark and Suzette's friends, plus a new neighbor's family. There was never an opportunity for Daisy to report on Tom's story or her meeting with Dave Olson. Back home that evening, she thought, "Maybe I've kept it to myself so long, I can't bring it up. Ellen was right that nothing's gained from rehashing it." Still, she felt burdened with the information she'd been given.

The writing of last wishes and obituaries was delayed until after the first of the year. "The topics blend well with resolutions," Daisy reminded them.

Donna remarked, "I might, just might be able to face that assignment after Christmas. But first, I'm giving flu shots for the rest of this month. It's my first holiday in Arizona, and I want to concentrate on it. I want to go to the Botanical Gardens and the Phoenix Symphony Pops Concert. I'm getting tickets, if anyone wants me to order more for them." Dave Olson and Alex brought her checks, and a few days later, Martha and Tom plus Mary Ann added their payments. Daisy enjoyed watching their interest in events she and Scott had frequently attended.

The Bunch of Daisy's talked over their Christmas plans and chose children's clothes this year. Boys & Girls Club sweatshirts ordered from a store downtown on Fifth Avenue were recommended. Their annual Christmas luncheon fell to Mary Ann this year, so Julio G's was the destination. "I'll get you gals eating Mexican food yet. You can choose anything from mild to wild," she promised.

On Saturday, December 10, they delivered their mound of packages and had lunch out. "Have you heard about those gals who formed a little club called OLEO, for Old Ladies Eating Out? They're trying all the restaurants in North Scottsdale."

"Sounds like the Red Hats. They eat in marvelous places. I guess we're all too content with our Ventura kitchen. I think the new chef's great, don't you?"

Martha spoke up, "Tom says he's from the Ritz Carlton in Phoenix, so he's used to pleasing hundreds of people."

"I gather these chefs move around a lot. Our former one is up at the Boulders in Carefree. Alex was raving about a meal he had there with his daughter."

"Daisy, you seem to see a lot of Alex. You Scotsmen stick together, don't you?"

"What a thing to say, Mary Ann. I've never thought about going out with a man, much less Alex MacPherson."

"I suppose not, since you still wear your wedding rings for some reason. He's a handsome man." She let the words drift across the room.

Daisy said, "I hear you're going to the concert with him."

Mary Ann fired back with, "Yeah, but I'm paying my own way. C'mon, girls, let's not carry this too far."

Ellen spoke up and said, "You know, none of us came here husband-hunting. When the love-bug bit, it was beautiful to watch. Let's just enjoy Martha's happiness."

That next Sunday afternoon, Bonnie and Malcolm invited a performing arts student from ASU to give a piano recital in the village dining room. Clarissa was on top of the world, and offered to host coffee and cookies after the program. The young man played beautifully, and the crowd was appreciative. Dave Olson came up to Daisy and invited her to join him at a table nearby. "Did you go to church this morning, Daisy?"

Quickly, she said, "Yes, I almost always go to the 9:00 service. How about you?"

He replied, "I'd like to, but most Sundays, my daughter calls and talks right past the time when the van leaves. I've told her I need to be out there before 8:40, but she rattles on and on."

"But you love hearing from her, don't you?"

"I do. As long as she's been in New Jersey, she's never been a churchgoer, so she sees Sunday morning as a great time to use the phone. One time I forgot to tell her something and called her right back. Her line was busy for four hours!"

Daisy laughed. "Our kids love the phone, don't they? I remember Scott was so impatient with long, chatty calls. 'Phone's meant for business,' he'd say. We should be glad our kids care enough to call us."

"True." They exchanged information about where their young ones lived. "Where do you spend Christmas, Daisy?"

"Wherever the brood is, usually at Julie and Matt's. What about you?"

Dave answered slowly. "Probably here. You know, it's so pretty around here, I have no desire to travel or get in that airport mess. Bonnie makes a fuss over those of us who are always in the dining room, and she and Malcolm are kind of family for me."

"That's good. Do you have long-standing friends around town?"

"Some. I've lost some too. Did you ever know Mike and Jeanette Nelson over at your church?"

"Sure. She was in my circle that last year before she died. Does Mike still play golf?" As soon as she said it, she regretted bringing up golf to someone who couldn't play any more.

"I think so. That's one thing I miss, but I've been playing more cards. That Clarissa is a demon at the bridge table. She doesn't let us get by with anything."

"I wish you could have known her when she was directing the chorale and playing the piano at the same time. Her hair was bright red, and she was a consummate performer."

"Really? When did she become such a card player?"

"Once the arthritis invaded her hands. Now that she spends winters here, she can play again, at least enough for Christmas carols and the like. But she played Chopin and Haydn so well; she had both feeling and technique."

"Interesting how people recycle after an obstacle, isn't it? I never thought about cards or listening to classical music until I lost half my vision."

"You seem to be so busy and active, Dave."

"I believe in putting the past right where it belongs! And I'm a better guy without alcohol. I was a noisy drunk, and I always assumed everyone wanted to party with me."

Daisy couldn't keep from smiling, and the time was not right for revelations. She wanted to enjoy Dave as a friend. Everyone liked him, and he deserved to carve out his new life like all the rest of them. "I'm glad Bonnie and Malcolm make the holiday festive for you!"

"You'll have to come back from your kids' place and join us here for some fun."

"I'll see how their timing develops on Christmas day. Thanks."

"You're lucky you've kept in touch with your old friends," he said.

Daisy nodded. "I knew they must be going through the same situation I was in, you know, when couples don't include you any more, and the single men drift away to live near their kids' families."

"Is that the way it looked to you? Funny, but to me, it seemed as if the ladies were always busy with the hobbies and charities they'd worked in for years. You all knew how to cook and keep house. We guys are the ones who'd forgotten when it's time to buy socks or shampoo. I never knew how much Shirley did for me."

Daisy smiled. "I'm sure that's what my Scott would have said too. Habits from mothering just keep us going after we're alone."

"If I hadn't moved in here, I'd have to get married again." He laughed broadly. "That's good; I'll have to tell Malcolm I figured out how to keep from getting married."

"I've thought a lot about living here alone without being lonely. Interesting, isn't it?"

"That's true. But see, you women think about those things and have all the answers. The rest of us bumble along, happy to discover life's still pretty good. Accidental answers keep us going." He looked around the room. "Daisy, we're the last ones here. Come on, I'll walk you home." As they neared her unit, Curly let out his best defense bark. "That's your dog? The one you take up to visit people in the Nido?"

"Curly's my counselor, companion, and now he's learning how to be a service dog."

"What does that mean?"

"He's being trained to help disabled people, you know, to lock a door, turn on light switches, and pick up pencils or pens. He's already passed the cuddling lesson, when he's invited up onto someone's bed or into a chair. Tough part of that lesson was to stay on the floor until he's invited."

"He's a beauty. Makes me feel better just to pat him. Next time I feel disabled, I'll come for some help. Take care, Daisy."

"Good night, Dave." She closed the door and leaned against it. "Why did I say *disabled?* That's always been a far-away word. Now it's so close, with this nice man and now maybe with Pete."

CHAPTER 29

There's a Time to Write

After the holidays, the Thursdays at Three group made out a new calendar of their writing topics, starting with last wishes and then obituaries. Ellen proposed, "Let's write our last wishes as letters to someone who will outlive us, and keep them personal, in our own files. Isn't that what Alex encouraged us to do? You all don't care how I distribute my mother's jewelry and so on."

"You're right, Ellen. But we need to put the pressure on each other to do it. Is two weeks long enough to figure it out?" Mary Ann seemed keen on moving ahead with this project. "It'll take me every day of two weeks to do my own, but let's get it done. I think the next project sounds like more fun."

Tom and Martha agreed and encouraged the deadline. "How about if I buy a packet of manila envelopes so we can each make a final copy and mail it to the right person or file it here?"

Daisy spoke up, "It would be great, Tom. We can all chip in, but you make the purchase and then stand here waiting for our papers to be sealed and deposited. You're in charge!"

Donna was the only one frowning and shaking her head. "Count me out. I may leave an order about my medical care, as Daisy suggested last fall. I already had some of that written down. But I don't have anything to leave to anyone. Any charity can come and get it all. I've already arranged my cremation and where the remains will be put. So, I'll start with the next writing project, O.K.?"

It was quiet in the room. Then Alex said, "Donna, you're way ahead of us. More power to you." He turned to the others and suggested a format, beginning with an inventory of valuable items. "Then we could describe the process we hope our heirs will use in distributing the goods. If there are special things with a story to them, write it out, and put someone's name on them. That's helpful if insurance is needed. Choose wisely, because once a kid inherits something, he can do anything he pleases with it."

"What if he doesn't want it? Can I suggest a second person?"

Alex laughed. "Sure, I guess so. But you could also make a blanket statement of what to do with anything unwanted, you know, like the hospital auxiliary shop or church rummage sale, etc."

"So, you're telling us to make this as readable as possible, without too many restrictions?"

"Exactly." Alex sat back in his chair and smiled over the group. "I've already done my assignment, so I can relax for the next two weeks. In fact, I'm talking this up to everyone at dinner. People can get the idea without coming to this group. When you get this old, you have to do certain things, like it or not." As they were leaving, he added, "Dave Olson wants to join this group. He's a believer in written wishes. Guess his wife died without any plans. He said he was lost."

"Bring him up to date and invite him," Ellen said.

Two weeks later, the Hedgehog Room was filled with laughter and people bragging about all they had written. Alex took charge of the discussions, since he had organized the format for their writing. "And did you think about sending a copy of this to anyone else?"

Daisy ventured, "I showed it to Julie, my daughter, but she wasn't very interested. That proved to me just what you said earlier, Alex, that they don't want to think about it, and they probably won't want to deal with our stuff later either."

They all nodded and agreed. "But we'll sleep better knowing it's all written down." Tom went on, "What about ideas for a funeral?"

Ellen said, "That's where I started. Tradition in our family has always followed certain patterns, and so, I made notes about that. Then I listed my treasures, and finally some specific things I wanted Emily to have. My son in Atlanta mailed me the safe deposit box papers, with his lawyer's help."

Beth was listening but not offering any comments. She took the envelope from Tom and dropped a thick fold of papers into it. "Now I feel as if I've done what Bruce and I should've done together years ago. He could never bring himself to talk about death or his illness or anything in a terminal sense. He assumed I'd outlive him, and if I'd died first, I wonder if he might have ended his own life. It all came back to me as I wrote these lists. I marvel that I was so practical at the time. I took over all the responsibilities as if it were perfectly natural."

Daisy spoke up. "It was natural for you, Beth, 'cause you'd watched him failing so gradually. You were the stalwart, and he knew you'd tie up all the loose ends." She paused and went on, "I admired you so much during those years. I knew at the time I should learn from your experiences, but I didn't. I never toughened up for what surprises lay ahead of me."

Ellen tried to rescue Daisy from her monologue. "You're being hard on yourself, Daisy."

"No, I know I just haven't overcome my grief yet. I thought I had it all worked out with this move, but here I am, still weepy and feeling sorry for myself. Sorry, folks."

Alex interrupted. "Daisy, your way of dealing with your loss was to rescue everyone else, and we all appreciate that! So, dry your tears, and let's talk about the problems anyone had about their lists and choices." Daisy smiled broadly and looked relieved to have someone take over.

Robert looked uncomfortable in this discussion. "I just wrote down all the stuff I've collected on my travels and then went 'Eeny, Meeny, Miney, Mo 'with my kids' names. Once in a while, I had to adjust so one of the granddaughters didn't get my five-foot-long peace pipe." They laughed with him at his simple process.

Alex asked Dave if he had anything to share. "Well, I'm here because I know how important it is to deal with end things. Hard to picture the next life, but we know we have to say goodbye to this one. Written ideas will sure help our kids. I wrote what Alex told me; it wasn't too bad. Thanks for including me."

Mary Ann tried to wrap up this project, offering to take the envelopes to the office, if that's where they should be filed. "I guess Bonnie has all the addresses of next-of-kin, so she can send these out when they're needed."

"Thanks, Mary Ann. Now, wasn't that fun?" Chuckles and mild applause followed. Alex asked who would begin the obituaries. "There's no required form; make 'em creative!"

It was quiet until Clarissa spoke up. "Since I'm often the first one called on, alphabetically, how about if I start off next meeting, and anyone else who's ready can read theirs too."

Daisy smiled and said, "Good for you, Rissa. I promise to try a rough draft by then too."

Alex stood to leave and then said, "Don't forget that what we enjoy in the newspaper pays some nice tribute to the deceased. Include something about how you hope to be remembered. Be good to yourselves!" As he was walking out the door, he said to Beth, "Otherwise, I may have to add a paragraph to each one, and you wouldn't want me to do that." He winked at her, and she chuckled.

CHAPTER 30

It's a Tough Assignment

WHEN THE THURSDAY AT Three group met again, everyone was talking at once about how difficult the assignment was. Alex started out saying, "I was the one telling you to do this, and I had already outlined what I'd say about myself. But it's tough to get it to sound smooth."

Robert chimed in, "Damned tough to write about myself. I don't think I care what's in the paper after I die. Donna was right. She said she'd never know anyway."

Daisy listened with a smile on her face. "You were the one who said you'd know what to say better than your kids. But isn't it hard to make your life sound as interesting as the ones we read every day? Ellen, you're so philosophical; what did you write?"

She answered quickly, "Oh, just the facts, I guess. I tried to embellish them, but it sounds like bragging."

Clarissa spoke up. "I said I'd start out, and I will. Did everyone get coffee? O.K., let's start. This is what I wrote:

"Clarissa Jane Benton, born on Sunday, July 8, 1923, in Cleveland, hummed her last musical note on ___________. The youngest of five girls, she grew up in Cleveland, St. Louis and Seattle, eventually settling on the Olympic Peninsula at Silverdale, Wash., before retiring to Scottsdale. Miss Benton was a graduate of the University of Washington, College of Music. Her first love was teaching her piano students, 143 of them over thirty-eight years. She later became a master bridge player and continued that interest until her death. With her colorful wardrobe and performers' stage presence, Miss Benton brightened the lives of her friends at La Ventura Retirement Village. She was preceded in death by her parents and sisters Elizabeth, Margaret, Louise, and Florence. She is survived by her beloved nephew Richard MacKinnon and his family of Poulsbo, Wash. Ms. Benton willed her body to Science Care of Phoenix, whose motto is 'Today's Research Yields Tomorrow's Cures.' A memorial service will be held on ___________ in Silverdale."

"Bravo," shouted Alex. "That's perfect! Clarissa, I admire you, because you know how you cheer us up with your bright clothes and energy. You're our fashion plate!" The others agreed and clapped for her.

Daisy added, "And you made it read like the ones we see in our papers. I loved the bit about humming." Clarissa beamed with all the praise.

Beth asked, "What professional groups did you belong to?"

"Oh, I forgot. I suppose readers might like to know and tell a friend who's also a member. I'll fix that before we file them away. And I'll get a picture. Don't you think people enjoy seeing a picture of the dearly departed one?"

The group fell silent. Tom spoke up. "I don't think that's necessary, not at all. How would you decide if you wanted a young-looking picture or one that shows you now that you're sick?"

Ellen said softly, "I like the ones that show a person in recent years, mainly so I might recognize the clerk at the drugstore or my insurance agent or a nurse at the hospital."

"Ellen's got a good point. No one puts a picture in the paper taken at the hospital, but one that's within the last few years is better than high school graduation!"

"Well, who's going to share next?" Mary Ann looked around and offered, "Want me to read?" They voiced approval.

"Mary Angelina Morelli Martinez, born in Chicago on May 30, 1930, died peacefully in her sleep last Saturday at her home in Saguaro Shadows. As a graduate of the School of Social Work at the University of Chicago, she devoted her life to working with children, in Chicago, Albuquerque and Roswell, New Mexico. She founded The Roundup program at La Casa de la Familia Social Agency in Roswell to prepare immigrant children for public school. In 1960 she married Lt. Jaime Martinez who died in 1996 in Guadalajara, Mexico. In 2003, Ms. Martinez retired to the La Ventura Village in Scottsdale and became a valued bilingual volunteer at the Boys and Girls Club. In 2006 she accepted the responsibility of organizing a new children's agency in Casa Grande, now known as Safe Haven where she served as Executive Director. She is predeceased by her brother Paul and her parents. She is survived by her brother Guido and sister Martha C. Gable of Scottsdale, plus three nephews and one niece. She will always be remembered as a foster mother to seven young boys in the Roswell area. Friends will gather at the Safe Haven to celebrate her three years' leadership on Wednesday evening at 7:00 p.m. Following cremation and committal in Memorial Cemetery, Casa Grande, a second memorial service will unite friends in the chapel at La Ventura in Scottsdale to say, 'Vaya con Dios, Mary Ann.'"

The silence was broken by Daisy who gasped and said, "What's all this about Casa Grande?" Others murmured their surprise.

Mary Ann sighed and explained. "All this has come up so fast that even Martha hardly knows when and where I'm going. But it's too exciting a challenge to turn down. I've helped Martha get settled here. I've done a lot of volunteer work here, but this is certainly the last time I'll get to start a new agency. The committee in Casa Grande is all set to blossom out, but they need experience, and that's what I have."

"Well, yes, but you own a place here."

"I know, but it can be sold."

Martha came to the rescue as she said, "I think it's very brave of Mary Ann to do this, and I hope I'd have the courage to move if a wonderful job came along. The people in Casa Grande have found her a place to live, in a nice community like this." Martha stopped, looked right at Mary Ann and started to cry. "I'm going to miss her terribly." Tom leaned closer and put his arm around her.

"We're all going to miss her terribly. Mary Ann, I know we should be saying congratulations and Godspeed, but how can you leave here?" Daisy looked around the group and saw that everyone was stricken by the news.

Mary Ann quietly said, "I don't know if I can make this move or not, but my brain and heart both tell me to do it. I'm needed there; *children* need me. That's what keeps me alive."

Ellen rose and went over to Mary Ann and gave her a big hug, followed by all the others. Tom said, "Her work is done here. She found Martha a new place to live, and now I'll try to protect Martha the way her sister did." They all nodded and hoped he would.

"Well," said Alex, "where do we go from here? Can anyone top this?" No one offered to read an obituary, so they all had another cup of coffee and sat around talking. "Next meeting, we'll have lots of ground to cover. In the meantime, pray for rain. Here we are in Arizona: 142 days without a drop!"

Two weeks later, the Hedgehog Room was filled with conversation and eager smiles. "I think everyone is speculating on what surprises might come out today," observed Alex, as he called them together. "Well, folks, at least your prayers for rain worked. Things look better everywhere, don't they? Do we have a volunteer to start us off?"

Martha spoke up and said, "Maybe I should be next, because I have no news to announce!" She unfolded her papers and began. "Martha Morelli Costello Gable died on Wednesday as a result of injuries sustained in a tragic traffic accident in Scottsdale a week ago. She was born in Chicago on September 13, 1933, and raised her family in Madison, Wisc., where she was a Certified Addiction Counselor at Aldersgate Methodist Hospital. She moved to Scottsdale in 2003 to join her sister Mary Ann Martinez. Ms. Gable dedicated her life to guiding people through the Twelve Steps of recovery from substance abuse. She will be missed by her numerous clients and colleagues. No one knows how many lives she has turned around and saved. Survivors include her devoted husband Tom, her sister and her brother Guido, as well as sons Paul, Frank, and Louis, and daughter Mary, all in Wisconsin. Her parents and her brother Paul predeceased Ms. Gable. A memorial service will be conducted at La Ventura Retirement Village on __________ by the Reverend Thomas Andrews of the United Methodist Church. Memorial gifts may be made in Ms. Gable's name to M.A.D.D., Mothers against Drunk Driving." She sighed and commented, "Whew, that was hard to write. And yet, no one else would have known how to describe my work or to name my kids."

Alex agreed. "You did a great job, especially that last touch about the memorial gifts. That always tells something, either about the cause of death or someone's favorite charity."

Tom cleared his throat, and when everyone looked at him, they saw tears in his eyes. "I thought this exercise would be good for us. Instead, it reminded me of what a short time we've been married. I wish we had longer."

Martha quickly said, "But Tom, there's no date on these obits. Maybe mine will be in ten years."

"Why did you choose an accident as the cause of death?"

"I don't know; I've always thought driving around here is dangerous. Everyone has come from different places and has different habits."

Daisy agreed. "It gets hectic in the winter, doesn't it?"

Tom offered to be next. "I agree with my sister-in-law Mary Ann in a peaceful death scene. Here's what I wrote: Thomas Vincent Gable died peacefully in his sleep on the night of __________. Mr. Gable was born in Bend, Oregon, in 1929, and eventually made his home in Eureka, California. He attended Northern California Culinary Institute and co-authored a cookbook titled *Secret Recipes of the Golden Bear,* named for his restaurant in Redding. Mr. Gable came to Arizona to join his brother Allan in his business, Mom's Office & Grill, in Scottsdale. When his brother died in 2002, the business was sold, and Mr. Gable retired to La Ventura Retirement Village. His proudest moment was when he reached thirty years of sobriety and was honored by his AA group. He has organized numerous groups and was a popular speaker on behalf of recovery programs. He is survived by the joy of his life, his wife Martha, her children and many customers. Memorial contributions may be sent to Valley Presbyterian Church to encourage their support of AA, Al-Anon and all recovery programs. A prayer service will be held in the El Nido Garden at La Ventura, 7375 N. Via de la Romeria, Scottsdale on Sunday afternoon at 4:30.

He sat back and smiled over at Martha. "Isn't it neat that we survive each other?" Everyone chuckled.

The door opened an inch or two, and Donna quietly slipped into the room. Alex reached over for the empty chair near him and motioned her toward it. She looked around tentatively and said, "I heard you all laughing in here, and I couldn't resist coming in."

Martha explained, "I just read my own obituary, and it's really cool to read about yourself and still be sitting here listening."

Donna frowned. "I thought all this would be so depressing. Well, go on."

Beth spoke up, "Before the other men decide to follow Tom, I'd like to read."

Alex smiled and said, "I could tell you were anxious to be done with it. You must have a different story."

"I do. Here goes. Beth O. O'Donnell, born on November 2, 1928, in Chicago to Mary Frances and Timothy Paul O'Brien, died last Friday after a prolonged illness. She graduated from St. Mary's School for Girls, Xavier Prep School and Elmhurst College. In 1953, she married Bruce O'Donnell, attorney-at-law. They made their home in Geneva, Illinois, until his death in 1990. Mrs. O'Donnell, C.P.A., retired from her own accounting firm, sold the business and moved to Scottsdale to be near friends in 2003. She was honored as Businesswoman of the Year in Kane County in 1970, served as president of the local chapter of Soroptimist International from 1980-1984, and was one of the first women to become a Rotarian in 1986. She is survived by sisters Mary in Florida and Colleen in Detroit, and brother Sean Francis in London. Services will be on __________ at Our Lady of Perpetual Help. In lieu of flowers, memorial contributions may be made to the Boys and Girls Clubs of Greater Scottsdale for their after-school programs."

Ellen clapped, and soon the others joined her. "Beth, I had no idea you were so prominent. You've never mentioned a thing about your business."

Daisy added, "I tried to tell you all what a success she was in Geneva. But what troubles me is that you spoke of a long illness. Do you really think you'll be sick?"

"Well, I've had cancer once, and it was pretty serious then. I just figure it'll probably come back and get me. It's always somewhere in your mind that if your immune system gets low from some other reason, the cancer could recur. I don't know why, but the doctor indicated that I'd had the tumors growing for maybe nine years, and that dated back to when Bruce was so ill, and I was so worn out. So, I try not to let things get me down, and I try hard to stay well, hoping to fight it off."

"Good. Just keep it up, and let's hope that long illness is just a literary expression." Daisy smiled again.

Alex looked thoughtful. "Beth, for someone fearing a terminal illness, you are the most radiant, beautiful woman I know. Get rid of your fears! You're much too healthy to leave us yet! All right, who can sound more important than Beth?"

"Well, since I was the one who sounded so ambitious in my recipe for success, I'll take the challenge next." Robert stood to read his words. "Captain Robert Hughes Newburn set sail for the next world at noon on __________. He served on the cruise ships of the Holland American Line, principally on the west coast of North America. Captain Newburn was born in 1925 overlooking the harbor of Gloucester, Massachusetts, where his father operated a fishing fleet. He traveled the globe with a keen sense of adventure from the age of sixteen on, including four years in the United States Navy. In 2002, he spent the winter in Scottsdale, Arizona and was impressed with the new retirement center, La Ventura at 7375 N. Via de la Romeria. He moved to La Ventura in 2003 and has been active in YMCA work, particularly in water safety issues. For twelve years, he was an instructor in the Power Squadron in San Diego. He was preceded in death by his wife Elaine in 1965, as well as his parents and a brother Richard Harold Newburn. He is survived by a son Nelson in Daytona Beach, Florida, and a daughter Victoria N. Russell in

Bangor, Maine. At his request, his ashes will be scattered over the Pacific Ocean off the coast of Mexico, a stretch of coastline he called 'God's gift of paradise.' There will be no services, but his friends are asked to remember him kindly." He looked around the group, then said, "How does that sound?"

"Captain, it sounds good. You never mentioned your schooling, and yet you became an officer, so you must have had some college work."

"That's right. I forgot all about it. I went to U. Conn, long before they had good teams. It wasn't where I wanted to go, but it was where my uncle offered to pay my way. You know how those things go. At least I was in the right place to enlist."

"So you'll add that to your obit? Any other comments, writers?"

"How come you don't want any services?" asked Ellen.

"Well, I really wish I could be buried at sea, but that won't work anymore, now that I'm stuck on land. I always like that Navy hymn they sing. Maybe you all can sing that for me, after I'm gone."

"I thought you wanted to hear it."

The Captain laughed and declared, "I will," and waved off any further comments.

"Well, folks, we still have four more of us to hear from. Shall we save us for the next meeting? Donna, do you want to come up with something too?" They all nodded and smiled at her as they stood up. It was time to take papers home and think about dinner.

CHAPTER 31

More Tough Writing

THE LOYAL BAND OF WRITERS gathered again to hear from Daisy, Ellen, Dave and Alex. He offered to be last and Daisy decided to begin. "I hoped mine would be the briefest, but there were things I wanted to put in print, at least for my grandchildren. So, I took a long shot on living for a while." She sipped her coffee and began. "Daisy Jones MacDuff died on Friday, June 13, 2014, just two days before her eightieth birthday. She was born in Franklin Falls, Iowa, to the Reverend and Mrs. Walter B. Jones. An only child, she learned young to be resourceful, creating handmade items all her life. She graduated from the University of Iowa in Home Economics and married her college beau, Scott MacDuff, a civil engineer. His assignments sent them to Poulsbo, Washington; Davenport, Iowa; Oklahoma City; Amherst, Massachusetts; Minneapolis; Madison, Wisconsin; and Aurora, Illinois, before they retired to Scottsdale. The MacDuffs were honored in 2000 by the Presbytery of Grand Canyon as outstanding volunteers in church mission programs. Mr. MacDuff died suddenly in 2001. In 2003, Daisy was instrumental in bringing together six of her out-of-town friends to live at La Ventura Retirement Village. They have become a team of volunteers for the Boys and Girls Club of Greater Scottsdale, primarily at the Rose Lane and Via

Linda-Lakeview Houses. She was an elder in the Presbyterian Church USA and remained active in Seasoned Seniors and choir events, Chapter BA of the PEO Sisterhood and Delta Gamma sorority. Mrs. MacDuff is survived by her daughter Julie and husband Matt Bryan and their son Mark, and by her son Peter and his wife Susan and their daughter Suzette. A memorial service will be held on Wednesday at 3:00 at Valley Church, 6947 E. McDonald Drive, Scottsdale."

Immediately, Beth noted, "I'm glad you named those things you belong to. I was afraid you'd forgotten your mother's advice about keeping your own interests alive."

Martha added, "I'm glad you included your travelogue, Daisy."

"It's so much a part of our lives, as I look back. I think I knew to begin with we would-be nomads, so that's why I worked hard to keep in touch with old friends."

"Dear friends," Ellen corrected.

"Yes, very dear friends who will be forever young. Now, Ellen, it's your turn."

"No, I'm going to defer to the newest writer, Dave."

"Just like that, eh? O.K. David Russell Olson, longtime resident of Scottsdale crossed from this life onto the shores of life eternal on Sunday evening in El Nido Care Center at La Ventura Retirement Village. He was born to Inga and Oscar Olson on Santa Lucia Day, January 6, in 1928 in Rockford, Illinois. He was a graduate of Northwestern University in Economics, followed by two years in the U.S. Army. Mr. Olson was a member of the Chicago Board of Trade for twenty years. He and his wife Shirley moved to Arizona where he joined Dean Witter brokerage. Widowed in 1997, he retired and concentrated on his love of golf. He was a member of the Gold Medallion Roundtable, Arizona Country Club, Ascension Lutheran Church and Scottsdale Rotary. In 2004, he moved to La Ventura where he especially enjoyed the bridge group and many new friends. Mr. Olson is survived by a daughter Sandra in Summit, New Jersey, son Donald and wife Amy in Minneapolis, and a daughter Laura and husband Bill Grant in Phoenix. Also, a brother Richard and his wife Edna in Rockford. Services will be held at Ascension Lutheran Church on Mockingbird Road on __________ at 4:00 p.m. A reception will follow at the Grants' home on Boulders Drive. Now, Ellen, no more delays; you're next."

"All right. But first, let me say I thought you wrote that very well. I had no idea you had always been in the financial world. You have a daughter in Phoenix?"

"Oh, sure. She's wonderful, beautiful, kind, you know, all the things a daughter's supposed to be." He smiled with pride.

"Well, I'm a real transplant from the south. Here's my story." She began to read softly. "Ellen Ferguson Crane, who died this week, was born on Tuesday, March 1, 1927, to Jack and Shirley Ferguson in Louisville, Kentucky. She attended the University of Indiana at Bloomington where she was affiliated with Kappa Alpha Theta sorority. After marrying Joshua Crane, she studied with him at Louisville Presbyterian Seminary. Ms. Crane was a Christian educator, assisting her husband in his ministries in Red Hill, Kentucky; Oak Park Illinois; Scottsburg, Indiana; Minneapolis and Atlanta. She was always an advocate of women's rights, especially in leadership in the Presbyterian Church USA. She will be remembered as an active member of AAUW and local Presbyterian Women's organizations. Widowed in 1997, Ms. Crane retired to Scottsdale in 2003 and became a member of the Valley Presbyterian Church. A memorial service will be held there in Kilgore Chapel at 4:00 p.m. on __________. In lieu of flowers, contributions may be made to the Hope Agency to the Crane Fund for Women, which assists women returning to the work force after family changes."

"Ellen, that was a real plug for the ladies. I never knew you were such a fighter."

"I'm not. I just point out possibilities and opportunities and try to find support for them."

"O.K. The strongest people in my family were the women. They outlived all the men and often were better educated and earned more money." He pointed to Donna and said, " Now or never, my girl. What's going to happen to you and your stuff?"

"I just want a simple notice of my passing into the next world. I have no heirs and no living relatives. I've become so fond of a little boy in the after-school program at the Rose Lane Boys & Girls Clubhouse that I've decided to leave any money that's left after my cremation costs to a fund for his college education. I want this to be a complete surprise to his parents and to him, so a man in the trust department of the Chase Bank over here has set it up for me."

Ellen clapped her hands and said, "Donna, that sounds like such a wonderful idea for you. What's his name?"

"The kids all call him Mophead, because his curls are tow-head, you know, almost white. His real name is Evan Allen, and he thinks it sounds too dull or too grown-up. He has a ready smile, and he's the first one with an answer to any question. Before I arranged all this, I talked to his fourth grade teacher, and she may suspect that I had a serious reason for asking about his family situation and about his grades. But I didn't tell her my plans. You all are the first to know about it."

"We'll keep your secret too, Donna. It's a great plan. You're a volunteer beyond all expectations! So, now it's my turn to wrap this up, eh?"

"Please, and Alex, it's been good of you to moderate our meetings. I'm almost sorry this topic is finished."

"Wait till you hear this; you may be glad! Alexander James MacPherson, attorney-at-law, died suddenly in his home at La Ventura in Scottsdale. He was born on April 1, 1928, in Dallas Texas, but grew up in Las Cruces, New Mexico with two brothers and three sisters. He graduated from the University of Arizona and was affiliated with Sigma Alpha Epsilon fraternity. He served in the United States Army during the Korean War, returning to Clear Springs, Texas, in 1955 where he married Doris Matthews, practiced law and was elected a judge in 1965. In 1971, he returned to Tucson to practice law for thirty years. He was a Rotarian, holding officers' positions and becoming a Paul Harris Fellow. In 2001, he lost his wife Doris after forty-five years of marriage. In 2003, Mr. MacPherson retired to La Ventura where he became active in a writing class and enjoyed athletic and cultural events in Scottsdale. He is predeceased by his brothers Angus and John. He is survived by his son David and family of El Paso, Texas, and daughter Betsy and family of Carefree, Arizona. Also surviving are sisters Emily, Barbara, and Janet of New Mexico. His last wishes were for cremation and for his worldly goods to benefit the Salvation Army. A memorial service will be held at the Desert Hills Presbyterian Church in Carefree at sunset on __________."

After the readings, Daisy expressed the general mood. "Whew! I feel as if our whole history together has been summarized, and yet here we are, still alive and well."

Martha added, "Isn't it eerie how final those words sound? We believe in an afterlife, and yet not one of us wrote anything about it. I wanted to add a P.S. to mine, 'Free of worldly cares, Mrs. Gable will now be able to tour the great cathedrals of Europe, her childhood dream.' Is that too odd?"

Tom gazed at Martha. "I never knew you wanted to travel. We can do that; we can do a big trip in this life, Martha."

She smiled broadly and eagerly asked, "Could we really? I'd put that dream out of my head years ago, never thought it would work."

Daisy said, "See? This made us think of those things, like the things I want to get finished in case I had to leave unexpectedly."

Ellen laughed at Daisy. "You were the smart one to give yourself another half a dozen years to accomplish your projects."

"Well, that was guesswork backed up by that web site that projects your life span. I told it my age, and I chose to die after eighty on a Friday the thirteenth. That's just to test my mother's superstitions."

"It's a good lesson for all of us to have our ducks in a row and then get busy doing what we've put off." Heads nodded all around the room.

Mary Ann said, "I had no idea I'd feel this way after hearing all the obituaries read aloud. We've survived this exercise, and we're free with another chance to do something. Now I really believe I'm meant to accept that job in Casa Grande. Moving again will make me simplify my life too. That never hurts!"

Ellen laughed out loud and said, "I'm going back to Atlanta for a week to tie up all the loose ends I left behind. And I'm going soon!" Captain Newburn agreed and offered to fly with her, on his way to Florida to visit his children.

Daisy asked around, "Shall we put these in the same envelope we left in the office safe? Maybe we should make a copy for ourselves first, in case of revisions."

Alex concluded the meeting. "Let's see if there's something we ought to add, like recent pictures."

Mary Ann said, "There should be a note at the bottom of each one that reminds a relative or someone close to add a few words to personalize or update the information. Don't you agree?"

Alex nodded. "Yes, I'll do that and then make copies, and give them to Bonnie and Malcolm by the beginning of the week. All right? It's time for a glass of wine at my place and then some dinner. Anyone want to join me?"

Dave fell into step beside Daisy. "This is a great group you've put together."

"It just evolved. We started with four of my friends, but they didn't know each other."

"But there are seven of you gals."

"More arrived and joined us."

"Then Alex said he and the Captain invited themselves to join you."

Daisy laughed. "Not exactly. They were in the writing class, along with Tom, and we just kept meeting after the teacher left."

"Thanks for including me. I'd never have so many friends without you, Daisy."

"Oh now. Don't forget the bridge group. You'll never get away from Clarissa. She keeps lists and records you wouldn't believe."

"Really?"

"She supported herself all her life on her piano lessons. She's a business woman through and through."

"Amazing. I gather Beth is too."

"C.P.A., ours in fact, back in Illinois. Here's my unit. Mind if I toss these papers inside before we go to Alex's place?"

"Fine. It'll give me a chance to see Curly." He held the screen door open and heard Curly's greeting on the inside. "How's it goin', Boy?" Curly was excited to have two people at the door.

Daisy checked his water. "Bye, Curly, we'll see you later." They locked up and left for Alex's promised refreshment.

CHAPTER 32

Beautiful March

MARY ANN'S UNIT SOLD immediately, and by March first, Bonnie and Malcolm had planned a farewell party. "We've never heard of someone retiring away from our retirement center, so we'll wish her *bon voyage*."

Mary Ann replied, "Romeria means a pilgrimage or a voyage, so at this address, you're on a journey somewhere too."

"But I hate to see you leave, especially now that we've become so close. Will you promise to come back to visit?"

"Of course. I can't let Martha and Tom get too distant. You know it's only about 58 miles to my next open door, so you could get together and drive down."

Alex was quick to pick up that invitation. "Tell you what, we'll be down on your birthday, no joking. I'll drive my daughter's minivan. She keeps it for the baseball team, but they won't need it till school's out."

"That's a good goal for me to get settled and ready for you. I hate good-byes, but here it is. You've all been great, and I'm going to miss you every day. But I'm going to be so busy, there won't be time to cry. Bye-bye." And with that, she waved and went out smiling.

The group was still facing the door when Martha said, "You know, she's looking forward to this like her first job. What a terrific sister I have!" The party continued without her.

Two weeks later, Daisy slid into her usual pew just as the organist began the prelude of joyous Palm Sunday music. A steady stream of people came down the aisle. Suddenly she heard a man's voice beside her. "Pardon me, is this seat taken?"

She looked up right into Dave Olson's smiling face. She slid over and said, "Join me."

He settled himself, and laid his cane on the floor behind his feet. Turning to her, he said, "I guess my daughter must have gone to church. So, I decided to celebrate the day. It's always been a favorite of mine."

Daisy smiled. "The palms are beautiful, aren't they? The children usually march down the aisle with their offering boxes."

"They're lining up outside. I saw them, the biggest first, then down to the ones holding the teachers' hands."

During the service, they shared a hymn book until Daisy had to excuse herself and fish a tissue out of her purse. Tears were spilling down her cheeks. The hymn ended, and Dave gently put a hand under her elbow to help her sit down. "I don't know what's wrong with me. I don't usually weep."

"It's a beautiful song. No apology needed." The service proceeded, everything on schedule. After the benediction, they stood to leave the sanctuary. Dave leaned over and said softly. "Perhaps I shouldn't have sat here."

Quickly she said, "Yes, you should have. It was perfect. I guess it just brought back a lot of memories. Scott died on this date, but after six years, I should be stronger than this."

"It's not a matter of strength, Daisy. It's just plain old love. We're all like that, at least those of us who had happy marriages."

"Thanks for understanding. Shall we get some coffee?"

"Sure. Let me get my cane and lead me in the right direction." They shook a lot of hands and greeted some of the Seasoned Seniors. "It's a beautiful day, isn't it? I should be here more often. Makes me feel good to get into an old routine."

"Dave, how did you get here? The bus left before I did."

"I took a cab."

"A cab? You could have come with me."

"Yes, but I waited to be sure I didn't miss Sandy's call."

"Well, don't let that happen again. How about a ride home?" They walked on toward the parking lot and Daisy's car.

Dave commented, "I remember this little car. It's a lot easier to get in it today than that day you brought me home from the hospital."

"You know, I forgot to ask how your knee healed. You seemed to recover so fast."

"I did. I never think of it now. But I don't do the pool exercise anymore. Maybe I'll join you dog-walkers for some exercise."

"That would be O.K. Another man has tagged along some times for the same reason. Except he claims it's because he's afraid of getting lost in the neighborhoods near us. Says all the houses look alike."

"He's got a point. I loved our old place down on Lafayette, because we had a shake roof and a flagpole out front. It was unique. And the citrus blossoms were like the ones near the church, filling the air in March. Oh, well, there I go, reminiscing. I'm as bad as you, Daisy."

They shared a laugh. Both were quiet on the way back to La Ventura. When they reached Daisy's parking space, Dave reached over and patted her hand. "You sit tight there, lady. I'm old school." He opened his door and got out with his cane, then hurried around the car and opened her door.

She smiled and thanked him. "It's been a long time since anyone did that. Are you walking over to brunch?"

"Sure. I'm starved after all that activity this morning." They walked along and caught up with other friends.

Later in the afternoon, Daisy tipped her recliner back and muted the TV. "What a lovely relaxing day. Curly, I think I'll catch a quick nap."

CHAPTER 33

"If only we had known. . ."

AT THE FIRST MEETING in April, Daisy said she was still amazed at how well-acquainted and close they had become. "Are there some things we wished we had known in the beginning?"

Captain Newburn spoke up first. "Yeah, I believed all that promotion about Arizona's having more boats per person than any other state. Where are they?" There were chuckles around the table. "If we have more rain, I may buy a raft, but I miss seeing a harbor."

Donna surprised everyone by saying, "It's awfully hard to make new friends at our age. I don't mean to sound so old, but you know what I mean. People act as if they want to keep their previous life a secret. Oh, they'll always tell you where they used to live, but not much more. You know, Alice and I have gone to the movies every week for the last year or more, but I just learned last week that she's been married and widowed three times. And she's talking about some guy over in the casitas who's handsome enough for her likes. She's thinking of asking him to take her out sometime." She laughed and looked around. "I should never have told you all that. Please don't let on you know." They all assured her that Thursdays at Three was a solid, confidential group.

Beth spoke up. "I had trouble being in a crowd all the time. You know, I lived alone so long and then planned when to go out on errands or with friends. It wasn't *all* the time like here."

"You're right. But I have to admit I haven't had any blue days either. It must be good to know someone is expecting you in the dining room. I'm sure it's good to have a reason to get dressed, or put on some makeup."

"I still have some days when I wish I could just be by myself." Donna shook her head sadly.

"Why don't you just sign out for lunch on those days and go some place, to a museum or the mall or the library? I get a break by working at the church."

Martha understood. "I think that's why Mary Ann started to volunteer so often at the Clubhouse. She needed to be with the kids she had worked with in Roswell."

"At first, I resented the lack of privacy," was Tom's comment. "And here I'm the one who completely gave up privacy and got married! So, it was just a new experience to live with so many close neighbors. I'd always been pretty solitary."

"That's funny, because I'd been a loner too after my first marriage blew up. I think that's how I got into such a drinking habit." Martha moved close to Tom and leaned against his shoulder. "Or maybe booze made me into a hermit."

Ellen asked Daisy a question. "What would you have done if you'd stayed in your own house and not written to us?"

"Oh, boy, I don't know. I think the lonely evenings were the worst. I might have taken to sleeping a lot. Bed always seemed like an escape. But I've heard depression and long hours of sleep kind of go together. I think some of the church people might have rescued me."

Ellen persevered. "But you really have to get into some group to get going again. Isn't that true?"

Again, the Captain spoke. "Ellen's right, but I don't think we men are as good as you gals in joining an organization or volunteering. It's too easy to sit around and watch TV and read."

Beth perked up on that comment. "I could have lived in my house in Geneva forever, just talking on the phone to all my old friends. They would have thought I was fine and would've left me alone. I suppose I could have kept doing some taxes for a little pin money and just to feel good."

"But, what if you had to go through the surgeries back there?"

"Hm. Hadn't thought of that. No, I'll always be grateful Daisy wrote me. She knew what would help me."

Daisy jumped on that. "I thought I was helping solve your problems. Instead, you all rescued me from mine."

Tom asked, "What were your problems, Daisy? Did those old days look better to you too?"

"No. But it was my link to these old friends. Everything was going perfectly in Scottsdale. We built our dream house; the kids live here too. Happy grandchildren. No complaints." Daisy hoped her answer didn't sound defensive, but after Tom's revelation about Scott, she found herself avoiding conversations with him.

He continued. "I think a lot of people in a retirement place put on masks of contentment or confidence, so no one will invade their past lives or wonder about their bank accounts."

Alex took offense at that. "I've found quite the opposite here. My daughter persuaded me to move here, so I wasn't red hot about it. But I found people to be very open, aware of being on the same plane as the others. Sort of like building a new house on a new street; everybody's in the same boat, needing neighbors."

Tom shrugged. "Maybe I look at people differently. I've always thought people are hard to please. My customers always made me feel threatened, kind of inferior; I was afraid I might not have what they wanted. So, I tried to analyze them before they spoke."

"Hey, that's dangerous to label people before you know them." The Captain's words surprised everyone. "I always assumed my customers were counting on me to have exactly what they wanted or they wouldn't have come aboard."

Dave interjected, "Tom, people often put on masks for better reasons than hiding. They want other people around them to be happy. What good would it do to complain about the past? We've all had disappointments, losses, pain. Who wants to hear about the past?"

Tom looked down and took a deep breath. "I guess I was being too critical. I never had much happiness, just hard work trying to make a living. I always wonder if other people struggled as much as I had to."

"Maybe you hope they did. But others may want to forget those tough years. That's the beauty of moving into a new place with all new friends. A guy who worked for me at Witter's was always reminding the rest of us about stocks we had pushed that had lost money, years ago. He never wanted anyone's life to be too smooth or perfect. I used to tell him to leave the rain cloud at the door."

Ellen commented, "Maybe this isn't where Daisy wanted us to take her question."

"Not to worry. Our conversations keep us going. I started all this when I asked if there were things we needed to know when we got here."

"Some of these places have an orientation session. I sure didn't know what to expect. In fact, I had some wrong ideas. I was afraid someone would be checking up on us. You know, I was tired from that long drive, and I'd been sick. I just wanted to be left alone for a bit."

"Donna, I still remember when you blew in here that Saturday night." Alex made them all smile. "That gorgeous cat wasn't at all tired. She just took over the place as soon as she found an audience."

"And in all fairness, I remember Bonnie offered me food even though it was way past dinner. I'm glad we don't have to sign in and out like nursing school. That would be annoying!"

"Well, what about celebrating? Maybe next month before anyone leaves for the season. You'll still be here, Clarissa?"

"Oh, yes, because our big tournament is May first. And I haven't said much, but I want you all to know I think you're amazing. You all fit together so well. I wish we'd known each other years ago."

"I'll second that," said Alex. "And I appreciate your including us menfolk. As Captain Bob said, we don't jump right in and join groups. But this has been interesting all along. Dave, I'm sorry we didn't get you in here sooner. Did I hear you're writing a book?"

"I am. It's great therapy, because life changes so much with the loss of your partner and a sudden disability. There's still so much joy left, wonderful people to meet, and I'm afraid people don't realize that."

Alex said, "That's quite a testimony. You're right. So, what's the title?"

"Don't know. I'm playing around with venture or adventure, probably influenced by the name of this place."

"Don't forget that Daisy calls all of us remnants." Ellen's words interested Dave.

"Really? Remnants, huh? I guess we are, in the Biblical sense. I like that. Spared to carry on or do something new?"

Alex chipped in, "Daisy, what in the world did you put in that letter? I keep hearing about your invitation, but I've never seen it."

Daisy laughed. "I don't know. It wasn't very literary. I just announced I was moving here and asked them to join me."

"Yes, and you reminded us of happier times when we used to have coffee and belong to the same groups and stuff, when we were thinner, richer, and had all the answers."

Beth was quick to add, "Daisy saw us as remnants like her sewing materials, so she knew we could be recycled into a new life. I think she's right!"

Daisy smiled and brushed aside all the compliments. "On that high note, let's get ready for dinner. Keep thinking of our next writing topic."

CHAPTER 34

More Worries Arrive

TWO WEEKS LATER, the group assembled with easy chatter, because no one had to read anything. "These idea sessions are always fun, aren't they?" Beth commented to Alex. "Once we get into a topic, the hard work begins."

"You mean we're really working hard in this writing business? That's nice to think we can still take life seriously."

Before they came to order, Malcolm popped in the door. "Daisy, I have an urgent call for you. It's your daughter."

Daisy looked startled and dropped her pad and pen on the table to follow Malcolm to the office. "Did she say what's wrong?"

"No, but I gathered it's serious. Take the call at my desk, and I'll close the door."

Inside, she sat down and punched the lighted button. She listened and nodded, reached for a pencil and Malcolm's note pad. "Say that number again, Julie." She wrote carefully. "He can't have visitors?" She paused. "Matt can get in, but only as his attorney. O.K., I've got it. Julie, where's Susie?" She listened a long time. "Fine. I'll be back at my place in ten minutes." She stood to leave the office.

"Everything O.K., Daisy?"

"Not really, but under control. My son has a problem, but Julie's husband can handle it, I'm sure."

"Both those men are lawyers, right?"

"Yes, but sometimes, even a lawyer needs a lawyer. Thanks for getting me to the phone."

Daisy returned to the room, sat down and broke into tears. "Please don't ask me what's wrong. It's just some family news I need to take care of. I'll be steadier tomorrow. Don't worry." She dried her eyes and gathered up her things.

Dave came to her side at the door. "You probably want to be near the phone. I'll come by later with a CARE package from dinner. You just take it easy."

"Thanks, Dave. That's nice." She stepped outside with Beth who was holding the door open for her. "That was Julie. Pete was. . . he was. . . arrested." She choked up again, then cleared her throat. "Julie said he called her *from the jail* in Phoenix. Her Matt left right away to see if he could get him out. Can you imagine Pete in jail?"

"Now, Daisy. He's a man and quite able to take care of himself. Why was he arrested?"

"I don't know exactly the wording, but it had to do with some outstanding warrant, like some ticket in the past that just came to light."

"Sounds as if he needs Matt to sort it out."

"I guess so. I just want to get home and sit by the phone. Surely one of them will call me soon." When they reached Unit 7, Beth gave her a quick hug and helped her with the door.

"Call me if you need company."

Inside, Daisy walked over to the blinking light on the answering machine. Curly must have sensed trouble, because he shadowed Daisy with every step. "Old Boy, your Pete has a real problem today. I bet he wishes you were beside him right now." She punched the button to listen.

A computerized voice announced "This is April twenty-first, 3:35, p.m." Next was Susie's voice, filled with sobs, "Mom, it's Pete. The police are holding him, in a jail. I don't know where, and he can't see me. Joe Crandall called me. They were leaving the Cork and Cleaver on 44th Street. Joe turned north and Pete had to cross traffic to go back downtown. Joe looked back and saw an accident, so he turned around and came back. He said

Pete's fine, but the other guy's car is totaled. Oh, Mom, what next?" Her voice dissolved and then there was a click as she hung up the phone.

"I'd better call her, but I wish Julie would call back first." Then there was a knock at the door. "Just a minute." Daisy brushed her hair back and opened the door.

"Room service, Madam." Dave stood there, holding a small tray with a glass of white wine on a blue paper napkin. She opened the door and invited him in. "Alex prescribed this, and I am your personal waiter."

"You know, that looks so good right now." Curly thumped his tail against Dave's legs and then parked himself beside the empty chair. "I just listened to Pete's wife reporting that he's been arrested. Sounds like an accident on 44th Street, just above Camelback. He's O.K. but in jail." She set the tray on the coffee table, and they both sat down. "I should call her, but I don't want to."

"I can believe that. But it was Julie who called you during the meeting?"

"Yes. I suppose Susie had called her first. Oh, woe, these kids are grown up and yet still calling for help." She shook her head in disbelief.

"Daisy, there's not much you can do, unless they can bail him out. It takes hours for a judge to determine if he's bondable. Do you s'pose he'd been drinking his lunch?"

"He told me once that he was through with martini lunches, when he was in the hospital that same week you were."

"I'll tell you, I had more close calls like that. Never caused an accident, but I sure could have."

Daisy felt as if she might faint if this conversation continued. She reached for the glass and sipped the light, tart wine. "This is tasty, Dave. Thanks. How did you manage the tray with your cane?"

"Oh, I've memorized the path to your door without a cane, lady." He chuckled. "I remember times when I needed to relax. My kids have kept me in hot water lots of times. It's worse now that I'm alone."

"You're so right. I felt like turning from the phone and telling Scott the call was for him."

"This is when we need friends. And I know where that accident happened. Do you want to go and look at the place?"

"Heavens, no. Pete wasn't hurt, but I guess the other car's a wreck. How about a cup of coffee?"

"I'd like that. How about if I go over to the dining room and get two dinners packed for carry-out?"

"That'd be wonderful! I sure don't want to go over there tonight."

"Me neither. Keep the coffee hot; I'll be back in about an hour." As he left, he heard the phone ringing but kept going.

Daisy approached it with caution. "Yes? Hi, Julie. I'm all right. A friend was just here, and I listened to a frantic message from Susie. Have you seen her?" She waited. "Matt will be the best messenger, since he knows what to do. Where's the jail?"

Curly began to bark. Ellen was at the door and gently let herself in, patting Curly as she entered. Daisy nodded and gestured to a chair. "Yes, I'm here, dear. Another friend just came in. Well, you'll keep me posted, any hour. It doesn't matter. I'll worry more if I don't know what's going on. I especially want to know the charges. All right, and thanks, dear. 'Bye."

Ellen began, "I'm not here to pry, but I want you to know that no family news can shake me up. I've heard it all, after forty-six years in the manse."

"You must have heard terribly sad things. This is about Pete. He wasn't hurt but must have caused an accident. Something about the police checked his license and found there was a warrant against him. Susie's taking Suzette over to bring his car home. That's the only thing she can do at the moment."

"Can he be bailed out?"

"We don't know yet. Matt called Julie and told her something about a few DUI records. Why didn't we ever know about those?" She shook her head. "I feel so distant from their lives, and yet when something goes wrong, they're on my doorstep. It doesn't seem fair."

"And since when is life fair? God never promised a fair life. But you have the strength you need because you have faith. That's the promise."

"I know. I just had a little spark of anger there for a minute. Why would he do such a dumb thing as to ignore a ticket? He's an attorney. Wouldn't that show up on his record somewhere?"

"Don't know, Daisy. Well, I'll make excuses for you at dinner. You're waiting for an important phone call from Pete. Everyone'll assume it's about his health. I'll fend that off with a 'test results.' Take care. Shall I check in later?"

"No, thanks. If something monumental happens, I'll call right away." They hugged, and Ellen left. Daisy fixed Curly's dinner and added fresh water for him. "What's the matter, Curly? Can't you eat with me watching you? Oh, go on. Try it." He sat and looked at the bowl, then at her. "Do you need a persuader, a little piece of cheese?" His tail came to life, and she took a block of cheese from the refrigerator. Several small pieces tumbled into his bowl, and that temptation was too much. He had barely finished when Dave arrived with two plates wrapped in foil and a plastic bag of rolls dangling from his wrist.

"I never thought to ask if you have silverware and maybe some butter."

"Of course I do. The coffee's made too. Let's see, how about this table? I have another place mat. Will that chair be comfortable? First, I need to let Curly out."

"Looks like a party to me. Wish we had better news to celebrate. However, good friends make the best of all news, as long as the burden is shared."

"Thanks, Dave. You're lending me a lot of strength, and I appreciate it. I'm afraid I don't deserve it. If you knew. . ." The telephone sprang into life, and cut off Daisy's budding apology.

"Hello?" Daisy settled into the nearest chair. "Yes, I'm sitting down. What do you mean?" She listened intently. "Not until midnight? Strange hour for a hearing." She frowned. "Matt can't get him released? What do you mean, it might be a month? What?" Daisy's voice rose an octave. "But he hasn't hurt anyone. He has the money. He can't walk well. It's the law?" She dropped her head and said silently, "Oh, no, not my son."

As she hung up the phone, Dave said politely, "Shall I leave?"

"No, please don't. That was Julie. Matt's with Pete, but he told her he may not get him released. The legislature has mandated a four-year probation with four months' incarceration for the number of DUIs he had. Can you imagine he was driving on an expired license?"

"Maybe a revoked license?"

"Yes, that's what I mean."

"Well, yes, I almost did it myself one time. I've had five DUIs in my adult life. Can you believe it? The difference is that I always paid my fine and always had an attorney at my side. I wish I had the money I spent on getting myself out of trouble!"

Daisy looked intently at Dave, and then she said, "I can't believe that, Dave. You're too smart to do that."

"Smart has very little to do with it. When drinking was part of my life, I was not smart. I was addicted. The laws applied to someone else." Dave reached over and let Curly in from the patio.

"Yes, but he's a lawyer."

"I know, Daisy. But he's a man first, a human being with weaknesses like all of us."

"But he has a wife and a daughter. He was earning good money."

"I finally realized that having money may have made it easier for me to be a drunk." He ate a few bites and then continued, "Not that it's an excuse, but it was easier to hide my bar bill if I had cash that Shirley never knew about."

"You and I have another matter to talk about, Dave. I felt so betrayed when I learned that Scott drank too much."

Dave reached across the table and covered Daisy's hand with his. "Daisy, not tonight. O.K.? I know we have a past to talk about some day, but not tonight. There's enough going on without all that." He squeezed her hand and patted it, before he went on with his dinner.

Daisy tried to eat but found the food sticking in her throat. "What will happen to Pete?"

"Pete's a grown man, and he'll take his penalty as it comes. No doubt, he's thought about cutting back or quitting the booze before now. This'll get him started."

"Yes, but can Susie and Suzette get through this?"

"They'll have to. You know, people can endure a lot more than they ever thought possible. Does Susie work?"

"No, she's big in the volunteer scene."

"Maybe she can parlay her experience into one of the staff jobs at those places, you know, like the hospital or the library or wherever."

"She'll really have to be strong about it so Suzette keeps going to school. She's in her senior year and applying to colleges."

"Can she get a scholarship?"

"Why? Will this cost Pete a lot?"

"Hm. Well, maybe. Depends on the fines and the charges. Tough to say." Silence fell across the table.

Daisy nibbled small bites and finally began to feel more optimistic. "She said something about probation for four years. Four years? Why?"

"It's the law, Daisy. All of a sudden Pete's just like some kid who's caught smoking pot. If he ignores his court date and gets caught again, it all adds up."

"But he's not a kid, and he never smoked pot. Well, I don't know about that. That was a long time ago."

"Trouble is, the law never forgets."

Daisy poured two cups of coffee, and they pushed the plates aside. "Thanks for bringing dinner over. I'll try to face the crowd by noon tomorrow. Ellen came by while you were gone, and she knows what's going on. It's so embarrassing. Then I hate myself for saying that. I should be thinking how Pete feels."

"He knows he's hurt you, as well as his wife and girl. He made a bum choice once and never recovered from it. Now he's getting a new start. Pay the piper and move on." Dave stood and patted Curly. "Come on, Big Guy, I'll take you out." They moved to the door where Dave pulled a plastic bag from the holder by the door, while Daisy gathered the dishes and went to the kitchen.

Once they were back inside, Dave said, "I'll be going now, but I'm on call as a friend, day or night." He gave her a quick hug and closed the door.

Daisy sank into her usual chair and reached for the rest of the glass of wine.

CHAPTER 35

Life Moves Along

EACH DAY DAISY HAD MANAGED to trust others to help Pete. She encouraged Susie and Suzette to keep strong and to pray. She tried to set a faithful example.

She had recovered from the initial shock of Pete's problems. Whenever she talked with Susie, she found herself balancing on a fine line between her own disappointment over Pete's lack of good judgment and defending him to his wife and daughter. One day, Susie exploded at Daisy, "Why didn't you stop him from drinking so much in college?" Daisy was hurt and speechless.

Dave continued to be a good listener, often walking her home from the dining room and coming in to talk. "It's good for me to see the family's point of view toward a drinker. I was always so focused on myself and my problems. My poor wife must have suffered the way you are. There's never an easy answer to the 'why?' question. I had a million excuses. Most of them began with 'if only' and ended with 'tomorrow'."

"Couldn't Susie have helped him stop drinking so much?"

"No, he has to make up his mind to quit, not just taper off, but quit. Alcohol is his way of thinking now, but he has to learn all the symptoms and the triggers to find a new point of view."

"You said you stopped drinking, but how?"

"When I finally got it through my head that I'd die if I drank again. There I was, in the hospital, couldn't see, couldn't remember a thing about the accident. Shirley's car was totaled. I was about to be discharged from the hospital with bandages all over one side of my head, my arm in a sling, no clothes and no one to bring me any. I was washed up, a complete disgrace!"

Daisy was overcome with sympathy and could not think of a thing to say. She reached over and laid her hand on his arm. He covered her hand with his. "All, I can say is, you are one strong man to rise above that day. I pray my son can climb out of his disaster."

"He can, if he wants to. I learned that day how much I wanted to live. I'd never thought much about it before that accident."

"You say you can't remember the accident?"

"Nope. I read in the paper that I swerved to miss a car that crossed the centerline; I didn't slow down and lost control. The only thing I remember is hanging almost upside down, my face a few inches above water and my left arm stuck in the steering wheel. Someone strong had a hold of my foot and kept telling me to stay awake."

Daisy shuddered at the picture. "That's awful. When did help come?"

"Well, that guy hanging onto my foot was the biggest help. Blood was running up my nose, and I wanted to vomit. I've always been afraid of deep water. You know, it was just a nightmare. I must have blacked out, because the next thing I knew I was in a hospital bed surrounded by nurses, and I had a blistering headache. Doctor told me right then and there I'd lost my sight in one eye, but my arm was just twisted and sprained at the elbow. The next morning I began my recovery. By the next day, I knew I had to live a new life."

"Yes, but that's not easy. Weren't you depressed, or sad? Did you call Sandy? Or Laura and Bill?"

"No, it was all up to me. Most of us drunks know deep down that this might happen. I'd sworn off a couple of times before. I didn't want Laura to see me until I was ready."

"Did you begin to feel better, I mean clearer in your mind? I keep thinking how preoccupied Pete is. His mind is always somewhere else, but he knows the right thing to say and covers up real well."

"That's what we specialize in, covering up. We're so clever, so full of excuses and explanations. But what a relief it is not to have to make excuses for being forgetful or late. My family must have wondered how I could ever make it in the business world. They used to say I was lucky, but I was just a good con artist!"

"You know, Dave, we're all con artists in some ways. I painted such a glowing picture of my perfect life that I almost lost my friend, Donna. She told me she hated me years ago for having such perfect kids and such a perfect husband. I even deceived myself into thinking everything was bliss."

Dave patted her arm and said, "Listen, this isn't true confession time. I just wanted you to know why I'm a happy man today. You don't have to pour anything out to me. I like you just the way I see you. I *really* like what I see."

"Good, but you said something that made me think. Your family called you lucky and didn't want to know the truth. I called Scott my ideal and defended him from the kids and their criticism. They saw his flaws, but I kept him on a pedestal. I stifled him to the point he couldn't share any problems with me. I never asked him if something was bothering him. In fact, I can hear myself saying, 'Another great day at the office, dear?' when he came home."

"Yeah, Shirley was the same way. She idolized me for keeping the checkbook and servicing the cars, all the man's stuff. She always told me she couldn't do a thing without me."

"We put a lot of pressure on you men. Now, young women take on some of those jobs and the men pitch in around the house. Maybe better times are ahead if they each keep some independence."

"Let's hope they talk more. As you say, no one ever wanted to admit any doubts."

Daisy's phone rang, and she moved to answer it. "Yes, dear, how are you? Suzette's at a friend's? Sure, come on over. I'd love to hear everything." She listened and laughed. "I'll open the door." She hung up the receiver and said to Dave, "Susie's on her way here, like on the sidewalk." With that, the door knocker rattled.

"Susie, dear, come in. Meet my friend, Dave Olson." They shook hands, and Dave started toward the door. "Dave, why don't you stay a minute. Then I won't have to repeat everything Susie tells me."

He nodded and sat down again, letting Susie and Daisy share the short sofa. "Mom, how can this be happening to us? I can't imagine what I'd do without Pete coming home at night."

"You'll manage just fine. It's amazing how we adjust to the things we have to accept."

"That's easy to say, but you never had to go through this. He called this afternoon and told me to get a job, can you believe it? He never wanted me to work. Where would I get a job? He's always had a wonderful income. And here it's Suzette's year to graduate. What will she tell her friends?" At this, she buried her head in her hands and groaned. "How could he do this to us?"

"She may have to tell them the truth. Her dad made some bad choices. Pete told Matt he put your family needs ahead of paying his fines; he thought there'd be a period of grace on the deadlines."

"Why didn't he tell me?"

Daisy looked over at Dave and said, "Dave's been telling me a lot of things about Pete's way of thinking. He never wanted to disappoint you or Suzette."

"Well, he sure has done it now!"

Dave cleared his throat and said, "Pete has done the bravest thing he's ever done, if he's admitted to being an alcoholic. It takes courage to face it and pay the penalty."

"He's an alcoholic? You mean he'll never be able to drink at all? He's sick? He's not like that. I've known other people who were drunk all the time, but he's not like that. He's a gentle nice guy, always trying to keep everyone happy at the office."

"The nicest people I knew in college became alcoholics. They lost their self-esteem along the way, and it's darned hard to find it again. I know, because I am one."

"Really?" Susie looked at Dave, then turned her attention on Daisy and asked, "Mom, did you know that?"

"Yes, and I'm learning that Pete's dad was probably a serious drinker too."

"Does Pete know that?"

"Maybe, and maybe not. We haven't talked about it lately, but we will."

"I have to go and pick up Suz, so we'll talk tomorrow. Pete's being held until the hearing on Wednesday." She stood. "Goodbye, Mr. Olson. I'll think about what you said."

After the door closed, Dave also made his farewell. "I'll see you tomorrow. Call me if you get down in the dumps and need to talk. Pete's wife is lovely, so immaculate in every detail. Does she ever relax?"

Daisy chuckled. "No, not much. You saw her at her typical best, except when she was sad about having to work. She's very dependent on Pete. She won't want him to use a cane or be guilty of anything."

Dave gave Daisy a quick hug and left, saying "Relax, it'll all work out."

As Daisy let Curly back in, she reviewed the last few days. "Curly, you know something's wrong, don't you? I guess there's not much we can do about it either, just keep loving Pete and pray for him to be strong."

Daisy was leaving the mailboxes one morning when Martha opened a letter from Mary Ann. "She's so happy down there! Listen to this:

> *I miss you all, but I'm sure this is where I belong. The first two board meetings were pretty stressful, but now that I can report on some success, they're happier. I have ten more kids registered to start in May. We're still working on the plans for a summer program. I'll keep you posted.*
>
> *Love to you and Tom. I hope your dreams are still on track. Give me the dates of that big trip. I want to picture right where you'll be each day! Keep cool, M.A.*

"She sounds wonderful."

"She does, but I miss her cheery face at meals and our meetings. You know what else I miss? She could always alter my clothes. She spoiled me. Now I've gained weight, I need her."

"Well, I miss her too. About your alterations: I can help you. I know how to make things fit. It's better to adjust something than spend time feeling bad about a few more inches. Bring your problem to me. You know I sew almost every morning."

Alex appeared at her door one afternoon. "Daisy, I've come to find out what I can do to help you and your family. What's going on that keeps you looking so serious?"

"Thanks for your concern. I can't seem to shake off a certain gloom. I wake up in the morning with my usual gratitude for another day of life and my prayer for the day ahead. Then it hits me. *My son is in prison.* He never hurt anyone, never disturbed the peace, was a good father and husband. But my son is in prison."

"I've been a concerned parent too. I know what you mean; I know how you suffer."

"What got you over it?"

"Talking with people, admitting my fears. You know, fear is usually at the bottom of depression. You're afraid the situation may get worse. Or Pete may get hurt or relapse. Or Susie will give up. Or your granddaughter will escape into the street world."

"There are so many things to fear, aren't there? Susie isn't taking this well at all. And therefore, Suz is worried about her mom, her dad and I suppose about herself maybe not going to college."

"She has to keep going too, you know."

"I know. I could sell some of Scott's retirement investments and pay for ASU. I'm afraid she wants a more exclusive college."

"Well, that's what may need to change. She has to compromise too. Can you talk to her about your idea? What's Pete going to do about retraining himself?"

"I haven't heard him say anything. He writes very sketchy notes. Ever since his stroke, he's had trouble writing. He even has some difficulty with words, I think."

"One thing's for sure. You can't give up your life while he's struggling along. He made this mess, remember."

"Oh, that sounds harsh."

"I meant it to be harsh. Daisy, you're our leader, our best friend. We're a happy bunch here, thanks to your energy and ideas. We can't stand to watch you decline in health because of your kids. I was elected to come here and tell you this. It's not easy."

Daisy's eyes filled with tears. "Alex, I didn't know I was slipping. Does it show that much?"

"Yes, it does. You have to perk up and come back to life. Today!"

His demanding words made Daisy smile. "All right, I'll try. Where do you need me most?"

"On Thursdays at Three. We only have a few meetings left before some of our friends leave town."

"I know, and I always wonder if they'll all want to come back."

"Really? I don't sense unhappiness anywhere. But some of your old friends want you to perk up and let them cheer you up." He stood and put out his hand to her.

Daisy took his hand and impulsively hugged him. "Thanks, Alex. New friends are as valuable as the old."

CHAPTER 36

Summer Melts Away

As usual, early May was beautiful weather, warm and clear, with an occasional hot day to preview what lay ahead. The chef turned Kentucky Derby Day into a cause for celebration. On Saturday, May sixth, he served a pie that made everyone forget diets and healthful eating. The southern favorite was a big hit, no matter which horse had won.

The real estate market in Scottsdale slowed down as the weather warmed up. Fortunately, La Ventura had a good spring season for sales as another building of apartment units neared completion. June was very warm, often topping record high temperatures.

Thursdays at Three continued, with friendly conversation and quarts of iced tea. Occasionally new people visited a meeting, and by the time Daisy left for her vacation, she felt confident the group would go on providing a comfortable place to make friends. If they decided to write something, all the better.

Bonnie was showing new residents, the Ansons, around the property one morning. "Summer's going quickly and quietly around here. The workmen are indoors now, finishing up Building Five, and some of our residents are off visiting their families in cool country."

Bill Anson asked, "Do your meal plans allow flexibility when people go away like that?"

"Oh, yes, we have several options for you to consider."

"Good," and he nodded approval. "I think we'd be very happy here, so we need to choose a place."

Malcolm had joined them and offered to start the process of becoming a "resident manager."

Mid-July brought the monsoon season along with some blowing dust. Early morning pool aerobics became more popular, and the ice cream parlor added some tables and chairs in the corner of the adjacent hallway. The chef kept the menus light and cool. Malcolm ordered a few extra movies for the theater, and the residents agreed that siesta time should be a permanent item on the schedule.

By August, the Bunch of Daisy's had caught up on their families and were content to slip back into a relaxed hot weather mode. Tom declared it a time of "No brain drain."

Schools opened in the third week, and the Boys & Girls Clubs fall schedule started. Beth offered to keep the volunteer sign-up sheets circulating. She invited new people to visit a club once before committing to a whole season of after-school hours.

At dinner one evening, Daisy mentioned her ongoing concern about helping people fit back into La Ventura after they had spent time 'back home.' "You know, when this place was new to us, we were excited about starting our new life. What if it isn't a good fit anymore?" No one else seemed concerned.

"Speaking of fitting," Martha interrupted her, "I can't squeeze into my travel suit. Could you help me with your magic sewing machine?"

Daisy laughed. "Come by tomorrow morning, and I'll try."

While it was still reasonably pleasant outside, Martha arrived with her lovely grey pant suit. "I'm embarrassed to admit I've put on these inches since I bought it. What can we do?"

"If I move these two buttons and ease out some of that fullness in front, I think you'll still have your favorite travel suit, Martha. I'll fix this today, and tomorrow you can pack for your dream trip!"

"Thanks, Daisy, you're my best friend, next to Tom. We'll be back by October." She started to leave, and added, "Don't worry about those people who went back home. When they get back here, they'll know they're home with all of us."

CHAPTER 37

Reunion Time

WALKING OVER TO DINNER ALONE, Daisy realized how eagerly she looked forward to seeing familiar faces, especially the Thursdays at Three friends. Her pet economy for July and August was eating lunch at home rather than buying into the lunch plan. Her place stayed cool. She and Curly ate lightly and took a siesta.

Now she stood at the dining room doorway, reminding members of the Thursdays at Three Writers' Group of the meeting in the Hedgehog Room at 3:00 the next day. "I think we'll have seven there," she reported later to Ellen. "Martha and Tom aren't due back until next week. Clarissa might even show up; who knows?"

"Won't it be fun to hear about the vacations? I can't wait to tell you about Emily, little Emily." They chose a table and sat with Donna and Alice.

Alice said, "You know, I saw some new faces near the mailboxes. I was only gone ten days. How could I have missed meeting them?"

"Well, the Ansons moved in during early September but didn't want the meal plan, only for Sunday brunch. So, we won't get to know them for a while."

"I didn't know you could do that."

"Evidently you can. They came from Costa Rica. They retired there two years ago and then didn't like it. Clarissa will love them, because they're serious bridge players."

Donna added, "If they speak Spanish, we could use them at the Boys & Girls Clubs, couldn't we?"

Daisy nodded. "Then that younger-looking Ms. Farley works almost full time over at the hospital, so she said she'd just be here for dinner on the weekends until January."

"My, oh my, we're getting diversified, aren't we?"

Daisy's face suddenly lit up, as she pointed toward the main door. Clarissa popped through the door as vigorous as ever. "Can you believe she's eighty-three?"

Ellen laughed with Daisy, and they waved Clarissa over to their table. "How was the trip?"

"Absolutely wonderful. Kind of warm here, but I'll get used to it again."

"Sit down, and tell us all about you."

She sat down, hanging her huge purse over the arm of the chair. Her hair was shorter and smoothly coiffed. She shed her jacket and straightened her collar, all coordinated in a becoming shade of rose. "Well, I'm ready for some food. I forgot to warn Bonnie I'd be here. Think they'll have enough for me too? Alice, how are you, and Donna, you're looking so tanned and young."

"Thanks; you're looking good too. Tell us about your friends in Washington. Are they still so timid?"

"Worse than ever. I'm older than all of them, but they worry about everything. I keep telling them to find a place like La Ventura, but they never will." She was the dose of energy they all needed, and she went on, "My old neighbor Betty had to give up her car, and everyone was pretty relieved about that. I wonder if some of the folks here should consider giving up driving too."

"What about Jan, your nephew's wife?"

"She had a bad summer, poor dear. I tried to help, but I've become such a lazy cook. All I could do was go to the store and buy some dinner. How about the rest of you?"

Donna volunteered, "You missed a lot of excitement in the Phoenix news, Rissa. A serial killer was at large, scaring the wits out of everyone in the Phoenix area."

"Really? Did they get him?"

"Well, two men are in jail who seem to be the right ones, but the paper says it'll be at least sixteen months until the trial comes up. And they're looking for a third one."

"But they are in jail, for sure?"

"Yup. Nasty pictures. Then there's a rapist going around attacking sleeping women, but that seems to be south of here."

"My word, I'm glad we're in a gated place, aren't you? I think about that when I'm up north and see all my old friends walking alone or the group's driver has to go home alone. I don't mean to scare them, but I'm always talking about finding a safe place for them to live."

Daisy was nodding, and added, "Even with my guard dog, I never liked the nights alone."

"Daisy, how's your son?"

"It's a long story, Rissa. But he's home, so anything is better than last spring. He seems to have trouble reporting to someone regularly. You know, lawyers are pretty much their own bosses, and he's terribly depressed over the probation the court ordered."

"Is his wife helpful?"

"Perceptive as usual, Rissa. No, she's a complainer, about her part-time job, about not seeing Suz often enough, just about everything. I alternate between feeling sorry for Pete and being mad at him for upsetting the whole family."

"I can believe that."

After dinner, they all drifted in different directions, some to the theater and others toward the casitas. Daisy and Ellen fell into step. "Daisy, are you really worried about Pete?"

"Not too much. He knows what he needs to do, and he doesn't need his mother nagging at him. I might drive him back to drinking, and I'd do almost anything to prevent that."

"What's Julie's take on the situation?"

"My daughter's pretty wise. She was mad at her brother at first; then she realized he was addicted and couldn't help himself. He had to admit he needed help, but he wouldn't do it. So, it took a crisis to stop him. We both believe he's a strong guy and can make it through this. He's finding his faith again."

"Have you missed having Dave to talk to about Pete?"

"I have. He called last night from Minnesota and said the doctor is giving him a thirty percent chance of seeing in that eye again. Wouldn't that be wonderful?"

"Does he get along well with his son and wife?"

"Yes. Don and Amy are both in management of the biggest hospital in Minneapolis, so Dave feels he has extra support from them. In fact, they were the ones who begged him to come and meet this famous eye surgeon."

"So he's having surgery?"

"That's what he said, when the doctor can fit him in."

"Did you know he'd be gone so long?"

"No, I didn't. He's been a real comfortable kind of friend to have. I learned a lot about understanding my son from him."

"I know, and I'm glad." Ellen put her arm around Daisy's waist.

On Thursday, shortly before 3:00 in the Hedgehog Room, Malcolm added ice to the pitchers of tea and glasses, and poured a few glasses. "Expecting your usual ten?"

"Only six or seven. Clarissa is back as you know, but she may be too tired."

"Boy, she keeps going, doesn't she? This morning she called the office and reminded me that they'll be playing bridge tomorrow, just a warm-up she called it."

Robert was the first one to come in. "Hi, Malcolm, Daisy. How's it goin'? Keeping cool?"

Malcolm replied, "Not yet, but the days are getting shorter. How are you feeling, Captain?"

"Oh, some better. Don't know what got into me this summer, but I've been dragging."

"Bonnie says we need to get back into routine to feel good. We'll get the aerobics bunch going again and start some new groups. Will you need anything else today?"

"No, but thanks for your help."

Beth arrived next, with news that Alex had been sighted in the parking lot. "I waved, and he called out something about seeing us later."

"Good! We've all slowed down. Must be the heat. We expect summer to be over, but it never is until October."

When Donna came in, Beth asked about the cat population. "So far, my queen has been pretty tolerant of the youngsters. Terri used to bat at them when they came too close that first week. Now she kind of yawns and stretches and just glares at them. Hansel is the most aggressive, but he's learned. This is my second round of kitty-sitting, you know. First when Martha and Tom spent a week with Mary Ann and now while they're in Europe." Everyone smiled at the report.

The door burst open, and Alex came in with hugs for everyone. "It's good to be here, folks. Let me tell you, Texas is not the place for a summer vacation. It rained and then it steamed and then it rained some more. I've really become a desert rat. No more humidity for me. Now, how did the rest of you do?"

Beth agreed with him, "Illinois was damp this summer too, at least where I was. I've been back here for a month and glad of it. I'll think twice before I go next summer."

"Daisy, what'd you do, stick it out here all summer?"

"No, Curly and I went with Julie and her kids to San Diego, along with half of Phoenix. They coaxed me into staying ten days this year. It was beautiful, I must admit. I worried about my son Pete and his girls, but Julie kept telling me they needed time to be alone."

"I s'pose so. Any news about Pete?"

"He's doing all right."

"Okay, I understand. Have you been over to the Rose Lane Club lately?"

"Yes, just last Friday. They've had a bumper crop of kids this summer, and they really thanked us for sending some volunteers. Beth put out a sign-up sheet for the after-school hours."

"What's new from Tom and Martha?"

"Not a word. Had a note from her sister Mary Ann; she had a card from them in England."

"Wasn't that a great trip for them? They deserved it, like a late honeymoon."

As if on cue, Clarissa swept into the room, carrying a shiny pink bag marked Seattle. "I brought cookies and candies from my favorite shop. Let's just rip open the bag and dig in."

"Clarissa, you haven't changed a tad. How do you do it?"

"This climate makes me younger. I have to tell you, I just heard some really hot gossip."

They all chuckled at her announcement. Beth asked, "How could you hear something so fast? You've only been here twenty-four hours or so."

"Doesn't take long, once I see some of the bridge players. Did you hear about the Berringers?"

"About the divorce?"

"Yeah, isn't that sad? Why on earth would they split up after all these years?" The Captain shook his head.

Ellen replied, "I know what my husband would tell you. The toughest years are the first five and the last five."

"Why? You can't predict when the last five start."

"I know, but that was his wisdom. He said those are the years when people nit-pick about little habits and what he called 'peculiarities.' You know, those things that begin with the words, 'Why do you always. . .' and neither one knows the answer."

"Interesting."

Beth added, "I guess he's giving her the unit and going to live with his son. So, is she going to live alone in that big unit?"

Clarissa smiled and coyly suggested, "Maybe she'll find a new roommate." She passed the cookies around again.

Daisy raised her voice and said, "Seven of us are here, so let's sit down and talk about one thing at a time. Okay?"

Alex cleared his throat and announced loudly, "Meeting's starting. Come to order."

With a little fanfare, Daisy began. "Vacation's officially over, except for Tom and Martha. Dave can't be here, because his son and wife have arranged for him to be treated by a famous eye doctor at their hospital in Minneapolis. He says there's a thirty percent chance of his vision coming back in his bad eye. That's good news, so we'll keep him in our prayers. Any other concerns or joys we should celebrate?"

Ellen's hand shot up, and she said, "Yes! Sweet, young, little Emily has been elected Captain of the swim team, and that makes her a sure bet for a scholarship, at Georgia and maybe even at Indiana. Isn't that amazing?"

"Good for her. She's a leader, I could tell."

"Really? I guess I just thought of her as my sweet little granddaughter, forever fourteen."

"I think she'll surprise you. Any other news?"

Alex spoke up and asked, "How are we going to bring these new folks into our groups?"

Clarissa offered, "I've already met a few and recruited three new bridge players. One more and we'll have a new table."

"I'll play," Robert said. "I played some this past summer and kind of enjoyed it. Kind of. It's not my favorite thing to do, but I need something to get me going again."

"We'll get you going, sir. Before you know it, you'll be going to the senior prom over at St. Barnabas." There were laughs around the table, and he blushed.

"Alex, what did you do in Texas for five weeks?"

"Hey, I'm retired from my office, and I'm not a property owner any more. What freedom! My kids needed some help in their business. They got me involved in building a new office for them, and it felt good to be back in legal stuff. I got them set up better, tax-wise, and it was fun being with their kids too."

Daisy nodded. "The next generation grows on you, doesn't it? I have to be careful not to get too involved with my college freshmen. Mark ended up at ASU, and he's living on campus. Suzette had a tough time accepting her changed plans, but she'll be all right at Scottsdale Community for this year. If they can foot the bill by next year, maybe she can transfer to Claremont."

"I had a note from Mary Ann and she's fine. Loves what she's doing. The place has expanded, and she's into some counseling with the mothers of her children."

"Boy, she really has the experience to do good things for people. I envy her those skills!"

Clarissa spoke up, "Bob, you could do those things too. You could go to the Club after school and teach the little boys to do something good. Are you a good swimmer?"

"Well, yes, I am. I never thought about teaching someone else to swim. Don't know how you do that."

"Think about it. Couldn't you build model boats to sail over at the park there?"

"Gosh, Clarissa, you're full of ideas, aren't you. What vitamin pills do you take?"

So the afternoon was a reunion of the friends who had come together as Daisy's remnants.

CHAPTER 38

New Neighbors

DAISY AND CURLY WERE out early, hoping to beat the heat, which was still intense. "Come on, Old Boy, get back on the walk. Curly, come, now!" Daisy bent down and patted him. "What's bothering you over there?" She squinted toward the front window of Unit 23 and saw something round and shiny on a small table. "C'mon, Curly. Someone lives there now. We can't be snoopy." However, she was curious. "Maybe it's a small aquarium. That'll drive the cats wild."

As they were coming back, Beth flagged her down. "Come in for coffee, you two." Curly was welcome everywhere, so Daisy accepted Beth's offer. "Have you been down this side of the green?"

"Sure. We started out that way."

"Did you see anything unusual?"

"No. Well, wait a minute. Curly saw something new in the window of Unit 23."

"That's what I mean. Last night I strolled out after dark, just to get some fresh air before bed. A small candle was burning in that window. Beside it was a big crystal ball. Did you see it?"

"Well, I didn't want to be too nosy, but Curly seemed very interested in it. Does it have fish in it?"

"Of course not. It's the kind of solid glass bowl that fortunetellers use."

"Seriously?"

"Yes, Daisy. I'm trying to tell you what I saw. A woman came toward the candle and that ball and sat down at the table. She put her hands on the ball. Then she blew out the candle, so I couldn't see anything more. Isn't that odd?"

"Maybe. Do we know who she is?"

"I'm going to find out. What if she tells fortunes and gets everyone around here believing in spirits?"

"Now, Beth, isn't that a bit of a stretch? No one can have a business on the premises, so she can't go too far."

"Nevertheless, I'm going to find out about her."

"Fine, and be sure to tell me too. Wouldn't it be easier just to pay her a visit and take her some cookies or something?"

Beth looked a little sheepish and said, "I guess you're right. I don't know why it bothered me so much. Well, yes, I do know why. Bruce actually consulted a seer one time when his father was ill. His mother said she knew why, but said she'd go to the grave with that secret."

"Heavens, what a thing to tell her son."

"I know. It bothered him. But the gypsy he met with didn't know anything either. It was such a waste of time and money."

"There are people who would argue with you."

"Yeah, I know. I'll keep still about this. See if you can find out anything, Daisy."

"We'll try. Curly, it's time to go home and start the day. Thanks for the coffee, Beth."

As Daisy left for the church Saturday morning, she found a business card on her windshield. She pulled it out and read:

Violet Vance

Readings, Tarot Cards

Channeling

Your confidante

On all spiritual levels

480-777-0121

"Oh, my, won't Beth be interested in this!" She went on her way to check over the choir robes.

When she returned, there was a beautiful pot of yellow mums at her door with a note tied to the ribbon. She read aloud, "I'm back and hope to see you tonight. Dave." The word *see* was underlined. Daisy smiled and wondered if it meant his sight was improved. "Well, Curly, we might have company before the day is out. We'd better tidy up around here. I might even brush you again today."

News of the business cards of Violet Vance spread through the community by noon. Beth commented, "She must be nice to choose a card that matches the interior of my car." Then she laughed heartily.

"Now, Beth, be nice. Maybe people think I'm strange to work on sewing projects all the time. And you do spend a lot of time reading mysteries. That's what makes you so suspicious."

"It is not. I'm just a detail person and like to put together all the little clues."

Ellen joined them and accused them of whispering in the dining room. "You two look as if you're up to mischief."

"Us? Never. You don't have a car, so you don't know what we're talking about. Daisy, show her the card."

Daisy handed it to Ellen and said, "We don't know who she is. We must be careful not to say anything out loud."

"This was on your car? So it's someone who lives here?"

"Yes, in Unit 23. Remember, the place where Mr. Hoover ended it all?"

"Beth, we really must never refer to that event."

"I promise, I won't breathe a word of it. But someone else is sure to tell her."

Donna slid into an empty chair, followed by Alice and Clarissa. "What a great table we have this noon! Donna, have you had any First Aid patients lately?"

"Not many. A few blisters from a hiker last week, and some medical references for the new couple, the Ansons. They seemed very pleasant, very well-traveled. She mentioned they speak Spanish and hoped to start a class here. Wouldn't that be useful?"

"Definitely. I wish they ate with all of us so we'd get acquainted."

"You're right; the dining room and the pool are the best places to meet people."

Clarissa added, "Or the beauty parlor. Now that's where you really get all your questions answered. Recipes, diet tips, news about TV shows, almost anything you ask."

Phyllis Fenton asked if she could sit with them, and of course everyone agreed. "I'm having a very bad day," she confided.

"What's troubling you, Phyllis?" Ellen was always ready to help.

"I have a new neighbor who's trying to frighten me. I put two new towels outside to dry yesterday afternoon, and they're gone today. That means someone was on my patio."

"Wouldn't you have seen a person right outside your door?"

"Oh, no. I keep my blinds closed against the sun."

"Do you lock your gate?"

"Well, no. Do you?"

Daisy replied, "Not locked, but closed so Curly won't wander away."

"As if Curly would leave you! But seriously, at night you lock up, don't you?"

A few nodded in agreement. Ellen continued, "Phyllis, do you have some idea who might have borrowed your towels?"

"No, they're stolen, I'm sure. Last week I lost a letter that Bonnie swore she put in my mailbox. I set it down right beside me at the movie, and when the lights came on, it was gone. See? Someone is trying to scare me. It must be that new person living in Unit 23. That's a haunted place. My telephone rings at odd hours, and no one is there to talk to me."

Daisy rose to the challenge. "Why don't you make an appointment to talk with Donna? She has been so helpful to others around here. She's a good friend to all of us, and I think she'd have some ideas to comfort you." Privately, she exchanged a nod with Donna and thought Donna would be able to analyze the symptoms.

Donna immediately offered to chat with her. "How about this afternoon around 3:00?"

Phyllis seemed doubtful but said, "Really? You think we could figure out what to do?"

"We'll try. Please, come see me at the First Aid Station."

Daisy, Beth and Ellen strolled across the grass, enjoying the cloudy afternoon. "That was good of you, Daisy, to suggest that Phyllis could talk to Donna."

"Well, she can talk about having the lock changed on Phyllis' gate or changing her phone number. She's dealt with these things before."

"Do you think Phyllis is getting a little fuzzy in the mind?"

"Maybe. She's been very fearful as long as I've known her. Jane Simpson was a neighbor of hers, and she told me at church that Phyllis *needed* to be in a guarded community."

"We probably all *need* to be." They laughed, but then Ellen went on. "It's so hard to see some changes in people here. I never knew them before, but I wish I had. It must be important for Bonnie and Malcolm as Directors to be observant of the changes."

"I told Martha last summer when I did some alterations for her that it's easy to alter clothes to fit, but it's tough to make this place and its programs fit all of us as we age."

"You're so right."

CHAPTER 39

November's Here Already

Ellen greeted the group on Thursday in the Hedgehog Room with a signal to be quiet and hide around the corner of the closet. In the center of the table stood a beautiful chocolate layer cake with one large candle. Then it dawned on Daisy that it was Beth's birthday. By the time six of them had huddled in the corner, Ellen hummed a note and became the choir director.

Beth gasped at the scene and the others appeared, with Clarissa following Beth. Robert came along the hall and joined the Happy Birthday chorus. "Once more," shouted Clarissa, and they all sang with gusto as she directed them.

"How did you remember? I haven't told anyone."

Ellen confessed, "During our life stories, I made a note about each birth date. Now wasn't that fun?" She lighted the candle and told Beth and everyone to make a wish. "See, at least one of our wishes is bound to come true."

This was their fourth meeting, and they still hadn't chosen a formal topic for the fall. They considered ideas like the best thing about La Ventura or the best Christmas they remembered. Then Alex suggested they write about the person who had most influenced their young lives. "We could put these short pieces together and maybe give out copies down at the Clubhouse to the youth group. Aren't they the junior high school age? It might be like mentoring them."

The idea sounded good, and they agreed to try to write a page before the next meeting on November sixteenth. The meeting dispersed in time for dinner.

The knock on Daisy's door startled her but sounded familiar. She opened it cautiously, and there stood Dave. He stepped in and engulfed her in a bear hug. "Daisy, dear lady, why are you crying? I meant to make you happy."

"You do, Dave. I am so happy to see you." She dabbed at her tears. "Come in and tell me about your summer. I started to call it a vacation, but I guess it was more serious than that."

"It was, and it's good news. I can see light and shapes with that eye, and it's changing every day. Even if it never gets better, I feel more normal. I can see you better. Now tell me about you." He reached over to her and gave her another hug. "I didn't know I'd miss you, and all the rest of them."

"We've been comparing notes, and we're all the same way, critical of where we went and asking such caring questions about each other. It's amazing."

"Curly, Old Boy, I didn't mean to ignore you. You're a patient beast, aren't you?" All this time, Dave had been rubbing Curly's ear and patting him. "Daisy, tell me. How's Pete? You didn't sound very confident about him when we talked a few weeks ago."

"I'm always afraid. I can't build up my trust that he's really sober, and yet I never knew he wasn't. I used to talk to him, and he was often in a hurry or in the car. But I never suspected he was drinking. Now that I know what's at stake, I'm really fearful."

"I can believe it. He's home?"

"Yes, but he's having physical therapy for the stroke damage to his left foot and hand. Susie takes him, and one of his partners picks him up and brings him home on his lunch hour. It works really well."

"She's working still?"

"Yes, but she hates it, feels it's degrading. Can you believe it? I didn't know she had those notions about working women."

"And Suzette? You said she's at SCC?"

"Yes, and doing very well. She's determined to get a scholarship for next year. She lives at home and grumbles about that a lot. I feel sorry for Pete on that score."

"Yeah, that's too bad. Makes him feel guilty. Doesn't help his self-image. Does he seem to think and talk straight?"

"I don't know, I mean, about legal talk. He speaks a little slowly in regular conversation."

"Any speech therapy?"

"No, and I've learned he doesn't want to talk about any treatments. He about flipped when the therapist offered him a cane, but he took it home and uses it only when they go out."

Dave smiled knowingly, and said, "I know. When I left the hospital seven years ago, my cane was white. That's the worst. Tell me about our buddies, the writers."

Grateful for the change in subject, Daisy started with Clarissa, the most colorful one. "Now she's organizing a tournament, because two of the new residents are champions. She has Robert playing too, can you believe it? He sounded depressed one day, and that's all it took to get her started. She calls him Bob now. She has him signed up to give a program about his life as a ship captain to the youth group at her church."

"And he's thriving again?"

"Oh, yes. And Donna looks good. She was kitty-sitting while Tom and Martha were gone. They got back from the cathedral tour and three weeks in England in mid-October. Donna's still in the nurse's office and loving it. She and Alice Turner hit the movies at least once a week. Dear Ellen is full of news about Emily. I'll let her tell you all about her. Beth is upset about a new woman down her way, in Unit 23."

"Wasn't that where that guy lived who was so depressed?"

"It was, and that's hard to forget. The new gal is named Violet and she's into spiritual things like predicting the future for people."

"No, really? Tea leaves and stuff?"

"Yes, and Bonnie and Malcolm are keeping an eye on her business. She's quite popular at the county fair and some of the art shows, but in a very kind, pretty way. She's beautiful and wears lovely sweeping sorts of garments. She's modeled at some luncheons at the Camelback Inn, and you know, there's nothing amiss that I can see. Beth just took it too seriously, I think."

Dave reached for Daisy's hand and said, "I feel as if I've been gone a year instead of four months. Do we still eat at the same time? All right if I come by here and walk you to dinner, Lady?"

Curly rose from the floor at the sound of the word *dinner*, and they laughed together. "It would be nice, Dave. I still need your advice, and I'm so thankful for your help last spring."

"Hey, what are friends for? You included me in your life even though I was a blind, back-sliding Lutheran who couldn't drive or get out of the pool gracefully. Thanks for that." He stood and went toward the door. "I see the flowers are doing their best."

"I forgot to say thank you, and they're wonderful. This place could stand some color after the hot summer."

"See you in an hour, Daisy, my lass."

She sat down in the loveseat and called Curly over. "What do you think of that, Curly? My friend Dave sounds like a date, doesn't he? I'm glad you approve of him, Old Boy."

As Election Day drew nearer, Beth once again complained about the political ads on TV. "The politicians are making me *sick*. I may not vote this year!"

Alex tried to calm her. "If you don't vote, you're just being one of the lazy voters who think one vote doesn't matter."

"Well, I can't stand lazy people, so I'll vote, but it may not be for my old friends the Republicans."

"I'm not telling you how to vote. Just get over there and be counted. You're registered, aren't you?"

"Oh, yes. Count me in."

Probably Beth's vote was one of the 399,000 new votes for Governor Janet over her 560,000 in 2002. Dinner table talk avoided local politics; so many residents were from other states.

No one overlooked the results of the House and Senate races, however. Ellen's comment to Daisy was, "Your dad and my husband would have been pleased with the outcomes, right?"

"Probably, but ministers learn not to be too vocal about their votes."

As Thanksgiving approached, Daisy noted it would be the first family gathering since Pete had been ill and then arrested. Would it be a tense scene? The family rallied nicely, with Susie helping in the kitchen and Suz setting the tables. Her best friend was with them, and Mark brought a girl who couldn't get home to Nova Scotia. Matt carved the turkey. Pete was unusually quiet, but Daisy thought it was a nice change from the more boisterous years when he and Matt tended to become live entertainment.

Julie packed her a C.A.R.E. package of turkey plus pumpkin pie. By 4:00 she was ready to say farewells and thank you's to the crowd.

When Daisy let herself in and Curly out, she picked up a telephone message from Dave. "How about a glass of wine and a turkey sandwich at 7:00? Your place or mine?" Curly let himself in and listened with her. His tail was wagging; he was a sociable dog. "Well, Curly, where do we go from here?" She punched the play button again and smiled as she listened.

She took her things to the kitchen and noticed Julie had included two pieces of pie. "That's my part of the deal," she said softly to herself. She dialed Dave's number. After four rings, his answering machine came on. She left a message: "I accept your offer, but I can also offer pumpkin pie. Your place or mine?" She hung up and laughed at herself. "Daisy, you're having fun over this. You haven't had fun in so long, you've almost forgotten how to laugh! C'mon, Curly. I'll fix your dinner early."

CHAPTER 40

Holiday Highlights

RESIDENTS WERE INVITED to a special Tuesday Night Social Hour to meet new people. The lavender name tags identified ten new arrivals. Bonnie made the introductions and added certain information, mostly about where they had recently lived.

Daisy sat with Clarissa and watched her make notes about the new names. "You're still watching for more card players, aren't you?"

"Sure, but also listening for anyone from the Northwest. Don't you like to find people from your old territory?"

"I do, but remember I'm the one who lived all over."

"That's right. I forgot. I do remember the year when Martha was new and she met Tom."

"So do I. That's a real success story, isn't it?"

Then Bonnie was talking about a Doctor Richard Ruggles from San Fernando, California. "He's eager to get back to the land of golf and steady ground beneath his feet. Ask him where he was during that last little quake." Robert was quick to move over to talk to the doctor.

Daisy was waiting to hear about Violet Vance since her cookie visit had been so brief. "I'm not being a good Chamber of Commerce this year, Clarissa."

"You've had enough on your mind, dear."

Dave pulled a chair up beside Daisy and whispered, "I just met Vi." Daisy turned to look at him and saw the mischievous look on his face.

"Where?"

He replied, "About four rows behind you and near the far wall."

She shifted around in her chair and soon was able to look that way. Today Vi was even prettier in a soft shade of green gauze. "Are you thinking about consulting her?"

He said, "I'm concerned about my future, aren't you?"

Daisy could hardly suppress her giggles. "Hush."

Bonnie continued, "Violet Vance is another new member of our village, and she comes from Los Angeles. Be sure to ask her about her work in the studios. She knows some of the most fascinating people. I meant to ask you, Violet, why did you leave Southern California? It's not nearly so warm over there."

Violet stood and said, "To tell you the truth, I came here to leave all that celebrity glitz behind." She smiled and shrugged. "I know it's hard to believe, but I think Arizona people are more down to earth." A few people clapped and laughed. Someone called out, "Welcome."

The door opened and a woman entered tentatively. Bonnie called out to her, "Hi, Gen. I'm glad you got home early enough to join us." She turned to the crowd and went on, "Gen Farley works at the hospital until eight, usually. She has future plans to join us, however, as soon as they let her retire. Now, why don't you all mingle around and greet these new managers. The punch bowl tonight is pineapple and orange mix. The usual drinks are in Ben's care."

Dave stood and offered to get something for Daisy. "I think I'll have a glass of chardonnay. I'll keep our seats here." While she waited, Martha sat in Dave's chair. "How are you, Martha? Do you have any new recruits in the twelve-step group?"

"I do. Isn't that amazing? The group keeps going. When some drop out, others seem to arrive. I know it's important to have the meetings available."

"Definitely! I think Bonnie and Malcolm handle the subject well too. They always provide something special to drink at these meetings and announce it. Where's Donna tonight?"

"Haven't seen her all day. Haven't seen Alex either. Did he have a good summer?"

"Yes. He was with his kids in Texas and does *not* recommend Texas in the summer."

"Too hot and sticky? I don't miss that at all. Madison usually had cool, lovely months, but if it once got hot, it was steaming hot. No air conditioning either."

"I remember. Thanks, Dave. Martha, just slide over here. Dave has another chair."

"Well, world traveler, did the cathedrals measure up to your dreams?" he asked.

"Yes, indeed. I'll never know how the people built those huge places without the machinery we have today."

"It's amazing. There are a couple of great novels written about the workmen who lived at the site for years while they cut the stones or built the platforms to raise the beams."

"I'd like to read one now that I've seen them."

Dave turned to Daisy. "Did you ever get to Europe in all your husband's assignments?"

"No, never. All of Scott's work was for a government office, state or national."

"We'll have to do that someday. Excuse me a minute. I want to meet Bill Anson. I've known him somewhere else."

"I've never laid eyes on the man. Are they guests or owners?" Martha had missed their arrival.

Daisy explained what she'd heard about them and their meals. "I don't know if they have allergies or diets or are just reserved people. They'll join us for Sunday brunch."

"Tom and I like having lunch at home. Dinner over here seems more like a party when we've been home all day."

"Except you're not home all day."

Martha laughed and agreed. "We've had more fun down at the Boys & Girls Club. Mary Ann got us into the best part of it, the after school program. Tom has the best teaching job; the boys are learning how to cook in a micro. They learn to use paper plates and plastic wrap. It's much healthier food than fried stuff. I'm teaching a knitting class, so the girls can make a Christmas gift for their moms. First they made a scarf for themselves."

"I'm glad to hear all that. It makes me feel good that we share our comfortable lives and free time."

Martha and Tom proposed that the expanded Thursdays at Three friends plan what to do for the clubhouses this year. "We could find out what they need the most and then report to you all. Could we still have the annual Christmas lunch for the ten of us after we deliver the gifts?"

Tom said, "We could go down to Mom's Bar & Grill."

"Great idea, Tom. I still remember that good pizza from there on your birthday," Ellen encouraged him.

Daisy kept very still, waiting to see if Dave had anything to say. She carefully avoided looking at Tom. She had succeeded in putting the 1999 accident in the back of her consciousness, but now all the details flooded into her mind. She was grateful to hear Ellen's question.

"Is it a big enough place for a big round table of ten?"

"As a matter of fact, it might not be. Is that the kind of seating you'd like?"

"It's what we've done before, but we could do it differently."

Then Dave spoke up. "How about Arizona Country Club? I could arrange it, and you all could chip in later when my bill comes. It's such a pretty place at Christmas."

"Hey, Dave, that'd be super. I've never been there, but I've heard it's good."

"I know enough people there to set it up. Still go the barber there when I can get a ride." As he talked, Daisy realized there was a lot she didn't know about Dave's life. "Martha, you two can plan the gifts, and I'll do the food. Do we exchange gifts too?"

"No, that first year we decided we all had enough stuff to wear and take care of, so we'd give to an agency. Every year we collect money to buy whatever they say they need. Daisy was our first contact, and then Mary Ann. I'll ask about it tomorrow afternoon when we're working at the Clubhouse."

Daisy's telephone was ringing as she unlocked her door. "Donna, what's wrong, dear? We missed you at dinner last night and lunch today." She listened. "Terri's dying? She's at the vet's? Oh, Donna, I'm so sorry to hear this. What can I do to help? Sure, I'll call the others, right away. You're waiting to hear from the vet?" Daisy looked at her watch. "Want me to come over and wait with you?"

Daisy turned from the phone and patted Curly. "Time for you to go out, friend." I have some calls to make before dinner."

Amid the preparations for Christmas and sympathizing with Donna over Terri's demise, the Thursdays at Three writing plans were tabled. "Probably just as well the fall schedule never blossomed," Daisy commented to Ellen. "How do we get so busy?"

"We thought we were coming here to be lazy. Your letter reminded us of all the things we wouldn't have to do any more, and we'd have our meals prepared for us. You didn't know we'd get so involved with the town and our churches."

"But isn't that wonderful?"

"Yup. It's just surprising. You and your remnant idea."

"It was you who referred to the remnants in the Bible. You knew we'd have to do something since we were being spared."

"By the way, did you write a Christmas letter?"

"Very short one that I folded inside the new card from the church."

"Is there anyone else who might come because of your first letter?"

"No, I don't think so. Sue would never leave Boston. Betty is immersed in Santa Fe and her artist's life, and Evelyn could never get away from all her responsibilities."

"You didn't invite anybody new?"

"Nope, because we have such a great bunch right here."

"Whoa, check the time. We need to get ready for dinner. See you over there."

Wreaths appeared on most of the doors, and there were lots of signs about 'Happy Holidays' to combine Jewish and Christian celebrations. Incoming mail increased, much to everyone's pleasure. Clarissa polished up her holiday music and played in the Great Room several times a week. The Bunch of Daisy's delivered three carloads of hams and turkeys, fleece coverlets and warm jackets plus an assortment of toys. At the last minute, Robert bought a huge train set, took it to the Rose Lane Clubhouse and set it up for the younger children. The spirit of the season revived their four-year tradition. Daisy recalled someone's cutting remark about the seniors who retire in Scottsdale being so self-centered they act like permanent tourists. Her reply was, "Not my friends!"

Dave suggested that a group of them go to the Christmas Eve service at Valley Church. With four cars, they were able to transport fourteen others. The Ventura van took another dozen to Our Lady of Perpetual Help and St. Maria Goretti. Back in their assigned parking places around ten-fifteen, they said their farewells. Dave walked Daisy back to her Unit 7. Curly greeted them royally and bounded out into the crisp night air.

"Daisy, you've become my closest friend. Does that bother you?"

She laughed and replied, "Of course not. I've always been the kind of person to have loads of friends, but no one really close in the last ten years. Do you know what I mean?"

"Yeah, me too. I think that's what comes of having a good solid marriage. That's the person you confide in or trust with your feelings."

Curly wanted in, and they both followed him inside. "Want me to make us a cup of coffee?"

"I'd like that. Even better if you still have any of those cookies."

"Sure. Let me get the pot started first." She noticed how easily he moved over to the counter with the cookie jar and helped himself. "I like your kitchen better than mine. I can't figure out what makes it different. Our floor plans are about the same, aren't they?"

"No, this first building is attached at the back to the hall leading to the mailboxes and the bank. See? I don't have that little window you have."

"Okay, I see. It gives you one more cabinet and more counter space."

"I'm glad now that I'm here, but when I saw the place, there was no choice. I picked this unit because the patio had a bit of a view and was two feet wider than the one next door. Malcolm accused me of picking lucky seven."

"It's been pretty lucky, hasn't it?"

"True. End units are quieter too, and the man in Unit 6 is La Ventura's accountant, you know."

"Yeah, I've met him. Nice guy, probably quiet."

"He is. He told me Curly is can defend his place too."

"Coffee's good, and those cookies are really good."

"I'm glad you like them, because they're the easiest to make." They sat comfortably in separate chairs with Curly between them hoping for a crumb.

"It's getting late, and I'd better be going." Dave stood. "I never want to leave here, but I don't mind the walk home. I review everything we've said. You're that important to me." He gave her a hug and was out the door before she could say anything.

"Curly, I'm doing the same thing, thinking about the meaning of every word." She put away their dishes and put out the lights. In the flickering light of her miniature table tree, she found herself wondering what it would be like if Dave lived next door. Or maybe even closer.

CHAPTER 41

Happy New Year, 2007

THE NEW CLASS SCHEDULE was posted in the hall. The choices were: Crochet for Beginners, Investment Club, Arizona Politics, Line Dance, Writing (Topic TBA), and Opportunities to Volunteer. Watercolor and Wood Carving were continuing favorites. There was a sign-up sheet for water aerobics as well as the Driver Safety Class offered by AARP. "What a lineup!" said Alex. Others gathered around to read the notice. "Daisy, did you reserve our Thursdays at Three room?"

"Yessir. I wasn't sure when to start again, but we've done well on the first and third of the month. That would be this week on the fifth or wait until the nineteenth."

"Thursdays, you mean?"

"Yes. That doesn't conflict with the others, does it?"

"No, I think they know we're a permanent organization, so I'll ask our friends about a starting date. This extra sign-up looks good too: Digital Photography for New Camera Owners. I should take that."

"So long as it isn't on Thursday afternoon, go for it. Do you think we should advertise our group? We don't want to be snobbish." Daisy shook her head as she spoke.

After dinner that night, Martha came up to Daisy and said she'd heard about two of the singles moving in together. "Do you think they should?"

"What could we possibly do to stop them? Or should we? Do you know who it is?"

"No, I heard about it from Tom who heard it from another guy at the pool table."

"Pure gossip, in other words."

"Yes," she said slowly, "but it could give the place a bad name, don't you think?"

"Let's find out who's involved and if it really is a permanent arrangement."

"Okay, I'll see if Tom can find out more."

"You know, that goes on in other communities, I've heard, because the people don't have to change their Social Security status. It's not as if they're going to have families. I know two who actually did have a wedding ceremony, very quietly, but they kept their former names, and I don't think it was a legal event, more of a personal promise."

"I knew a couple of women back in Madison who shared a home and pooled their resources. I guess that's about the same. They said they saved money on food and utilities. But we don't have those bills."

"It's good we have Directors here to watch over all of us, not just the Resident Managers like us who might change the rules on a whim."

Martha looked stunned at Daisy's words. "It's not just a whim, Daisy. I'm concerned about the proper way to live. We have a reputation to maintain."

"Only our own, dear."

"You're telling me to mind my own business, aren't you? Tom is very concerned about the appearance of things too."

"Well, let's give it some time and see what the whole story is." Daisy thought to herself that perhaps Tom had often let himself get too involved in other people's lives, including hers.

On the nineteenth, the Thursday group arrived in the Hedgehog Room with papers and pens, eager to talk about their mentors or people they had admired. Ellen asked where Beth could be, and then said, "Have we invited anyone new to join us?"

Silence prevailed until Donna came in. Robert spoke quickly, "Let's just call Donna our newest member, and then we can feel good about being an open group."

Donna laughed and said, "You can't get away with that, Captain. Either we're open to new people or we're not. You were all so quick to urge me to join you, and I don't even like to write."

"But you wanted to be part of the Bunch of Daisy's?"

"I do belong to Daisy. When I lost Terri I was glad to have friends who understood why I was so sad. You all had heard my life story. A couple of people told me just to go out and find another cat, as if they're all the same." Tears came to her eyes.

"You know, that's not a bad idea, even if it was said all wrong. Why don't we go and look at some kittens, or maybe visit the Pound, whatever they call the place for lost cats."

Donna looked at Robert as if she'd never known him before. "You would do that with me?"

"Sure. Want to go now?" The group chuckled at his enthusiasm.

"Do you honestly like cats?"

"Don't know. Never had one on shipboard. I imagine they're pretty good company."

"I accept your offer, Robert. Maybe tomorrow afternoon? I have to work in the morning."

"Sure. After lunch. I'll find out the address and stuff later this afternoon."

Alex came in and took the last empty chair. "You're all waiting for me to pound the gavel and call us to order. Well, consider it done." He pounded a fist on the table in fun. "Is there any more coffee?"

Daisy found another mug and poured a hot cup for him. "Alex, did you think of someone to write about?"

"Not yet. Have a couple of ideas, but I wasn't sure what you wanted to know about them."

"Maybe we could make a list of what traits make someone a strong influence." With that, Beth offered to write on the white board if they would dictate ideas. "Remember, no one is wrong when we brainstorm."

Writing about their mentors and memories of teachers and coaches kept the group talking and comparing notes for the rest of January. Alex summed up their efforts well when he said, "This makes me realize that we could be important to some of the kids we meet. Lots of the boys have told me they only see their dads once a month or at the holidays. You know, we grew up in years when most of us had two parents. We were lucky to hear their opinions on what's important in life. Some of these kids are only with their moms and just at the end of the workday or early morning."

The group agreed to take this assignment more seriously and put it in writing.

Valentine's Day in 2007 was announced as The First Annual Art Show. "Why haven't we ever done this before?" Malcolm asked Daisy. "Those dear people have been painting in the craft room ever since we opened."

"It's because most of us are just interested in our hobbies as pastimes, not careers. I'm still surprised that our writers are willing to share so much personal stuff in our group."

"That's because you were the organizer, Daisy, and everyone knew you."

"Yes, but I don't write!"

"You do now."

"We all have to make changes. In fact, that's a good thing about this place. As Directors, you and Bonnie always seem interested in new ideas."

"Speaking of changes, we're adding another concert series this spring. And I bought us thirty tickets to the Rembrandt show at Phoenix Art Museum. Think I'm going too far?"

"Heavens, no. Our little bunch will probably take ten of each."

"They're expensive, you know."

"Yes, but people will pay for quality entertainment."

"What else needs changing around here?"

Daisy looked thoughtful. "Do the new people get the same information sheets we got, you know, about policies here and suggestions for getting along with your neighbors? I remember thinking that was a great one, since most of us hadn't been in community living for a long time."

"Sure, they get them. We've added some color and put them into a packet, but it's about the same. Have you heard complaints?"

"Once in a while someone asks me what I think about some rumor."

"Such as?"

"Well, a while ago, Martha asked me if there were rules about someone moving in with another person."

"Does she regret marrying Tom?"

"No, no. But they did get married, officially, and they think others should too."

"Hm. I heard some of that too. By the time Bonnie and I had worded an announcement, I was pretty sure the problem was over. Not that it couldn't happen again, but we're not trying to be the housing police."

"That was my comment at the time, especially since I heard it was just a 'trial run.' If that happened in our old neighborhood, no one would pay any attention. What were you going to say?"

"Words to the effect that small units are designed for single residents, and if anyone wishes to find a larger unit and join forces with another resident, please see the Directors."

"Very cool wording. You two are great!"

"Thanks. Well, keep me posted if you hear something I should know about."

Daisy surveyed the whole campus as she walked home and thought again what a good place she had chosen. A message was waiting for her. "Could you and Curly make one of your friendly visits to El Nido to see Phyllis Fenton? She's a new resident in the D Unit and doesn't seem to talk much. Thanks for your help, as always."

"Curly, did you hear that? We're needed again. Maybe around three we'll pay her a visit. She's frightened of everything but you and me." Curly stretched and acted ready to go.

The landscaping around El Nido began to look mature, and the entrance had a welcoming look, even though the door also had an automatic lock that clanged shut behind them. They rang the bell and were admitted. Curly had become accustomed to the elevator, so they went up to the third floor and found Phyllis.

"Daisy, you're a dear to come and see me. I should never have consulted that fortuneteller about my future. Everything has gone wrong since then." Phyllis began to look weepy.

"Now, Phyllis, don't cry. This is a lovely place to stay. You're safe here and can rest easy that no one is trying to frighten you."

"But she was. I'll bet she knows someone else she wants to have living near her, not me."

"I doubt it. She's a very busy lady, attending all the local fairs and art shows. She helps a program at the Veterans Hospital in Phoenix, by analyzing handwriting. She's been consulted by the police in missing person cases."

Phyllis's eyes widened as Daisy spoke. "You mean she really knows something about the spirits?"

"She knows something about people. Did she tell you something scary?"

"Yes, she said someone who is eighty will die this year, someone with white hair and a little overweight. It will be a big surprise and very sad."

Daisy smiled. "That could be one of forty people here."

"Yes, but she patted my hand in a knowing way. I'm not ready to die, Daisy."

"No matter how much someone feels ready to die, it's always a surprise, Phyllis."

"She told me she had predicted that a big old cat would die before Christmas. Isn't that when Donna's cat died?"

"Yes, it was. But you can't live every day in fear. Donna wouldn't have enjoyed her cat the day before Terri died if she had been fearful."

Phyllis took a big breath, frowned and said, "I guess that's true. What will happen to all my things when I die?"

"You should take some time and write instructions. You'd find that was fun. I did it, and I felt much better."

"You mean, really plan?"

"That's right. Just review in your mind each piece of furniture or china and think about who would get the most use out of it. I left instructions to send a lot of my things to the Salvation Army or the church mission sale."

"Did you? What a nice project. Do you think a nurse could bring me paper and a nice pen?"

"I'll ask as we leave. Curly needs a pat on the head. You know, he was brave to come up here in the elevator."

"Well, dear Curly, come closer." At that, he was on the bed, snuggling in beside her. "Oh, dear, I didn't know he'd do that so fast."

They laughed, and as soon as she'd patted him, Daisy called him off the bed and pointed to the doorway. "Bye, bye for now. We'll be back to see you."

"Don't forget the paper and pen."

CHAPTER 42

A Visit from Pete

FRIDAY AFTERNOONS WERE usually quiet. A few of the residents went away on weekends, and others went shopping for food in one of the vans. Daisy strolled home from the library with a couple of new books and found Pete waiting at her door. "How great to see you here!" she exclaimed. "Come on in." Curly was all over Pete with barks and jumps.

"I decided it was time for me to get out of the house. Suzette was going back to the campus and gave me a ride. I thought maybe you'd give me a lift home."

"Of course. Now tell me all about you. How are you feeling? Curly, settle down."

"The physical therapy is going pretty well, and. . ." A sharp knock at the door stopped him and started Curly's barking again.

Daisy opened it to find Dave standing there with a single red rose and a rolled up piece of pink paper in one hand and his cane in the other. "I hoped you'd be home."

"Come in, please. I want you to meet Pete. Pete, this is my friend, Dave Olson."

"Hi, Dave. I can see you're on a timely errand. My daughter helped to save me from forgetting the date." They laughed, and Dave handed Daisy the rose and the paper.

"I'm late, but only by two days. The Art Show filled Wednesday, and then I had a writing assignment for Thursday.

One big deal per day, you know." He turned toward Pete. "I've looked forward to meeting you, Pete." They shook hands and sat down. Dave went on. "Your mother's a very special friend of mine, and she's shared her concern about you. Yes, yes, Curly, you're a special friend too, Old Boy. Now sit down here."

"Concern might be a weak word. I imagine she's been as mad at me as my wife and daughter are."

Daisy tried to protest, but Dave took over. "No, she's given me a great picture of how my wife and daughter might have felt over the years."

"Oh? Whatever it was, you've lived through it and look good."

"I am healthy, thanks, but I made some rotten choices in my life."

Pete looked down at his hands and didn't speak right away. Finally he looked at Daisy and said, "Mom, I'm so sorry for what I've caused. I'm more than sorry; I'm ashamed. I'm embarrassed. I regret so much."

Dave smiled at Pete and said firmly, "My boy, you're well on the road to recovery. You've just turned the first corner. Don't quit, because that first one is the hardest. You never want to turn it again."

"Yeah, it was the toughest for me to admit I couldn't fix Humpty Dumpty. I still can hardly believe how much help I need. I've always been the helper."

"Thank God, there's help out there. If you ever, and I mean *ever*, need a buddy, you have one right here in old Dave Olson."

Daisy broke the tension, asking if they'd like some coffee. Both nodded yes.

Pete added, "That's one taste I've developed at AA. This one guy makes all the coffee, buys it at Costco, and it's always so good."

"It's fresh. That's the difference I learned. We used to make pot after pot until everyone had enough caffeine to speak up."

"Yeah, it took a lot of caffeine to get me to open up."

"I watched for a while, really impressed by the old timers."

"Amazing isn't it? One of our guys just celebrated his thirtieth birthday, and he never misses a meeting."

Daisy returned with the coffee cups. "So, he's younger than you, Pete."

"No, Mom, he's been *sober* for thirty years. Those are the birthdays we mark."

"Oh, I see. You have to stay there for a year at least to make the judge happy."

"But I get some chips along the way to inspire me."

Dave smiled as he heard the old familiar pattern described.

"So, Mom, how are you doing here?"

Before Daisy could respond, Dave said, "She's just fine. We couldn't get along without her. Have you met the Bunch of Daisy's?" Pete frowned and said he hadn't. "Well, they're the ones she'd known long ago and who came here to live. Then they adopted some of the guys who never learned how to make friends after their wives died."

"Good for you, Mom. You were always the best organizer in town."

"No, dear, I really was pretty quiet."

"Mom, you've never been quiet. You always needed to start something, at church or with the neighbors. I'm sure I do know some of the bunch, from years ago."

Dave was nodding all this time. "She's been taking care of all of us, as you say, just getting us started."

"Yup. Have you met my sister Julie? She's the same way. Dad and I just enjoyed being engineered, well-fed and entertained." Dave was laughing by this time; so was Daisy.

"I'd better put that beautiful rose in water. Excuse me."

"Pete, call me any time. As soon as my eyesight is better, I get to take a driver's test and apply for a license. Then I could be more help to you."

"At this point, I need courage, and you seem to have enough to spare."

"Knowing your mother has boosted my morale and I s'pose, courage."

"Yeah. I need to see her more often too."

Dave stood and announced, "I'm heading home. The wind has come up." Curly went right to the door. Dave snapped on his leash and let him out.

Pete watched with interest. "I think I'll go out and talk to Curly for a few minutes. Give you guys a chance to talk."

Dave cleared his throat and said he'd like to read what he'd written about his mentor. He picked up the pink paper. "I've had some men I admired as I grew up, but they came and went in my life. More recently, I've come to value someone who sets a pace for me and keeps me from mourning my old life, you know, the one I had before La Ventura days. It's a mystery to me why an old man could still need a mentor. I think it proves to me that as long as we live, we grow, and as we grow, we need a guide.

"My mystery mentor has a knack of bringing up a philosophic subject that gives me ideas to chew on. Then my ideas expand, and I become far more creative and confident about my life. To challenge us to think differently in our seventies is a big order! To live alone is something new. To have complete use of family income forces solo decisions. To have reached one's goals and yet still be alive raises questions of faith. I need my mystery mentor more than I ever dreamed." He looked at Daisy, and added, "That's about you, my friend."

He gave her a little salute, went to the door and left before she could wipe away the tears that had collected as he read.

Pete came back in and said, "What a nice guy. I think he really meant he would help me. I can tell he understands. C'mon, Mom, drive me home, O.K.?"

CHAPTER 43

Big News from Dave

AFTER THAT DAY, the channels of talking seemed to open more often. Daisy called Pete when she knew he was home, and he called her regularly too. Her sewing hours were more productive, and Ellen was the first to notice she was in better spirits.

"Daisy, what's your secret? You act as if you've found a new source of energy."

"I don't know, but ever since the day that Pete came to see me, I've felt better about our family. I was trying to avoid too much contact with them, and I was really afraid of Susie's temper."

"Has she calmed down?"

"No, but I know she isn't mad at me. She's unhappy with their life right now."

"There are times like that, right?"

"I remember a few. Speaking of being more cheerful, have you seen Donna? I think she's back in stride again with the new kitten."

"What did she name him?"

"Robert said it would be Fantastic, Fanny for short."

"Oh, my, that seems odd, but it's not my pet."

"Curly is still my favorite. I'm not sure I'd replace him if he got sick."

"Why? He's your guardian angel."

"True, but I don't know if I'll have the strength to take care of a puppy."

"You're right. I remember starting with a puppy when the kids were young, and it was frantic. Maybe if you could adopt a grown Golden."

"Maybe." As they approached Unit 7, Curly joined the conversation. "He must be eager to go out. He doesn't know how windy and cold it is." She opened the door, and he bounded out to greet Ellen. "Curly, be nice."

"Curly's always nice."

"I think he must have heard a phone message or something. That's the way he gets when he wants me to come inside. Come on in for a minute."

Sure enough, the message light was flashing. Daisy pushed it in, and Dave's voice filled the room. "Daisy, I have news I need to share. Call me as soon as you get in. Please."

Ellen's face lighted up with a smile. "So, Daisy, Dave sounds pretty excited. I think he's talking about more than Pete's case."

Daisy said, "Well, that urgent voice got Curly upset."

"But not you? Aren't you going to call him?" She frowned at Daisy. Then she said, "Oh, I think I'd better leave so you can find out his good news. Bye-bye, you two."

Daisy tried to stop her, but Ellen kept going.

Curly sat by the phone table, and Daisy deleted the message. "All right, Old Boy, I'll call our friend and see what's new." She dialed his number, and there was an immediate answer. "I'm home, and Curly and I want to know what's new."

She listened and smiled. "You're sure? Of course I'll take you." She waited. "Yes, you can use my car if you have to. O.K., give me five minutes." Curly waited at attention. "I have to run an errand. You hold the fort, Curly."

At dinner that night, Dave sounded like a fifteen-year-old boy with a temporary driver's license. "Can you believe I passed that vision test? Man, I was so nervous. The officer finally told me to take a big breath and sit back."

Alex laughed. "So you can drive now? But you don't have a car."

"I can fix that in a big hurry. Daisy's going to drive me down to the dealer in the morning. I bought about ten cars from them. Won't they be surprised to see me again? It's been eight years, no maybe nine or ten, since I bought that little blue convertible."

By Thursday at noon, Dave was ready to take everyone for a ride in his new Hyundai. "You know, it's a new model, and I'm a new driver, so it just feels good. It's a good price, and Daisy's son said a lot of good things about Hyundais."

"They say the police are always watching for little red cars, so I don't think you picked the right color, Dave."

"Hey, they're looking for kids driving sporty cars, not old duffers like me."

"Glad you got a four-door, so you can give us all rides. Where do you park it?"

"Well, that's the rub! First Malcolm said there were no spaces left near this building or the next one. Then he sized up my general condition, I guess, and asked if I still limp. I said yes, but I'm trying not to. Then he said he might have one. By dinner last night he assigned me to #30. It's only about five units away from mine."

"Sounds pretty good."

CHAPTER 44

Spring Is in the Air

"MARCH CAME IN like a lion, but it's gone out like a lamb, hasn't it?" Beth was admiring the beautiful lawn and the geraniums that were blooming everywhere. "I can't decide whether I like the beginning or end of winter the best. Last year I thought May was the loveliest weather I'd ever lived through. But this April day is a gem!"

Daisy agreed. "This makes me think of Easter when I was young. We had to plan what we'd wear to church that Sunday. I had to get my hair cut two weeks ahead, so my hat would look right."

"I remember. The dress is so casual out here. But the little girls at church wear a dress and the boys look as if they've been scrubbed and put in a buttoned shirt. It's the school clothes that drive me wild."

"Good thing I quit teaching when I did."

"Good morning, ladies." Malcolm had a business look on his face. "I have some news that's not pleasant. I'm calling a meeting right after lunch. If you see some of the people who don't eat with us at noon, be sure to tell them. Thanks." And he turned off the path toward El Nido.

"What do you suppose that's all about?"

"Maybe somebody's moving out."

"Daisy, you always worry that someone isn't happy here."

"Well, I want everyone to fit in somewhere, maybe not in my group of friends and maybe not in the Writers' Group."

"That's Malcolm and Bonnie's job to keep us happy."

"I know, but I think the rest of us can help. I'd like to see us form a team of Super Friends, friendly people who could be like our Stephen Ministers at church."

"We have them at Our Lady too. You mean one-to-one assistance in driving or consulting with a doctor."

"That's it. Like Rissa needs help writing her checks every month. My hands don't hurt, so I offered to help her. She's thrilled. You'd think I'd given her a huge present."

"I heard one of the men saying he's supposed to give up driving, but he won't because he doesn't want to depend on the vans."

"Let's talk to Bonnie about it. Maybe she could coordinate it, or maybe Donna knows people in need of help."

"Good thought. What else could be on Malcolm's mind?"

"Could the chef have quit? Oh, I hope not. I did see a new secretary in the office."

They went in to lunch and joined all the others who were speculating the same way. The Captain and Alex came in but hadn't heard about the meeting. "We should call Tom and Martha too," Daisy remembered. "We need morning announcements like in school," she said with a laugh.

The meeting started at 1:00 and almost everyone was there for it. Malcolm had set up the speaker system, so they knew it was important. He called on Bonnie first.

"Dear friends and resident managers, it's good to see you all in one place. Our family has grown over the past four years, and so our staff has had to multiply too. You know how fortunate we've been to have a congenial work force. Thank you for treating them kindly and with respect.

"It's with regret that I report on several losses this week. One resident has reported missing jewelry, heirlooms that were valuable. The very next day, the branch bank here discovered a damaged wall and safe. Nothing was stolen, however. Now this morning a resident has signed a complaint against our security guard over a broken window and missing laptop computer.

We called the police; they have a warrant to search the whole property. Until the police have gathered evidence and released the crime scenes, we're asking you to remain in this building, either in the library or the ice cream parlor, the first aid station or the main lobby. This room will be open all afternoon. We expect the search to take an hour or two. Thank you all for your cooperation."

Malcolm thanked her and then said, "In cases like this, it's easy to blame the maintenance people, you know, the gardeners and cleaning crew. Someone was certain he saw the security night man lifting the screen out of one window, as if making it an easy break-in. We put him on temporary leave as the police suggested."

Daisy turned to Beth and said, "Does he mean Joseph?"

Beth nodded. "Probably."

Malcolm continued. "We hope the jewelry will be found in the same hiding place where it was placed by the owner. We all misplace things occasionally. Petty cash was taken from the office a month ago, and that taught us to keep it under lock and key. The bank will make repairs to the wall and carpet as soon as the police have finished in there. When we get the all-clear, I hope you'll make your personal possessions secure and remember to lock your doors when you leave home. It's also a good habit to lock your doors when you're inside alone. Are there any questions?"

"Should we lock our cars too?"

"By all means, yes. Our night security guard moves around the campus and watches the parking areas, but he can't be everywhere at once. Our bright lighting is the best protection for cars and people, so Joseph checks the lights every night."

"Who's taking his place now?"

"We've hired a temporary service to patrol the area."

All eyes turned when a small woman at the back of the room said, "I lost my passport, right off the kitchen counter, last week. But I didn't think anyone would believe me, because I'm forgetful."

"Please report anything like that to Bonnie or me, Mrs. Norton. I'll stop by your unit later today, and we'll look for it together."

She continued in her frail voice, "I went to Violet, and she told me it's in a white car."

"I see. Well, we'll talk about it at your place. Any other comments?"

"I always lose things in the laundry room. Is there a lost and found place?"

"Yes, Mr. Eaton. In the office there's a large drawer of things found by the maids and cleaning crew. Right now, there are at least half a dozen pairs of sunglasses and some sweaters. The whole list was in the last newsletter. Be sure to tell us as soon as you lose something. We're happy to help you track it down."

Policemen came into the room, and one went to the microphone. "We're pleased to report that we found some important evidence and this case may be cleared up soon. In the meantime, please watch your valuables and if you hide something, write down the hiding place and keep that note in your wallet. If there's yellow tape near your place, please leave it intact so we can continue our search of that particular area. Thanks for your help, folks."

Malcolm stood and called out, "You're free to go."

As they walked along, Ellen said, "Well, that was a first, wasn't it? I don't really have any fine jewelry anymore."

Daisy replied, "Yes, and I kept thinking how nice it was that Phyllis is in El Nido and not frightened by this news."

"Does the cleaning crew go in her unit even though she isn't back yet? She might have left all kinds of good things lying around."

"Yes, but I think they have to be bonded to go in when she's not home. I don't know; maybe I'm too trusting."

"You have Curly, and he wouldn't let anyone steal your diamonds. Would he?"

"In exchange for a new chew bone, he might. Pets can be silenced, you know." She turned in to her patio and waved. Inside, she looked down at her hands and her beloved engagement and wedding rings. "I should find a nice safe spot for these. Mark could use them when he finds the right girl. I have some other rings it would be fun to wear now and then."

When the telephone rang, Daisy was surprised it was Susie. "Pete's doing so much better, so I wanted you to know. How about dinner on Sunday after church?"

"Wonderful, dear. My service ends at 10:00. Maybe after the later service at 12:30?"

"12:30 would be perfect. Suz will be home too." She paused and then added, "Would you like to bring your friend Dave? Pete thinks he's a good friend to have."

"Thanks. I'll ask him and give you a call back. Take care now."

"Well, Curly, that was a nice invitation. Too bad you can't come along, but you'd bother Susie's cat, and we can't have that." She reviewed what Pete must have said about Dave. "A good friend to have, for me or for him?"

She poured her iced tea and sat by the phone to dial Dave's number. "Hi, Dave. I just received a nice invitation that includes you." She described it, leaving out the explanation of friends. "Good. You want to drive? I know why. The church folks haven't seen your new car much. That's great." She listened a while. "Tonight? O.K. I'll be ready at 5:30."

No one had said much about seeing Dave and Daisy together so often, but Ellen finally cornered her one afternoon. "Do you know how much you mean to Dave?"

"I know how much he's helped me understand Pete's problems. Yes, we've fallen into a habit of walking to dinner."

"You know I mean more than that, Daisy. He worships the ground you walk on."

"I don't know about that, Ellen. He was lonely, and he gives me credit for including him in our groups. Now that he can see better, he's doing a lot more things with other people too."

"Daisy, look at me. He adores you. How do you feel about him?"

"I don't know." She could feel a blush coming up her face. "I was quite touched by what he wrote about me."

"Were you his mystery mentor?"

"He brought me a copy of it with a rose."

"A red rose?"

She blushed again. "Yes. Pete was here. He didn't say anything special about it."

"Pete's too wrapped up in himself to notice."

"Susie just called and said Pete is doing so much better. She invited me to dinner! That's really news. She also invited Dave, because Pete has appreciated Dave's advice."

"See? She knows it too."

"Knows what?"

"She and your son have noticed how special Dave is."

"Well, he is special, but that doesn't mean we're. . . we're *involved.* We've just shared a lot of worries."

"I hate to ask, but have you told him Tom's story about the accident?"

Daisy frowned and looked down. "No, but I think he knows. I tried several times to get into it. Each time he said something that blocked me from saying another word."

"Hmm. That's interesting. You know, I told you not to dig it up, and I think I was right. It would just bring back all he's been through. He looks so much brighter and alert with both eyes focusing. And to be driving again must feel good."

"He seems more energetic, doesn't he?"

"O.K. So, how do you feel about him?"

"I don't know. I thoroughly enjoy his company. We go to the same service, and we eat at the same table a lot. But I also value my time alone. I'm used to sewing and reading my e-mails every morning. I read the paper inside and out. I have my kids around town."

"You don't feel as if you're missing anything?"

"No. He's just a very nice addition to my life."

Ellen sighed and stood to leave. "If you're satisfied the way it stands, fine. But I have a feeling you'll find him on your doorstep more and more. Think ahead."

After a few minutes, Daisy sat down by Curly. "Well, my furry friend, that was a different kind of conversation, wasn't it? I don't want to think ahead. Let's just wait and see what tomorrow brings."

CHAPTER 45

Easter Traditions Bloom

WITH THE APPROACH OF Easter and school spring break and warmer days, grandparents began to talk of Easter baskets for children and hunting for decorated eggs. Bonnie came up with a new idea. "We have the largest lawns of anyone in the neighborhood. Would it be fun to sponsor an egg hunt that afternoon for all the little ones who live around here in the apartments?"

The lunch crowd started to talk all at once, and she continued. "We could post invitations in the lobbies near their mailboxes, for kids from three to eight. Would that be a good age group?"

Alex stood up and said loudly, "We'd be the best neighbors they've ever had! Let's do it. Can we all color the eggs? I'll donate a dozen."

Other hands went up and they were all excited about the idea. Clarissa clinked on her glass until the uproar died down. I'd be happy to buy fifty of those cute little buckets at Walmart."

"Me too" rang out all over the room.

Malcolm tried to be heard. "If we do this at about 3:00, would nap time be over, for the little ones?"

One loud reply was, "For us too."

A flyer was printed and before long everyone wanted to ride the van to the store to buy eggs and magic markers. Those who didn't want to boil the eggs bought plastic ones and filled them with coins or candy. Instead of remarks about missing their family traditions, the residents all looked forward to borrowing the neighborhood children. Bonnie planned to have pitchers of punch for the kids and iced tea for their parents. Eggs were due in the office by noon on Saturday.

At lunch, Malcolm announced he had sixty-two dozen eggs, 120 buckets and baskets and at least a hundred small stuffed chickens and bunnies. "How many children will we have, Bonnie?"

"The apartment managers in the four places estimated about twenty, twenty-five, eighteen and twenty-two, eighty-five in all. I think we have enough to make it fun."

"Thanks, folks, for getting into the mood of this. Maybe we can make a new tradition for these people."

By 2:30 on Sunday, the lawns and shrubs were covered with eggs. Volunteers held back the children until each had a container. At the stroke of three, Malcolm rang a big bell and the rush was on. "Amazing how they seem to stay out of each other's way," commented Beth. "I was sure there'd be some bullies and lots of tears."

"Some of them have already done something special today, so maybe they're not quite so desperate." Daisy caught one little boy just as he started to fall. "He didn't even take time for my sympathy," she laughed as he scampered off.

In the dining room for their light buffet that evening, all agreed that Easter was more joyous than last year. "We're celebrating our day of faith, and we're also making it fun for others. Those children were wonderful. They even remembered to say thank you." Clarissa was all smiles.

Daisy agreed. "It was good to be free to go to church and see my kids too, before this started."

"Right! The special dinner at our church was put on by the singles for the singles. It was delicious, and I didn't want to miss it." Clarissa managed to be attached everywhere.

"Dinner here was wonderful, best ham and turkey I've ever eaten. The flowers on the tables came from that big wholesaler in Mesa. Gorgeous!" Dave walked along beside Daisy. "Did you notice I left my cane at home?"

"Oh, Dave. I'm sorry I didn't see that."

"It's O.K. I just decided I feel steady enough without it, at least around here where I know my way." Curly barked as they approached. "Hey there, big boy. You want to take a walk?" Dave let him out the gate and watched as he galloped around.

They went inside and put on the lights. Curly bounded in and laid a pretty pink egg at Daisy's feet. "Curly, where did you get that?" They both laughed as he rolled it around the carpet with his nose. Daisy tried to grab it, but he was too quick.

Dave finally pounced on it and took it to the kitchen. "He wouldn't eat it, would he?"

She laughed and said, "I don't know. If I hadn't fed him at five, he might."

CHAPTER 46

April Showers Dampen Spirits

THE GLOW OF EASTER had hardly dimmed when sirens and paramedics clamored into El Nido in the early hours. Death was always an uninvited visitor on La Ventura's campus. Word spread quickly that Phyllis Fenton had died in her sleep. Her roommate was so upset that she had had a heart attack while the medics were in the room. Her condition was said to be critical, and that added to the gloom. Daisy called Phyllis' friend Sue and broke the news. Sue's comment was, "Phyl was never content anywhere. Did you ever notice how she'd try different chairs in the room? She had lived in four or five different apartments in town. I think she liked Ventura better than any other place. You all did a wonderful job of making her fit in."

"Thanks, that's the nicest thing you could have said."

"I suppose there are some others who don't fit in."

"Sure there are. Those of us who love it here try to make it fit for the newer ones. But it's not easy."

"Didn't you miss your old house?"

"I did! I was so homesick for that family room. But I couldn't move again."

"I can't even think about moving. They can carry me out of here feet first."

"If you get lonely on a rainy day like today, you might remember you're welcome here."

"Thanks, Daisy. I'll tell the other gals about Phyl on Craft Day."

Ellen surprised the Bunch of Daisy's one Thursday by announcing she had signed up for a Constant Comment friend. "She's a volunteer who lives over in Building Three, and she'll help me any time I call."

"But Ellen, you're the one we rely on to explain our problems. Do you need her?"

"I think so. I need a ride once in a while, and she's good with numbers, so she'll come once a month and balance my checkbook. And every time she comes, she brings a Constant Comment tea bag for us to share."

Daisy walked around the table and laid her arm around Ellen's shoulders. "Are you sure we couldn't help in the same way?"

"Positive. I thought about it a long time. I talked with Donna, and she approved."

"Well, we approve, but wish we'd known you wanted help like that."

Martha looked the most concerned. "I'm surprised you would trust a stranger."

"You know, there are times when a stranger handles things more businesslike. The Super Friends program helps the new residents, but I need more than attitude help."

Clarissa spoke up, "I agree. That's what I notice about my nephew. He always has a suggestion a little different from mine. He knows me too well. A stranger won't argue with you."

Beth said, "Can we still consult with you when we wonder what to do or say?"

"Of course. I just feel better having someone know my business matters. And once in a while, I'm a little light-headed. She'll come and sit, day or night."

"Is this the service advertised in the newsletter? Bonnie coordinates it?"

"Yes. Lots of people are part of it. They only get paid if they drive somewhere or stay overnight."

The Captain stuck his head around the doorway. "Got anything exciting going on today, girls?"

"C'mon in. You men don't seem to join us unless we have a writing assignment."

"Busy guys like us have lots to do."

Clarissa laughed at him. "I know where you've been. Lois told me you were taking bridge lessons from her. You trying to beat me at my game?"

"Not at all. But if I happened to improve, I might challenge you, just a quarter at a time."

No one mentioned what they'd been talking about with Ellen. Daisy liked that. "What was the movie you saw yesterday?"

"Donna and Alice picked out that one about Queen Elizabeth. Boy, was she good in that role! Well, gotta get going. See you at dinner."

Beth said, "I'm on the committee for new people this month. Have you met any of them yet?"

"I didn't know there were any." Donna looked surprised.

"Always someone new or one who missed last month's party. There's also a new couple whose daughter is bringing them to the meeting Tuesday night."

"Do you need more help on the committee? The health station can always be closed for an hour."

"Thanks. I'll see what Bonnie needs from us."

At dinner, Dave turned to Daisy and remarked, "I'm making progress on my book at last."

"Wonderful. I thought maybe you'd given up on it."

"No, just dragging my feet. I can't decide between two titles."

"Oh, tell me about it."

"*New Vision* or *A New View* or even *A Better View*."

"Interesting. Has your story changed since your surgery?"

"Of course! I thought I knew the adventure in my life, but it all changed."

"That's good. I remember what you said when we were trying to write our last wishes. But now all that has to be revised too."

"Gladly. No wonder people hate to believe every diagnosis. Medicine changes too, more than many fields."

"Aren't your kids happy about the success of the operation?"

"Yeah, they are. I've been talking to them about coming out here in the summer for an anniversary celebration. First birthday for my new vision."

"Good idea," Daisy exclaimed.

Beth was listening and silently thought about celebrating her new figure after losing both breasts. "Not for the dinner table," she thought and smiled. "Private celebration."

On Thursday afternoon, everyone was caught by surprise with an early monsoon sky and blowing dust. "The weather around here has always been so predictable," Daisy remarked. "But this year has been odd all over the country. What's happening to us?"

Alex nodded. "It must have something to do with the warming you read about, or about that current in the Pacific. Weather doesn't really bother us here, does it? We're pretty lucky to have roofs and ramadas to duck under." With that, noisy drops of rain pelted the windows of the Hedgehog Room.

Beth smiled and said, "Do you remember the thunderstorms we used to have in Illinois?"

Daisy nodded. "Usually when we had a picnic planned. Must be a Midwest thing."

"Madison was famous for the storms that whip across Lake Mendota," Martha said. "The warnings for boats were so important, but new students never believed they could drown."

"Nope. Can't let you claim all the noise and lightning." Donna continued to describe the storms that preceded and followed tornadoes in Oklahoma. "There's a good reason we had storm cellars. We kids learned to scurry down there the minute the town siren went off."

Robert interrupted. "Let me tell you, there's nothing quite so terrifying as a vicious storm at sea. A typhoon is enough to make you say your last prayers. I've made more promises to God in a howling wind, clinging to a hatch."

Ellen agreed. "I guess that would be more frightening than crouching on the basement floor, listening to the roar of the wind. That's where we had to go. You could hear furniture crashing around on the porch."

Alex said, "It's hard to be told to leave where you're sitting or eating, and to leave right that minute. Four years ago, we were just sitting down to dinner when a truck with a loud-speaker pulled up next to the cabin and ordered us to evacuate Summerhaven because of the fire. I felt myself wanting to say, 'Just a minute. Let us finish dinner first.' And we stuffed some food in our mouths, and I grabbed the car keys and the dog. My wife took her phone and a notebook she carried all the time. We didn't even lock the door."

"Where did you go?"

"Back home, into town. Watched TV the rest of the night and the next day."

"Did you lose the house?"

"No, but everything in it was so smoked we couldn't stand it. Sold it the next summer to some developer who was picking up all the bargain property."

"Have you been in a bad earthquake, you know, one that registered more than a five or six-point?" Dave looked around, but no one had. "I was at a meeting in the late eighties, over near Whittier, on the ninth floor. Couldn't believe the noise and the windows rattling, lamps falling over. I remember I tried to stand up and fell flat. Nobody ever told me to lie down, under some piece of furniture." He laughed lightly.

"What a bunch of stories we just told!" Alex exclaimed. "Maybe that's what we ought to write about." Just at that moment, there was a crash outside the glass doors. "That's a lounge chair from the pool," he shouted over the storm. "Daisy, get away from that door. You too, Beth." They moved quickly over to the inside wall of the room. The lights blinked once and then went out.

Robert commented loudly, "Yes, but the floor is steady under us!"

"Right, but this storm lasts a lot longer than a quake." Tom remembered some big quakes. "That's the only good thing about an earthquake."

"But aren't there aftershocks and more damage later?" Daisy admitted she'd never been in a quake, "But I remember the news warning people to stay away from windows and such."

The lights flickered on and then off again. Rain was beating hard against the building. When Alex opened the door to the hallway, they could hear the first hailstones on the roof over the main entrance.

"Thank Goodness for covered parking," Beth said, and Dave cheered too.

"Imagine hail falling on my new little red jewel!"

"You know, it's practically time to get ready for dinner, but I don't think I'll go home first."

"Me, neither. Why don't we just pile all our notebooks and stuff over here on the counter and pick them up later, or maybe tomorrow?" Daisy led the way by clearing space in the corner.

Clarissa had been quiet through all the talking. Now she ventured, "I'm really afraid of storms and having to walk around in the dark. I hate to admit it, but it's true." There was a rush to stand close to her and assure her they wouldn't leave without her. She sighed and said, "Thank you, friends."

Alex opened the door again and suggested, "Why don't we move out toward the living room and join some of the others there?" They followed him.

Daisy whispered to Ellen, "Funny no one wondered how the kitchen crew could fix dinner without power." They both laughed. "The best thing about our storms is that they don't last long, and they're so spotty. It may not be raining at Julie's at all."

CHAPTER 47

Daisy Blooms in May

When Daisy opened the door, she was delighted to see both Susie and her daughter Suzette. "Come right in, dear ones. How are you?" Curly nuzzled in between them for his hugs.

Susie spoke for both of them. "We're fine, and we have such good news about Pete, we decided to stop and tell you in person!"

"Wonderful. Go on."

"The doctor says he has recovered the full use of his arm and that foot too. He has only two more weeks of therapy, and he can go back to work fulltime. Isn't that just great?"

Daisy felt tears coming into her eyes, but said, "I can tell how much that means to both of you, and me too. Now how can we keep this from happening again?"

"Grandma, you sound just like Aunt Julie. We saw her at Walgreen's, and she said the same thing."

"Well, it was so scary, and we didn't see any warning ahead of time."

Susie cut in, "Yes, Mom, but there were signs. Pete says now that he knew he wasn't feeling as steady as he used to. He knew he was drinking too much and too often."

"Will he have his old place in the office?"

"He doesn't know. He called them this morning, but there was some big meeting, so no one could talk to him. I think he could go to some other firm if he has to."

"Let's hope it works out well. I never had the nerve to ask him what his chances were about returning." Curly sniffed around the door, as if he expected Pete to join them.

"They kept him on the insurance plan, so I think they expect him back. The doctor says he can read and write just like he used to. He'll still have to go to AA all the time. The court won't change that sentence."

"Can he drive?"

"Um, no, not just yet. I may have to be his driver."

"I can help too, Mom."

"How about your college plans for next fall, Suz?"

"Oh, Grandma, I don't know. This scared me a lot. I don't think I want to leave Daddy right now, or maybe not in the fall either."

Daisy nodded. "I can understand that. My mother got sick once when I was in college, and it made me so sad. I finally came home early for the winter break. I know how you feel."

"How are your friends, the ones from long ago?"

"They're mostly O.K. Beginning to talk about summer plans, of course. Clarissa always leaves July first or so. Beth is good. Ellen seems to be feeling her age a bit more. Know what I mean? She's paying someone to help her with some business things."

"What about the couple that got married?"

"Martha and Tom are fine. And her sister Mary Ann, the one who moved down to Casa Grande, loves where she's working. We miss her."

"Which one had the cat that died?"

"That was Donna, and she has a new Persian cat, named Fantastic, Fanny for short."

Susie hesitated and then asked, "How is your special friend Dave?"

"Dave's just fine. His vision has improved so much."

Suzette added, "Now he knows how good you look, Grandma. Maybe he'll ask you out."

Daisy smiled at the idea, and actually felt herself starting to blush. "I think we all have enough to do around here, dear. We're just friends, like lots of other people here."

"Sure, sure. I think he's pretty cool, and you are too."

"Your grandma lives with a lot of good memories of your grandpa, Suz. Why would she want go out with Dave, as you put it?"

"Grandpa would approve of Dave. He sounds a lot like him."

"No, Suz, he's nothing like Grandpa."

"Now, you two stop planning my life. I'm doing fine. Let's just concentrate on getting Pete up and running again."

"We're off, Mom. We'll keep you posted on Pete. Tell Dave we said hello." With two big hugs, they were out the door, leaving Daisy a little breathless.

At dinner, Ellen posed a question for the table. "I kept thinking about all our stories about storms yesterday. It struck me that we're so lucky not to be alone in a storm. Clarissa isn't the only one who's afraid of storms and the dark."

Martha answered immediately. "That's the wonderful part of being married. Tom and I can weather anything, we think."

"Is that a pun, or did you mean it?"

"No pun intended. I think I'm the luckiest one here." She turned and patted Tom on the arm.

Alex spoke out. "Yeah, I'd be glad to share my house, my life for that matter."

The table was quiet, as people started their salads. Finally, Beth said, "I may be the only one who really likes living alone. I have to admit, it's nice to have a friend near, if I can't solve my own problems. I'm not afraid of weather storms, but personal storms are serious. I couldn't have handled the cancer alone."

"We all learned from your crisis, Beth. You pulled us together so fast." Daisy continued eating and then added. "My dad had a favorite comment about growing up. He always told people they had to put down strong roots, wherever they went. They could always pull them up and take them along to the next place, but wherever one lived one had to dig right in as if it was forever."

Alex agreed. "See, that's why I said I'd like some company. I feel as if I've put in some deep roots here, and now I'd like to build on them." Once again, silence prevailed.

Malcolm passed the table and commented, "You guys are pretty quiet tonight. Where's Clarissa? You need her to liven up this table." As he left, they chuckled.

"Where is Clarissa?"

"And where's Donna? She's always near if not at our table."

"I'll check on them after dinner and let you know."

"Thanks, Daisy." The rest of their food arrived, and they concentrated on the meal.

About ten minutes later, Donna and Clarissa came into the dining room. Donna appeared to be helping Clarissa. One of the young assistants helped them find places to sit. Daisy rose and went over to their table, inquiring about them. When she returned, she explained, "Rissa didn't feel steady on her feet and called the health office. Donna was still there and picked her up for dinner."

"Is she O.K. now?" Ellen frowned.

"I think so, maybe a little pale."

"Could she really have been frightened about that storm yesterday?"

"I suppose so. I thought a dust storm might blow in again today. But the breeze died down."

"Life seems more unpredictable this year." Alex took a drink and continued, "I think I'll go up and visit my daughter tonight."

"Do you have to call first, or can you just drop in?"

"They always tell me to stop by if I'm in the neighborhood, but I usually call, at least from the car before I get too far." He stood. "See you tomorrow, folks."

After he had left, Beth observed, "Something's troubling him. He seems lonely, maybe aware of his age."

"Isn't it strange how that feeling creeps over you once in a while? Then the least little thing like a phone call or someone at the door breaks the spell."

Daisy replied, "Yes, Ellen, but Beth is right. He's concerned about something more than just the blue mood."

Beth nodded. "He may be one of these people who really prefer living with someone. Maybe being with his family all summer felt good to him."

No one commented until a cascade of laughter from across the room filled the air. Then Ellen smiled and said, "Well, at least Connie has solved her loneliness. She's with Ed Shapiro all the time, I mean *all* the time!"

Beth turned to watch them too. "My, oh, my. They've become quite an item. How old do you think he is?"

Daisy put in, "Ten years older than she is would be my guess. Heavens! What are we talking about? We're *gossiping*, girls. I can't believe I said that."

"Well, Daisy, he may be the best man she can catch."

"If she wants to catch one. Her ex is living in L.A., according to the nail girl in the salon. I used to think they made a good-looking couple." They prepared to leave the dining room.

On the way home, Ellen caught up with Daisy and asked, "Now, how's your love life?"

Daisy shook her head and answered, "Ellen, you're determined to marry me off, aren't you?" When Ellen didn't respond, Daisy looked around and saw that Dave was right behind them.

"What were you girls giggling about over at your table? Sorry I was late getting back from the dentist and missed out on my favorite seat." He slid his arm around Daisy's waist and kept pace with her.

She laughed and agreed. "We did get silly, mostly after listening to Connie and Ed having so much fun."

"I noticed how close they are. I'll see if I can pry any news out of him at the pool in the morning." They drifted their separate ways as the shadows grew longer.

Daisy let Curly out and stood in the doorway enjoying the evening air. "I couldn't go home." Dave's voice caught her by surprise. "I just felt as if I had unfinished business here with you."

Daisy smiled, called to Curly and led the way inside. "Come in and sit down. What's on your mind, Dave?"

"May I sit beside you? We just need to talk."

"Well, where shall we start?"

He took her hand and leaned closer. "Daisy, I love you. I want to be with you and know you better. Walking to dinner or going to church just doesn't satisfy me anymore. I want to be right here, close."

Daisy felt herself getting warmer, and finally she blurted out, "Me too." As they came together, Curly pushed in with them, and that made them both laugh.

"Curly, old buddy, there will be ground rules. First, you go and sit over there." Dave pointed to Curly's usual guard spot. Curly slowly moved back and went there, turning around once to make it his nest. "Now, Daisy, what can we do, together I mean?"

Tears rolled down her cheeks, as she said, "Dave, I'm so bewildered by my feelings for you. I just never thought I'd be interested in being close to anyone new. I'm not lonely. I'm not even feeling left alone. I don't know what's come over me."

Dave grinned and whispered, "Me too." They both laughed softly. "I never planned to date anyone or fall in love or even think about living with anyone. I was just perfectly happy with this place and a few friends, good food, same old town and getting better after the accident."

The word *accident* jolted Daisy, and she sat up straight. "Dave, we have to talk about that accident. I'm carrying a load of guilt about it."

He moved closer and said, "I know about the accident. Tom told me who was driving that car. Maybe he shouldn't have been, and I know I shouldn't have been driving. I could have forced him right into a telephone pole. It's over; it's done. It was a wake-up call for me, and I needed that. Thank God, good folks came around me and nursed me back. Then I met all of you, and the rest is history, as they say."

"Yes, but Dave, it could. . ." His hand covered her mouth and turned her head toward him.

"Nothing is going to come between us, not Curly or an old accident. Now, make me a cup of coffee, and pour yourself a glass of wine. Let's talk like two kids who've been given a second chance."

"You always manage to turn the conversation into something good. What would I have done without your support last year?"

"I don't know. I'm just glad no one else came around to help you. Let's talk about us."

"I may be too shaky to make coffee and pour wine. You'd better help." They got up and moved toward the kitchen.

Dave's hug became an embrace, and they enjoyed their first loving kiss.

Curly's friendly bark alerted them that someone was opening the door. They separated and returned to the living room just as Pete's voice called out, "Hi, Mom."

"Pete, how good to see you. You know Dave too."

"Sure. Hi, Dave. Good to see you. I hope I didn't interrupt anything?"

"Well, yeah, Pete. I was just about to propose to your mom. What would you think about that?"

Pete looked right at his mother and blurted out, "Mom, that would be great! You're much too young to live alone."

Daisy was stunned at the way the talk was going. She leaned against Dave and smiled weakly. "I think I need to sit down. The world is spinning too fast."

Dave eased her into a chair and went back to the kitchen, talking as he went. "I'll make us a cup of coffee, Pete. Stick around a minute."

"O.K. I will. I'm feeling a lot more hopeful about the future today, so I wanted to share that with Mom. Suz dropped me off here."

Daisy recovered her wits and spoke in her usual voice. "The news is so good, honey. Your girls were here earlier and they're so excited."

"Yeah, they were pretty upset with me for the last year or more. I'm sorry I ruined a lot of plans."

"You'll find yourself wanting to say you're sorry a lot, Pete, but the best thing is just to get yourself going again, one day at a time." Dave returned with a little glass of wine for Daisy. "This is what the doctor ordered for you, lady, and our coffee will be ready in a minute."

"Thanks, Dave." Daisy felt as if her living room had turned into a stage set with actors saying their lines, but no one had given her a script.

"So, Mom, when are you and Dave getting together?"

She sipped her wine and said, "I don't know. I don't even know if we are."

Dave came to the rescue and said to Pete, "You really did arrive just at the moment I was about to *suggest* we *consider* our future together. We've never talked seriously, except about you, my boy." Curly was restless and nudged at Dave's legs. "O.K., Curly, I'll sit down too."

"I'll get the coffee, gentlemen." Daisy had recovered from her confusion and poured the mugs and delivered them.

"So, what are you two planning?"

Silence settled on the room. Finally, Dave spoke up. "I really meant it when I said I was just about to sit your mom down and propose to her. Fortunately, you saved me from getting down on my knees."

Daisy smiled and went on, "I was absolutely speechless, and I still am. Pete, you bailed me out of all my problems when your dad died. Lately, I seem to be coasting along smoothly, alone. Now I have this wonderful friend who wants me to consider a whole new lifestyle. It's taken me six years to reach this point by myself."

"Pardon me if I interrupt, but you and Curly are in a rut. You still do all the stuff you used to do, but six years is a long time to sew for the church, clean the choir robes, and go to all the same meetings. Wouldn't it be fun to do something new?"

Daisy was taken aback by Pete's outburst, and she studied his face intently. "Is that really how it looks to you and Julie? As if I'm just going through the motions of living without any fun?"

"Yeah, more or less. Even the kids ask when you're going to get married."

"They do?" Daisy's voice squeaked.

Dave looked a little amused at this exchange. "Well, what do you say we postpone our serious discussion until tomorrow afternoon? This is a good chance for you and Pete to talk, and I need to get home and look up some information for Alex. After lunch, tomorrow, O.K.?" He stood, picked up the two mugs and took them to the kitchen.

"All right. I'll see you at lunch, and I promise I'll have a clearer head by then." She took Dave's extended hand and squeezed it. The door closed quietly.

"Gosh, I'm sorry I arrived just then. But you know I have to take a ride out here to see you whenever it's offered. Suz is my best driver, since her friends live out this way. She's picking me up in, oops, she's probably already waiting for me."

"But we never got to talk about your return to the office. Do you have the same space?"

"I think so. I'm going in tomorrow morning at ten. Then I'll know more. I'll let you know." He was getting up to leave when they heard a tap at the door. "That'll be Suz. Gotta run. Bye, Mom, and take Dave seriously. He's a great guy."

Curly ambled over to Daisy, laid his chin on her knees and looked up at her expectantly. "Yes, Old Boy, let's take a little stroll. I definitely need fresh air. Oh, do I ever!"

CHAPTER 48

Decisions, Decisions

At lunch, Beth complained that the Thursdays at Three group had drifted from its purpose. "We used to meet faithfully and make ourselves write something thoughtful. We're getting lazy!"

"No one seemed to suggest any new topic, and we always find so much to talk about." Daisy realized she too had fallen into other patterns, like joining the knitting group and giving a pep talk to the residents over at El Nido. "There are other things on Thursdays now."

"It was our afternoon to keep up with each other. That's how we got to know Alex and Robert and Dave. I guess I just miss it."

Donna caught the end of the talk and agreed. "I vowed I wouldn't be stuck in any small groups, but this one is so special. I wouldn't even have Fanny if it weren't for knowing Robert."

Daisy took a deep breath and suggested they meet the next day, at three as usual. "We need something to look forward to during the hot weather, don't we?" They passed the word around the tables, and Daisy offered to order the iced tea and reserve the room.

Dave sat at another table and then joined Daisy's group for dessert. "These cookies are not like yours, Daisy, but they're not bad. How about if I stop over around 1:30?"

"That's good. I'll put out the cookie jar."

As Daisy entered Unit 7, she took a critical look around. She let Curly out. Her thoughts wandered from liking the room to seeing it through Pete's eyes. "It's not very perky or cheerful. I haven't added a thing to it in four years here. I just walk through it to the sewing room. Funny that I know how to make alterations with thread, yet I'm afraid to change how I live. Hmm."

She went out to the kitchen and checked on the pitcher of tea and lifted the cookie jar lid. "Oh, what am I going to say next?"

The telephone interrupted her thoughts. "Hello? Yes, hi, Susie." She listened and nodded. "Pete looked great. How did this morning go for him?" More listening. "Good. That sounds so good for the future. *My* future?" She sat against the arm of the loveseat. "Well, dear, my future looks interesting."

The door opened a crack, and she motioned to Dave to come on in with Curly. "Did Pete tell you to call me? I didn't think so." She waited several minutes, nodding occasionally. Dave smiled as he figured out who was calling and what she was saying. "Susie, now don't be upset. I've managed quite well here for the last four years. I'm not feeling pressured by anyone. I have a very complete life here with lots of friends." She took a deep breath. "Susie, my finances are fine. I planned this move to suit myself, just what I could manage easily." She paused. "No, I never even considered moving in with either of you. Have you talked with Julie?" Daisy shook her head and exchanged a glance with Dave. "Susie, slow down. Call Julie and tell her your concerns. I'll let you all know if I have any news to share. Thanks for calling, dear." She put down the phone with a sigh.

"I'm sorry to keep you waiting."

Dave stood and came over to give her a hug. "Let me guess. Susie disapproves of me or us."

"Right. She doesn't know what she thinks I should do, but first she didn't want me to move out of the big house. Now she doesn't want me to 'move again,' as she puts it."

"She may be one of those people who are often wrong, but never in doubt. What she really doesn't like is that you didn't consult her first."

"If I was going to consult anyone, it would be Julie or Pete, my own children. Have you spoken with your kids about your idea?"

"No, I've told them I love you and want to spend the rest of my life with you." With that, he held her close, and she began to mellow.

"That's what I meant. It still seems like *your* idea to me. I spent hours last night, mulling over every word you said. I tried to picture both of us in this little place. This morning I wondered what you'd like for breakfast. I just can't seem to believe I know you well enough to share my whole life with you. Does that sound odd?"

Together, they eased down into the loveseat. He looked thoughtful and then said, "No, it's not odd, but I wonder if you think we can go on as good friends without being closer."

She leaned back and looked at him. "You're right. I've denied any so-called next step. That's kind of immature of me, isn't it? The only way I recovered from my loss of Scott was to convince myself I was able to live by myself and help other people do the same. You know, make big decisions about money and housing, etc."

"And you succeeded."

"Yes, too well, maybe. I admit, when you leave here, I'm sad. I'm lonely, but I put it out of my mind, knowing I'll see you tomorrow."

Dave smiled and said, "At least I'm somewhere in your life, just not front and center the way I'd like to be."

Daisy impulsively reached out to him and embraced him tightly. She whispered, "I think I can learn. I know I can."

After a long kiss, he said, "Can I believe that's a yes?"

"Yes, with a teeny-tiny but, can we figure out the details one at a time?"

"Absolutely. What detail first, lady?"

"Well, when do we tell people our plans? Shouldn't we make some plans first?"

"I heard about a unit that's going to be available at the end of the summer. A bigger place, with plenty of room for both of us and Curly."

Curly who had been snoozing in his corner came to life and snuggled into the conversation. "Curly, go back to your spot. You're so warm. Move." Daisy shooed him off. "Where did you hear about this?"

"This morning, over at the pool table."

"Did you act interested? If you did, a rumor has already gone around the whole place."

"No, no, I didn't say a thing. I just heard Bill Hawkins ask Jake if he was really moving to the coast. He said he was going to his daughter's place to help run her business. He's all excited about it. She's building an apartment for him over the garage, so he has to wait until August to go."

"Where is this place?"

"Unit 77, over near the emergency gate at the back."

"You mean we'd both sell our places?"

"Right. I don't think either of ours is big enough for your hobbies and Curly, plus me. You know, I'm used to spreading out with all my books and stuff. I'm a messy writer."

"So, who'll take Jake's place in the fitness room and pool room?"

"I don't know. They wouldn't need anyone for several months. Maybe run an ad in July?"

"I suppose so. People have liked him, haven't they?"

"Yeah, he's a good guy. I don't think we keep him busy enough. Maybe he can make more in his girl's business." He stood up and stretched. "How about a cup of coffee or some tea?"

"Good idea. I have a pitcher in the fridge. And I have cookies."

"Wonderful! Then tell me what's the next detail to plan?"

"Well, that sounds like an August plan. What about our kids and their plans? Did you really tell yours about me?"

"Of course. I told them I didn't need their approval, but I needed to tell them what I was going to do."

"Didn't they ask about their inheritance or their mother's dishes or anything?"

"Nope. Not a word. They're probably relieved I have no intention of moving in with them, *ever.* I told them I'd set up a trust fund for the grandkids, and they mumbled something about 'Gee, that's great, Dad.' They've been away from home for years, you know."

"It may be stickier with mine."

"Pete seemed pleased, didn't you think?"

"I don't remember. I was in such a state of shock."

"Trust me, he seemed pleased."

"Where would we get married?"

"Ah, now that may be more of a problem. Would your pastor marry you to an old Lutheran?"

Daisy laughed. "Why not? You've been coming to my church more than yours for the last two years."

"Do we have to go through all that pre-marital stuff?"

"Well, I should hope so!" Daisy jabbed at him with a grin. "The pastor might want to know your intentions or how you're going to keep me in the manner to which I'm accustomed."

"He's your father?"

"No, but I've heard my dad go through all that. I had to kid you a little bit. You're so serious."

"I have to be. Last night you were the serious one. I finally went home, remember?"

"I know. I am sorry, but I was just caught off guard. It still makes me giggle to think about announcing this to our friends, or to my circle. What will they think?"

"I'd like to say I don't give a hoot what they think, but I know better. They'll be happy for us and maybe even a little bit jealous. How does that sound?"

"Wonderful. I need you nearby when I tell my friends. I want to know when we'll announce this. And how do we live from now till August? It'll take me that long to digest all this."

"Well then, first I'll buy you something to 'aid your digestion,' as the ads say. Then we'll behave calmly as we do now."

"The group is meeting tomorrow at three. Are you coming too?"

"Of course. What's our assignment now?"

"It's what we've read recently that offers the most hope for the future." Suddenly that sank in on Daisy, and she started to laugh. "You knew that and wanted me to fall right into that topic."

"I remembered something like that, but does it have to be what we've read lately? How about something we've done recently?" He folded her into his bear hug, then headed toward the door. "I'll be back at 5:30. By then, figure out what we'll say tomorrow."

CHAPTER 49

Announcement Time

CLARISSA WAS THE FIRST ONE in the room, so she busied herself setting up the glasses of iced tea. She adjusted the ceiling fan and sat down at the head of the table. The group arrived, glad to be together again. Beth asked, "Why did we miss a meeting in early May?"

Alex answered, "Because I was in such a funk and you were all afraid to ask me why?"

Ellen picked up on that. "We agreed you were down about something, but we wouldn't be afraid of you, Alex. Or would we?" Laughter filled the room, and she went on. "There were a lot of tense moments two weeks ago. That double suicide attempt was just unbelievable! Does anyone know how Walter is doing? The bullet missed his heart but hit his shoulder?"

Donna knew he was out of the hospital. "Something like that, but he's not returning to us. His son came and cleaned out his unit. The Big Brothers truck came for the furniture. Bonnie said they'll put the place up for sale, but not until it's redecorated and completely renewed."

"Are there people on the waiting list for a two-bedroom unit like theirs?"

"A few. But it takes a while to find the right people. You know, they have to pass that physical test as well as sell their home and have their financing in place."

"Not easy today. There are so many places on the market. It's probably a good time to negotiate home sales, but this place never needs to."

Robert spoke out. "Wouldn't it be awful to live the rest of your life knowing what you did to your wife?"

Tom agreed. "I can't imagine making a pact like that and being the only one with a gun. A policeman there said the note explained it all and was signed by both of them." He shuddered after saying that.

Ellen said, "I only brought it up to explain why I think we totally forgot about meetings. The woodcarvers skipped three days, in honor of Walter, and of his wife's death. I guess he had done some nice work with them."

Alex shrugged and looked glum. "I'd really like to do some socializing, but when I hear stuff like that, it makes me wonder."

"You could join that dance school that the girls go to. They say it's more fun than the bridge club," suggested Clarissa.

"Are those the gals that danced last year at the party in May?"

"Yes, and they were terrific. Imagine, almost ninety! Well, I expect to be playing bridge in my nineties, maybe beyond!"

"You will, Clarissa, I'm sure you will." Alex changed the subject. "Now, who's going to tell us about something hopeful? We need to cheer up a bit."

No one spoke up. Ellen finally offered, "I have a lot of spiritual reasons to be hopeful, every day when I wake up. Hope is the one attitude that no one should be able to take away from you. If you read the book I just read, about a man who was a prisoner of war for five years, you see that he chose to keep hope alive, for himself and the others. No one could see inside his mind to know that, so they couldn't take it away from him. That's not news of the day, I know, but as I'm feeling so much older each day, I have to hang onto my faith in little pieces, well-worn, experienced pieces."

"Ellen, as always, you enrich us with your faith. My hope for right this minute is that you feel younger today." Alex always admired Ellen's thinking.

"It's not that I feel so old as that my body is giving out. But I can choose how to think about it, and I choose to be hopeful about finding comfort in each day."

"Amen to that. Does anyone else have some thought to add that will give us all hope?" He looked around the table.

Dave cleared his throat. Daisy felt her heart thump, knowing that this really was a beautiful time to share their plans. He looked her way, and a smile spread across her face. His joy was so contagious!

"I haven't read much in the past few days, because I've been busy *hoping* that Daisy MacDuff would consent to marry me." There was a communal gasp around the table, and instant applause. Daisy felt her face burning with a blush, and she stood up beside Dave. He put his arm around her, and they both were radiant.

Ellen was the most exuberant, shouting out, "I knew it, I knew it. Congratulations, both of you." Others were asking when and where and all the usual questions. Tom and Martha hugged each other, and Martha said something about how happiness is catching.

Daisy and Dave both tried to quiet the group. Daisy found her voice and said, "I simply can't believe this is happening to me. But my inner joy is just suddenly bursting out at the seams! Dave knows more about the future than I do."

He began to explain how their kids were aware of their decision, how they've talked about a place to live, and when they might put it all together. "I found out that Daisy has never been to Europe, and we're going there in the fall."

Tom and Martha offered advice on September travel. Robert recommended a cruise in the Mediterranean. Alex offered ideas on their future tax situation. Their words went far ahead of Daisy's vision.

Finally, Dave said, "We're taking one day at a time, trying to get our priorities straight. Even though life seems so simple here, with no decisions about who pays the bills and what'll we have for dinner, there are a lot of details to work out."

Daisy laughed and said, "How does someone move from one unit to the next? When I got here, Mark drove his truck right to the front door and took in the furniture. Now we have sidewalks and bushes and all sorts of obstacles."

"Don't worry." Martha began to describe Tom's move from his place and Mary Ann's departure. "Those men are so strong, and they figure out how to handle things."

Alex posed another question. "What does Curly think about all this?"

"He's been my buddy all along," Dave replied."

Daisy quickly added, "Maybe Dave just wants a watchdog that happens to belong to me."

Nobody believed that, of course. "Oh my, think of the fun we'll have over this event. Do Bonnie and Malcolm know this?" Beth was immediately organizing her thoughts.

"No one knows but all of you, our very best friends. I think we'll find a larger unit to share, so this will be a major çhange. You know, sell two units and change parking places and addresses and telephones, etc., etc. That's why we're just moving slowly."

Clarissa cleared her throat and stood, all four feet ten inches of her. "I'm so thankful you announced this today, before I leave for the summer. I'll have to know the wedding date as soon as you set it, so that I get my reservations made early."

"I hadn't thought about your being gone, Rissa."

"Well, who else would play for the ceremony?"

"Ah, let's see. The church organist, maybe," Then Daisy saw Clarissa's crestfallen expression and added, "but I'll try to make this an exception.

"Good. I'm often an exception to the rules," she said with a mischievous look.

Alex checked his watch and reminded them that it was after four-thirty. "How about a glass of wine at my place right now? Last time we did that we were on time for dinner. Can we do it again?" They all agreed and started for the door.

CHAPTER 50

Signs of Hope

MARTHA HAD AN IDEA during the next few days, "You know, I'm one year and one day older than Daisy."

Tom started to protest, "Really? I'm sure she's older than you."

"No, no, now listen. How about if we plan a party for me, supposedly, and then really have a shower or something fun for her, a surprise party. I'm sure we could fool her, if you could pretend to be surprising me."

"That's right. She'd do all the preparations for her own party." He laughed out loud at that thought. "It would be fun. Should we take Dave in on the idea?"

"Maybe," she said slowly. "Would he keep a secret?"

"Yeah, I think so. He's sure excited about all this."

"Well, weren't you too?"

"Sure, but I didn't have all the complications he has, or that you had. Children to tell or money to divide up."

"True. We were lucky too, because I had no strings attached. Even my Mary is completely on her own financially."

"So, what day of the week are we talking about?"

"Thursday is my actual birthday, so could we celebrate on Friday, or would she suspect something?"

"Yeah, she'd suspect. We'd better do it on Thursday. That's not a week when we usually meet, so I hope that's O.K. How many people are you thinking about?"

"Just the Bunch of Daisy's plus Four."

"Oh, you have a new name for us, eh?"

"It just came to me, that's all. Ten of us. Maybe have it in the Hedgehog Room where we always meet? Remember you have to be the one making the plans."

"I can do that. I'll reserve the room for the evening? Or we could have a luncheon? How about just a cake and drinks? I'll order the cake."

"Perfect!"

"I'll just whisper to Daisy that I'd like to surprise you at our meeting with a cake, and maybe some salted nuts and pretty napkins. She'll take over from there, won't she?"

"Only problem might be that she'd wonder about marking my seventy-fourth birthday. Tell her I told you I'd never had a birthday party, so you're making up for lost time. O.K.?"

"I can do that. Now we'd better get over to dinner or someone will wonder where we are."

Daisy passed the word around easily about Martha's birthday, and Ellen began to scheme with Beth about making a poster to decorate the room for Martha. Then a few days later, Martha told Dave the real plan to surprise Daisy. He loved it. "She's already making an embroidered apron for Martha with her birthday and hearts and flowers on it. Twice she's told me how sad it is that Martha never had a party."

"Good. I've invited everyone to a shower for Daisy. Since we're writers, we're going to write something memorable for her."

"She'll love it, because you know that we don't *need* anything to set up housekeeping."

"I know that, but we have to celebrate somehow. You do know it's her birthday the next day, don't you?"

Dave looked shocked and said, "No, of course not. That never occurred to me." Then a happy look crossed his face. "I have the ideal gift in mind. Don't worry about a thing. Thanks for the tip-off, though. Whew, that was a close call."

June 14th brought out all the flags for Flag Day. At lunch, when Martha and Tom weren't there, everyone was buzzing about the afternoon meeting. They knew Tom had ordered a cake and would pick it up. They all had cards ready for Martha. Alex reminded them the theme was Signs of Hope Today.

Daisy arrived early to help Tom, and Martha was conveniently delayed by a phone call from her sister Mary Ann in Casa Grande. When she arrived, they showered her with good wishes and sang Happy Birthday with gusto. She acted surprised and carried on beautifully.

That was the cue for Tom to arrive with a cake. They all watched as he opened the box very dramatically. Then Martha announced that this was her gift to Daisy, whose birthday was the next day.

Daisy sputtered out, "But this is your party, Martha. We all want you to feel special today. You were sad you'd been born on a Wednesday, remember?"

"That's all very true, but we have to share this party. This was a ruse." Suddenly there was a shower of cards tossed onto the table with *Dave and Daisy* or *D and D* on them. Bonnie and Malcolm slipped in and added their cards.

Dave clapped his hands for attention. "I brought a gift for Daisy that she can't take back and exchange, because it was made especially for her." He produced a small square box which was enough to force Daisy to sit down to steady her shaking knees. She finally realized the contents and all the attention focused on her.

"Dave, I don't know if I can open this." She fumbled with it until Martha produced a small pair of scissors to cut the ribbons and expose a sparkling diamond. "It's the most beautiful thing I've ever seen." Dave removed the ring from the box and put it on her finger. He planted a kiss on her cheek, and everyone applauded. The ring was almost the loveliest piece any of them had ever seen.

"Time to cut the cake. Then let's see what all these cards say." Alex piled the cards in front of Martha and Daisy.

It was close to dinner time when all the cards had been read and shared. The leftover cake was wrapped tightly, and Beth and Donna took charge of the cleanup.

Daisy was still speechless. Martha was excited about her cards and her original idea. Tom was praised for his part in the plan. This was indeed a Sign of Hope for all of them to enjoy.

CHAPTER 51

More Hope

A WEEK LATER, THE EARLY summer heat was the first topic of the Thursdays at Three group. Martha commented, "This heat always surprises me. Yesterday, my little pot of petunias just gave up the ghost and collapsed."

"It's the end of the season pretty soon for all these plants. Even the geraniums don't really survive very well. I kept two going last year by taking them inside." Daisy smiled and said, "I told you we'd never have to shovel snow or rake leaves or clean the pool. Did I forget to mention being thankful for air conditioning?"

Alex thumped his fist on the table and said, "All right, everybody, let's think positive and talk about hopeful things in our lives today. Who's ready to talk?"

Clarissa spoke up. "I'm always first alphabetically. Couldn't we invite the Ansons to join our little group?" No one answered until Alex laughed and caught on to her idea.

Beth joined in and said, "We need you to start us off, Miss Benton, because you're always clever."

"I wish I could be clever about seeing hopeful things today. But I'll be honest, I'm depressed over the political scene in the capitol, and I'm opposed to war. I don't drive, but if I did, I'd object to the gas prices. The taxes on cigarettes are astounding, so I'm glad I quit smoking. On the local scene I'm disgusted with the way children are abused and yet no one starts a crusade against child abuse. On Sunday morning, for about an hour, I feel a spark of hope. I should go to church every day." With that, she laughed and sat back in her chair.

Alex frowned and said, "Clarissa, you have so much enthusiasm for life, and that comes from curiosity plus looking ahead with hope. Don't be depressed; go to church again. We all need your spirit!"

Dave waved his hand and said, "When I first met Daisy, she told me about her friends, and she especially told me you were perceptive, Clarissa. She's right. You're looking at the big picture and relating it to yourself. I took this question the other way around. I pictured myself surrounded with all sorts of good things: Daisy, this place, seeing out of both eyes, driving my own car, and sunshine most of the time. To me, my immediate surroundings speak of hope."

Ellen nodded and offered her observation. "You're both on track. If Rissa had kept talking, she probably would have itemized what she thinks about in church, all the same things you mentioned, Dave. Likewise, if you had continued, you'd have expanded beyond La Ventura into the world. Hope is free to everyone, but it can be invisible. It starts out so small that we miss it in the big picture. It's so quiet we can't hear it unless we know to listen for it. That's the teaching of Jesus, the promise of God, the assurance of the Holy Spirit in us. When the newsman tells us how many were blown to bits today, we have no measuring stick to tell us that thirty thousand soldiers completed their tasks today and are resting safely tonight. I think the media reports have smothered our hope." She nodded again as if to say Amen!

Alex had to comment on how the conversation was going. "Lots of truth in what you said, Ellen. Donna, you're awfully quiet over there. What have you seen recently that's hope-filled?"

"I don't know. I think the thing that lifts my outlook every day is seeing all the old people, me included, around here, going about their business, and laughing and loving life. When I came here, I was so suspicious of everyone's intentions. I was tired; I'd been sick a long time; I had lost my only child. Gradually, and I mean it took a long time, I found myself in control of my life. From that perspective I could see other people managing their lives. My fears moved to the back burner, and I began to admire some of the residents. The ones using walkers and wheelchairs seem pretty pleasant now. Even the ones I see over in El Nido smile and talk about what they'll do tomorrow. That's it! Thinking about tomorrow gives me hope."

Tom applauded. "When you got here, Donna, I thought you'd leave soon. You didn't seem to like any of us, and I just assumed this was a mistake for you."

"You did? Wow, I'm glad I didn't know that."

"Now, wait, let me finish. You have exactly the right approach about planning tomorrow. That's all we have to do. When we're kids, it's important to have a vision as a guide, but once we're this age, I believe we just are responsible for today and tomorrow. We can dream ahead, but that's almost too much to hope for. What should reinforce that hope for tomorrow is that today is what we were hoping for yesterday."

"Hey, we're getting so philosophical that it's way past our stopping time. Can the rest of us wait two weeks to pontificate?"

Clarissa said clearly, "I had my say. Next thing is bye-bye." She waved her jeweled hand and grinned. "I'll fly away, but don't talk about me. I'll be back early, remember?" And humming the first four notes of the wedding march, she left them laughing.

At the dinner tables, they found small cards reminding people that this was the longest day of the year. *Make the most of it!* was printed on one for each person. "Speaking of hope," remarked the Captain. "I haven't really done much today, but I think I'll use this as an excuse to call Nelson and Victoria. That ought to shake them up. If we didn't have emails, I'd never know they were alive. Or vice versa."

Alex agreed. "My kids have been so busy with the end of the school year and vacation plans. When I went out there last week, I sensed the feeling 'Oh, hi Dad, you're still here, aren't you?' when I rang the bell and let myself in."

Daisy couldn't let that rest. "Alex, you understand their lives. If they had known what you told us before you left that evening, they'd have perked up right away."

He chuckled a bit. "Was that when I dropped that bomb about looking around for someone to marry?"

"Yes, it was! How's your research coming along?"

"Nil, zero, zip, nada. I'm not up to it. If someone moves here and finds me, that's good."

Daisy laughed and said, "I know what you mean. Except I had never thought of it."

"So Dave really surprised you? He's a good man. I have a feeling you two will have some good years together." He returned to his meal, and no one looked up until the wail of a siren came close. "Whoa, that sounds like it's here."

There was a flurry of activity out around the main door where two uniformed men deposited a gurney. Bonnie was talking, while Malcolm was assisting a man toward them. Daisy spoke out, "I think it's Mr. Anson; I believe his name is Bill. Yes, there's his wife Joanne. Gosh, they've only been eating dinner with us for a couple of months. She told me it was getting too hot to cook in their unit. It faces west, and you know how hot that room can get."

"That's Dr. Ruggles over there with them. He's a great guy. I took his photography class in January and really liked it. He's had a lot of field experience."

"Field meaning where?" Beth asked.

"Oh, on tours with a research team in Cambodia and once or twice to Malawi in Africa."

"How did he choose La Ventura?" Beth wanted to know.

"I think his sister lives in Carefree. She's a nurse and retired from Healthcare up on Shea."

"Well, Alex, she's a lady you might invite down here from Carefree for dinner. She'd feel real comfortable with her brother right here as a chaperone." Beth giggled like a sorority matchmaker.

"Boy, am I going to regret saying I was looking."

"We tried, Alex. We want you to be happy."

All this time, the paramedics were tending to Bill Anson, but not taking him away. Donna observed, "I think I should go over there and at least introduce myself to Mrs. Anson." The others agreed, and she rose and left the table.

Once the paramedics packed up their gear, everyone stopped watching and relaxed, thinking Mr. Anson had maybe choked or felt weak. "Nothing serious," was Donna's report. "He tends to choke or not be able to swallow. Joanne says it goes with Parkinson's, and he's been a patient for a long time. I gathered they had consulted with Dr. Ruggles earlier."

"It's reassuring to have both Donna and a doctor on board, isn't it?" the Captain remarked.

CHAPTER 52

Summer Flies By

"THIS IS A SUMMER TO break the records, isn't it?" Tom said to Daisy as they picked up their mail one morning.

"Boy, it sure is. I think we're all lucky to have new air conditioners and shaded doorways. Not many units face west."

"I guess you and Dave will be moving in together soon? I'm glad you two settled all the problems from the past, but it's a big way to show you feel sorry for him."

Daisy hesitated before replying. "Dave and I will be moving the day before the wedding. That's August 9, when I'll go over to my daughter's and he'll be arranging furniture." She chose to ignore the reference to problems and pity.

"I suppose he forgives your husband for the accident."

Slowly Daisy replied, "Yes." She turned around before she could say anything she'd regret and purposefully strode toward the open door.

When she reached her door, she was trembling. Curly's usual happy greeting eased her nerves, and she sank into an easy chair. "Why does Tom enjoy meddling in other people's business?" Curly didn't answer her, but she felt as if she had handled the scene properly. "I don't feel sorry for Dave. I feel *really* sorry for Tom and his bad attitude! Now if I can just avoid being alone with Tom again."

At lunch, Bonnie announced that this would be the last opportunity to wish Annabelle Parker well in her move. There was a bit of a murmur around the room, as questions were asked about why she was leaving. Several of the women went to her with hugs and happy faces. But Annabelle looked very downcast.

Donna was able to enlighten the Bunch of Daisy's. "She came to me several times with complaints that really should have gone to the directors. I tried to offer some ideas about how she could use her space and feel comfortable. She kept calling La Ventura a nursing home or just 'the home.' She felt angry that her good friend had talked her into coming here, and then at the last minute her friend couldn't afford it. She moved here alone and wonders why nobody knows her. Yesterday she told Bonnie that she'd been so lonely until she said she was leaving. Then everyone was solicitous."

Daisy said firmly, "Those are the people we seem to miss. Why don't they try to fit in?"

Beth answered, "Because they think this place should fit into their needs. They're always the ones who won't change how they do things. They want the meals at their hours and lawns mowed in the morning so they can nap after lunch. I don't see how any community can adjust to them."

Donna agreed. "It's hard to explain to someone like Annabelle, so it's better if she finds another place to live."

"Has she found one?"

"A freestanding house, yes. I asked her about caring for the place, and she said it would be no problem. So, I wished her well."

Dave arrived promptly at 5:30 to walk with Daisy over to the dining room. "I had the best morning. Did you miss me at lunch?"

She smiled affectionately and said, "Yes, of course. But you had told me you might not be back in time."

"Well, I signed some papers and you need to also. The unit will be cleaned and painted, with new carpet, by August fifth. That gives us time to move in and get married on schedule. Then we can have our places cleaned out and ready for them to show in a couple of weeks. Sound good?"

"Yes, but what if we can't sell ours right away?"

"Don't worry about it. I can handle that." Inside, he continued, "Jake is thrilled to get out of here before it gets any hotter. I offered to help him with anything, but he's already got movers coming and other people to help him. How are the arrangements at the church?"

"Fine. Pastor is ready to advise us whenever we can make an appointment. The organist is willing to stand by in case anything happened to Rissa's arrival the day before. My circle will make cookies and serve the punch. Everyone is quite excited about our plans."

"Are you?"

"Yes, dear, don't worry about me. I'm getting used to having other people direct the show." She laughed, and Dave gave her a quick hug.

The bridge players had just come out of their room, and Robert was smiling broadly. Ellen asked him if he'd won the prize, and then asked again. Finally she laid a hand on his arm, and he turned to face her. "Robert, I asked you if you'd won the prize today, but you didn't hear me."

"I know. My battery is out on one side, and I think I need more help on the other. These invisible hearing aids may not last for me."

"I didn't know you wore any aids."

"Oh, yes. I was one of the first to try these little guys, but I need more help now. Darned expensive things! I'm going to a meeting this afternoon with an audiologist. She comes every month to check up on all our equipment."

"No kidding? I didn't know there was a group of you."

"It's probably the biggest crowd of medical needs. The glasses people go to their own doctors, but we just have to muddle along with new batteries." He laughed at himself.

Daisy turned to Dave and asked, "How are we going to decide what to move and what to give away?" She nibbled at a roll. "When can we talk about the furniture, like the table and stuff in the bedrooms? Your desk is really big and heavy."

Dave smiled and answered, "I wondered when you'd begin to get down to the details, the little pesky stuff we have to decide."

"Well, those are the things I just want to avoid, but now I can't. Like, where will my sewing machine fit?"

"You're the one always talking about people making changes and fitting in. I guess we're going to find out how we fit in together."

"You're being obtuse. I mean it seriously. I can't just wake up some morning and move that day. I have to plan. Don't you?"

"Yeah, but I've already done it. I can picture the whole place furnished. Do you want to walk over there again and look at the unit?"

She thought a minute and finally said, "O.K. I know I have to deal with this." Others were listening to them with amusement.

Beth said she'd be glad to come along and chaperone. Robert offered to bring a yardstick and measure each wall. Alex even joined the fun and said he'd bring some champagne if it seemed a good time to celebrate. Martha and Tom just watched, since they'd already been through this process.

"Let's go over there in the morning and take some notes so we know how to direct the movers. If we go now, we're going to be swamped with free advice."

Daisy agreed. "Maybe I'll sleep better tonight."

"Is there anything I could do to help you?" Dave whispered in her ear.

She sputtered, "No, Dave, don't be silly."

"I was just trying to be trustworthy, loyal, helpful, friendly, courteous, kind."

"Stop. Stop. I'm sure you were a wonderful Boy Scout, but you're overdoing the friendly stuff. What happened to obedient?"

"That was coming next. You just couldn't be patient, could you?" He put an arm around her shoulders and whispered in her ear, "Obedient, cheerful, thrifty, brave, clean and reverent. There!"

"Somewhere in that list are some tough words to explain to the little guys learning them."

"Right! Physically strong, mentally awake and morally straight. Did you have to coach Pete?"

"Oh, yes. Those were the days." She shook her head wistfully.

CHAPTER 53

Hope Shines Through

"DAISY, DO YOU REMEMBER Clarissa told us about the Berringers and their divorce? Well, I just heard that Adele is getting married again. Can you believe it? I'll bet the ink isn't dry on the divorce papers!"

"Now, there you go, Beth, jumping to conclusions. Did you really hear this?"

"Not exactly. I heard she had the place completely repainted and new carpet put in."

"She might be going to sell it."

"No. She told Ruth who told Jenny that she let Raoul choose the colors. Do you know who Raoul is?"

"No, but I'm sure you're going to tell me."

"He's the manager of the gardening crew. He speaks Spanish!"

"The gardeners here?"

Beth was nodding her head vigorously. Jenny said that Ruth told her that Adele's sister is blowing a fit over it. Raoul is moving in!"

Alex had just come into the meeting room, and asked, "Who's Raoul?"

"He's the future husband of Adele Berringer, that's who he is."

Jack Berringer's ex-wife?"

"The very same."

"Wow, that didn't take long, did it?"

Daisy laughed at the expression on his face. "Alex, you have a few mixed emotions about this news, don't you?"

"Yeah, because I can't seem to see anyone available to date, much less marry. And then someone else right in our midst makes a decision overnight."

Beth observed quietly, "Maybe it wasn't overnight."

As that sank in on the group, Martha and Tom arrived. "My, you're all so quiet. Are we in the wrong room?"

Daisy took over and said, "No, we're just teasing around. Come on in and cool off. Tea for both of you?"

"Yes, thanks."

Alex changed the subject with, "Any hopeful items in your recent reading? We got pretty solemn that last time we talked."

Ellen came in and sat, fanning herself with a piece of the newspaper. "I'm hoping that the new Social Director will be someone we like. I can't say any more, because I talked the last time."

"New Social Director?" Robert hadn't heard that news. "Do we have a name, a man or a woman?"

Alex jumped in with a name and lots of information. "She's Marcy Craig, about forty-five, I'd guess. She's done this same kind of work in two other communities, originally from Colton, California, near San Bernardino. She's a former phys. ed. teacher and then a social worker."

"She's changed jobs pretty often, then."

"Could be she's been looking for us!" Alex was good at putting a new spin on any subject. "Her last job was as an assistant to the director over at the Beatitudes. That's a big place, so she must know what she's doing."

"Right. When do we get to meet her?"

"At dinner tonight, I think."

"By the way, how did you learn all this?" Beth looked a little miffed that there hadn't been a general announcement that such a position was open.

"I spent some time with Bonnie, just chatting."

"I see. Well, it all sounds good, just so long as she doesn't disturb the Bunch of Daisy's."

"No one would dare uproot us!"

"Or prune us in the fall?"

At dinner, Marcy Craig was introduced. The applause was huge, and that was a truly hopeful sign. Donna slid into the chair next to Daisy and apologized for missing the afternoon meeting. "I was called over to Gen Farley's unit, because she hadn't been seen for a couple of days at the hospital. She's only working fifteen hours a week now, but they were still worried about her."

"Goodness, what did you find?"

"I found she'd fallen and dislocated her hip. She was in a lot of pain and evidently just passed out so she couldn't even get to the red help button. She thinks it happened early in the morning. I got her into an ambulance and off to the ER. When I got there, the doctor told me he thinks she had a stroke. She's having trouble talking. Her hip has been adjusted, but the nerves that were pinched are very painful. She was admitted, and now she's under a lot of sedation."

"Gosh, we think we've taken all the precautions by living in this guarded place, and yet something like this still can happen!"

"She's younger than all of us, isn't she?" asked Beth.

"Yes, she is. I picked up some literature about a service all over the country, called Life Alert. I'm writing an article about it for the next newsletter."

"What is it, some kind of insurance?"

"No, it's a pendant worn around the neck. It can be down inside your clothes, and all you have to do to get help is push a button."

"What if you can't get to the button?"

"This is a wide part that moves. I think you could roll over onto it, or use your fist or your knee. It's a good design."

Daisy chipped in, "I bet Curly could use it!" They all laughed at that, but Donna agreed.

"So, what can we do to help her?"

"I wish we knew her better." All the comments and questions reminded Daisy how important the get-acquainted evenings are.

Alex chimed in, "You missed the new social director's introduction. We think she'll be good at combatting the problems here."

Donna smiled and asked what he meant. "Problems?"

"Oh, it seems some people are getting gossipy and minding other people's business."

"Alex, you aren't turning into a grouch, are you?"

"I may. But tomorrow I'll be smiling, because I have a dinner date."

"Wow. Do we get to approve of your choice?" Robert was sounding like a father. "How late will you be out?"

"Who knows? I may be out until dawn. How early is the front door opened?"

"It's not like the dormitory. You can come home anytime, but watch out for security guys. They might be armed. Be sure you know the password."

Dave interrupted this line of questioning. "Speaking of password, I'm having a heck of a time with my computer. Who's the best guru around here?"

"Probably Doc Ruggles," suggested Alex. "He explained that little camera of mine in about five minutes. He prints out his own pictures and illustrates articles he writes. Give him a call."

"That might be extra nice, since he's sort of new around here," said Martha. "If he likes to write, do you suppose he'd put up with all of us amateurs?"

"I'll catch him at dinner. We're pretty slow right now with the writing, aren't we?"

"I'm still thinking about hope. Like, I hope I behave myself properly tomorrow night!"

"We *hope* you have a wonderful dinner date. But maybe we could get more philosophical by Thursday afternoon."

Daisy added, "In our writing, we've learned so much about each other and living here; I want us to continue, and I never thought I'd hear myself say that."

Donna said, "Me too, even though I have a bad time writing an assignment. I have to listen to the rest of you to get any ideas."

"You seem to be a hopeful person, Donna. You were real optimistic when we went looking for a kitten that day, even though you were sad to lose your old one."

"You were so nice to take me on that errand, Robert. You know it's hopeful to watch an animal grow, like a child. The future is built into living animals, just like into us. Who ever thought we'd get to be so old and still changing?"

Ellen summarized, saying, "That's very spiritual of you, Donna. It's a hope-filled process we have very little control over. Lower forms of life reach the adult form and maybe don't have a reason to continue living, have a short life span. But I believe God intended for us to keep growing, with gusto!"

Alex assured them, "By Thursday, I shall be profound. How about the rest of you?"

Robert offered to remind Martha and Tom about the topic for Thursday, and they all went their separate ways. "And try to be good to yourselves so you act nice to others."

As they walked along, Daisy said to Dave, "That was a lot out of Robert, wasn't it?"

"You know I think he's opening up more with that bridge group. They seem to kid around a lot."

"See you tonight? I'm trying to finish up two doll quilts this afternoon. I hate leaving things unfinished."

On Thursday, Daisy announced that her most hopeful sign of the day was her progress in packing. "A week from today, the movers will be here."

Dave nodded. "In fact by this hour next week, I'll be moved in, and you'll be on your way to Julie's house!"

There were smiles around the table. Alex said, "Let's get going on this hopeful note, and see what Martha and Tom have to be hopeful about."

"I'm the wrong one to start with. I'm pretty depressed about a lot of things these days." Tom propped his head up on one arm bent at the elbow.

"Now, Tom, don't be." Martha turned to the rest of the group and went on. "We're sad about the way the war is going. We're sick of the political news, fifteen months before the election. But we both laughed at the story about a cat who sailed from Hawaii to the mainland, packed in a movers' crate for nineteen days. She jumped out and settled in the family's new house in California! Now that was a hopeful tale."

Others were laughing and clapping. Alex quizzed Tom for his answer. "I guess I feel hopeful that we're getting clouds and some showers. Summer will finally end. I haven't read any books lately that I liked. The writers are so shallow and use so much crude language. I don't know. I'm just depressed these days. Sorry."

Usually, Ellen would have come up with some words of encouragement, but today she was silent, sorting through several sheets of notes in her lap. Alex finally said, "I'm sorry too, Tom. We all hit these stages every so often. Robert, wasn't it you who called this the doldrums?"

"Right. It's time when you need a good wind to get you moving. Nothing brings it on faster than summer here, or severe winter if you live up north."

Martha moved closer to Tom and whispered something to him. They both stood up, and she said aloud, "If you'll excuse us, we'll see you at dinner." Everyone nodded assent, and they slipped out the hall door.

"Alex cleared his throat and said, "Well, maybe someone else can rescue the conversation here. Beth?"

"I did write something down that interested me the other day. Did you read about the smell test that a research team has developed, to identify people who are fifty percent more apt to remain mentally alert and fit?"

"No, I didn't, but I agree that would be very hopeful. What were the smells they used?"

"That's the list I wrote down: onion, lemon, cinnamon, black pepper, chocolate, roses, banana, pineapple, soap, paint thinner, gasoline and smoke. So, if you missed identifying four or five, you might be losing some of your faculties. But I thought it was so hopeful that research is getting somewhere about Alzheimer's."

"It's the scariest of them all, isn't it?"

"You heard that Mr. Eaton has just been diagnosed with it? He's moving over to El Nido next week. Thank Goodness we have that kind of care."

"Thanks, Beth. That was really interesting. Well, I guess I'm last as usual. It's sad that the most hopeful thing this week is how well the D-backs are doing! But, I notice that when the home teams are thriving, the mood around town seems to be up. So, let's keep them winning!"

After a little applause, Alex went on. "It's time to go over to the dining room, folks. Remember: every single one of you better be front and center next Friday. Right, Dave?"

He wrapped his arms around Daisy and said to the rest, "Remember, two o'clock, Valley Church, up at the Chapel end of the place." He planted a kiss on her cheek, and the group squeezed through the door and hurried toward the smell of roast pork in onion gravy, one of the community favorites.

CHAPTER 54

Moving and Marrying

AUGUST NINTH DAWNED bright and hot. Daisy looked around her Unit 7 and shook her head at all the boxes. "This was such a pretty little place until I packed everything. Oh, God, I hope I'm doing the right thing." Her moment of prayer was cut short by the telephone. "Hello?" She smiled. "I'm up, dear, and admiring my boxes." She laughed lightly. "Yes, I have the coffee made, so come on over." She hung up the phone and smiled again. "Yes, I'm doing the right thing!"

The movers were cheerful young men. One of them teased Dave and Daisy about combining their households. "How are ya gonna decide where to put everything? You've got a lot of stuff here."

Dave pointed to Daisy and said, "She's the moving boss. She knows where to put it all."

Once they had the furniture and boxes inside at Unit 77, the movers disappeared. Dave and Daisy were left to make decisions. By lunch time, they walked out on the clutter and locked the door. "It's wonderful to have a place to go and eat and forget this," he said.

"We can't forget it. This is the day we have to settle in. Do you know where we'll be tomorrow at this time?"

"Yup. Looking for the right clothes and the car keys and the rings."

"I'll be at Julie's, and I can let her take over! Thank Goodness for daughters."

"I don't know. My daughters are acting as if they're going to a party tomorrow. I think they're just having fun seeing each other again."

"No questions about your getting married again?"

"Nope. Sandy said she'd stop calling me early on Sundays, but I'd have to call her every week. Laura's easy, since she knows you and this place."

"Well, let's eat." They found a table near the door and started at the salad buffet right away.

"Daisy, Daisy," floated across the room. "I'm here and ready to practice tonight."

"Rissa, how did you get here?"

"I flew in, of course. Took a cab, because I knew you were too busy moving. What time is the rehearsal?"

Dave chose to answer her. "We thought we could skip that. We're just supposed to be there half an hour early, in the parlor next to the chapel."

"Well, that's different! How will I know what to play, or where the organ is, or what the pastor wants?"

Daisy to the rescue said, "I have it all written down, Rissa. It's very simple, really. You know exactly what and when to play."

"But I've never seen the organ. Is the organist nearby to help me?"

"As a matter of fact, she's an old friend of mine, so she's standing by. She'll meet with you in the chapel at one-thirty."

Clarissa sighed. "I suppose it'll all work out. You people in Arizona are so casual about things. How many people are expected?"

"We think about twenty will be there."

"Twenty? Is that all? What about all these folks?" She spread her arms wide to include the whole dining room.

"They'll all be part of a party afterwards, right here, at three o'clock. Just the family will be at the chapel, and our closest friends."

"The Thursdays at Three bunch, I hope."

Dave agreed. "I'm sure they'll be there. And our family will come over here after the first little reception at the church."

Finally, Clarissa seemed satisfied. "Be sure to eat a good lunch, you two. Have to keep up your strength, you know!"

By the end of the afternoon, both Daisy and Dave were wearing down in energy. "The place looks pretty good, don't you think?" Dave was the usual optimist.

Daisy agreed, but she had her doubts about keeping house easily until the kitchen things were unpacked. "It's just as well we're not leaving town for two weeks. By then, surely we'll have ourselves organized."

When the telephone rang, neither one knew where it was. The ringing continued as they rummaged for it. Curly was poised beside the loveseat, tail wagging. Daisy caught his message and picked it out of the cushions. "Hello?" She listened and finally spoke up, "Susie, we're fine. We've done as much as we need to do." She paused. "Dave and I will see you over at Julie's in about an hour." She shook her head silently. "No, dear, it's just a casual dinner for the seven of us. Dave's going over to Laura's and eat with his family. So, I'll see you at Julie's."

To Dave she reported, "They just can't believe we're doing this our way. A wedding is a wedding, she said. So, we're supposed to have a rehearsal dinner and dress up. You're not supposed to see me tomorrow until the wedding, et cetera, et cetera."

Dave chuckled. "I probably won't, since you're having your hair done and a manicure in the morning. I'm getting a haircut and picking up those engraved picture frames we ordered. Well, we have to give the kids some fun too. One more day of letting them call the shots won't hurt us."

They tackled one more stack of small boxes, taking time out occasionally for a hug and some smiles when they came across some superfluous item. He said, "I think that makes three colanders and four can openers. Hey, how about checking that wine you put in the fridge? The sodas are all cold too. We've earned a rest."

They pushed aside some pictures and sent Curly to his new corner. Dave proposed a toast. "Here's to our last moving day. May we live here happily ever after!"

"Oh, that's nice. Let's hope that's true."

The evening went as planned, and their wedding day started out smoothly. Dave called from Unit 77 to declare, "This is my last morning to wake up here alone!"

Daisy laughed and admitted she hadn't slept very soundly. "I kept wondering if I'd remembered everything. Did you remind Bill to be there early?"

"Yes, Laura promised to be on time for once!"

"Julie is so prompt that she's already told me exactly when to be dressed and when we're leaving."

"Tomorrow, let's not even look at a clock."

Daisy felt a small lump in her throat at the thought of tomorrow. What would it be like? Aloud, she said, "We probably should unplug the phone. I can imagine someone calling to find out if the choir robes are ready."

"Forget the details, my dear. Let's just think about this afternoon. Bill wanted to know what time we'd be leaving the family reception to come over here."

"I don't know. I told Bonnie we'd start the party at three. After all, the service will only take about fifteen minutes, max. Then half an hour for a little family fun time and pictures, and a few minutes to drive out here. I think we'd leave the church before three, don't you?"

"Sure. That's what I told him too. Well, lady, I'll see you at the church. I love you."

"And I do love you, Dave. I'm getting used to this whole idea just in time, I guess." She laughed and hung up.

When the pastor introduced Mr. and Mrs. Olson to the little crowd, they saw all the Thursday friends and their families wreathed in smiles. Some applause broke out, and Dave and Daisy clung to each other. It was a defining moment! Clarissa swung into the recessional, and the pastor ushered them up the short aisle, into the narthex and then the parlor. The guests followed them and were greeted by Daisy's circle friends with cookies and iced tea. Several toasts were raised and very soon, someone was telling Daisy and Dave that it was 2:45.

Daisy was trying to thank the cookie bakers and servers, and Dave was giving the attendants' gifts to Julie Bryan and Bill

Grant. Congratulations and hugs filled the parlor! Suddenly the couple was being propelled out the door toward a sleek white limousine. The driver opened the back door and helped them inside the air conditioned luxury.

"Dave, where did this come from?"

He leaned over, gave her a kiss and whispered, "From our kids or our friends. Who knows? Let's just revel in it for the seven-mile drive home."

The driver turned and indicated a knob on a small door. When Dave pulled it, it turned into a shelf with two flutes. Quietly, an automatic door opened beside it, revealing a chilled small bottle of apple cider champagne. They both laughed, and the driver nodded and smiled. Dave did the honors and poured. "To us," he said. And they began to move toward La Ventura.

As they drove up to the main entrance, Dave remarked, "La Ventura has a new meaning, doesn't it?"

CHAPTER 55

What's Next?

ON THE FOLLOWING THURSDAY, as the group gathered at the Hedgehog Room, Tom said, "I suppose the lovebirds will join us today."

"Of course." Ellen spoke confidently.

"Well, they may have outgrown their old friends."

"You know, we didn't treat you and Martha any differently after your marriage. We were so happy for you."

"Hm. Well, I s'pose."

Alex sensed the sarcasm floating between them and broke in. "Let's see what plans we have for the fall. It's always like the beginning of the school year, isn't it?"

Beth answered with an excited "Yes!"

Robert came in and chimed in, "I vote with Beth. Whatever she was approving, I'm with her."

They laughed and Alex continued. "I've decided to learn something new this year."

"What? Another hobby or club?"

"In a way. I'm going to be a tutor to three boys over at the Rose Lane Clubhouse."

"What subject?"

"Math, of course. They're not quite ready for law. They use calculators as well as their computers, so I'm going to the fifth grade class at Kiva to see what it's all about."

"How often will you meet with them?"

"Every Monday, Tuesday and Wednesday, after school."

Daisy and Dave came in, and the group all clapped and shouted out their greetings. Martha stood and gave Daisy a hug. She whispered, "Isn't it nice not to be alone any more?"

Daisy laughed and said, "The jury is still out. So far, we're still running into each other in the kitchen and fussing over who's going to feed Curly. Poor thing, he's so confused in a new place with two people to guard."

Dave pitched in, "We have to move some of the furniture, you know. The table's going the wrong way, and the phone is never handy. We have two remote controls, so she can shut up the announcers or ads when she's had enough. It's tough living with Proverbs 31. Seriously, life is wonderful!"

Tom said, "It's just different, isn't it? No more secrets."

While Dave looked puzzled about that comment, Martha cut him off with, "Daisy was a Home Ec. graduate, remember? So she knows how to do everything domestic. Lucky Dave." They all nodded in agreement.

Alex resumed his chairman's role. "We were starting to talk about this fall and new things. I'm trying to fit into the community better by being a tutor to some boys in math. Do any of you have some new ways to fit into life around here?"

Donna said, "I'm still busy with the First Aid Station, and I may teach a class or two in the new schedule. Marcy has asked about some exercises and a program for weight loss."

"I think both of those would be marvelous." Beth's response was shared by the others.

Ellen announced she'd be leading another grief support group, starting in October. "We want it to run through the holidays, since those are tough days for many people."

"Do you think I should try to promote written last wishes and wills again?"

"That was so well attended last year. Do it again."

"No, that part was about what people should do with their possessions."

"Wasn't that all part of the same program?"

"No. We were the only ones who wrote the last wishes. Incidentally, do we need to update anything?"

A knock at the door precluded an answer. Alex opened it and said, "Well, come right in. We have a distinguished visitor, folks. Marcy, this is known as the Thursdays at Three round-table, or some such title." He brought another chair up to the table and seated her.

Marcy smiled and began, "I'm visiting all the existing groups, and Bonnie said I should start here."

"She's absolutely right. Let's go around and introduce ourselves." One by one they gave names and something personal.

"Thank you. I know you've read about me and my experience. Now I'm trying to plan the season ahead with some interest groups. The biggest gap I saw in previous years' plans is in the medical area. I think it could be useful to offer a time when people with like medical conditions could meet."

Donna helped out by adding, "A special technologist will still come and explain about new hearing aids. But there may be some folks who'd like to share their concerns about Parkinson's or high blood pressure or diabetes."

"And Donna will provide some guidance for weight loss and keeping limber and strong. Are there some other things you'd like to have us include?"

"Some of us liked the tickets to the Christmas shows last year. Maybe you could reserve a block of seats?"

Marcy made a note of that. "Of course we can. Any other topics? Do we need a second book club?"

Robert jumped in. "Yes, one that reads men's books, you know, sports stories and those sea adventures. Maybe biographies of men."

"So noted, Captain. Is that what they call you?"

"Yes, ma'am. I was that for so many years I almost forgot Mister Newburn or Robert."

Daisy put in, "Only the bridge players call him Bob."

Marcy replied, "I think Captain is a great reminder to stand up tall and be at attention. It'll keep you young!"

"Yes, ma'am."

"Are there enough former military men and women to make up a group, just for conversation, that is?"

"Probably so. I'd be glad to help recruit. Ha ha! Just for talking, that is."

"I'm making notes. Now, are there some plans you already have that I should know about?"

"Our pet charity, if you want to call it that, is the Boys & Girls Clubs of Greater Scottsdale. Daisy got us interested in it. At Christmas we make a big deal of buying warm jackets or a special toy for the kids who need them or food for their Christmas party. Robert bought them a train set last year and set it up just for the little guys. Computer stuff rates high with them. One of our gals used to work at the desk, because she spoke Spanish. We try to pitch in at whichever clubhouse needs us."

"Tell her about our Easter Egg Hunt last year, Alex."

"Yeah, that was sure fun." He proceeded to describe the afternoon and all the children.

Alex reminded Marcy to ask Dr. Ruggles to teach the camera class again. "That was a Godsend after Christmas."

"Ah, yes, with new cameras. How many attend this group on Thursdays?"

Daisy answered, "About ten of us. Clarissa's in California, but she was here earlier for the wedding. Martha's sister Mary Ann moved to Casa Grande, but she used to be one of us, and we still talk about her."

"If I list this group with the other classes, is it all right to have new people join you?"

Looks were exchanged around the table, and Alex served as spokesman. "Of course we're open to new people. But we've become pretty much of a family. Look at us, two weddings out of the group, and we often share tables in the dining room." He laughed and shook his head.

Ellen added, "Yes, we're open, and every year we talk about this same thing. That's how these men came into the group, through the writing class one year."

"I've heard you're all writers. Is that true?"

"We've had fun that way, and that's how we know each other so well. I mean, if someone new starts to come to our meetings, he'll have to read us his autobiography."

Daisy said, "Whoa, Alex. Then we'll have to read ours to the new person. That would take weeks."

"Oh, you're right. I guess we'd have to take someone new on faith! Likewise, he'd have to be brave to join this group."

"Hm. So, Daisy, you were the founder?"

"Not exactly. We grew out of a writing class one winter."

Enthusiastically, Beth explained, "We wrote our autobiographies, then our last wishes and our own obituaries and advice for the kids at the Clubhouse. We shared our so-called recipes for success, and lately, we talked about what seems hopeful in the world today."

"Wow, what energy you all have! No wonder Bonnie started me off with you. What other groups are there?"

"Woodworkers, and they meet all the time. There's a book group and the artists had an art show that was great, last spring I guess. The knitters have been making little sweaters for a church mission on the Navajo Reservation. Some quilters make lap covers for a hospice in Flagstaff."

"I'm impressed! I think we need a little publicity and a lot of thank you notes to these people. I'll see what I can do. It might stimulate some similar interest in other retirement centers. Well, I should be going, and I'm sorry if I interrupted your planning session. Let me know what you decide to do next." Marcy slipped out quietly.

Alex commented, "She's nice, isn't she? Seemed really interested in what we've done. So, what shall we keep doing?"

"It better be good," said Daisy. "We have a reputation to maintain!"

"Should I see if Doc Ruggles would like to join us? Donna, you could ask Alice if she wants to come along."

"I could, and also see what Vi thinks about writing. She gives a lot of talks, so maybe she'd be willing to share with us." She looked around for approval.

"Give it a try. No one ever has too many friends."

Dave announced it was time to get back to work on their projects at home. "Daisy and I are busy people, you know." His eyes twinkled, and no one took him seriously. "We leave next Tuesday, the twenty-first, for London! We'll keep you posted where we'll be and when we'll be back. See you at dinner tonight." Dave gathered Daisy with a broad smile on his face, whispering, "A honeymoon! Think of that."

After the couple had closed the door, Martha observed, "A year ago when we were going on a trip at the end of summer,

Daisy altered a suit for me. She said it was easier to alter clothes than people's habits and attitudes to help them fit in here. Alex was talking about fitting into Scottsdale, and I got to thinking about new people adjusting here."

Beth spoke up. "Maybe that should be our next assignment, to put together a collection of essays on the topic of 'adjusting to a new way of living after seventy.'"

"That could be really helpful to new residents, or people thinking about moving here."

"Yeah, it's not easy at first," said Tom.

"What if the remnants don't match, or blend?" Everyone smiled at Ellen's question. "What happens if there's a flaw in the weave? Or if we begin to fray around the edges?" Ellen always thought in terms of problem-solving. "You know, our bad habits seem to be magnified as we age."

"I read a sign in the men's store the other day: *alterations are free.* But I thought to myself, no, they're not. There's always a catch." Tom looked unhappy.

Martha returned, "Yes, but with Daisy, the alterations *are* free. She did wonders with a suit of mine, and in fact, with all of us remnants."

"You ended up hosting a party for her, so you paid her back."

Martha looked shocked at Tom's remark. "You're getting grumpy again. What's wrong?"

"Nothing. I'm just surprised that Dave is so fond of Daisy. It's ironic, isn't it, when you think of what that awful accident did to him."

Alex interrupted and said, "Let's get back to the project of our ideas and reflections that might help the newcomers." He led them to choosing the next topic. "We could call it 'expectations vs. our adjustments.'"

Ellen liked that. "I had no idea what to expect, beyond the old-fashioned nursing homes."

Robert added, "Yes, but we've had to make some changes to fit in. I admit it."

Alex closed things by saying it was a great idea. "See you on the first Thursday in September, the sixth I think, with a personal essay. See you at dinner tonight."

CHAPTER 56

Life Changes

BETH ARRIVED AT THE Hedgehog Room early to be sure there were a few extra chairs, in case some new people came. "I hope we grow, but I wish Daisy could be here to welcome any new ones."

"Talking to yourself again, Beth?"

"Alex, it's not nice to sneak up on people."

"Hey, it's good to know you can't hear my knees creak all the way down the hall. You know any good ortho doctors?"

"Seriously? Are you thinking of replacements?"

"Yeah. My daughter says I should do it before it gets real bad. I used to walk miles, but not these days."

"I heard the same advice, before my hip joint just quit. Your daughter's right. It would make the therapy easier afterward."

"Hmm. I'll think about it. Probably Daisy's girl can give me a name. What's her married name?"

"Bryan. Husband's Matt and the son is Mark, I'm sure."

"Thanks. I'll look her up. Have you heard anything from the honeymooners?"

Beth laughed. "No, and I don't expect to. Do you?"

"No, I guess not. It's different around here without them, isn't it?"

Beth nodded. The others began to drift into the room, including Alice with Donna. She looked a little tentative, but everyone began to greet her and treat her just like a regular member of the group.

Alex looked around and cleared his throat loudly. "I feel as if I should pour the tea and pound a gavel to get us started." The group clapped and agreed.

"So, folks, we were going to talk about expectations and adjustments. Before someone makes a comment, let's welcome Alice to our Thursdays at Three meeting. Alice, we've all shared a lot about our past, such as where we're from and some words about our family. Bring us up to date on you, please."

Alice looked around uncertainly, and then she said, "Well, I'm a transplant from Nebraska, from Omaha to be exact. It seemed like a big city to me, but this is much more sophisticated."

"You just like having so many theaters to choose from!" Robert knew she loved the films.

"Oh, you're right. It's so much fun to read about the new films and then actually get to see them right away. And Donna has been such a good friend to drive. I have almost no family, just one brother back on a farm. He didn't approve of my coming out here, but I couldn't stand another winter there. I'm afraid of the ocean, so the desert is my style." She smiled and that was the end of her story.

"Welcome. We also hoped to have Doc Ruggles joining us, but he usually plays golf on Thursday. He said he might always be a bit late. We'll see. All right, what about our proposed topic of our expectations about living at La Ventura? Anyone ready to comment?"

It was quiet for a minute, but Ellen said, "Clarissa should be first, because she always offers to be. But since she's still away, I'll start out."

"Good! Is it cool enough in here for everyone? O.K."

Ellen explained, "First of all, it's not at all like a nursing home! I like being able to sit with different people at meals. There's always someone to talk with. The movies are great, because I don't have to drive or take a bus to see a good one. It helps to have a lot of interests, and this place offers all kinds of ways to keep learning. I could never get bored here."

Ellen paused and looked toward the window wall wistfully. "Josh would have loved this place, being close to neighbors and meeting new people all the time. I wish we'd thought about retirement living years ago.

"Well, that's all I wrote, and maybe I'll keep adding on to it." She leaned back and looked around at the group.

Martha ventured, "You're such a leader to all of us in your faith. I thought you'd tell us this place was an answer to prayer."

"You're right, Martha. I should have thought of that!"

Alex smiled and said, "There's time to add anything you want. I expect we'll all get ideas from each other. Who's next?"

Robert said, "It was my suggestion, so I'd better act like a captain and speak up.

"I didn't know what to expect in Scottsdale, but when I came here to visit about five years ago, La Ventura was under construction. A young guy named Malcolm came out to greet me and showed me the plans. I thought it would be neat to be in on the beginning, so I signed up. I often wished I hadn't, until I actually got here and other people began to arrive.

"It was pretty dull until I met Daisy. For one thing, she had a wonderful dog. She seemed pretty down-to-earth, and she knew the town. She got me interested in the Boys & Girls Clubs and another agency downtown called Vista. I've always liked working with kids. I liked the pool, so I met some people there.

"Yes, I changed. I learned how to do a lot of things, like fix breakfast and do my laundry. On shipboard, everything was done for me. That's why people began to kid me about being the captain. I ordered the daily paper, and I bought a new TV. I needed to organize my life in new ways. I had to remember to introduce myself to people. Everyone knew who I was before. Working at the Y, everybody knew me. Now I was seventy-seven and in danger of getting fat and lazy.

"Would I recommend this lifestyle for other people? Damn right! It's a great investment in the future."

"Bravo, Captain. Any comments, folks?"

Ellen spoke first. "I still can't imagine why you chose to live inland. You were born near a harbor and spent your life on water."

Robert shuffled his feet a bit and looked out the window. "I never told anyone this, but my aunt in Connecticut told me that all the men in my family had dementia, hardening of the arteries or whatever you want to call it. When my wife Elaine died, Aunt Lou told me I should find someone to take care of me. She said I was just like my uncle, and he died at sixty."

"How awful. How old were you?"

"Let's see, about forty-five."

"So you went to sea again?"

"Right. I was alone. I had good benefits. I could work for twenty more years, and I loved the water."

Alex cut off this exchange with, "Captain, that's a moving story. I think that prophecy should be included somewhere in your essay. I bet you're not the only one who chose a place like this to prepare for the worst."

"Alex, that's a harsh way to put it."

"Well, it's true. We all fear an illness we might inherit, and especially once we're alone." Others looked thoughtful, and most nodded in agreement.

After they settled down, Beth spoke up. "I'm one of the ones Daisy helped the most. So, I'd like to speak now."

"Fine, do so!"

"I was afraid I'd be the oldest one here and maybe the only one with a cane. Scottsdale always sounds like a swinging place full of golfers and tennis people. I got here and couldn't believe how pretty the place is. The rooms looked way too small, but the common rooms were nice. When I got out and saw the town, I realized there are all kinds of people here, all ages with varied health status.

"It's a terrible loss of independence, and I'd been alone a long time. I sold my car with my house, so that left me in a new situation too. Then I was here about six months and was sick, seriously so. These new friends rallied around me more than my own family. I don't know what I'd have done without them.

"Yes, I adjusted to the small quarters, meals on a schedule, new friends and new doctors. I had no choice! Now it feels as if I've always been here. I share a lot more of my opinions than I used to. I bought a car, and that's nice to have. I was too lonely back in Illinois and didn't even know it. Winters are more confining there than summer is here. I love La Ventura!"

Alex clapped and said, "Beth, we're so glad you stayed, even if it meant you had to change a bit!"

"Alex, you always cheer us on. Now, isn't it about your turn?"

"Well, to begin with, retirement is a huge change. Not owning my own home means I don't get to use my tools any more. I mean my own tools. I can go to the workshop over in the basement of El Nido, but it just isn't the same. I miss having conversations with other tax people and attorneys. But I have time to read a lot, and I've been writing with this group for three years.

"I had to learn to do my own laundry, and I have to go out for groceries regularly. These are all the things my wife did for me. It's an interesting town, but I miss Tucson. All new doctors and a dentist make me nervous. I guess I'll get used to them.

"I'm sure glad to have lunch and dinner served. This group of friends is great, and I look forward to sitting with them at meals. Meals alone are bad. I learned that I need to initiate action if I want something to happen. Now I'm going to volunteer as a tutor. The Boys & Girls Clubs have been a good connection for me. This is a good place too; it's big enough to have new faces all the time, and the directors are good folks.

"I guess I wish Daisy were here so I could thank her for making a difference in how I get along. I only came here to make my kids happy. They don't like Tucson, and they can't move their business. So, if I wanted to see them often, I had to move up here. Yeah, I get lonely some evenings. That's when I think I ought to get married again. Then everybody tells me I should forget it."

"Who told you to forget it?" Beth asked.

"Oh, the guys at the fitness center. Even Jake who used to run the place said life is a lot easier alone. I've always had people to talk to, at the office and then at home."

Beth continued. "Daisy would suggest you get a dog. She talks to Curly like a buddy."

"Hey, speaking of Curly, who's taking care of him now?"

"Daisy's son Pete has him. After their move here and now to Pete's, the poor dog must be completely confused."

Alex shrugged. "I bet he's just fine. Dogs are better at adjusting than people." He cleared his throat and said loudly, "That's it for today, folks. Anyone for a quick glass of wine at my place before dinner?"

Donna turned to Alice and explained, "Alex lives so close to the side door of the dining hall that we can slip in at the last minute. He's always our host."

"What if we're late for dinner?"

"No one seems to mind if you and I are late coming from the show."

Alex nodded. "That's true. Come on along with us." Alice looked uncertain but she followed the group.

CHAPTER 57

More Essays

On Friday, the fourteenth, Ellen came to lunch waving a postcard from Daisy and Dave. "They're on the way home. Isn't that exciting?"

"How's the trip going?"

"Here, she wrote it. 'Wonderful places to see and lots to tell when we get back. Julie will meet us Sunday night, 16th. See you at lunch, Monday.' It must be this coming Sunday."

"That's great," commented Alex. "I bet they had a good time. Such a change of scenery, and I don't think Daisy'd been overseas at all."

Beth affirmed that. "I was afraid it would be a tough way to start a marriage, but they seemed to be rarin' to go."

"The only person who threw any rain on their parade was Tom. Wasn't he funny about the wedding?"

"Now, Alex, you have to go easy on Tom these days. He doesn't seem to be relaxed about anything. I just hope there isn't any problem with Martha."

Ellen shook her head, "I don't think that's it. She told me he's had a lot of headaches. Pain makes one critical and cranky."

"You're right. Well, what do we have to eat today?" Food talk took over, and Beth and Ellen were ready to change the subject.

By Monday noon, the room was abuzz with people watching for the newlyweds. When they came in the main door, there was a round of applause. Dave grinned and waved at the crowd. "Glad to be back among friends. Thanks for the welcome."

Daisy was all smiles too. "Beth, Ellen, hello. Oh, and Donna, how are you?" They settled at a table and began to pass the rolls and butter. A server asked which soup they preferred, and things seemed to be normal. "When are we meeting again, and are you still working on essays?"

Alex took over. "Yup, more essays. Doc Ruggles has joined us."

"Alice too," Donna added. "And Vi promised to come this week. We're meeting Thursday."

"My Goodness, things moved ahead."

"But we missed you. Alex read his essay and said he wished you were here to be thanked."

"We'll get back to this time zone and be there Thursday."

And so they were, right on time. Alex called the group to order and said, "We still need to hear from Vi, Alice, Rich Ruggles, Daisy and Dave."

"Don't forget Clarissa; she's still over at the beach."

"Did you write and tell her our assignment?"

"Sure did. And she usually blows in about the end of the month. You know, with this big a group, we may have to print up our essays. Rissa has missed all of them, and Daisy and Dave have missed the first four."

"Weren't we going to print them up anyway? We thought they'd help some other people adjust, or not feel too bad about taking some time to fit in."

"You're right, we did say that. So, we'd better have things in readable shape. I'll type Clarissa's when she gets back."

"O.K. We'd better get started reading aloud. Who's first? Doc?"

"I'll jump in here. I haven't been here very long, but I'm already convinced I made a good move. It's hard to retire from medicine, but I'm officially out of the practice. The climate brought me here, with the chance to play golf all year. I hate mold and dampness, so the desert is the place for me.

"I still have trouble mixing with strangers at meals. I tend to treat everyone like a patient or a colleague, as if I'm in the hospital cafeteria. It's hard to adjust to mailboxes in another building. Same with the parking spaces. Malcolm told me that a space may open up nearer my unit, and I'd appreciate that. I keep a lot of sports stuff in my car.

"I like the looks of El Nido, and if I ever need care, it looks good. I'm always checking out the care situation now that I'm eighty." He sat back as if he'd finished. "I'm afraid I haven't changed much, but I will."

"Rich, how did you find this place?"

"On the Internet. Looks good, and the fact they're still building appealed to me. I like new places, new carpet, and drapes, and things."

"You lost your wife recently, you told me."

"About two years ago now. Alzheimer's, really sad."

They all nodded and looked interested. Alex thanked him and asked, "Who's next?"

"I love living here!" Alice was just bubbling with excitement. "I love cable TV and the theaters in Scottsdale. I've never cooked much, because I always worked or was married to a man who traveled all the time. So, I feel as if I'm living in another hotel. The flowers are so pretty here. I'm so happy I haven't had to change at all.

"I'm always curious to meet new people. To be able to give little presents to the boys and girls is such fun. I never had any of my own, just various stepchildren.

"Did you ever read the book called *Passages*? She said the most important way to achieve well-being is to reach out beyond yourself. That's what keeps us happy. Remember what fun we had at Easter?"

The group was all smiling as she chatted on. Dr. Ruggles was especially attentive. "You're absolutely right. We all benefit from the exchange of ideas and opinions. You were married?"

"Oh, my, yes. Three wonderful men. They all died." She shrugged and looked sad for just a moment. Then she went on, "We had lots of fun together, but they hadn't taken good care of themselves. You know, they smoked and drank, and just wore out young." She chuckled lightly, and clasped her hands together like a little girl. "My daddy disappeared when I was four, so I guess I was always looking for an older man. At least that's what my brother said."

"And where does he live?"

"Back on the farm in Nebraska, alone. I don't think that's healthy. That's all I know."

Alex said, "Thank you, Alice. You really do add a light touch to all of us. Your joy is contagious." Several of the group laughed along with her.

"Vi, how about you? You're the newest resident among us."

"I don't have a thing ready to read, but I'll write down some of my impressions. You've all been very friendly, and I appreciate that spirit. I'm still working now and then, so I won't be around all the time. I know why I came here."

Alex picked up on that. "And why, may I ask?"

"I read about this place in the *Tribune.* I used to advertise in that paper."

"What was your company?" Alex asked tactfully.

"I worked for an agency that staged fashion shows for stores. The same place also provided entertainment for conventions and state fairs and the like. I can read cards and tell fortunes. Call me if you're curious about your future."

Dave nudged Daisy and whispered, "I told you I was anxious to know my future, but you laughed at me."

"I'll tell you about your future if you call her!" she whispered back.

Alex was asking who would speak next. "Donna, what have you done since you've moved here?"

"Well, I was a solitary person, always working to support myself. I was sick all one summer and into the fall, so I knew I had to make a retirement plan. I got so lonely, I told my old friend Daisy I'd try this place for one year. However, I've come to like it here, very much!

"I had a hard time getting used to people talking about bad health and money problems. I already knew enough about those subjects. I didn't like the meal schedule. I've always had my own washing machine. But now I like shopping just for breakfast food, and we worked out a laundry time schedule. My car is still O.K., but I lost my beloved Terri. She was my talisman, my reason for living at one point when I was so sick.

"Two places have been turning points in my life: one was a fishing shack where I learned the truth about my failed marriage. The other is La Ventura. Oh, yes, I've changed, and what a relief it is!"

"Donna, you always surprise me!" Alex stood up and went over and gave her a hug. "I can't believe you were so physically weak that you needed us."

"By the time I drove out here, I wasn't so weak. It was just that weak feeling that warped my thinking."

"I see. What do you all think? Shall we wait until October fourth for the last five comments?" Heads nodded, and people shuffled papers and prepared to leave.

"Daisy, you and I lucked out again!" Martha was laughing, but Tom looked downcast. "Come on, Tom, let's get ready for dinner. Our stories can wait two weeks. Come on, dear. Let's go." Reluctantly he rose, and they went to the outer door.

Daisy and Dave combined their papers and headed to the hallway and the dining room. "I need to stop at the office and fill out that form for Malcolm." They walked along slowly, enjoying the relaxed tempo they loved.

Back in their new place, Curly greeted them as if they'd been away for another three weeks. Daisy went to the kitchen, assuring Curly that his dinner was about to be served. He watched her intently as if he needed her permission to begin eating. "So, you need a bite of cheese to tempt you?" To Dave, she said, "I think someone's been spoiling Curly with extra treats. The dry kibble isn't what he wants first."

"The kids probably fed him table scraps and anything they didn't like."

"That's all right, Old Boy, you had good care while we were gone, and that's all that matters." She patted him lovingly. "You know, we need to allow more time to walk over to the dining room from here."

"Yeah, I noticed we were a little late last night. I'm ready; are you?" They locked up and set forth.

Walking home from dinner, arm in arm, Daisy observed, "These essays are really filled with bits of wisdom and faith, aren't they? I still marvel at how people can adapt at our ages."

"The thing I notice most is the way we've become so interwoven. As I got older and lost Shirley, and therefore her friends too, there was no one around who knew about my kids or grandkids or where I'd worked or what I was reading."

"I know. Being here has expanded our world again. I loved that quote from *Passages* about having a purpose beyond oneself results in a feeling of well-being. Well-being encompasses a good life, and that's what we're all looking for."

"La Ventura's a good venture for all of us, not just lucky old me!"

"You're right, dear. Dave, who's that shouting over there? I don't have my glasses on."

"It's Clarissa. Where's she been while we were gone?"

"She was going to visit a cousin of her father's in La Jolla until it cools off here. She must be back to stay."

Clarissa came closer and was puffing by the time she reached them. "You two look wonderful!" She fanned at her face. "My, it's still warm here. Daisy, how did you like the long flight?"

"Well, it was exhausting, but it got us there. You'll have to see our pictures. I'll find them by tomorrow. And how was the beach?"

"Beautiful, just beautiful. But after two weeks of it, I was ready to come back here. She didn't have air conditioning, and a couple of the days were really hot. So, what have you all been doing here?"

Dave took over. "Unpacking and sorting out the little gifts we bought for the kids. You know, we all need to get writing again. There are still five of us who need to read our ideas. Have you done anything yet, Rissa?"

"No, of course not. I forgot the topic."

"What were your expectations of this place, and have you changed since living here?"

"Oh, that'll be easy to write. I'd better get back home and think about it. See you tomorrow."

CHAPTER 58

Good Memories

ALEX BROUGHT THE GROUP to order for the first meeting in October. "Let's finish up this topic, folks. We have a lot to listen to today. Who's ready?"

Daisy asked, "Could you stand a lighter mood? I made up my mind more easily than the rest of you, I'm sure."

"Go ahead; tell us your story again."

"I had no problems moving here, except for missing my family room. I liked space to entertain the family and friends. I have my kids in my hometown of ten years, my dog, my car, my church and a few friends there. I knew I could settle in here. What I didn't know was that my grief was still very fresh and unresolved. I was so happy organizing everyone else's single life that I hadn't accepted my own. The books people gave me about being a widow were like textbooks to me. I read them and applied the information to all *your* lives. More than once, someone here has reminded me that my counseling services aren't welcome.

"Then love came into my life in a new way. I didn't even recognize it! I could have lost Dave, because I had myself convinced that I was fine. I liked going to meals with friends. Our volunteer activities kept me feeling useful. My friends were drivers when I had cataract surgery. The kids came by to see me occasionally or invited me to their homes. I'd merely changed my address.

"Bless Dave for making me take an inventory of my life here. He helped me to define my comfort zone and see that I needed to make changes like the rest of you. I had to let go of the past and move ahead. Thank you, dear Dave, and thank all the rest of you for helping me."

As usual, Daisy put everyone in good spirits. She knew she was surrounded by friends. Alex added, "You two have made the biggest changes in your living arrangements, like Tom and Martha. You're a good recommendation for the place!"

Dave spoke up. "Maybe I should respond to the challenge next. I was so needy when I came here that everything was wonderful to me. The caring people, the food, the pretty new surroundings all made me happy. I couldn't see very well, so small rooms seemed safe. I found I could pay someone to do my laundry. My daughter shopped for things for my breakfasts. I just felt lucky to be accepted here, because when I bought the place, I expected to be hale and hearty. Instead, I was still using the white cane. I'm grateful they made an exception and bent the rules for me.

"I've changed so much in three years that I hardly know where to start. I like the place and the new Dave Olson. And I *love* the new Mrs. Olson!"

Everyone laughed and clapped for that remark. Alex reached out and shook Dave's hand. "You've shown a lot of courage, my friend, to walk around with a blind eye and to keep your spirits high."

"The surgery was really the miracle, though. And you know, no matter how bad that accident was, the result was an answer to prayer, years of prayers."

Alex looked around the room and stopped at Tom. "How about your thoughts, Tom?"

"Sure. I've changed since moving here. I'm married after being a bachelor for fifty years. I still like AA meetings; they feel like home to me. I kept my car and some of the furniture from my apartment. I like Scottsdale.

"At first, I didn't like having everyone know what I do every day, but I got used to it. I don't like to talk all the time. I've never been a happy person, so I'm surprised I fit in here. Meeting Martha helped me the most. She says I worry too much about other people, but I still wonder why all of you seem so lucky and happy in life.

"I'm concerned that our investment here keeps its value. That's why I try to be aware of what's going on. I follow rules, and I want everyone else to act that way too. I think my changes are for the good, mostly where Martha is concerned."

"Tom, I think you need to give yourself permission to retire, to relax. Keep your focus on the two of you and having some fun. You're blessed with a beautiful wife, so keep her happy." Alex turned to Martha and said, "Beautiful Wife, it's your turn."

She smiled and began to read her words. "I was really fearful of moving to La Ventura, even with my sister's help. I found a friend here, a soul mate, and we started a twelve-step group. It's small, but so strong. Then I found love again and have been married for three years. Our shared interests and the two cats keep us involved with other people, as well as the other friends of Daisy.

"I started out being anxious about living here and promised my sister I'd try it for three years. Then she left for another job. Now I'd hate to leave. This is truly home. Dinner out every night is nice, and my housekeeping and shopping don't take much time. We've been doing a lot of volunteer work over at the Boys & Girls Club. Those kids have become *our* kids.

"What a wonderful group of friends we have now. Moving here has been my lifesaver!"

Daisy clapped, and the others began to thank Martha for what she had written. Tom had tears in his eyes, and Martha squeezed into the chair beside him. "I didn't mean to make anyone cry."

"I know. I guess I got caught up in your story instead of my own thoughts."

Alex thanked them both for sharing their stories. "Now, Clarissa, you usually start us off, but this time I'm counting on you to wrap it up."

Vi spoke up. "If you want her to be the closing, you'll have to listen to me right now."

"Oh, Vi, I apologize. Of course, I want to hear what you wrote. You told us you'd write, and I forgot. Forgive me?"

"Sure. I wanted to read this, because you all don't know me yet. I bought in here, because I lost my job as a model. I have a bad foot, and I have to walk very carefully. I was diagnosed with pre-diabetes, and it scared me. I'm all alone. My dear partner died after I had cared for her for seven years.

"I guess my biggest problem is curious neighbors. People keep asking me where I came from. Last week, I went to Malcolm and asked him why people keep looking in my window. Then he told me about having a death in that unit, and about all the remodeling that was done. That doesn't bother me a bit, now that I know the story about Mr. Hoover.

"I'm from Phoenix originally. I never made it as an actress, but the modeling business paid well until my foot pains began. It's a solitary sort of career, so I never had a lot of friends. Now I have lots of clients in the psychic world, and I still enjoy meeting people at the state fair and at art shows. People's palms hold many secrets, and sometimes the cards can shed light on personal problems. I've found my real gift. My mantra for happy living is to be myself, with no false expectations, no depressing baggage from the past, but just what gives me pleasure today. That's why I'm so delighted to meet all of you, to share meals and an occasional glass of wine, to join you in classes and then retire to my own little nest at the end of each day."

Alex was enthralled! 'Vi, that was a beautiful statement of optimism and confidence in the future. Talk with Donna about your painful foot, and keep on writing with the rest of us. Now, Clarissa, deliver your message, please.

"Yes, I shall. But first I want to thank Vi for her reminder to be positive about ourselves. Now for my story. At eighty, I was invited to join a dear friend in Scottsdale at La Ventura. The concept of a village, a complete small place to live, in a warm climate, appealed to me. I hated to give up my lifelong home in Washington state, so I just came for the winter. By August, I sold my home and planned to spend the next summers with my nephew and his wife. That was a big, big change. My friends in Washington didn't need me year-round, and all my piano students were long gone.

"Here in La Ventura, I found new friends who wanted me to teach them to play bridge. They made me feel needed. The first changes I had to make were for my crippled hands. I needed laundry help, check-writing help, and transportation. Gradually, the pain eased up, and I developed some new interests.

"Dinner is fun instead of hard work. At eighty-four, I'm thrilled to think I can still change my attitudes, and occasionally a habit! I've framed that letter, that magic letter from Daisy, and I'm grateful to her and to this place. Those lovely double doors opened into a new life for me."

"What did that letter say?" Vi had never heard about the remnants.

"Ask Daisy. Maybe she has a copy of it."

"No, I'm afraid not. I remember making nine copies for my nine distant friends. Maybe you could read Clarissa's if she can bring the framed one to our next meeting."

Dr. Ruggles asked Daisy, "Did you compose it on your computer? Maybe it's still there."

Daisy's face lit up. "Yes, I did. You're right. I'll look for it tonight. But don't expect a great literary thing, Vi. I thought I'd found a way around my loneliness and my responsibilities with a big house and property. I simply thought everyone else must have the same problems. I was wrong in some cases, and I hadn't solved my own situation either. But I'll show you the letter. Let's see, I'd need seven or eight copies."

"Daisy, you do that, and I'll put together all these little essays. Be sure I have a copy of each of yours."

"Mine's not typed, Alex. Can you read it?"

"Yup, I'll do it."

Daisy offered, "Let's have the next meeting at our place. It's a bit of a long walk over there, but it would be nice for all of you to come and visit us. Let's invite Marcy too."

"Wonderful idea, honey!" Dave stood up and announced the number of the unit and which walkway to follow. He ended by saying, "Three o'clock at the Olsons' home. Wow, doesn't that sound good?"

CHAPTER 59

The Letter, Updated

DAISY AND DAVE STOOD AT their open door to greet all twelve of their guests. "Welcome, and c'mon in, friends. Choose a chair, and we'll get the iced tea served right away." Together, they owned exactly fourteen seats for the living-dining area. Daisy brought out the pitchers and her cookie jar.

"I baked yesterday, because I think Dave married me so he'd have a steady source of these cookies." Gradually, they each picked up a glass and a cookie and took a seat.

Alex began by saying, "This is a happy day, folks. We've grown to fourteen with one non-resident member."

Quickly, Marcy spoke out. "Now, I'm not a writer, and I'm sure this invitation was a courtesy."

"Not true. We'd be honored to have you in our midst. No one ever has to read aloud anything we've written, but we think we should all leave a written trail in this world."

"Well, I'll think about it. That idea does appeal to me, since I have two grandchildren far away who'll never know who I am."

Several asked about the next topic. Clarissa especially seemed eager to find out today. "After all, my nephew is coming for the holidays, and we all get so busy at the Boys & Girls Clubs. How about something that goes with Thanksgiving?"

Ellen said, "That's not a bad thought, Rissa. We could put together food ideas or family traditions or travel stories."

"We could even make it into a little booklet."

Marcy suggested the office could make copies. "It might serve a second purpose, other than just fun, as a treat for those who have no family close by, something to read and think about."

"Could we even open it up to other people to send us something already typed that we could include?"

The Captain was quick to say, "That would make us seem like a real open group. You know, we never wanted to sound 'closed.'"

Daisy responded, "Since everyone wonders about that letter I sent in 2002, we could end with a copy of it. Or does that sound too corny?"

"Great idea! Clarissa, did you bring your framed copy today?"

"I did." She passed it along her side of the room.

"Oh, it's such a short note. Is that all you sent, Daisy?"

"Yes, it is. See? That's why I keep telling people that the letter was just an idea, a Christmas card note, not a miracle."

Alex interrupted, "And if I had read that letter, I might have said 'no, thanks' to it. What you did right was to send it to *friends.* You jogged their memories of happier times."

"That's what got me. She made it sound so easy." Beth laughed softly.

Dave cleared his throat and asked, "Could we update Daisy's letter with a sort of a group response?"

Ellen agreed, and Beth said, "Or could we make it an invitation to more friends?"

Marcy said, "Remember that we're developing a waiting list now. I wouldn't want someone to pack up and move, thinking that we have an open unit."

Ellen looked thoughtful. "I liked Dave's idea of a response to that early letter. Maybe say something about 'some of the friends who accepted Daisy's invitation now express their appreciation. This is their fifth shared Thanksgiving Day.' Would that make it fit in with the Thanksgiving idea?"

Daisy pounced on that. "Yes, that's nice."

"If you assemble some short reflections or essays or poems, I'll see that we make enough copies for everyone." Marcy stood.

"Right now, I'll say my farewell for today. Thanks for including me, and I might have more free time at your next meeting."

Alex thanked her and urged her to plan on joining them at the usual meeting in the Hedgehog Room.

"So, Daisy, you're willing to phrase the group expression? And each of us will produce a few words about Thanksgiving? Can anyone write a poem, or tell a joke?"

"Don't forget the idea of a favorite old recipe. Or maybe one from the chef here?"

"Hey, that's an idea. The food last year was just great." Then Dave looked hesitant about going on. "Maybe this year I'll have some new family to eat with."

Daisy smiled and said, "Don't worry, I'm trying to forget how to cook a turkey and make stuffing and gravy. But a recipe would be good. Also, maybe a special prayer?"

"Good, Daisy. This is beginning to look like a nice project to end the year." With that, Alex stood and thanked the Olsons for their hospitality. "Now, Dave, keep your eyes open for another single girl for me."

"That could be a risky assignment, friend. Are you trying to get me in trouble?" As usual, they departed in good humor.

CHAPTER 60

Thankful Hearts

A WEEK LATER, DAISY LOOKED UP from her desk and said, "I found that Christmas letter from 2002. Did you ever read it?"

"I never saw it. Let me see it." Dave took the letter and scanned it. "No wonder your old buddies decided to join you."

"Not all of them did. In fact, Betty in Santa Fe would probably be a great match for Alex. Oh, well, can't change history. But I guess I can write some generalization of the ones who didn't or couldn't accept the invitation."

"Then the rest of the pamphlet would be written by some of the ones who did move here. Right?"

"I'll try. In the meantime, why don't you go have a visit with the chef about your favorite part of last year's feast?"

"O.K. Be back in a bit." Dave closed the door behind him, glad to have an errand outdoors in another beautiful October morning.

Daisy re-read her original letter. She mused to herself, "This will be the fifth Thanksgiving season together for some of us. What a blessing!"

When Dave returned, Daisy put on the TV news and heard more reasons for being thankful for their life at La Ventura. Pictures of raging wildfires in California filled the screen. Homes were swallowed up in flames and smoke. "Thank Goodness we're right here, safe in our home!"

Dave came out from behind the Sports Section and smiled at her. "This is our home, isn't it? We all talk about our *units* or *apartments*, but I like the sound of *our home*."

Daisy felt a tear coming into her eyes, and she simply nodded. Curly, with his instinct for detecting emotion in the air, arrived and rested his chin heavily on her knee. "Yes, Curly, you're thankful for our home too."

Special Thanks

EVERY BOOK COMES INTO PRINT with the support of a professional team. I appreciate the hard work of Patricia L. Brooks and Earl L. Goldmann at Brooks Goldmann Publishing Company LLC, in guiding me through the process. Their endorsement and encouragement kept me going! Bob Kelly, Wordsmith at Wordcrafters, Inc., was the most complimentary and kindest editor I've ever met. I'm grateful to the patient cover and interior designers at 1106 Design. This whole team earned my respect and sincere appreciation.

The cover shows another great team. Thank you, Mary Lorenz, for posing as the main character, Daisy, who truly invites you to come to Scottsdale. I give thanks to Nancy Thomas for sharing pictures of her beloved "Taffy" to portray Curly, a talented Golden Retriever. Thanks also go to JoAnn's Fabrics & Crafts at the Pavilions in Scottsdale for the mountain of remnants pictured.

My advance readers, Gene, Emily, Norma, Ted & Pat added greatly to my finished product. Thanks to all my readers and new friends!

— Kiki Swanson
www.kikiswansonbooks.com
kikiswan@cox.net

ORDER FORM

Please send me:

Quantity		*Total*
_____	*Remnants: Ready for New Life* ($20)	_________
_____	*My Will Be Done* ($20)	_________
_____	*Dearly Beloved* ($18)	_________
_____	*The Legacy of K. Don Fry* ($10)	_________

Enclosed is my personal check or money order for $ ___________.

Name ____

Address ____

____

Mail to:

Kiki Swanson
7933 E. Sandalwood Drive
Scottsdale, AZ 85250

or contact at
www.kikiswansonbooks.com
kikiswan@cox.net

THANK YOU! HAPPY READING!!